Copyright

© 2026 Christian Hurst

Published by Outpost Books

Produced by Christian Hurst Publishing

www.churstpublishing.com

Distributed by Ingram

Additional distribution by Draft2Digital and Amazon

Cover design by Max Young and Christian Hurst

Set in Ethnocentric by Ray Larabie (Typodermic Fonts)

and Allumi by Jean François Porchez (Typofonderie)

ISBN (Digital): 979-8993932729

ISBN (Paperback): 979-8993932705

ISBN (Hardcover): 979-8993932781

For retail, visit: LilyStarlingBook.com

Author blog: christianhurst.substack.com

Instagram & TikTok: @churstpublishing

Second Edition: July 2026

Lily Starling
and the Death Machine

By Christian Hurst
Book 3 in the Lily Starling Series

• • • •

For the ones who search for Tembreabrezi

LILY STARLING
AND THE DEATH MACHINE

CHRISTIAN HURST

THE WIND HIT LILY HOT and hard as she ran, dragging sweat across her skin. She shoved her hair out of her face without slowing, lungs still burning from the last sprint.

"Two more coming over the ridge," Xynn said in her ear. "Go east. It's the clearest path back to the caves."

Lily didn't answer. She skidded in the mud, boots sliding, then caught herself and pushed on. The sting in her legs flared sharp and bright. She was sure she could hear something behind her now—footfalls, too many of them—but she didn't look back.

"Come on, damn it," she muttered through her teeth. "We're so close."

She slapped the side of her scanner. The screen stayed black. The scorch mark along the casing was still warm to the touch, a souvenir from her earlier run-in with the locals.

"How much further?"

Silence. Then a faint hum over the comm—Xynn, tongue pressed between her teeth the way she did when she was thinking too fast.

"Xynn?" Lily snapped.

"Just—keep going," Xynn said. "There should be an entrance nearby. I'm trying to clear the interference."

A ground transport roared somewhere in the distance. Too close. Lily ran harder.

"Fucking hair," she said, shoving the damp strands off her forehead again.

"Second thoughts?" Xynn teased, breathless but smiling.

Lily made a low sound in her throat.

"For the record," Xynn added, "I think it's cute."

She'd cut it for the heat on Gherion Prime—blistering days, cool, sticky nights where she and Xynn would work up a sweat together.

Air whistled past her now. Moving. Focused.

"I feel a draft," Lily said. "Like a wind tunnel. Must be the cave."

"It's just ahead," Xynn confirmed.

The breeze pulled at Lily's skin, sudden and familiar, and for half a second her mind slipped—a crisp draft from the bedroom window, Xynn's body, the shock of night air on her breasts before everything else drowned it out.

She shook it off and wiped her hair from her eyes again.

"There," she said.

The entrance yawned open in front of her.

She skidded to a stop.

"Problem?" Xynn asked.

"You could say that," Lily said, heart hammering.

She stared into the dark opening.

Straight down.

The bottom too far down to see.

And whatever was chasing her was getting closer.

Introduction

LILY'S EYES STUNG FAINTLY. The light in the lift was too bright—too white, the kind that pressed flat against her skin and left nowhere to look away. She glanced at Xynn, and they exchanged one of those looks that said a lot without saying anything at all, the kind that only worked because no one else could decode it.

She realized, a little to her surprise, that she had butterflies.

Not because they were about to see Caris, exactly. More because they were about to see *anyone*. It had been a while since they'd been around other people—really around them. Longer than Lily liked to admit.

The shuttle ride in had been as turbulent as she remembered from her last visit to Bimini. She was relieved this trip came with far less risk of weapons fire, but that didn't stop the restlessness from settling in. She didn't want to lose the focus she and Xynn had found together, the narrow, efficient orbit they'd been moving in.

The lift slowed. The shaft opened onto a broad force field, and Lily stepped forward instinctively, drawn to the view.

Field generators sparked just beyond the barrier, arcing with energy as they maintained the cloak—an invisible curtain that kept Bimini's inhabitants unaware they were being watched. Past it, the planet glowed. Coppery light rippled across the landscape, brighter even than the lift's harsh white illumination, but warmer too. Alive in a way the artificial light could never be.

"Look," Xynn said softly, pointing.

Along the rock face, red vines flowed through seams of crystal as if the stone itself had liquefied, the tendrils moving like something swimming—slow, deliberate, impossibly graceful. Lily felt the familiar chill of it, the reminder that Bimini's beauty was inseparable from its violence.

The doors swished open, loud and sudden.

Lily jumped.

"You okay?" Xynn asked, amused. "Need a tranquilizer or something?"

Lily shot her a glare through her bangs and stepped past her.

"Just nervous to see your girlfriend?" Xynn teased.

Lily didn't turn. She refused to give Xynn the satisfaction.

The hallway beyond was sterile and cold, the air scrubbed so clean it felt thin. Xynn jogged to catch up with her, the teasing fading as quickly as it had come.

"Hey," she said. "Say something. I'm sorry for teasing."

Lily exhaled, then smiled, genuine this time. "I'm just not really up for people. I want to get back to the mission. Or back to Adius II." She paused, then added, "Preferably with fewer clothes."

She tugged at the straps on Xynn's halter—

—and the door slid open.

Caris stood there, perfectly composed, her face as symmetrical as Lily remembered. She smiled, already shaking her head.

"You two."

They hugged.

"I really am sorry to call you all the way out here," Caris said.

The lab felt busier than Lily expected—not loud, just dense. Motion layered over motion. Screens blinked in tall vertical stacks, lines of data scrolling like rain. Glass cylinders lined the walls, each filled with drifting particulate suspended in pale amber light. Cables curved across the ceiling in bundled arcs and disappeared into the floor again like roots.

No one looked up.

The three of them stepped inside and threaded their way between workstations, and the dozen or so Union scientists continued without pause. Hands moved over instruments. Lenses adjusted. Something that looked halfway between a seismograph and a heart monitor ticked in slow, patient beats.

Lily felt the familiar unease of being present and unseen.

Unregistered.

Caris walked ahead of them, voice level, posture clipped with focus.

"We've been measuring the cycles for the last seven months," she said. "Tracking the fluctuations after the renewal we witnessed. The surface patterns are predictable—measurable. The vines continue to feed life throughout the planet."

They passed a transparent floor panel.

Beneath it, veins of copper and red pulsed faintly in the stone.

"Even though the next event shouldn't occur for approximately fifty years," Caris went on, "we're already seeing micro-variations in the planetary core. Drop-offs in the output of the Caronite life form."

Xynn's expression tightened. "Like a battery draining?"

Caris nodded once.

"Exactly. Nothing severe enough to interrupt function—but enough to imply the energy output is finite."

Lily glanced around the lab again.

Bodies in white coats and jumpsuits, heads bent toward their work.

Screens charted downward slopes. Gentle at first.

Then steeper.

The hair on the back of her neck prickled as Caris pulled up a live feed from one of the Bimini towns.

"It's unsettling, working here every day," Caris said softly—almost reverent.

On the screen, children ran through narrow streets, laughing as they chased one another beneath the copper light—their wiry silver hair catching and burning against it. The living red vine threaded through the background, always there, always moving.

"Hard to believe they're all doomed to annihilation by design."

Lily swallowed. "I imagine it takes a toll on you." There was a heartbeat of silence. "Leena... why did you need us to come out here?"

There was a look on Caris' face then—something halfway between nervousness and glee. A brightness that didn't quite reach her eyes.

"We discovered something," she said.

Lily waited.

Caris glanced back at the screens. "We've been monitoring individuals who were present during the renewal seven months ago. The ones who remained on-planet during the blast cycle. Their genomes are... shifting. Very slightly. Minor epigenetic changes across tissue samples. Nothing detectable in behavior yet, but measurable at the cellular level."

Lily's stomach tightened.

Caris hesitated, then added, almost too casually, "I didn't want to interrupt your honeymoon."

She looked at the floor as she said it.

Lily caught the flicker in her expression and couldn't quite place it. Embarrassment, maybe. Not jealousy. Something closer to curiosity—like Caris was trying to understand a question she hadn't asked out loud.

Caris straightened. "I couldn't raise King Zayir. He hasn't responded to my last three transmissions. And I needed another subject—someone I could trust." She turned back to Lily. "Can I run some tests on you? Just scans, initially. Inside a clean room. Then a controlled exposure to ambient radiation outside the barrier."

Lily nodded before she let herself overthink it.

She glanced at Xynn.

Xynn gave a small, reassuring smile. "I'll be fine waiting here. I have my own methods of torturing you."

Caris huffed a quiet breath that might have been a laugh.

Lily followed her toward the inner corridor, the lab lights brightening as they walked—screens reflecting across the glass like constellations. And somewhere beneath it all, she felt the faintest tug of unease, like something in the room had shifted direction without anyone saying so.

The clean room was colder than the lab.

Light washed across every surface—flat, clinical, almost colorless. The air smelled filtered, stripped of anything organic. Panels lined the walls in seamless planes, each one pulsing with a faint internal glow. In the center of the room, a narrow examination platform rose from the floor like a fragment of sculpture, cables disappearing into the base.

Lily stepped up onto it and rested her hands at her sides.

Caris adjusted a set of instruments overhead, the metal arms gliding into place with a soft hydraulic hum.

"Are the genetic changes dangerous?" Lily asked.

Caris shook her head. "No. Quite the opposite, actually." She studied a floating display, lips pressed thin in concentration. "Cellular repair markers are trending upward. Mitochondrial performance shows a slight improvement. It's almost like..." She hesitated. "Like we're getting a little younger."

Lily raised an eyebrow.

Caris caught it and allowed herself a small, rueful smile. "Only a very tiny bit. But there is some measurable health benefit."

She tapped a control and a new spectrum of light swept across Lily's skin—cool, blue-white. The machine whirred softly, recalibrating.

"So," Caris said, too casually. "How's married life?"

There was a note in her voice Lily recognized on instinct—suspicion, shading into concern.

Caris sees through me.

She felt her shoulders tighten.

"Well," Lily said carefully, "we've been really enjoying helping with the rebuilding efforts on Gherion Prime. Tevya's made a lot of progress." Her voice softened. "I wish Datch were there. We're both afraid to leave her alone for too long. She acts strong, but... she's hurting."

Caris nodded, accepting the shift in subject without pushing it.

She switched a lever and a different color light bathed the room—warmer, amber at the edges. A soft vibration shuddered through the platform.

"I never knew androids could be so... passionate," Caris said, without the slightest hint of irony.

Lily almost laughed.

There was so much she wanted to say—wanted to shout—but that was how the last six months had been. Every truth tucked behind timing. Every confession stalled.

"It isn't about that," she said quietly. "I love Xynn. You know that, right?"

Caris smiled. "I know. I've known since that day in zero-G training when you went as red as that sky out there at the mention of her name."

Lily felt heat climb into her cheeks again.

"I just wanted you to know," she murmured. "You seem... worried about it."

Caris drew in a slow breath.

"Look—it isn't that at all." She hesitated. "But I know it's selfish. I want you to stay in the fleet. I want to work with you on the Salamander again when we're recalled." A pause. "Calan is with Joren now. And I see that look in your eye."

"What look?"

Caris' smile tilted. "You hate authority."

"What? I do not— I mean, what does that have to do with—"

"I just…" Caris winced, as if she regretted bringing it up the moment the words left her mouth. "I worry this life isn't what will make you happy. Alrek is too—"

"Wait," Lily said. "You two are talking about me?"

"Forget I said anything."

Caris flipped a cylindrical instrument upward like an old periscope and powered it down. The lights in the room dimmed by a fraction.

"Let's get some fresh air," she said, nodding toward a hatch that led to a narrow observation platform outside.

By then, all Lily really wanted was to finish the scans and get out of the lab. There would be time to catch up later—time to talk, to laugh, to pretend things were normal—but the longer she stayed, the more she felt like she was risking something slipping loose. A word. A look. A truth she couldn't take back.

Caris led her out onto the observation platform.

The heat hit immediately.

It wrapped around her like a wet cloth, heavy and relentless. Even Gherion Prime, with its humid nights and metal-scorched afternoons, felt like a spring picnic by comparison. Sweat prickled across her shoulders and along the back of her neck. The light above the planet burned copper-bright, bleeding across the horizon.

Caris adjusted the portable scanner, its lenses ticking softly as they recalibrated in the open air.

Beyond the cloaking field, Lily could just make out the tiny shapes of the Bimini people moving through the distant settlement—figures crossing courtyards, children darting between doorways. They were close enough to see, too far to touch.

And completely unaware.

"Do you think they know?" Lily asked. "That their life cycle depends on nuclear destruction?"

Caris pursed her lips.

"We've learned the cycle doesn't benefit the people," she said. "Or any other surface life. Only the Caronite life form at the planetary core."

Lily felt her heartbeat climb.

"Wait—what?"

Caris kept her eyes on the scanner. "The detonation recharges the Caronite. In turn, it restores what was destroyed. But based on everything we've mapped so far... they're not a symbiotic species."

The heat pressed harder. Lily swallowed.

"So... what happens if it dies out?"

"In all likelihood?" Caris said softly. "Life would simply continue."

Lily stared out at the settlement.

"You mean they all die," she said. "They all really die. And what comes back after? Them? A copy?."

Caris didn't answer.

The silence sat between them—heavy, deliberate, impossible to step around.

Lily thought she might be sick if not for the overwhelming urge to leave, to get away from the heat and the light and the impossible truth of this place.

"Did you get what you needed?" she asked.

Caris lowered the scanner and gave a single, crisp nod.

"Yes. Let's get you out of the sun."

They stepped back into the lab's cool light.

Lily's gaze drifted immediately to the central monitor, where Xynn stood watching a live feed from one of the towns. Children ran through the streets, darting between low stone arches and crimson-shadowed walls. The vines threaded through the background like veins beneath skin—alive, patient, ever-present.

They laughed as they played.

Small bodies. Quick feet. Silver hair flashing copper in the light.

Children running and laughing in the shadows of inevitable destruction.

The knowledge hit her differently now.

Not as horror.

As certainty.

Every one of them would die—truly die—and whatever came back afterward would only look like them. Only move like them. Only echo what they had been.

Lily's chest went tight.

Caris said something to lighten the mood, something professional and kind, and the room drifted back toward the rhythm of work. Xynn brushed

Lily's arm and smiled as if to say *we'll talk later*, and Lily nodded, because that was how they survived these days—by threading humor over the hollow places and pretending it held.

But the image lingered.

Children laughing beneath a sky that had already written their ending.

On the shuttle ride out, the adrenaline finally wore off.

Xynn sat beside her and said nothing at first, one hand resting over Lily's knuckles. Lily blinked hard against the sting in her eyes, wiped at them once, tried again. It wasn't grief, not exactly. It was six months of restraint cracking at the edges. Six months of secrets. Six months of pretending the ground was still solid.

Xynn leaned closer and touched her cheek with the back of her fingers.

"Hang in there, Lily," she murmured. "I've got you."

Lily let herself rest against her, head on Xynn's shoulder as the shuttle climbed toward the upper atmosphere. The hull rattled with turbulence, metal shuddering around them. The world below shrank to copper light and red veins and distance.

A small purple light flickered to life on the black box clipped to Lily's belt.

She felt it before she looked—her breath tightening, her spine going straight. She glanced down at the display, eyes scanning the signal code.

Her grief folded itself away.

Her focus sharpened.

Lily sat up, sniffed once to clear her throat, and turned to Xynn.

Their eyes met—steady, aligned, no hesitation.

"We're close," she said.

Chapter 1: The Dream of the Dead

THE JUNGLES OF BIMARA breathed.

Not with wind—there was almost never wind—but with heat and life and the slow, patient pulse of things that had been growing for longer than anyone could measure. The leaves were thick and waxed with moisture, their edges beaded with droplets that clung and refused to fall. Vines twisted around the trunks of wide-bodied trees, red and umber and living-green, threading through the canopy like veins. Somewhere in the distance, something called out—low and resonant—swallowed again by the damp.

The air shimmered under the relentless light.

From orbit, Bimara looked gentle—a world wrapped in jade and gold, ringed in vapor like something holy. Below, it was dense. Clinging. Alive in ways that made you feel like you were trespassing just by breathing.

Lily watched it through the viewport.

The small jump ship vibrated around her with an energy that never quite became ambient—frenetic, insect-like—running through the deck plates and into the soles of her boots. The glass dimmed against the glare, but still the jungle glowed—layers on layers of foliage and rock, shadows pooling in ravines like dark water.

She thought of Xynn.

Not the Xynn sitting quietly across from her now—calm, composed, hands folded in her lap—but the Xynn who had endured Bimara. The one who had walked through the world's heat with a bruised spirit and a fire under her ribs, who had carried grief like a weight bolted to her spine and still stood tall.

Lily had been through her own storm here—fear, anger, guilt, the sharp ache of almost losing everything she'd only just begun to admit she wanted.

But Xynn...

Xynn had faced something else entirely.

Not just the planet. Not just the danger.

Ronin. The cult. The cage of expectation and devotion and threat.

The desperate thought that comes when you know you're being hollowed out, tic by tic—and you don't know if you will ever be restored.

Lily swallowed and tore her eyes away from the window.

The black box sat in her palm like a living thing.

Small. Matte. Edges smooth and cool against her skin. A faint seam ran around its middle, almost invisible unless she tilted it into the light. When she turned it, a single purple indicator pulsed softly—like a heartbeat under glass.

Her reflection hovered faintly in its surface.

The purple light steadied.

No longer pulsing—burning.

"Xynn," Lily said, already moving.

She slid the black box into the interface port beneath the console. Xynn was beside her in an instant, fingers flying across the controls, expression sharp and focused.

A chime cut through the cabin.

Then a voice.

Calm. Dry. Familiar in a way that belonged to another life.

"Good morning."

Lily exhaled all at once.

"Datch," she said, relief washing through the word. "I was beginning to think we lost you. You've been recompiling for almost a month since we last talked."

A faint pause—just long enough to feel like hesitation.

"My apologies," the voice replied. "Recovery has been...inexact. But successful to a degree that exceeds expectation. I have restored approximately nineteen percent of my cognitive programming."

"Nineteen percent," Lily echoed, barely above a whisper.

It sounded like a ghost of a person. A fraction. A survivor in pieces.

"I am grateful to be here at all," Datch continued. "When I initiated the data back-up, it was with the intent that the investigation not be lost. I did not anticipate that I would require the archive to recover...myself."

Xynn spoke softly, sincerity threading her tone.

"It's good to hear you again, Datch. Fragmented or not."

"Thank you," he replied. "Your presence is...appreciated."

Xynn keyed in a sequence and brought up a topographical sweep of the planet below. The terrain resolved in layers—ridgelines, cavern mouths, a dense lattice of tunnels spidering through the crust.

"We're in orbit over Bimara," she said. "Your theory about the underground ruins seems to be right on the money. The tunnels we found last time were only a fraction of what's down there."

"As I suspected," Datch observed. "Ronin required extensive subterranean shielding for his life-essence transfer array. It is efficient to reuse infrastructure where possible."

The display zoomed inward—a cavern system beneath a dense stretch of jungle, ringed with thermal distortions.

"And given that Nymara's Tear remains the most cumbersome element to transport," Datch went on, his voice fading in and out, "there is an even higher probability that he will return here."

Lily's hand tightened against the console.

"Nymara's Tear," she murmured. "As in...all the water in those underground rivers."

"Precisely," Datch confirmed.

Xynn's eyes lingered on the scan, then shifted.

"I still think we should have told Tevya."

Lily didn't hesitate.

"We agreed," she said. "Just the two of us until we verify he's really here."

A soft crackle passed through the speakers.

"I owe you a measure of personal gratitude for your discretion," Datch said. "There remains a non-trivial chance that my reconstruction will fail. If I decompile entirely, I would prefer Tevya not endure the loss a second time."

Xynn's gaze drifted to the small statue of the kitchen buddha fixed to the command panel—a good luck gift from Tevya.

Lily thought of her then. The quiet hospitality. The meals she made just for them. The way she moved through the kitchen with a kind of practiced joy—an old-world habit that didn't belong, not for someone who didn't eat.

"Let me go down," Xynn said, meeting Lily's eyes. "I don't like the thought of you running through those tunnels without me."

Lily shook her head — a small smile, a look of reproach flickering in her eyes.

"Absolutely not. I need you up here running the scanners. This is a great little jump ship — and honestly I'm still impressed the refugee mission trusted you with it — but these Saravethi controls give me a headache."

She unclipped the black box from the console and fastened it to a magnetic brace on her belt.

"Besides," she added, brushing her fingers across it, "I'll have Datch with me."

There was a faint ticking sound as the audio channel narrowed into a more localized field.

"Our likelihood of entering and exiting without detection is reasonably high," Datch said. "I calculate—"

"Don't you dare jinx this," Xynn cut in sharply.

The silence that followed stretched a beat too long.

"I cannot see your faces," Datch said. "Are we... joking? Not joking? Are we ready to depart?"

Lily shook her head, a smirk flickering at the corner of her mouth.

"Ready."

• • • •

Lily hated traveling by personal transport pod.

It felt like being sealed inside a very small elevator and then dropped off the side of Mount Everest. She'd only done it twice in simulations and once in real life—and she'd puked every time.

"A great way to start the mission," she muttered as the restraints tightened across her shoulders and chest.

The pod detached with a sharp metallic click and slipped free of the jump ship. Gravity vanished in a breath—then returned sideways.

"Did something go wrong?" Datch asked.

"No," Lily said tightly. "I'm just... not used to having a ghost around to talk to. So if it sounds like I'm talking to myself, I probably am."

"Noted," Datch replied.

The pod caught atmospheric drag.

Heat shuddered across the hull in waves. The craft pitched, then rolled, something rattling in the frame like bowling pins. The sound of wind wasn't really wind—more like pressure, screaming and compressing and hurling itself across the exterior plates.

Lily shut her eyes.

She counted her breaths.

One.

Two.

Three—

A warning tone chirped, rapid and insistent.

Landing cycle.

Her eyes snapped open as the pod slowed hard—except it didn't feel like slowing. It felt like falling in reverse, like her bones turned liquid and everything inside her slid the wrong direction.

Then—

Contact.

Soft.

Too soft.

Her body braced for an impact that never came—and the absence of it was worse; her gut felt as if it had been poured out across the floor and left there.

The restraints released with a hiss.

Lily folded forward, palms gripping her knees, willing the world to stop tilting.

No puke.

Maybe a good omen.

"Did the landing go well?" Datch asked.

"So far so good," Lily said, voice still thin.

The hatch cracked open and humid air surged in. The jungle pressed close—vines, low branches, a thick carpet of leaves shifting in slow, insect-laced motion. She dragged a few fallen limbs over the pod's hull, breaking and wedging them into place until its outline blurred into the undergrowth.

She slipped into cover, crouching beneath a wide-rooted tree.

Lily studied her scanner. "Xynn, I'm reading like... a million life signs."

Her earpiece filled with chirps, taps, and filtered data streams as Xynn worked.

A long second passed.

Then another.

"Yeah," Xynn said at last, voice tight. "There are a few dozen mercenaries in the area. But you're right—there's a lot of activity we didn't detect before."

The jungle hummed around her.

She could hear her own breath.

"Am I anywhere near the entrance we were aiming for?" Lily asked. "My scans are all turned around."

Xynn exhaled through her nose—frustrated. "It's that damn radiation from the underground springs."

Lily remembered almost dying here—more than once.

She pushed the thought aside.

"I thought we compensated for that."

"Yes," Xynn replied dryly. "Thanks for reminding me."

The jungle closed in around her as she moved.

Every step was a negotiation—roots twisting beneath the moss, leaves brushing damp and cool against her sleeves, insects stitching invisible threads through the air. Xynn guided her in small, precise murmurs through the comm, each course correction threading Lily deeper into the green.

Then the trees fell back.

The structure rose out of the growth like the memory of something ancient—stone blocks twice her height, edges softened by centuries of moisture and vine. The greenery crawled across it in living ropes, leaves trembling faintly as if breathing.

"Found it," Lily said.

She placed one palm against the warm stone and followed the wall until the carvings appeared—spirals, angled marks, clustered script—then there, half-buried beneath a curtain of vine.

"That's the one," she murmured. "The symbol for Veyrik."

"With your permission," Datch said gently, "I will transmit the sequence."

Lily nodded, even though he couldn't see.

Harmonics whispered through the stone—a layered hum that seemed to vibrate in the back of her teeth. Xynn's translated frequencies echoed through the channel, overlapping with Datch's reconstruction. The air shifted. Something deep inside the wall responded.

Stone slid.

The entrance opened like a wound healing in reverse.

Cool air washed over her—heavy with mineral damp and the faint metallic scent of still water. She stepped inside.

Her light cut through the darkness in a narrow cone. The walls were slick, etched with old reliefs lost beneath lichen. Filaments hung like thread from the ceiling—not quite spiderwebs, but close enough to make her skin crawl.

"I still don't quite understand," Lily said quietly. "Veyrik wasn't always a Gherionite?"

"Not precisely," Datch replied. His voice sounded different here, as if softened by the stone. "He was a member of the original Gherionite people—the organic race that predated my android kin. He led a rebellion against Leviathan's Hand, a coalition of species obsessed with the pursuit of eternal life."

Lily's boots splashed through a shallow film of water as she moved deeper. The echo followed her like a second heartbeat.

"When they captured him," Datch continued, "they sentenced him to serve as their first test subject."

The air grew colder.

"So they essentially sentenced him to eternal life?" Lily said.

"In android form," Datch answered. "The ancient storm-worshipers explored countless organic methods of prolonging their lives. Their attempts failed. They became... distorted. Monstrous. One by one, they went mad—and destroyed one another."

Lily swallowed.

"Only Veyrik remained," Datch said. "As Ronin, he transferred each inhabitant of Gherion Prime who pledged loyalty into artificial bodies. Those who resisted... were executed."

"Charming," Lily muttered.

She swept her light across a collapsed archway. Something skittered out of view, the motion gone before her brain could name it.

"But he never abandoned the singular goal," Datch went on. "A perfect organic vessel. One that could house his consciousness indefinitely—and replicate the sensation, emotion, and physicality of the body he lost."

Lily frowned.

"That just seems kind of... greedy. And honestly, insulting. I mean—to androids."

"I am not offended," Datch replied, entirely sincere.

Lily shook her head—a thin chuckle hissed through her nose.

She slowed at a branching corridor.

"What am I actually looking for? Xynn, am I going the right way? Xynn?"

A hiss of static filled her ear.

"Interference," Datch said gently. "The mineral density here is... significant."

Lily tightened her grip on the scanner.

She moved deeper into the corridor, boots whispering against damp stone. Her light skimmed along the walls—fractured carvings, half-collapsed alcoves, places where the ceiling dipped low enough that she had to duck. The air grew warmer the farther she went—heavy, metallic, humming with a subtle pressure she could feel in her bones.

The scanner flickered.

A spike—then noise—then another faint rise.

Lily slowed.

"Hold on," Lily whispered.

She lifted the scanner, watching the waveform jitter and reform. A faint thermal bloom edged along the right wall—subtle, but wrong for stone.

She stepped closer.

The surface wasn't carved like the others. It was smooth—tiled, each piece fitted so tightly the seams vanished unless you caught them in the light just right.

"This wall," she murmured. "I think there's a room on the other side. The temperature's different. Warmer."

"I may be able to interface with the lattice," Datch said. "Stand clear. I will attempt harmonics."

A low vibration filled the corridor—not sound so much as pressure. The tiles shimmered faintly, then began to separate, each segment sliding inward before lifting with a grinding, ancient groan.

"Datch, you did it," Lily breathed.

The wall rose—

And the world opened.

Sunlight knifed in through the gap, flooding the darkness with heat and dust and the sound of voices. Beyond the threshold, the corridor gave way to a wide open pavilion carved into the cliff face—and below it—

A camp.

Tents. Equipment racks. Power cells.

And no fewer than two dozen heavily armed mercenaries.

Every head turned.

Every weapon followed.

"Shit."

Lily spun and bolted.

"Datch, close the door!"

"What is the matter?"

"Close the damn door!"

Footsteps thundered behind her—shouts, metal striking stone, the snap-crack of weapons powering up.

"Lily?" Xynn's voice surged through the static. "What's happening?"

"We found friends," Lily hissed, lungs burning.

Blaster fire erupted—searing bolts tearing past her shoulders, scorching the stone beside her as she drove forward, legs pumping, heart hammering in her throat.

The jungle exploded into sound.

Blaster fire cracked through the trees—sharp, electric—scorching bark and sending birds erupting into the canopy. Lily ran, lungs burning, boots slipping in wet soil as branches slapped at her arms.

"Lily—east," Xynn called in her ear, breath tight. "You need to get to the next temple, about half a kilometer. I was trying to warn you that one was a dead end—I couldn't get through."

"But it had Veyrik's name on it," Lily shouted, ducking under a low branch as a bolt tore a molten scar across the rock beside her.

Datch cut in.

"'Veyrik' was a word used by the ancient storm-worshipers. Approximate translation would be: 'gateway.'"

Lily barked out a humorless breath mid-stride.

"Now he tells me."

Two speeder bikes burst over the ridge ahead—engines shrieking, riders leaning forward like knives.

Blaster fire rained down.

Lily dove behind an embankment. Dirt slid beneath her palms—another bolt struck hard against her hip.

She heard it before she felt it.

A sharp metallic crack.

The black box on her belt sparked—purple light flaring—then dying.

"Datch!" she hissed.

Static.

"Just my luck—just my luck—and don't you start on jinxes either," she snapped toward Xynn, jaw tight, as she yanked her blaster free.

She hated this part.

Hated the weight of the weapon. Hated the way muscle memory slid into place.

She was an excellent shot.

Most days, she hated that too.

Today... maybe not.

She fired—one rider spun sideways off the bike, the second clipped a tree and vanished in a shower of leaves and metal.

Lily slid down the embankment, boots skidding through mud, momentum carrying her into a steep spill of loose red earth. The jungle roared—engines, shouting, echoes ricocheting through the trees—closing in from too many directions at once.

"Which way?" she gasped, scrambling upright.

Her hair clung to her forehead—slick with sweat, caught in her lashes.

She shoved it back with the heel of her hand.

"Fucking hair."

The sound of pursuit tightened around her—circling—while the path ahead narrowed into shadow.

The jungle narrowed into corridors of pressure and heat.

Her scanner flickered in fits and bursts—direction collapsing and reforming as the signatures around her multiplied, circling, tightening like a closing fist. They weren't chasing her from behind anymore. They were ahead. To the sides. Above the ridges. The sound of engines came in waves, bouncing and returning, until it felt less like pursuit and more like a net being drawn shut.

Loose red earth slid out from under her boots and she rode it down, half-controlled, half-gravity, until her feet struck hard at the base of a jagged cut in the earth. The ravine opened into a vertical shaft—stone walls slick with condensation, roots dangling into darkness.

She edged forward.

The bottom was too far down to see.

"Xynn," she said, breath ragged. "Is there water at the bottom of that chasm?"

A heavy vehicle crested somewhere beyond the ridge—deep engine, industrial, close.

Static. Then Xynn's voice, strained.

"Yes. I think so. I'm... seventy-five percent sure."

Lily huffed out a thin, humorless breath.

"I sure hope you're right."

She tapped the control on her chest harness. The diving rig cinched tight—padding compressing around her ribs, helmet seal hissing into place. For a moment, the world narrowed to the sound of her own breath.

Then she jumped.

The air tore past her in a rushing column—cool, then cold, then nothing but blackness. She fell for what felt like forever, weightless and helpless and utterly committed to the choice she'd already made.

Something flickered at her hip.

The purple light sputtered back to life.

Datch's voice arrived with improbable calm.

"We appear to be falling."

"Ding ding ding," Lily muttered—then the world hit her.

Impact.

A shock of water—hard and enveloping—slammed into her from below. The suit absorbed most of it, padding blooming around the force, but the breath still punched out of her lungs in a burst of bubbles.

She kicked.

Floated.

Broke the surface with a ragged gasp as the breathing rig released and folded back.

Blue light pulsed faintly along the cavern ceiling—phosphorescent veins tracing the tunnel system in long, ghostly arcs. The underground spring stretched in every direction, quiet and echoing, like a cathedral drowned in stone.

Lily spat water and dragged in a clean breath.

"Glad to have you back," she said to Datch, voice thin but steady.

"Likewise," he replied. "We should avoid repeating that experience."

Xynn's voice cut in, cracking with relief.

"Thank god you're okay. Please don't ever do that again."

Lily treaded water, turning slowly, eyes searching the dim passages.

"Well," she said, breath soft but edged, "if you both stop leading me into armies of angry marauders... please tell me you can direct me which way to go."

"Straight," Xynn said—sure this time.

Lily secured her respirator and began to swim toward the light.

The passage stretched on and on.

The water narrowed into a shallow channel that fed into a stone causeway. Lily hauled herself out and onto the slick floor, boots scraping softly as she rolled to her knees. She released the pressure seal on her suit—padding loosening, the rigid plates easing away from her ribs—and drew in a steadier breath.

The air was different here.

Cooler.

Older.

It tasted like minerals and dust and time.

She started forward.

The corridor ran straight and long, its walls carved smooth by hands that had known precision and ritual. Fine grooves traced the stone in interlocking patterns, the lines catching faint blue light that pulsed from somewhere unseen. Water dripped in slow, patient intervals from the ceiling—each drop echoing like a metronome.

The sound of voices bled in from ahead.

Muffled. Layered. Too far away to distinguish words—only cadence, tension, breath.

Lily slowed.

Something lay against the far wall.

A body.

Face turned away, armor scorched and split across the chest, a weapon still clutched uselessly in one hand. She stepped past it carefully, jaw tightening as another shape emerged a few meters farther on.

Then another.

She remembered Bimara's last reckoning—Ronin had murdered his own guards. And then, ultimately, he had murdered Datch. Taken her friend—no—ripped him away from her.

Resolve settled into her like weight. Resolve and—anger.

"We're not leaving here without him," she said—quiet, but clad in steel.

There was a faint sound in her ear—Xynn's tongue tapping her teeth again.

"Lily..."

To Lily's surprise, Datch spoke over her.

"She is correct in her assessment," he said. "I am detecting a structure consistent with the consciousness transfer device. Ronin is within proximity of achieving his intended objective. If he succeeds—and if this... distraction is concluded—his potential for harm becomes incalculable."

The voice ahead sharpened.

Closer now. Almost words.

"He has to be stopped," Lily said. Water clung to her hair and ran steadily down her neck. "It ends here."

"You're right," Xynn said—the words stiff with worry. "But you know how dangerous he is. Do not let him see you. And if you have to—take him out."

Lily nodded.

Cold. Focused.

"I'll try to stun him. Restrain him. We'll call in the fleet. In fact..." She exhaled. "Maybe make that call now, Xynn."

"I already did."

More bodies lay scattered along the stone—Ronin's men, eyes glassy and fixed on nothing. The corridor widened by degrees—stone angling outward until the hall opened into a vast chamber.

Lily stopped just inside the threshold.

The room was enormous—two hundred feet across at least—and hexagonal. Light existed everywhere and nowhere at once—no lamps, no fixtures—only a diffuse glow suspended in the air, as if the room itself remembered how to be illuminated.

Ancient machinery lined the walls, fused into the stone—copper conduits, crystalline lattices, curved plates etched with spirals of unreadable script. Bones and mummified remains lay in clusters across the floor, some arranged deliberately, some collapsed where they'd fallen centuries ago.

At the center of it all—

Ronin.

Hunched over a device that looked as though a monolith had been carved open and taught to think. Part stone. Part machine. Part something far older than either. His long frame bent in concentration, hands moving across a bank of controls that pulsed with an inner, feverish light.

"In and out without detection, right, Datch?" Lily murmured.

"I am... eating my words, as Tevya would say," Datch replied.

Ronin's voice rumbled deeply as he worked—an old, fractal language that rose and fell in jagged poetry.

"Old Gherionite," Datch said. "Somewhere between a prayer and... a cry for help."

Ronin shifted a control.

A tall cylindrical column rotated with slow, deliberate weight, revealing a containment cradle tucked within its core—sleek, polished, unmistakably modern. The contrast was jarring—Union-grade preservation technology grafted into ancient architecture.

A cryo-pod, Lily was fairly sure.

It opened with a reverent hiss.

Inside stood a body—tall, powerful, rendered in muscle and line. The features echoed Ronin's, but refined, corrected, perfected. Youth and age at war in the same face. The skin was not the pale marble tone of the Gherionites—but warmer, clay-colored, as if sculpted from earth rather than plaster.

"The organic vessel?" Lily whispered.

"Indeed," Datch replied—his voice shifting, something like unease beneath its composure.

"Lily... I have an idea."

Lily moved along the outer crawlway as quietly as she could, keeping to the shadows that curved around the chamber's edge. She matched her steps to the drip of water and the low thrum of machinery, inching closer to a thick conduit that bridged several of the systems together.

Ronin remained lost in his work.

His attention was absolute—body rigid, voice murmuring in Old Gherionite as his hands traced reverent, ritualized movements across the console.

Lily crouched beside the conduit and lifted the damaged black box.

"The circuitry is failing," she whispered. "This is probably our only shot, Datch. Good luck."

There was a pause.

Then—soft, sincere—

"Whatever happens... thank you."

Lily swallowed.

She pressed the connector into the conduit.

The black box hummed—weak, unstable—and Datch began tuning harmonics through the failing pathways just as Ronin powered the machine fully online. The chamber brightened in violent pulses. The vessel inside the pod twitched, muscles responding to stimulation, breath rising in pre-programmed rhythm.

Ronin laid himself down upon the transfer cradle.

He positioned his head with deliberate care—hands folding over his chest, eyes shining with rapture.

He was ready to leave his body behind.

He may be in for a surprise, Lily thought.

The machine roared to life.

Energy rippled across the chamber—electric filaments crackling along the stone, the ground trembling beneath Lily's boots. Sparks burst from the black box. The purple light guttered—then died.

She held it in place anyway—fingers locked, jaw clenched.

The transfer field intensified.

Ronin's face softened into blissful anticipation.

And behind him—

The organic vessel stepped free of the cryo-pod.

It moved with weight.

With presence.

With awareness.

Ronin sensed it before he saw it. His eyes snapped open. He twisted upright in one fluid motion—staring into the face of the being that should not have existed.

"It isn't possible..." he breathed.

Silence.

Lily glanced down at the blackened shell in her hand.

"Datch!" she called. "Remember the plan—restrain him!"

She didn't know if he could hear her.

Didn't know if consciousness had landed where she hoped.

The being's mouth twisted into a crooked, unsettling grin.

Ronin took half a step back.

"Datch...?" he said carefully.

The being tilted its head.

"Well... close enough," it replied.

Then—without hesitation—it wrapped one arm around Ronin's throat and locked the hold tight.

Lily lurched forward, hand outstretched.

"Wait—!"

The crack echoed through the chamber.

Bone. Metal. Something between the two.

It was the kind of sound that made the stomach turn.

Ronin collapsed to the floor.

"Datch..." Lily whispered.

"What's happening?" Xynn cut in over comms—voice sharp with panic.

The new being nudged Ronin's body with his foot.

"It's alright," he said calmly. "It is safe to come down now, Lily."

She approached slowly.

Her chest felt hollow.

This... this wasn't how Datch acted.

Not her friend.

"Datch?" she said again—quiet, uncertain.

The being looked at his hands, then at himself—flexing fingers, testing breath.

"Not sure," he answered. "Mostly... I would say."

Their eyes fell to Ronin's body.

The being studied it with clinical curiosity.

"Very interesting."

His tone was cold.

Detached.

He prodded the corpse once more with the toe of his boot.

"It would appear... I have completed the assignment."

· · · ·

The shuttle descended fast, engines flaring as it fought the uneven air. Heat rolled across the landing site, dry and abrasive, crawling over Lily's skin and cutting through the seams of her jumpsuit. The wind tore across the stone in hard bursts, carrying dust and grit that stung her eyes and snapped against the hull. The noise filled her ears until they rang—but her heartbeat still cut through it, loud and insistent, faster than the engines ever were.

Xynn stood at her side. They hadn't had a chance to be alone since Xynn joined her on the planet—no chance to explain what had happened. Lily met her gaze and felt the weight of it settle between them. The worry in Xynn's eyes was unmistakable, and Lily didn't bother pretending she could hide her own. They held the look, both knowing the other could see everything.

Nearby, Datch—whatever he was now—carried the bodies out from the chamber. He moved carefully, efficiently, laying them out and covering them against the wind. There was something almost ceremonial in the precision of his movements. Lily didn't question the task. She welcomed the distance—at least until the Union arrived.

Then the light caught the livery, and Lily couldn't stop the faint curve of a smile as the shuttle touched down.

Salamander.

The hatch released and dropped onto the stone with a solid, echoing thud.

For a moment, it felt like all sound stopped.

Except for that incessant heartbeat.

Lily felt Datch's presence beside her before she looked. His shape was close enough to register in her peripheral vision, familiar and wrong at the same time. His appearance echoed other Gherionites she'd seen—but altered. More human. Not human. More *flesh and blood*. He didn't look like Ronin. Not exactly. But he didn't look like Datch either.

Boots clacked down the ramp. Lily lifted her head, squinting against the backlighting of the setting sun.

"Alrek!"

The relief in her voice escaped before she could stop it. He crossed the distance quickly, and she met him halfway. They embraced, hard and brief.

"What have you gotten us into now, Lily?" Alrek said, his tone testing, familiar.

Lily pulled back and glanced around. A few crew she recognized. A few she didn't.

And the captain.

"Captain Dalren." Lily straightened, the seriousness settling in as she processed who stood in front of her.

The last time she'd seen Dalren was on Starbase Twelve. She'd assumed he was on his way to indictment—cover-ups, smuggling, years of diverted Union resources, all in service of protecting his estranged son. She had not imagined him standing on a landing site, in command of a starship.

Her ship.

"Lieutenant Starling," Dalren said warmly. "Good to see you again. At last."

They shook hands.

"And you must be Xynn," he added, turning easily toward her. "I've heard quite a lot about you two."

Xynn bowed, heels clicking together in practiced respect.

There was a pause. Lily felt it stretch, then realized it was hers to break. She gestured toward Datch.

"And this is—"

She stopped. The words didn't come.

Datch wore a faint, almost playful smile, nodding encouragingly, as if helping her along.

"It's okay," he said lightly. "You can say it."

Alrek frowned.

"I am Datch," Datch said. For just a moment, the cadence of his voice felt familiar enough to tighten Lily's chest. Then his grin widened—too wide, too easy. "That wasn't so hard, was it?"

"Datch?" Alrek echoed, stunned.

"Well, it sure is," Dalren said, stepping forward. He took Datch's hand with open enthusiasm, pumping it once. "It's good to have you back, Commander. Truly. But how?"

Datch pursed his lips, considering.

"The object of my... resurrection is in the chamber," he said, matter-of-fact. "I've been clearing it out so we can detonate it."

Lily's stomach churned as they descended into the chamber again. Even without the violence that had taken place here, something about this space resisted reason. The air felt wrong—heavy, inert, as if it had absorbed too much and never learned how to let go. Very few things struck Lily as purely, instinctively immoral. This did.

Datch filled the silence as they moved, explaining the mission in clipped bursts—the tracking of Ronin, the reconstruction of his program, the transfer.

"I am lucky to be alive," he said, almost casually.

Dalren listened without interruption. Then, carefully, "This artifact. This machine. How does it work?"

Datch's posture shifted. He burst with an uncomfortable enthusiasm.

"It is a wonder," he said. "The ancient Gherionites, working alongside a kind of galactic cabal, discovered a path to eternal life. Consciousness transfer. A complete preservation of self. Unfortunately, the process destabilized them. They descended into madness and destroyed one another. Ronin, however, was able to stabilize the transfer. It would need much more study to fully understand."

"The Union scientists will have quite the time picking this one apart," Alrek said matter-of-factly.

Lily side-eyed him.

Dalren nodded. "A discovery of this importance—"

They entered the main chamber, and his voice fell away.

The space opened before them, vast and terrible in its symmetry. The structure dominated the room, its intricate surfaces catching the low light in ways that made Lily's skin prickle. For a moment, no one spoke. The machine did not hum or glow. It simply *held* the space.

"Sorry to be the one to put the brakes on this," Xynn said, stern but steady. "But I agree with Datch. No good will come from the existence of this... device."

Lily nodded once. "Destroying it was the plan from the beginning."

Dalren's expression tightened—not quite a smile. "Then you shouldn't have called in the cavalry."

Lily instinctively turned toward Alrek.

"Mr. Alrek," Dalren continued smoothly, "please assemble a team. We'll need a full scan before we begin transferring this equipment to the ship."

Alrek nodded sharply and turned away.

Lily stared after him. "Wait—you're taking this aboard the *Salamander*?"

She looked at Datch. His expression had darkened.

"Lieutenant," Dalren said, "I've formally requested your recall to active duty. Command will be in touch shortly. I recommend packing your things. The *Salamander* needs you."

Lily didn't speak.

"Fleet command trusted me with temporary command during this difficult time because of my background in logistics," Dalren went on. "I asked for you aboard because of your leadership skills—and your tendency to think outside the box."

Xynn stepped forward. "Difficult time?"

Alrek had already disappeared up the ramp. Lily could feel heat creeping up her neck.

"The news will hit the relays soon enough," Dalren said. "A highly lethal plague has swept through the Nullstorm Region. Thousands of citizens of the Krythar Ascendancy are already dead."

Lily's anger slipped away as quickly as it had arrived. "Thousands?"

Dalren paused. "Hundreds of thousands, I'm afraid. The pathogen is designated VEN-2E. An organosilicon retrovirus—it hijacks cellular structure, calcifies internal organs. Turns you to stone from the inside out. Nasty business." He exhaled softly. "It's spread through New Xyridren and into the outer belt of Union space. Civilians on Nassius IV are calling it the Shard—but they've always had a flair for dramatics."

Lily and Xynn exchanged a look.

"That's awfully close to the Saravethi colonies," Xynn said grimly.

Dalren's tone sharpened. "Which is why I don't have time for improvisation or cowboy judgments. Command will determine the fate of this... thing."

His gaze settled on Datch.

"Is that going to be a problem?"

Lily's mind finally went completely quiet.

Datch smiled—that same uneasy, oversized grin as before. "Of course not, sir." He met Dalren's eyes. "Eryk. Chain of command and all that."

Lily felt Xynn's hand close around her arm, steady and warm.

"What do we do now?" Lily whispered—though she already knew the answer.

Xynn would have to report to her duties with the Saravethi relief effort, and Lily would report to the Salamander.

Xynn smiled faintly. "You heard the man," she said. "We go pack. And knowing you, we'll have to do laundry first."

THE CLINIC WAS A CONVERTED community hall on the edge of town—low ceilings, dust motes drifting through slanted light, rows of folding chairs filled with quiet, watchful families. Outside the open doors, the square was full: people waiting in line, others standing back with their arms folded, as if distance itself offered protection. Lily couldn't make out words—only the low murmur of voices, the occasional cough, the scrape of shoes against the walk.

Dr. Thesari moved between stations, her white coat smudged with the day's work. She'd been here since dawn. She talked as she prepped syringes—soft voice, steady hands—a low, continuous stream of explanation that felt less like conversation than something she needed to keep herself anchored.

"People wonder why the Union vaccine is in limited supply—practically flying off the shelves," she said to Lily as they loaded doses. "I tell them the truth. It's familiar. Human labs. No synthetic bridge."

She nodded toward the cooler holding the matte-black vials.

"The Gherionite one is... generous. They developed it themselves to stem the spread of the plague—shared the formula freely. They had the incubation tech to fuse silicon components with organic tissue. It saved thousands. Countless, really."

Her mouth tightened, just slightly.

"But then the whispers started. 'Unnatural.' 'Why trust something made by machines?' Some people even claim the Gherionites started the plague. Poppycock, I say—just fear. But fear sticks."

Lily nodded, scanning the line beyond the doors. "We're supposed to give them what they choose."

"That's the order," Tess agreed. "Choice." She hesitated, then glanced back at the cooler. "But choice only works when people trust the options."

She checked the manifest again.

"We're down to twenty Union doses," she said quietly. "After that, it's Gherionite—or nothing."

Lily stepped closer to the open doors and looked out at the line winding past the square.

Tirium III. A small Ishrethi colony, quiet by Union standards. Cooperative. On the list of places that were supposed to be easy.

As the plague crept farther into Union space, more inhabited worlds slipped into danger. Tirium III was in the red zone now. It should have been a friendly stop. Stable governance. Good relations. No history of trouble.

And yet.

Lily watched the people outside. They weren't just afraid. They were wound tight with it. Arms crossed too firmly. Voices pitched low and sharp, as if restraint itself required effort. A few faces turned away when they noticed the Union insignia on Lily's jacket. Others watched her openly, with an edge she hadn't expected when the *Salamander* first arrived.

Friendly didn't look like this.

Lily felt the wrongness settle in her chest. Anger this early meant something else had already taken root—and fear, once it curdled, didn't stay contained for long.

Alrek stood at the front table, calm and methodical, and Lily couldn't help thinking how much he'd changed in the past year. He followed orders now. Cleanly. Like a proper soldier.

You're an engineer, not a grunt, she'd told him once. He hadn't laughed the way she'd expected.

Dalren had noticed him. With the Raath-Ka away at the Fleet Academy for the term, Alrek had been singled out—pulled closer, trusted. He'd been proud of it, even if he never said so out loud.

Now he handed out Union vials to anyone who asked, steady and efficient. Lily always offered the Gherionite option as well, careful to keep her tone neutral. When someone hesitated, Alrek would step in gently.

"Your choice," he'd say, already reaching for the blue vials, keeping the line moving.

Lily kept trying to work the line, keeping her voice low, speaking to those who lingered.

"The Gherionite vaccine is safe," Lily said. "It's the same one they used in the Nullstorm region. It didn't just slow the outbreak—it stopped it. We know what it can do, because we've already watched it work."

A man near the front—broad shoulders, tired eyes—met her gaze and held it. His wife stood beside him, one hand resting on the shoulder of their teenage daughter. The girl watched Lily closely, her expression open, curious.

The father spoke at last, his voice flat with decision. "We'll take the Union one. All of us."

The girl glanced at Lily. "Dad... she said it's safe."

He shook his head once. "You know what they're saying," he said. "I'm not taking chances."

Behind them, the line stirred.

"They're pushing the synth stuff again," a woman muttered.

"If it's so safe," someone else added, "why did the Union make a new vaccine?"

The words moved through the room like ripples—quiet, almost polite—but spreading all the same.

Lily kept her voice even. "No one's pushing. It's still your choice."

The girl looked from her father to Lily, then back again. "I mean..." She shrugged, uncertain. "I'll take the Gherionite one. Look, they're almost out of the other one."

She gestured toward the thinning row of blue vials. The gold bangles at her wrist clinked together as her hand dropped.

Her father's expression tightened. He turned toward Lily—not raising his voice, but the accusation landed all the same. "You see what you've done?" he said. "You put the idea in her head, my own daughter—"

He stopped, jaw working, but the moment had already tipped.

The low murmur behind him grew denser. People leaned in. A few stepped closer to the barriers, not aggressively—but close enough to change the space. Arms folded. Hands clenched and unclenched. The air felt smaller, tighter.

Alrek came to Lily's side. "Lily," he said quietly, the way he does when he's about to get under her skin. "We're following protocol. They decide."

She didn't look away from the crowd. "We're almost out of Union doses," she said under her breath. "If we don't start offering the Gherionite vaccine more clearly, people are going to leave without anything."

Alrek met her eyes, his expression apologetic but firm. "Then they leave," he said. "You know the orders. If they refuse, that's on them."

The father tugged his daughter back. She resisted for a second, then let herself be pulled in line. The next person stepped forward.

The line moved again—but it wasn't the same. People weren't just waiting anymore.

They were watching Lily.

Alrek turned to her. "Why don't you take the Gherionite stock in the speeder truck to the next site," he said. "Take Carter and Gomez."

Lily hesitated, her gaze drifting back to the line—families still waiting, shoulders drawn tight, children pressed close to their parents. A few of them were looking past her now, toward the door, as if measuring the space between patience and panic.

She didn't like being pushed aside.

She liked it even less when it was Alrek doing the pushing.

Lily nodded sharply.

They loaded the speeder truck quickly, efficiently, under the steady weight of watching eyes. No one spoke as the last latch snapped into place. Carter kept his head down. Gomez fixed his attention on the controls, jaw tight.

The truck was barely more than a reinforced utility rig—lightweight, open-sided, designed for short hops between sites. More cart than transport.

It eased into the narrow side alley, repulsor humming low.

For a few seconds, Lily caught her breath.

Then she noticed the looks.

Faces hardened as they passed—scowls replacing caution. A man spat onto the sidewalk. Someone else shouted something she couldn't quite catch, swallowed by the hum of the engine.

Another voice cut through, sharp and clear: "Synth lover."

Lily turned, too late to see who'd said it.

The first impact came from behind—a dull tap against the hull. Testing.

Then another.

A stone skidded along the side panel. Hands slapped against metal. Someone banged a fist against the rear frame. The noise multiplied, messy and overlapping now, no single voice in charge of it anymore.

"Should I hit the boosters?" Carter asked, fingers hovering.

Lily gripped the side rail. "No," she said immediately. "I don't want to risk hurting anyone."

The truck lurched as weight shifted against it. More hands now. Not organized—just momentum finding itself. The vehicle tilted, barely at first, enough for Lily to feel gravity hesitate.

Then the balance went.

Lily cut the repulsor, afraid the recoil would throw someone under the frame.

Metal screamed as the truck hit the pavement, crates breaking loose inside.

The world turned sideways—and stopped.

For a moment, Lily stayed where she was, braced against the tilted frame, breath loud in her ears. The repulsor whined and died. Dust hung in the air. Somewhere nearby, someone was shouting—too close.

Then hands appeared at the open side of the truck.

Shadows moved past the frame. The crowd was already closing in, faces pressed near, voices climbing over one another. Someone struck the hull with something hard. Another voice shouted again—angrier this time.

"Out," Carter said sharply.

They scrambled free, boots hitting road, barely clearing the truck before someone yanked at one of the loose crates.

That's when Carter and Gomez drew their weapons.

"Back up!" Gomez shouted, firing a warning shot into the air.

It didn't slow anything.

The crowd surged forward—hands reaching for the crates, bodies pressing in, anger finally uncoiling now that it had permission. Someone slammed into the side of the truck. Another cracked open a case, vials spilling across the ground.

Three Ishrethi men broke from the edge of the crowd, moving fast and without coordination—just momentum and anger carrying them forward. One still had an anti-synth placard clenched in his fist, the lettering smeared and flaking.

Carter reacted first. Then Gomez.

Stun rounds cracked through the air. The men went down hard, not gracefully—one stumbling before he fell, another twisting as he hit the earth. The sound of it landed heavier than the shots themselves.

"Cease fire!" Lily shouted. "Cease fire—what the hell are you doing?"

They lowered their weapons, but it was too late.

The moment the men hit the ground, something broke loose. The crowd surged—not all at once, but in waves—people pressing forward, shouting over one another, hands reaching for the truck and the crates. The focus fractured just enough to give Lily an opening.

She shoved her way through, catching Carter by the arm. "Fall back," she said, forcing her voice steady. "We can't salvage this."

They pulled away together, retreating down the alley under a hail of thrown objects—rocks striking the pavement, scraps of metal, shouted curses that chased them as the distance opened up.

By the time they reached the corner, the noise had dulled into something less distinct. Shouting blurred into a low, restless roar. Lily didn't look back. She didn't need to.

What had been a line was now a riot.

Lily's comm tag chirped. Dryst Amaris's voice cut cleanly through the noise.

"Lieutenant, please report back to the ship. Union vaccine supply is exhausted, and there appears to be some sort of unrest."

"Thanks for the heads-up." Lily slapped the comm tag dark.

The anger settled behind her ribs, hot and steady, refusing to burn out as they made their way back to the shuttle.

As it lifted off, Lily stared through the viewport at the shrinking town below. Smoke rose in thin, ugly plumes from somewhere near the square. The image branded itself into her mind. The girl's bracelets, clinking. The brief light in her eyes when she'd understood. The father's fear, tight and protective. The way the crowd had tipped so quickly into fury.

She looked across at Alrek.

He shifted his gaze from the window to his boots. Then back to the window. He didn't look at her.

Lily leaned her head back against the shuttle seat and closed her eyes.

• • • •

Steam filled the small shower in slow, curling sheets, clinging to the walls and beading along the mirror. Lily stood under the spray longer than necessary, letting the water run hot against her shoulders, her back—the places where the day had lodged itself. Dust slid down the drain in pale streaks. The sharp smell of salt finally gave way to soap.

She closed her eyes and breathed.

When she stepped out, toweling her hair dry, the familiar two-tone chirp sounded from her console—the one Caris always used. Lily smiled. Relief.

She tapped the screen.

"About time," Lily said.

"Hey," Caris said, her voice perfectly poised as always. "Yeah. I made it aboard."

"Is your replacement finally up to your satisfaction on the Bimini project?" Lily teased.

"It'll have to do," Caris said, without a trace of sarcasm.

"Well, welcome home," Lily said, surprised by her own sincerity.

Caris's tone softened. "You holding together? I heard things went... well. You okay?"

"Better after a shower," Lily said matter-of-factly.

She sighed. "They acted crazy, Leena." Paused, reconsidering. "They acted desperate. We were literally handing them the solution, and they just—"

"Weren't exactly grateful," Caris finished.

"Yeah."

"Hey," Caris said, rallying. "Dinner tonight? We can catch up. Burgers and fries? Catch up with ketchup? Eh?"

Lily grinned wide and squeezed her eyes with her fingers. "Ugh. Stick to operations, Leena."

They both laughed.

"To be honest, I'm not really hungry," Lily said. "But I could go for ice cream. Or something sweet. Just—don't tell Alrek. You know how he is about sweets."

Caris laughed softly through her nose. "0700?"

"See you then."

The comm went flat, and Lily rubbed the towel through her hair again, slower this time, feeling the last of the heat ebb from her skin. The quiet settled in—almost peaceful.

She stepped into the bedroom and wrapped the towel around herself just as the screen chimed.

Lily crossed the room and pressed the access panel, already smiling. "You know, Leena, we can share one of those chocolate cakes you like—"

She froze.

King Zayir stared back at her from the display, caught mid-expression as he tried—and failed—to school his face into something dignified. The grin slipped through anyway, wide and unmistakably amused.

Lily tightened her grip on the towel and drew it closer, suddenly aware of the lingering steam, her damp hair, the heat climbing up her neck.

She lifted her chin and assembled her least-embarrassed expression.

"Your Majesty," she said evenly, even as her cheeks burned. "I wasn't expecting a call."

Zayir cleared his throat, still smiling despite himself. "My apologies, Lieutenant Starling. I believe I... mistimed this."

She held his gaze, willing the flush to fade.

"Well," Lily said, steady now, "I appreciate the call. How can I help?"

"I wanted to check in," Zayir said gently. "After what happened at the colony. The *Salamander's* efforts. Your efforts, specifically, Lily."

Her name landed with a familiar discomfort. Lily let it pass. She could forgive—she'd learned how to do that—but she hadn't forgotten the stunts he'd pulled, the ways he'd overstepped.

"Don't mention it," she said evenly. "And thank you for checking in."

Zayir nodded. "I also wanted you to know the Ishrethi government remains one hundred percent behind the combined Union–Gherionite vaccine effort. Despite the rumors."

"Rumors?" Lily asked.

"Oh, yes," Zayir said. "For weeks now. That the Union plans to withdraw support from Gherion Prime. That their application for Union admission may be rescinded. All baseless, I'm sure."

Lily frowned. "I had no idea."

A familiar voice slid into the channel, smooth and dripping. "Oh, come now, dear. I've had my eye on you."

Lily drew a slow breath as Queen Veyshali entered the frame.

"Your Majesty," Lily said carefully.

"Oh, tsk. Come now," the queen replied.

"Queen Veyshali," Lily corrected, steadying herself. "You look well."

Veyshali's gaze traveled over her—lingering on damp hair, the edge of the towel, the bare skin she'd forgotten to be self-conscious about. The queen smiled.

"As do you," she said. "But don't pretend to be some naïve child. You know perfectly well the tension that's been building between the Union and Gherion Prime. All the goodwill earned—that business on Bimara. The Gherionite rebuilding efforts..."

"How do you know about that?" Lily asked.

Veyshali's smile didn't falter. "As I said—I've had my eye on you."

Lily couldn't help noticing that Zayir had gone completely still. His mouth was set, his expression unreadable as he deferred—entirely—to her.

"Any goodwill born of those efforts," Veyshali continued, "or of the Gherionites' generosity in developing the vaccines, has washed away with the tide of politics."

Lily realized she'd forgotten everything else—the towel, the steam, the room around her. She was fully, uncomfortably present. Why were they telling her this? Why call at all?

"Those poor, lonely robots," Veyshali said softly. "Unable to contract the virus themselves. And yet they diverted their own resources to produce a miracle. Some—myself included—would call that selfless."

Her tone shifted in an instant. The warmth vanished.

"But you know how others see it, don't you, Lily?"

Hearing her name from the queen's lips was worse than when the king used it.

"What?" Lily asked.

"Suspicious," Veyshali said flatly.

Lily held the queen's gaze. "What does this have to do with me?"

For a moment, neither of them answered.

Zayir spoke at last, his voice careful—almost tentative. "Lily... we're simply checking in. After everything that's happened. Making sure you're all right." He managed a small, earnest smile. "And to reassure you of our support."

Veyshali's lips curved. "Yes," she said smoothly. "Of course, darling."

She reached out and stroked Zayir's cheek—a slow, possessive gesture that made Lily's stomach turn. Zayir stiffened but said nothing.

Veyshali's attention returned to Lily, sharp and intent. "Lily, keep your head on your shoulders," she purred. "It's about to get worse out there." Her smile softened, just enough to feel intimate. Or threatening. Both. "You're going to need all the friends you can get."

The feed went dark.

Lily stared at the blank screen for a beat longer than necessary. Then she let out a breath—a quiet, rasping sound from the back of her throat—and shook her head.

Whatever that was, it wasn't reassuring.

• • • •

The bridge felt quieter than Lily remembered.

Not empty—never that—but subdued, like a room where everyone had learned not to breathe too loudly. Consoles hummed. Status lights pulsed in orderly rows. No one chatted. No one lingered. The *Salamander* moved through space with the same quiet grace it always had, but something essential had gone rigid beneath the surface.

Lily stepped out of the lift and paused, letting her eyes adjust.

Dryst Amaris stood beside the captain's chair—he almost never sat in it these days—shoulders slightly hunched, hands folded behind his back in a way that felt more like waiting than working. He looked... smaller. Not physically—The Dryst was as tall as ever—but somehow diminished, as if the brief gravity of command he'd once carried had been carefully, methodically removed.

He glanced over when he sensed her—his smile a bit weary.

"Lieutenant," he said. "I was wondering how long it would take you to come up here."

"I had questions," Lily said. "About the call."

Amaris huffed softly. "I can't say I blame you."

She joined him at the rail, lowering her voice. "You okay?"

He hesitated—just long enough to be honest.

"Captain Dalren prefers efficiency over... interpretation," he said. "Turns out leadership isn't a creative discipline anymore. It's a math problem."

Lily followed his gaze across the bridge. The crew moved with practiced precision, each action clipped, contained.

"He treats people like components," Amaris continued. "If we're not operating at one hundred percent, we're malfunctioning."

Before Lily could respond, the doors at the rear of the bridge slid open.

Captain Dalren entered without ceremony.

He moved with quiet exactness, uniform immaculate, expression pleasant in a way that felt practiced rather than warm. His eyes passed over the bridge—not lingering, not searching—just registering, like a man skimming a checklist he already knew by heart.

"Commander," Dalren said mildly.

Amaris startled, only then realizing he'd been leaning against the rail. He straightened at once, shoulders snapping back into place.

Dalren stopped beside him, tilting his head slightly, as if amused.

"Leaning again?" he asked, almost kindly.

Amaris flushed. "Apologies, sir."

Dalren smiled and paced toward the captain's chair, unhurried. "I've said it a thousand times—officers don't lounge about like children waiting for the bus."

He sank into his seat without waiting for acknowledgment.

Lily wasn't impressed.

"Captain," she said.

Dalren turned. Waited.

"Did you route a high-level diplomatic call to my quarters without giving me a heads up?" she asked. She kept her tone measured—procedural.

Dalren regarded her as if assessing a readout.

"Lieutenant Starling," he said. "I trust your conversation with our Ishrethi allies was... productive?"

"It would've been more effective if I'd known it was coming."

A faint smile touched his mouth. His eyes flicked to her damp hair.

"Catch you in the shower?"

Lily stood her ground.

Dalren turned back to the console, fingers gliding across the interface.

"We all have to be ready at a moment's notice," he continued lightly, as if reciting a script he'd repeated a thousand times. "We are three months into a fragile deployment. Emotional latency creates inefficiency. Inefficiency creates risk."

Amaris stared straight ahead.

Dalren finally looked back at Lily.

"I expect adaptability from my officers," he said.

Lily held his gaze for a beat longer than necessary.

Then she nodded once and stepped back.

"Sorry if you felt embarrassed," Dalren added, still not looking at her as she turned to leave. "I'm sure the king wasn't shocked by your casual appearance."

Lily stopped.

"I'm told you two are old... friends."

She turned back, ready to sting—but caught herself.

"Relationships, Lieutenant," Dalren said smoothly. "We are not fighting a virus. We are navigating political tension." His eyes finally met hers. "Relationships are going to make or break this effort."

Lily blinked. "Yes, sir."

Dalren tilted his head. "Something else?"

"What about our relationship with Gherion Prime, sir?"

For a fraction of a second, Dalren bit back a smile—one that said *touché*.

"Well," he said, pleasantly, "that, my young friend, is above my pay grade."

He glanced back at his display. "I believe you're off duty for another two hours. I promise not to interrupt you again."

Lily nodded, keeping her face neutral this time.

As she turned toward the lift, she caught Amaris's reflection in the glass—eyes dulled, jaw tight.

The bridge doors closed behind her with a soft, clinical seal.

• • • •

Lily rounded the corner too quickly and nearly went down in a heap.

"Whoa—sorry," she said automatically, steadying herself as something gelatinous shifted underfoot.

Charlie retracted himself with a faint, embarrassed ripple. "My fault," he said. "I've been... spreading this week. It's a new containment program."

Lily sniffed. "No, I should've been watching where I was going. How are you, Charlie?"

Charlie reformed into a more compact shape, his surface shimmering faintly as he settled. "You look like you're thinking too hard. Trouble?"

Lily rubbed her temple. "I don't want to dump on you." She forced a smile. "It is good to see you, though."

"Likewise," Charlie said.

There was a clatter down the corridor. Charlie shifted. "Hey—what's Datch doing?"

Lily focused her gaze down the hall.

Datch—*in his new form*—was several meters away, one arm buried elbow-deep in an exposed wall panel. He'd pulled a nest of optical cable and circuit filaments free, the strands glowing faintly as they flexed and twined around his fingers. He tilted his head, studying them with open fascination, as if listening to something no one else could hear.

Lily winced. "He goes by Eli now."

"Oh. Right." Charlie shifted again, his surface dimming slightly. "Thank you for reminding me before I made a fool of myself."

Lily drew a slow breath, watching Eli. "I doubt he would've noticed," she said. "He's been so... focused on himself lately."

She winced. "Sorry. It's just—I—"

"Miss the old Datch?" Charlie finished gently.

Lily nodded.

She took a breath and stepped toward the open panel. "Hey, Eli," she called. "Need a hand?"

Eli turned at once, smiling—wide, curious, delighted in a way that was almost infectious.

"Lily," he said brightly. "No, I'm quite all right. I don't require any assistance."

He tugged free a large power coupling.

Sparks flickered. The lights in the corridor went out.

"Ha!" Eli laughed, as if a revelation had just struck him. "I *knew* that would happen. And yet—it's so much more satisfying to see it actually occur!"

Lily wrinkled her nose. "Um, Eli. I don't think you're cleared for maintenance in this section of the ship..."

He continued pulling at wires as she and Charlie edged closer.

"Or any section," Lily added.

"No need to fuss," Eli said cheerfully. "I'll put it back."

He began shoving conduit into the wall in no particular order. "Honestly, everyone aboard acts like an ambient euphoria-absorption singularity..."

Lily smirked despite herself. "A fun sponge, really?"

Eli snapped the power coupling back into place. The lights hummed on.

"Charlie! You are not a—" He glanced at Lily. "—a fun sponge. Would you care to join me on the recreation deck?"

Charlie rippled, almost trepidatious. "Sure, Eli. Let's see what they've got going on today."

Lily continued on toward the commissary. She was grateful to Charlie for keeping Eli out of trouble—for now.

But she couldn't shake the feeling settling in her chest.

She was worried.

• • • •

The commissary was quieter than usual—less chatter, fewer bodies lingering between shelves. Lily queued her uniform request at the terminal, only half-focused, letting the white noise of the ship give her mind a break.

She spotted Tevya near the back counter.

Her posture was perfect. Head high. Shoulders squared. She looked composed in the way Tevya always did when she wanted to be unreadable. But Lily had spent too much time with her not to notice the difference—the stillness was tighter now, deliberate.

Tevya was signing for a small equipment case. Lily caught the label as it slid across the counter: *charge coupling, standard issue.*

"For your new quarters?" Lily asked, already knowing the answer.

Tevya turned, surprise flickering across her face before it smoothed away. "Yes," she said. "A power stabilizer. The outlets in that section are... temperamental."

Lily hesitated, then stepped closer. "I heard what happened," she said quietly. "I'm sorry. Datch—" She stopped herself. "I mean. Eli."

Tevya inclined her head, just slightly. "It's all right," she said. "Truly." A pause. "I chose to move out."

Lily frowned. "I just wish—"

Tevya lifted a hand, gentle but firm. "Eli is... exploring." She searched for the word, then let it settle. "Sensation. Experience. What it means to exist in a body that responds to the world differently." Her mouth curved, not quite a smile. "He was living despite me being there. Not *with* me."

Something tightened in Lily's chest. "Tevya—"

"I'm all right, Lily." Tevya met her gaze, steady and unwavering. "Really. You don't need to worry about me."

She picked up the case and tucked it under her arm. "You Union organics have enough to worry about right now."

The word landed wrong.

Lily shifted, caught off guard. She'd never heard Tevya refer to people like that before.

Tevya hesitated—then turned back.

Her composure narrowed, sharpening into something more deliberate. Focused.

"Lily," she said, lowering her voice. "You need to be ready."

Lily blinked. "Ready for what?"

"For what's coming," Tevya replied. "Keep your senses sharp. Don't let yourself get dulled by procedure."

Lily frowned. "You're the second person to tell me that today." She searched Tevya's face. "Why me?"

Tevya studied her for a long moment, as if weighing how much to say.

"Because you see more," she said finally, gesturing faintly around them.

"Everyone else has blinders on now. They see the way Dalren wants them to see."

She didn't elaborate. Lily didn't need her to.

"You won't let that happen," Tevya said. "You never have."

The words settled heavier than Lily expected.

Tevya's ivory hand closed around Lily's arm. Firm. Grounding. Intentional.

"There's more going on than a virus," she said. Not ominous. Certain. Her eyes held Lily's with an intensity that made it hard to breathe.

Before Lily could respond, Tevya pulled her into a brief embrace.

It startled Lily enough that she froze for a heartbeat before returning it. Tevya's grip was strong—anchoring, almost protective.

"I'm taking my leave once we reach Starbase Eight next week," Tevya said quietly. "Good luck, Lily."

Then she stepped back, nodded once, and turned away—walking out before Lily could stop her, or ask the questions already crowding her mind.

Lily stood there a moment longer than necessary.

Two warnings. One day.

• • • •

The shuttle rattled its way through the upper atmosphere, every loose piece of equipment complaining in protest. A crate somewhere behind Lily knocked once, twice, then settled into an uneven rhythm that set her teeth on edge. Someone hadn't strapped it down properly. She made a mental note to care later.

Right now, she focused on breathing.

She glanced across the narrow cabin at Alrek. He was strapped in opposite her, shoulders squared, jaw set, gaze fixed firmly on the viewport as the clouds slid past in bruised streaks of gray.

Lily leaned forward just enough for him to notice. When he finally looked at her, she lifted a brow and raised her voice over the noise.

"Can't do an away team without me, right, Alrek?"

The corner of his mouth twitched. A smirk, brief and restrained—but not a smile.

"Dalren made the roster," he called back. Then he turned toward the window again, conversation apparently concluded.

That gave her pause.

The memory surfaced uninvited: barely an hour earlier, her head had just hit the pillow in her bunk, exhaustion dragging her under, when the comm had chirped.

Lieutenant Starling, report for away team.

She'd sat up instantly, heart already racing.

Dalren had put her on the roster?

This was a routine cargo retrieval. No civilians. Zero risk. No reason for her to be there.

No *official* reason.

Her gaze drifted sideways.

Eli was strapped in beside her, legs bouncing slightly as he rotated a pair of data rods between his fingers, slotting and un-slotting them with casual fascination. The faint glow of their interfaces reflected off his face as he hummed softly to himself, absorbed, delighted.

Babysitting.

The realization settled in with a familiar mix of irritation and concern. Eli's first away mission since being cleared for partial duty. Supervised. Controlled. Watched.

Watched by her.

Lily leaned back against the harness as the shuttle shuddered again, the loose crate clattering in protest. She exhaled slowly, eyes closing for half a second.

Routine, she told herself with a frown.

As they disembarked the shuttle, Eli quickened his pace and fell in beside Lily.

"Lily," he began, a note of urgency threading his voice. "I wanted to give you something. I think—" He hesitated, then pressed on. "I want you to have it."

He placed a small device in her palm. Smooth. Cool. Flat and round, tapering to a subtle point at one end.

"Thanks," Lily said, turning it over. "What is it?"

"A Korolith disruptor beam emitter," Eli said. "They call it the Jewel."

Lily's brow creased. "You're giving me a weapon?" She wasn't afraid—but she was caught off guard. "Why? And where did you even get this?"

"Never mind that," Eli said quickly, already walking again. She matched his stride as they headed toward the depot site. "I'm concerned you may need it."

He glanced at her, searching her face. "I know everyone thinks I'm paranoid lately. But despite that—this disruptor..."

"The Jewel," Lily said, gently confirming.

"Yes. It's—" His expression brightened, that familiar spark flaring. "It's very cool. Extremely difficult to trace. Almost impossible to dampen." He lowered his voice, earnest now. "Just... promise me you'll keep it with you."

She studied him as they walked. The concern on his face was real. Unfiltered. It tugged at her in a way she didn't have time to unpack.

She would follow up on this later. With someone. She wasn't sure who yet.

"For now," Lily said carefully, "okay. Dat—" She caught herself. "Eli. Okay. I'll keep it."

She slipped the Jewel into her pocket.

They continued toward the rendezvous point, side by side.

The forest pressed in close around the path, trees tall and bare-limbed, their branches interlacing overhead like a lattice of bones. Snow lingered in uneven patches along the ground—not fresh, clean snow, but compacted and gray at the edges, churned into mud where boots and machinery had passed before them. Each step made a soft, wet sound, the earth giving a little underfoot, as if it hadn't fully decided whether it was still frozen.

The air smelled sharp and metallic, cold enough to sting the lungs. Lily pulled her collar higher and kept walking, breath puffing faintly in front of her. Branches shifted deeper in the woods, swaying back and forth with more than a gentle rustling. The forest wasn't quiet so much as watchful.

They crested a low hill, and the trees thinned.

Below them, the depot spread out in a shallow basin cut into the land. Semi-open. Functional. Ugly in the way only infrastructure could be. Parallel tracks crisscrossed the yard in rigid lines, steel rails half-buried in slush and dirt, disappearing beneath stacks of cargo containers arranged with careless efficiency. Some were Union-standard blue, others unmarked, their surfaces scarred and dented from years of use. A few sat open, yawning and empty, like the mouths of beasts left unfed.

There was no sign of people.

A pair of maintenance robots moved slowly between the tracks, their motions repetitive and indifferent—lift, scan, adjust, repeat. One paused, then continued on, apparently satisfied. Inside the main structure, a single overhead light flickered, stuttering on and off with a faint electrical buzz that carried across the yard.

No voices or engine sounds. No heat plumes rising into the air.

Just systems left running, an ambient electrical whine threading through the cold.

Lily felt the wrongness settle again—subtle but persistent. That sensation at the back of her skull, difficult to dismiss. The sense that she needed to be somewhere else.

She tightened the hood of her field jacket, remembering she was technically in command.

"Doesn't look like there's a welcome party." She gestured toward a small entrance, ajar—golden light pouring out onto the gray through the crack.

"Come on," she said, leading the group forward, boots squelching in the mud before giving way to gravel, then pavement, then the deck.

Inside, it was warm.

Not comfortable—just warm enough to make the dampness noticeable. The concrete floor was wet throughout the large space, tracked with muddy prints and dark streaks where water had pooled and never quite evaporated. Somewhere overhead, a pipe hissed faintly. The air smelled like metal, oil, and something old that had given up on being cleaned years ago.

They wound their way past awkward scaffolding and stacks of containers arranged in no obvious order. Long sheets of metal were balanced atop crates, forming makeshift worktables cluttered with tools, datapads, and half-empty cups.

And at the center of it all—

A single man, snoring loudly.

His chair was tipped back at a dangerous angle, boots propped on the counter, a crumpled brown lunch bag resting on his chest. Every exhale rattled.

They stopped.

The away team exchanged looks. Lily caught Ensign Lopez biting down hard on the inside of her cheek. Barely holding it together.

Lily was less amused.

She cleared her throat.

"Excuse me, sir."

Nothing.

She stepped closer. "Excuse me."

Still nothing.

Eli lifted a finger.

He made a soft, delighted sound—like a child who'd just solved a puzzle—and before Lily could open her mouth to stop him, he was already moving.

The brown paper bag was swiftly liberated from the man's chest. Eli puffed it full of air with exaggerated care, then—

Pop.

The sound cracked through the space.

The chair tipped. The man went down hard, limbs flailing, a startled yelp echoing off the metal walls.

"Bugger!"

He scrambled upright, swiping at the air, heart clearly still trying to catch up with reality.

Alrek stepped forward, arms crossed—his expression carefully disapproving, though Lily caught the twitch at the corner of his mouth as he fought a smile.

"We're with the starship *Salamander*," he said. "Weren't you expecting us?"

The man blinked at them. Once. Twice.

"Eh? Yeah—yes, of course. Tuesday." He rubbed the back of his neck, accent thick and unmistakably Australian. "You were supposed to be here Tuesday."

He glanced down at his coat, a string of curses tumbling out. "You've made me spill coffee all over myself."

Lily privately suspected the coffee had done the coat a favor. The smell in the room suggested very little had ever met soap and survived.

She stepped forward. "Sir—"

"Jackson." He thrust out his hand, encased in a suspiciously damp leather glove.

She was grateful for her own gloves as she shook it, firm and brief.

"Jackson, I'm Lieutenant Starling," she said. "You can call me Lily."

She smiled—sincere, but controlled.

"And today *is* Tuesday."

"Oh. Well—so it is," Jackson said, peering down at his wrist as if checking a watch that wasn't there. He squinted, nodded to himself. "Tuesday."

He shuffled over to a wall-mounted display, its surface streaked with dust and fingerprints old enough to qualify as sedimentary layers. With a swipe of his sleeve, he revealed a half-functional map beneath—grainy, low-resolution, and peppered with blinking red dots.

"Right. So. The vaccine crates you're picking up—they're split across a few storage sites." He waved vaguely at the screen. "Were meant to come in by truck tomorrow morning. But if you're here now, no reason you can't grab 'em tonight. They're all secured. Just... spread out."

He paused, then added, helpfully, "Bloody cold out there."

Lily studied the map, trying to make sense of the scale. The silence stretched.

"Damned cold," Jackson repeated, nodding with conviction.

"Okay," Lily said at last, pinching the bridge of her nose. "Three sites. How do we get to them?"

Jackson brightened. "Ahh, there's the ticket."

He pointed toward the far end of the depot, where two massive vehicles sat idle on recessed tracks. They were enclosed, boxy, and unmistakably utilitarian—part cargo hauler, part snow crawler. Lily thought they looked like something out of a Victorian fever dream, if Victorian engineers had access to antigrav plating and industrial suspension.

"The sleds'll take you," Jackson said proudly. "Automated. Warm. Keeps you out of this miserable excuse for weather."

"Great," Lily said, without enthusiasm.

"Only thing is—"

She closed her eyes for half a second. "Yes?"

"There's only two of 'em." He shrugged. "They're programmed for the far sites. The near one—" He gestured vaguely toward the tree line beyond the depot walls. "I always walk that one."

Alrek frowned. "How far?"

"Oh, 'bout two kilometers. Give or take." Jackson sniffed. "Despite the cold."

Lily felt the beginnings of a headache bloom behind her eyes.

Beside her, Eli smiled, genuinely delighted. "Cheer up, Lieutenant," he said. "I love a good walk."

Lily and Alrek exchanged a look so synchronized it might as well have been rehearsed.

"Fine," Lily said. "Eli and I will take the near site."

She added, dryly, "Despite the cold."

As they began downloading the map data to their units, Lily leaned closer to Eli and lowered her voice.

"I'll take the cold over the smell in here."

Eli tilted his head, thoughtful. "Oh, thank goodness," he said earnestly. "I was hoping that wasn't considered an acceptable collection of aromas."

Lily snorted before she could stop herself.

By the time they were halfway to the storage site, Eli had not stopped talking.

He filled the cold air with everything—updates from Taran about the Raath-Ka teaching rotation, half-formed theories about how long it would take for the enhanced food synthesizers on the *Salamander* to start "anticipating cravings," an enthusiastic aside about how sound traveled differently through bone and muscle than through synthetic corridors.

Lily listened when she could. When she couldn't, she nodded.

Just as she thought she might finally earn a pocket of quiet, Eli tilted his head, thoughtful.

"So," he said lightly, "did you ever hear back from Trish?"

Lily slowed a step.

She remembered mentioning Trish in the mess hall—barely more than an aside. Trish wasn't one for long calls, but she always replied to messages. Always. Even if it was just a single line, a joke, a check-in.

"No," Lily said. "Thanks for asking." She forced the words to stay casual. "I hope she's okay."

Eli didn't press. He just nodded, filing it away.

Silence crept in behind them.

It brought everything with it—Veyshali's warning, Tevya's farewell, the image of Trish's unread messages sitting untouched. Lily pushed the thoughts aside with practiced effort. Her head wasn't here. She needed it to be.

A rustle above her broke the spell.

She looked up.

Eli was halfway up a tree.

"What are you doing?" she asked, more exasperated curiosity than reprimand.

He dropped down beside her with a soft thud, boots sinking slightly into the damp ground. In his hand was a large, curved fruit, its thick red peel glossy against the gray of the woods. He peeled it back about an inch, releasing a faint, sweet scent.

"Care for a bite?"

Lily shook her head. "You know the rules. You shouldn't eat alien plants."

Eli took a bite anyway.

Immediately, he began to gasp, clutching his throat, staggering back a step as if his airway were closing.

"Eli!" Lily snapped, panic spiking as she moved toward him.

He burst out laughing.

"You are *too* easy, Lily."

She didn't blush. She just stopped. Closed her eyes. Exhaled.

"It's a gorch-fruit," he said cheerfully. "Like a chewy banana. Very sweet. You sure you don't want some?"

Lily was already several meters ahead by the time he finished speaking. He jogged to catch up.

"Ha. Sorry," he added, contrite but delighted.

"Shh," Lily said sharply.

They'd reached the edge of the storage site now—a loose sprawl of containers and barrels scattered unevenly through the trees. Old crates. Scrap. Shadows that didn't quite behave.

She slowed, listening.

Voices. Low. Movement. Something clattered.

Lily drew her blaster, grip steady, muzzle angled forward.

Beside her, Eli raised the gorch-fruit and aimed it like a pistol.

She shot him a look.

Then she swept her light across the clearing.

The beam landed on a cluster of figures.

Small. Bundled. Frozen mid-movement.

Kids.

Lily blinked and lowered her weapon.

She raised her light, sweeping it across the yard.

"Hey," she called out. "Are you kids supposed to be here?"

The words sounded strange in her mouth the moment they left it. What would seventeen-year-old, street-kid Lily think? She couldn't help it—she sounded like a cop.

Three figures stepped into the edge of the beam. Small. Humanoid. All wearing the same orange jumpsuits and thick coats, faces half-hidden beneath their hoods.

One of them shrugged. "Our parents work on the base," the kid said. The voice was flat—nervous, maybe. Or something else. A little too even.

Lily hesitated. A flicker of something old stirred—an echo of cold nights, borrowed warmth, the instinct to stay close to the lights.

"It's late," she said instead, firmer now. "And it's cold." She gestured toward the structure behind her. "You should head home. Please."

The kids stared at her.

"Our parents work on the base," another one repeated as they began to back away.

Lily exhaled and turned toward the storage unit door.

Of course.

A keypad. Dark, recessed into the metal frame.

She tapped her comm. "Alrek, looks like we need some kind of access code..."

Static.

"Alrek?"

She heard Eli's voice behind her, but it barely registered. "Umm, Lily..."

She tried again. Nothing.

Her jaw tightened. She switched frequencies, then stopped. She didn't have the depot channel.

"Great," she muttered.

She tapped her comm tag. "Lily to *Salamander*. I need the frequency for the main depot."

A pause.

"Sending it now, Lieutenant," Lieutenant Basco replied.

"Lieutenant..." Eli said again, closer this time.

"Just a second," Lily said, already punching in the new frequency.

"Lily." Eli's voice sharpened.

"What?" She spun around, irritation flaring hot.

Eli wasn't looking at her.

He was staring past her—eyes fixed on the space where the kids had disappeared.

His expression had gone strange. Focused. Uneasy.

"That's not right," he said quietly.

Lily followed his gaze.

The children had moved close together. Their bodies were... rippling.

"Our parents work on the base," they said again—but the voices overlapped now, garbled, wrong.

Not children.

Not people.

The shapes sagged, collapsed inward, like wax softening near heat. Coats smeared into the form that once held them. Limbs stretched, then merged. Flesh—or something like it—flowed together, pooling low to the ground in a slick, glistening mass.

"What the—" Lily took a step back.

The mass rose.

It pulled itself upward in stages—thick limbs extruding and locking into place, a spine forming in wet increments. A head followed, too large, jaw heavy, teeth extruding like half-remembered ideas of predators.

A monstrous silhouette. Something out of a nightmare.

"Shape wraith!" Eli shouted.

Lily didn't hesitate. She raised her blaster and fired on stun.

The bolt hit, splashing uselessly across the creature's surface. It recoiled—not in pain, but surprise—then swung a thick, semi-formed tentacle.

The impact took Lily off her feet. She hit the ground hard, breath tearing from her lungs as Eli went down beside her.

The world rang. Mud and old snow smeared across the side of Lily's face, packed into her ear.

"What the hell is a shape wraith?" she gasped.

It formed limbs faster now—five at once, maybe more—smashing and swinging. One slammed into the earth inches from her head.

"That!" Eli shouted back.

Lily rolled her eyes as she tucked and tumbled, narrowly escaping another blow.

"Hey, um—Union lady."

Jackson. Of course.

"I forgot to give you the door code."

Lily ducked as a tentacle slammed into the ground where her head had just been.

"Yes!" she shouted. "What is it?"

"You okay over there?" Jackson asked, sounding genuinely curious. "These woods are *not* safe after dark."

"Now you tell us!" Lily and Eli shouted at the same time.

"Just give me the code!" Lily barked.

"Okay, okay—no need to yell. It's zero, zero, zero, zero."

Lily let off a string of English and Saravethi curses as her fingers flew over the keypad.

Behind her, the creature charged.

The door unlocked with a heavy clunk.

Lily dove inside, grabbing Eli's arm and yanking him with her. The door began to slide shut as the shape wraith slammed into it, the impact reverberating through the metal.

The door sealed with a final, thunderous slam.

They stood there, breathing hard, the distant sound of something heavy and angry thudding uselessly against the other side.

Lily leaned back against the cold metal, chest heaving.

"...I hate this planet," she said faintly.

Eli, still staring at the door, nodded. "Yes. Strongly agree."

• • • •

The pounding at the door had stopped. On the monitor, they watched the creature recede, its shape thinning and unraveling as it slipped back into the woods.

"I recommend we remain inside the structure for a period of time," Eli said, studying the feed. "To ensure it does not return."

"You don't have to convince me," Lily said, giving herself a quick once-over. Surprisingly intact.

She steadied her hands and tapped her comm tag.

"Alrek, it's Lily. Just a heads-up—there are shape-shifting predators in the area. They mimic people. And they are not friendly."

There was a beat of silence. Then Alrek's voice cut through the static, tight with concern.

"Are you okay?" he asked. "Do you need us to rendezvous with you?"

"No—we're all right," Lily said. "A little bruised." Her hand went instinctively to her ribs. "We're inside with the vaccine containers."

Another pause. She could hear movement on his end—boots, voices, the sound of someone doing two things at once.

"Thank God," he said. "Listen—the *Salamander* is sending another shuttle to pick up your supply directly." A breath. "But we're stuck here overnight. A train is coming in at dawn with the rest of the containers from the far side of the landmass."

Lily closed her eyes and leaned her head back against the cold interior wall.

"Lily," Alrek said carefully, "what are your orders?"

Concern still threaded his voice.

"Understood," she said. "Approved. We'll meet you in the morning, okay?"

"Lily—"

She cut the channel.

Eli talked the entire time they waited.

About the creature. About the depot's structural inefficiencies. About how fascinating mimicry-based life-forms were, provided one removed the imminent threat of being eaten. His words washed over her without landing.

Lily's thoughts kept circling the same points, tightening like a knot she couldn't loosen.

Vayshali's warning.

Tevya's grip on her arm.

That look—certain, unyielding.

And Trish.

No messages. No reply. Nothing.

The shuttle finally arrived, engines whining softly as it settled into position.

Lily genuinely smiled when the hatch opened.

"Dante!"

Lieutenant Junior Grade Dante Basco stepped down onto the deck, his uniform as crisp as ever—though finally in the navy blue of the *Salamander*.

"Lieutenant," he said warmly. "Good to see you. You look a little banged up—are you okay?"

Something in Lily's mind shifted. She wasn't sure what triggered it—the familiar face, the weight of the last few hours—but the realization came clean and sharp.

She wasn't contributing anything here. She was just...

She looked at Eli. "Babysitting."

His brow lifted. "Babysitting?"

Lily laughed. "Never mind."

She turned back to Basco. "Actually, I should probably get checked out by Dr. Thesari."

Then to Eli. "You've got this, right?"

He blinked. "Lily?"

"I mean—you can stay the night," she said quickly. "Help Alrek finish up. You'll be fine." She smiled again. Softer now. "You're... more than fine."

A hesitation crossed his face. Small. But unmistakable.

"Uh. Sure," he said. "Yeah. Where are you going?"

Lily didn't hesitate this time.

"Earth."

Eli opened his mouth—then closed it again.

Lily turned to Basco. "Shall we?"

She stepped onto the shuttle.

The door slid shut behind them, sealing off the cold, the depot, the forest—and the look of surprise on Eli's face.

As the shuttle lifted, Lily stared straight ahead, jaw set, heart pounding.

That wrong feeling—

Was finally lifting.

Chapter 3: Wings of Refuge

THE RAIN IN WHAT USED to be the United Kingdom was the kind that didn't fall so much as arrive. It seeped into the city through the air itself, a patient mist that turned sharp corners soft and made every streetlight bleed into the pavement. Lily had expected it to feel different after two hundred years—different sky, different temperature, different smell—but some things refused to be edited out of the planet's memory.

Earth had always been a world with weather.

Sleep was intermittent with Xynn away on her mission. Lily had been reading about Earth's history, late at night, in the glow of her quarters, hunting for the shape of the place she'd left behind and the one she'd returned to. It was a habit she couldn't shake—like checking a bruise just to make sure it still hurt.

There had been a climate scientist somewhere in what used to be England, back when the planet's oceans were still sick and heavy with old mistakes. The records called him a pioneer. A visionary. A man whose work led to the filtration systems that cleared the seas, that pulled the poison out of the water and turned the tide of a century that had been tipping toward collapse.

Millions of people had lived because of him.

And Lily couldn't remember his name.

That was the strange thing about heroism, she thought. How easily it blurred. How history could rescue a planet and still forget the sound of the person who'd done it.

She stared at her reflection in the dark glass of the Tube window, the tunnel sliding by in a rush of black and flashing lights.

She was in London now.

Technically.

The signs still called it London. The map still drew the city in familiar lines. Even the underground system—the Tube—had survived in name and function, because Earth clung to nostalgia the way it clung to its myths. Not because the past was better, necessarily, but because it was known. Safe. A shape the mind could hold.

Today, she'd read, was a holiday.

Climate Day.

She'd heard it mentioned on the Salamander in passing—one of the offhand facts people traded about Earth when they were trying to sound worldly. It wasn't like Union celebrations on the core worlds, with shimmering projections and curated speeches. Climate Day was quieter. Strangely personal. The anniversary of the scientist's birth, commemorated in muted colors and short comm notices that encouraged Earth citizens to reflect on what they had.

Lily's lips twitched at the thought of it. Reflect. She pictured Earth herself sitting in silence, forced to consider how gratitude was supposed to work when the creatures who'd spent centuries poisoning you were suddenly asking to be thanked for the cure.

She tried to picture the man again, his face from the grainy old archives. His hands. His tired eyes. She could remember that—tired eyes and an earnest mouth and a posture like someone who carried the whole ocean on his back—

Zach.

She blinked.

Doctor Zachary Friedman.

The name surfaced like a bubble rising from the deep, sudden and absurd. Lily frowned at it as if it had personally offended her.

Zach Friedman.

Maybe that was why she couldn't remember it. Somehow it just didn't feel right that someone brilliant enough to save the oceans should be named Zach.

She knew her mind was guilty of wandering like this—leaps, sideways threads. It always had. Especially on trains. There was something about the motion, about being carried through a place without touching it, that made her thoughts drift loose.

She watched the other humans in the car for a moment. Faces lit by displays, by overhead panels, by the pale glow of tunnel lights streaking past. People wrapped in their own worlds. Their own private survivals.

Her thoughts slid anyway, as if they'd been greased, back to Caris.

She could still see her in the corridor outside Lily's quarters, catching her like nimble fingers plucking a dandelion pappus out of the air before it could drift away.

Lily had already packed. Not everything—just the essentials. Med kit, spare clothing, some gear. She'd kept it light on purpose—so weight couldn't be used as an excuse to hesitate.

The leave days the fleet owed her were a quiet joke at this point. A paper promise from calling her back from her honeymoon. "We'll make it up to you, Lieutenant." As if her life could be balanced on a schedule.

But she'd asked anyway. Pushed the request through official channels, through whatever bureaucratic membrane still existed between her and the command deck.

Dalren had approved it, quick and easy.

Oddly amenable.

Maybe relieved.

Maybe he really was happy to get rid of her for a few days if her head wasn't going to be in the game. Or more to the point—if she wasn't going to play his games.

Lily thought that was refreshingly honest. She'd expected at least some mild barking.

Caris made up for it.

She hadn't raised her voice—not at first—but her whole body had been tight with fury, her shoulders squared like she was holding herself back from doing something she'd regret. Lily had seen Caris in battle. She'd seen her coordinate evacuations under fire. She'd seen her calm in the middle of chaos.

She had never seen her look like this.

"Where are you going?" Caris had demanded, and there had been something in the question that made Lily's chest tighten. Not curiosity. Not concern.

Control.

Lily had answered anyway. "Earth."

Caris's eyes sharpened, her jaw setting. "You can't just—"

"I can," Lily said. She hadn't meant it to sound like that—sharp, defensive—but it came out anyway, like the words had been waiting in her mouth. "I have leave. Dalren approved it."

Caris's expression shifted, and Lily saw something flicker across it, quick as a shadow. Disbelief. Then anger, redirected.

"Of course he did," Caris said, and the bitterness in her voice surprised Lily more than the anger.

Lily's stomach sank. "What is that supposed to mean?"

"It means you're doing exactly what he wants," Caris snapped. "You're making it easy."

Lily stared at her. "This isn't about you, Leena."

The name came out like a blade.

Caris's face tightened. For a second Lily thought she'd gone too far—thought she'd cut something she couldn't stitch back together. Then Caris's eyes went colder.

"You're right. It isn't about me," Caris said. "It's about you."

Lily's pulse thudded in her ears. "Look, I'm going to check on Trish. I'll be back before you know it."

"And then what?" Caris demanded. "What are you going to find? You don't know. And you assume you can fix whatever it is yourself?"

Lily opened her mouth, then closed it. Because the honest answer was: I don't know.

Caris stepped closer. "You're not thinking straight..."

She put a hand on Lily's arm—gentle. There was something in her dark eyes that almost made Lily waver.

But then—

"Alrek and I are worried about you."

Lily's throat tightened. "What?"

She backed up instinctively, breaking the contact.

The anger that snapped through her was sudden and bright. Maybe it wasn't fair—maybe it wasn't even directed at Alrek, or at Leena, not really. It was the feeling of being cornered. Of being ganged up on.

Lily shook her head and looked away. "I'm done with this conversation."

Caris's voice went low. "Lily—"

But Lily was already walking, the corridor blurring around her, her heart hammering with the kind of anger that wasn't clean enough to be righteous. She hated herself for it. She hated Caris for pulling it out of her. She hated the ship for feeling suddenly small.

And she hated, most of all, the fact that she couldn't quite put her finger on what either of them were truly angry about.

The Tube slowed, brakes whispering through the car, and Lily blinked hard as if she'd been shaken awake. She glanced up at the station signage and felt a small jolt of panic.

Her stop.

She pushed to her feet too fast, shoulder brushing past a commuter, and slipped out through the doors just as they chimed their warning.

The station beyond was bright and impossibly familiar.

The old tiled corridors. The curved walls. The signage styled like something lifted from a film set and polished until it gleamed. She half expected to see an advertisement for a phone from 2010 plastered across the wall. Even the air smelled the way she thought it should—metal and damp and human bodies passing through.

Earth's habit of preserving itself was unsettling. Like a museum that lacked funding and imagination.

Lily moved through the flow of commuters, out of the underground and toward the escalators that led up into the city.

She pulled out her commtag as she walked, flicking through the holographic interface. Her pulse ticked higher as her messages loaded.

Still no reply from Trish.

Her stomach tightened.

Then she saw it.

A message from Valen.

She opened it, eyes scanning the words quickly and then slowing as meaning settled.

Lily! So good to hear from you, he wrote. The Capitol Complex is closed for the holiday, but I will be present for a private council session. I'd love it if you dropped by. I have arranged access for you. The code is below.

Valen Meris.

The only Hedonian official Lily had met who really felt human. At least in the way she knew. She was glad he'd become a friend. Earth still felt foreign to her—still unfriendly.

Lily swallowed.

She could feel the city above her, poised and humming. She hoped there might be something there for her, hidden in plain sight.

She slid the commtag away and stepped onto the escalator, rising toward the surface. Her hand drifted to her pocket and found the outline of the jewel—the weapon Eli had given her. She'd almost turned it in.

Now she was glad she hadn't.

The light stung her eyes as she stepped into the brisk London air.

She knew the way.

Two blocks to Trish's inn.

Two blocks to answers.

She came around the corner and saw it.

Scales and Feathers.

Except now it wasn't.

The windows and doors had been carefully boarded up—too neat to be municipal. Not rushed, either. Lily guessed—by the precision—that it had been Trish herself. Fresh graffiti marred the sign, the emblem of the fish and the wing half obscured by a tag Lily thought wasn't particularly well executed.

Her head spun for a second. Any hope of answers sank in her stomach like a stone.

She pulled out her commtag.

Xynn was still out of range.

Her finger hovered over Alrek's name for a beat. Then Caris.

Then she swiped and pulled up Valen's message and hit call.

A polite tone chirped back at her. Valen Meris was occupied.

Lily exhaled and lowered the commtag, mulling over her next step. She considered trying to find Eira, but she could spend days hunting for a Ludon leader and still come up empty. Delen had helped her during the Leviathan mission, but she had no way to reach him now.

No thread to pull.

Just dead air.

She stared at the boarded windows again.

She buried the part of herself that wanted to turn around and go back to the station.

"Let's have a closer look," she murmured.

She strolled around the corner into the dead-end alley beside the inn, careful not to stand out—any more than she already did. She scuffed past more boarded-up windows and trash skittering over the ground. A cat perched on a stack of crates gave her a look that clearly said *why did you just interrupt me?*

The red metal back door had seen better days. Scarred and dented, it looked like someone had literally driven a vehicle into it at some point and then simply reattached it without another thought.

Two-by-fours were nailed across it in an X. A chain adorned the door's hardware, heavy and ugly—almost dungeon-like.

But the chain had been cut.

The coil hung slack, still threaded through one handle like someone had started to secure it and then stopped halfway through.

Lily gave the door a gentle nudge.

It swung open.

Inside, the inn was dark. Quiet. Stale. But the shape of it was the same. The same narrow hall. The same worn floors. The same feeling it had when it had been a place where broken people could put their pieces down for a moment without being punished for it.

Some of the personal effects were gone—small things Lily prayed Trish had taken with her, and hadn't been carried off. Lily's instincts kicked in, and she went impossibly quiet. The kind of quiet where you nearly ceased to breathe.

She crossed the main hall, moving toward the back where the rooms for rent were. Before she touched anything, she turned in a slow, full circle—checking corners, shadows, the empty angle of every doorway.

Alone.

She tried the first door.

Locked.

She moved to the second.

Click.

Lily eased it open.

The room looked lived-in. Not abandoned.

A few pieces of clothing—feminine, neatly folded—sat in careful piles on the floor. A plate with the remains of a meal rested on a chair that seemed to function as a table. A mattress in the corner was the only other furniture.

A hand mirror lay near the mattress beside a large supply of makeup. The room smelled faintly of smoke, old and sweet.

In the opposite corner were empty liquor bottles and several prescription vials.

But it was the wall beneath the boarded-up window that caught Lily's attention.

Over two dozen books were stacked neatly, almost reverently. Lily recognized some of them—Trish's. She'd seen them in the lobby last time, lined up on a shelf like proof that someone still believed in learning. But others were less familiar, including a well-worn copy of the King James Bible.

"You looking for me?"

The voice came from directly behind Lily—commanding, raspy, and high-pitched all at once. Close enough that Lily's heart slammed into overdrive.

She spun.

A young woman stood in the doorway, small-framed but somehow taking up the entire room. Young, Lily clocked instantly. Too young to be standing like that. Like she owned the building.

She wore a clean dress that looked like it belonged to another world. It hung loose, and Lily thought it could use an undergarment of some kind. Her hair was chopped short, jaw-length like Lily's, uneven in a way that Lily wasn't sure was deliberate. Her hazel eyes burned the same color as her hair, copper and steel.

One hand rested on her hip as she took Lily in.

"Are you a client?" she asked. "I don't like people snooping."

Her gaze flicked over Lily's jacket. "You don't look like you have money. Union type."

Lily forced herself to breathe, still trying to steady her heart from being startled. "No. Not a client."

The girl's mouth twisted as she considered that. She narrowed her eyes like she was trying to decide what species Lily was.

"I'm Didot," she said. "You're pretty—but I usually only have male clients."

Lily cleared her throat. "I'm not a client. I mean, I'm not looking for… that."

Didot began to circle her in bare feet, with an innocent wobble—somewhere between a ballerina and a drunken sailor.

"You're friends with Trish," she said. "You looking for her?"

Lily's brows drew together. "How'd you know?"

Didot's eyes opened wider, sharp as glass. A smile, for the first time. "You look healthy, so you're not from this neighborhood. And that's a nice tactical vest you've got— not very well concealed under your jacket." Her gaze flicked past Lily toward the open door behind her. "Also you broke into her place."

Lily relaxed a notch.

"The door was open," she said defensively, though she wasn't really sure why. "How do you know Trish?"

Didot's expression shifted—something in it softening before it hardened again.

"She was helping my fam," she said. "My—" She paused, correcting. "The people I used to crash with. A vaccination program. That Trish." A small, fond scoff through her nostrils. "Bleeding heart, that one."

Lily believed her about Trish. It sounded exactly like the kind of thing she would be involved in.

"Do you have any idea where she might have gone?"

Didot lit a cigarillo of some kind. She took a long drag, and when the smoke rolled out of her mouth she said—an octave lower, suddenly serious—"Let's discuss."

She dipped into a small curtsy and opened the door behind her, turning the knob without looking. "Step into my office," she added, in a cheesy host's voice.

Reluctantly, Lily followed her.

The room was lit by an old desk lamp perched on a folding chair. A large ice chest sat against the wall, flanked by more folding chairs. The smell hit her—liquor and old vomit, layered with something greasy that had soaked deep into the wallpaper.

Didot dug through the ice chest with the lit cigarillo still in her mouth and produced an unopened bottle of vodka. She cracked it open and poured it into a juice glass balanced on the chair rail, filling it halfway.

"Drink?" she offered, holding it out.

"No thanks," Lily said, with all the sincerity she could manage. She claimed the least scarred chair in the room.

Didot shrugged, dropped into one of the hard metal chairs like she'd been born there, and downed half the glass in one swallow.

"Now," she said, wiping her mouth with the back of her hand. "Your lady. Lady she is. Lady be... lady with stubble." She waved a hand. "No judgment."

Lily's expression tightened, impatience flashing across her face.

Didot caught it. She straightened and cleared her throat.

"If I had to put money on it," she said, "she's in Lock Number Nine."

Lily frowned. "Lock Number Nine?"

"That's the one."

Without warning, Didot popped up like a jack-in-the-box, standing straight on the chair. She hopped down and bounded out of the room.

Lily was just beginning to think she should make her exit when the slender figure reappeared, cradling a book nearly the size of her head.

"Look here." Didot thrust it into Lily's hands, already open to a page showing a map of the British Isles overlaid with a dense schematic.

"This water system services the Hedon vertical complex," she said. "Originally built with twelve underground locks to compensate for terrain from Tidbury to London."

Lily glanced up. A scholarly focus had settled over Didot's features.

"Over the years," Didot continued, "some of the infrastructure collapsed. They bypassed Locks Eight through Ten. Lock Number Nine became... something else." Her eyes wandered. "An underground borough. For people like me."

Lily studied the map. Lock Number Nine sat near the Swanscombe Marshes. She let her finger rest there.

"And this is where Trish was distributing the vaccine?"

Didot smiled, and Lily didn't like it. "That's the place. We call it Ninebury."

She took another drag, eyes unfocusing as if she could see it.

"Dollars to donuts," Didot went on, "Trish is still there. The old lady's obsessed with saving everybody." Her smile thinned. "I can tell you how to get in."

She tapped ash into an empty bottle.

"For a price."

Lily's lips pressed into a narrow line.

She didn't like the sound of any of this. And she was fairly certain Didot was lying—at least about part of it. But the thread was there. Tangled. Real enough to pull.

And what were her other options?

Go back and beg Dalren for help.

Lily exhaled slowly.

"What do you want from me?"

Didot looked thoughtful. As if she hadn't expected to get this far.

She stubbed out the cigarillo and moved toward Lily, catlike. Too close. Her hands came to rest on Lily's thighs—light, testing, invasive in a way that felt practiced.

"I've got a client coming late this afternoon," she said.

Lily couldn't tell if Didot was trying to be flirtatious or threatening. Either way, it wasn't working.

"He's important," Didot went on. "Connected to the galactic shipping lines." She stepped back then, straightening, smoothing the front of her dress with something almost like embarrassment. "He owes me a lot of money. But it's bad business shaking down your own clients."

She composed herself for a beat longer.

"I had a business partner who handled that kind of thing," she added. "She kicked it a few weeks ago."

Lily absorbed that. "Sorry for your loss."

Didot's expression stayed steel, but her eyes went glassy.

"So," she said. "What d'ya say? You be my heavy, and I'll help you out."

"Or," Lily said carefully, "I could go figure it out myself."

She knew it was a pointless bluff.

"You won't get in," Didot said flatly.

Lily's gaze dropped to the floor. Then to Didot's bare feet on the stained rug. Something twisted in her chest—sharp, hard to name.

She exhaled.

"Okay," she said.

Didot extended her hand.

They shook on it.

· · · ·

The tramway to Swanscombe was little more than a worker's ferry.

Low-slung. Utilitarian. Loud in a way that felt almost violent.

Lily felt more out of place here than she had in the Footings District, which surprised her. This wasn't a place people passed through accidentally. It existed for a purpose.

Fortunately, if you didn't belong to that purpose, you were invisible.

No one looked at her twice.

By the time she stepped off the tram, her ears were ringing. The shift to the ambient sounds of the marsh—the wind, the water, the distant cry of birds—felt like pressure equalizing.

She followed Didot's directions carefully. Looking around, it seemed the land hadn't changed much from the way the hundred-year-old map had painted it. It matched Didot's description exactly. The marsh slumped toward the water in a tired way, grasses knotting and unknotting in the wind.

The Thames slapped the shore with cold impatience. Froth sprayed up as Lily picked her way forward, brackish water catching her face and lips—sharp, bracing, irritating.

What first appeared mostly flat opened up into layers of hidden topography—a graveyard not of bodies, but of hulls.

Ancient vessels lay half-buried in the muck, ribs exposed like the bones of animals that had wandered somewhere they weren't meant to go and never made it back. Between them yawned a man-made pit—precise in a way nature never bothered with. Concentric squares descended step by step into the earth, each level more choked with sea grass and weeds than the last.

She slowed.

This was it.

Didot had said to look for the heart.

"Well," Lily murmured, "I'll be damned."

The rock sat just off-center, partially buried, unmistakable once you saw it. Not a child's idea of a heart—but the real thing. Muscular asymmetry. Chambers. Ventricles forming a blunt arrow that pointed toward a faint disturbance in the ground.

A path.

She followed it and found the gap—almost lost beneath the overgrowth. A metal corridor, narrow and dark, barely wide enough for a single body.

Lily paused only long enough to steady her breathing.

Then she squeezed in.

The walls pressed close immediately. Cold metal at her back, at her shoulders. She turned sideways and slid forward, the panic rising just enough to remind her to force it down. This was not the tightest space she'd ever been in. Not by a long shot.

Still.

The light vanished faster than she expected. Her boots scuffed softly as she moved, inch by inch, until the darkness felt complete—total in a way that made time slippery.

She kept going.

When the pinprick of light finally appeared, it felt unreal. She moved toward it, emerging into a cube-shaped chamber—metal on all sides, vast by comparison. Maybe a hundred feet across. Maybe more.

In the center waited a hatch.

Heavy. Old. Circular. A wheel set into its face, and a locking mechanism secured by three dials etched with pictograms.

Lily exhaled.

Didot had warned her about this part.

She crouched and turned the first dial—three widening concentric rings. A ripple.

The second—a fluid spiral collapsing inward toward a dark center. A vortex.

The third—an inverted triangle.

"A tad dramatic," Lily said to the room.

The lock clicked.

The hatch loosened beneath her hands, and as it cracked open, the sound rushed up to meet her.

Water.

Fast. Heavy. Alive.

She descended.

The ladder dropped straight down into darkness, its rungs slick with condensation. Lily kept her back to the wall, moving carefully, counting breaths without realizing she was doing it. The light from above narrowed quickly, thinning to a pale coin and then nothing at all.

When her boots finally hit solid ground, she paused.

The space opened up around her—a platform suspended inside the lock's interior. She switched on her torch.

Water roared below.

Not a trickle. Not seepage. An enormous volume of it—black and fast-moving, churning through channels that should have been empty. Lily frowned, heart ticking up a notch.

This lock was supposed to be dry.

She replayed Didot's instructions in her mind. Don't stop on the ladder. Don't touch the rails too long. Follow the walkway to the end.

She moved forward, boots ringing dully against the metal grating. At the far edge of the platform, a staircase dropped steeply down along the wall, its steps disappearing into shadow.

Lily hesitated.

Then she started down.

The sound of the water grew louder with every step. By the time she reached the first landing, it had crept over the soles of her boots. Cold immediately, biting through the material.

That wasn't right.

She continued, more slowly now. The next level down, the water reached her ankles. It sloshed with her movement, tugging insistently, as if testing her balance.

Lily glanced up.

She was several stories below the hatch now. The ladder looked impossibly far away. The light above it was gone.

Another step.

The water surged higher, spilling into her boots. Her socks soaked instantly, the cold shocking enough to steal her breath.

That's when she heard it.

Not the constant roar she'd been tracking—but something else layered beneath it. A deeper sound. A pressure. A sudden, accelerating thunder that made the metal beneath her vibrate.

Lily turned just in time to see it.

A wall of water barreling down the channel toward her, filling the space completely. No gaps. No escape route. Just force.

"Oh—"

It hit her like a brick wall.

The impact knocked the breath from her lungs, slammed her against the railing, then tore her free entirely. She didn't even have time to fight it—only enough time to know, with stark clarity, that there was no getting out of this one.

Darkness crowded in as the water closed over her head.

She clamped her mouth shut, held what little air she had, her body pulled fast—unnaturally fast—by a current that felt like being fired from a weapon. Metal scraped past her. The world compressed into pressure and motion and the brutal need to stay conscious.

Then—

She burst free.

Lily shot out of a massive pipe and into open air, tumbling hard onto wet stone. She gasped violently, coughing, dragging air back into her lungs like it had been stolen.

Her torch skittered across the ground, still lit.

She pushed herself up, dizzy, soaked, shaking—and froze.

An entire city stretched out before her.

Underground. Vast. Improvised but permanent. Layers of scaffolding and walkways rose into the darkness above, lit by strings of salvaged lights. Makeshift shelters pressed close together, patched from metal sheeting, old signage, fragments of infrastructure repurposed into walls and roofs.

Shops, too. Stalls built from crates and panels, hand-painted symbols marking food, tools, medicine. Smoke curled from somewhere deeper in, carrying the scent of cooking oil and damp earth.

People moved through it all like this was normal.

A few glanced at Lily as she stood dripping in the open—Union jacket, soaked boots, wild-eyed. Their expressions flickered with irritation, suspicion, and then dismissal. Secondhand Hedon clothing hung loose on their frames, colors faded, seams mended too many times to count.

No one stopped.

Life simply flowed around her.

Lily swallowed, chest still burning, and understood with sudden clarity that she hadn't fallen into a hidden refuge.

She'd dropped into a world that had learned how to survive without ever being seen.

Lily picked a direction and started walking.

The path narrowed into a cluster of structures pressed together, lights strung low overhead. One opening stood out—less shelter than storefront. A wide counter made from repurposed plating. Crates stacked behind it. Goods arranged with a kind of tired care.

She stepped inside.

The floor was slick beneath her boots. Water dripped steadily from her sleeves, her hair, the hem of her jacket. The man behind the counter glanced up from sorting something unidentifiable into a bin.

"What d'you want, love?"

His voice was rough, but not unkind.

"Sorry," Lily said automatically, gesturing down at the floor. "Didn't mean to—"

He waved a hand. "End of the world, love. Little water won't hurt these floors."

Lily let out a small, surprised chuckle of relief.

She looked around. Packaged food items lined the shelves—labels in multiple languages, some so faded they were barely legible. Others were wrapped in paper or cloth. A few crates held produce that had seen better days.

"Can I ask you something?"

"Hm?" the shopkeeper muttered.

"Well," Lily said, "I just flew out of a giant pipe." She gestured vaguely behind her. "And everyone's acting like this just... happens all the time."

The man snorted softly. "Most people who come through here," he said, "doesn't pay to get to know 'em."

He looked her over more carefully now. Took in the cut of her jacket. The way she stood.

"And you look like some kind of cop," he added.

Lily bristled. "I'm not."

"Course you're not."

She shifted. "I don't suppose you have any clothes I could borrow."

He stopped what he was doing.

"Why should I help you?"

Lily reached for her pocket, checking the payment fob was still there. She and Xynn kept a small reserve of interplanetary exchange credits—habit born of too many outings that ended with them stranded on unfamiliar worlds.

"I have money," she said.

The man studied her for a long moment. Then he leaned back, considering.

"End of the world or no," he said finally, "money's always useful."

When Lily stepped back out into the thoroughfare, she was drier—and dressed for the place she was in.

The clothes didn't fit quite right. But that seemed to be the fashion down here. Layers draped and overlapped in ways that favored movement and comfort over modesty. Like Didot, the people of Ninebury didn't seem particularly concerned with what showed. Lily adjusted what she could, finding a configuration that worked for her.

She slung a canvas bag over her shoulder, stuffed with her soaked jacket and anything else that might draw attention.

As she moved on, she couldn't help noticing how many people were down here. More than she'd expected. More than felt possible.

An entire population, tucked neatly out of sight.

Lily slowed, scanning faces, paths, doorways—trying to decide where to begin.

Lily let herself drift with the flow of foot traffic.

The city narrowed, then widened again into something like a strip—neon signs buzzing and flickering against oxidized metal, music bleeding from doorways, laughter pitched too loud to be sane. Saloons. Clubs. Dens of light carved into the underground like wounds that refused to close.

And then she saw it.

A large neon sign flashed overhead, its letters stuttering slightly with each pulse.

DIDOT

Tall, unsubtle and impossible to miss.

"Of course," Lily muttered. It hit her then that Didot wouldn't use her real name.

She headed towards the sign.

Out front, a hand-painted placard swung lazily from a chain:

END OF THE WORLD PARTY

CYRANTHIANS DRINK FREE

Inside, the club was everything she'd expected—and worse.

Bodies pressed together in a low-ceilinged space soaked in color and heat. Dancers moved on raised platforms, their skin painted or tattooed in elaborate Hedonian patterns that shimmered under the lights. Makeup clung unnaturally to faces, exaggerated eyes and mouths until people barely looked human anymore.

Lily counted three scans of her payment fob before she finally pushed her way into a section of the club quiet enough to think. Her tolerance for paint-stripping music had always been pretty low.

This room felt different. Slower. A sort of thickness in the air you could almost swim through. Cushions littered the floor and low platforms, bodies draped across them—mostly topless, regardless of gender. Body paint smudged from earlier activities. Several people sat in loose circles, dipping slender instruments into a glowing powder. The powder hissed softly as it heated, releasing small clouds of vapor that they tried to catch in their mouths, laughing when they missed.

A couple of people lay sprawled on the floor, eyes closed, breathing slow and heavy.

Lily decided they'd overdone it.

She spotted someone who looked like security—broad shoulders, neutral stance, eyes that tracked movement rather than music—and approached.

"Hi," she said, raising her voice just enough. "I was hoping you could help me."

The guard turned his head slowly, deliberately, until his gaze met hers.

"I'm looking for a friend," Lily continued. "Her name is Trish. She was distributing the vaccine here in Ninebury."

The guard barked out a laugh.

"This ain't Ninebury, kid."

Lily's stomach dropped.

"What do you mean?"

He leaned closer, breath sour. "This ain't no place anymore. This is hell. And we're all about to be dead down here."

Lily frowned. "Dead how?"

The guard snorted. "What, did you fall out of the sky or something?" His eyes slid over her. "Now go enjoy yourself. Pretty thing like you."

The word *thing* scraped against her nerves like broken glass.

Lily swallowed the response rising in her throat and scanned the room instead.

That's when she saw him.

A man sitting alone at a low table, wrapped in a bulky sweater that looked absurdly out of place. A book lay open in front of him. He read calmly, as if the chaos around him didn't exist at all.

She crossed to him.

"What about you?" she asked. "You going to tell me to go dance too?"

He didn't look up. "I'm flattered," he said mildly, "but I'm not much of a dancer."

"No," Lily said, exasperation bleeding through. "That's not—never mind." She took a breath. "What's with all this end-of-the-world talk? And don't tell me I should already know. Pretend I'm new."

"Of course," the man said. "You're the young woman who came through the secondary pressure valve earlier today."

Lily stiffened and sat down across from him. "How do you know that?"

He turned a page.

"I know everything that happens down here."

She stared at him.

He closed the book at last and looked up at her.

"But to answer your question," he said, "I'm afraid it's true."

Lily felt the room tilt slightly.

"We're all going to die very soon."

He extended his hand.

"Arsenal Combs," he said. "I'm—well. The founder of Ninebury, if one insists on titles."

Lily took his hand. His grip was dry, confident. Unhurried.

"Lily," she said.

She knew immediately—beneath the cable-knit sweater, beneath the calm affect—that this was a dangerous man. Not loud. Not cruel in obvious ways. Dangerous in the way systems were dangerous. In the way inevitability was dangerous.

"You see," Combs went on, folding his hands as if they were continuing a pleasant academic discussion, "the Hedonian government knew we were down here. Of course they did. They simply chose not to acknowledge it."

He smiled faintly.

"Then, without warning, they rediverted the water back to Lock Nine."

Lily's jaw tightened.

"No notice. No evacuation window." He shrugged. "I'm trying not to take it personally."

He gestured vaguely, toward the ceiling, toward the roaring infrastructure Lily had just survived.

"As you experienced firsthand, anything attempting to exit through the main aqueduct is now pulled back toward our little sanctuary here at remarkable speed. Physics is such a loyal servant."

He chuckled, soft and almost fond.

"I'm afraid you're trapped here with the rest of us."

Lily looked past him, through the haze of the club, through the bodies and lights and smoke. The words registered. The logic followed.

Still—she knew herself well enough to recognize the thought forming immediately after.

I'll find a way out.

"I'm not dying down here," she said.

Combs tilted his head. "Very noble, Ms. Lily. But I assure you, there is no way out."

She didn't respond.

"I'm looking for my friend," Lily said instead. "If you know everything that goes on down here..." She gestured lightly. "Then you know Trish. She was running a vaccine program."

"Oh, certainly." His smile returned. "Trish. Such a charming person. Less Red Cross, more drug dealer, I'd say. But yes—technically she was providing the vaccine."

Lily kept her expression still.

"I'm afraid she left about a month ago," Combs continued. "Before all this unpleasantness."

Left.

She sunk back, the chair creaking beneath her.

"What about a young woman," she asked carefully. "She might go by Didot. Or something else. Hazel eyes."

Combs's brows lifted with recognition.

"Ah. Liza Roberts," he said. "A terrible tragedy, what happened to her parents. She left around the same time." His gaze sharpened. "Is that who sent you?"

Lily didn't answer.

She didn't have to.

"I see," Combs said mildly. "Then you'll want to meet her sister. She works for me, actually. Cordelia. A lovely girl."

Lily straightened. "Can you help me get in touch with her?"

"She cleans the rooms with the other girls," Combs said. "Best to keep them out of harm's way." His eyes flicked around the club. "Barbarians everywhere."

Lily's fingers curled slowly against her knee.

"Spectre," Combs called, lifting a hand.

The large guard Lily had spoken to earlier stepped forward.

"Take her to see Miss Ferrick," Combs said. "Over at the Chapter House. And be nice."

Spectre grinned, showing teeth. "I'm always nice. Ain't that right, sweetie?"

Lily rose from her chair.

She'd navigated worlds with rigid hierarchies before. Patriarchies, empires, councils that spoke in absolutes. Somehow, though, these humans—these *specific* humans—were finding every wrong button with surgical precision.

She followed anyway.

· · · ·

The church shouldn't have been there.

That was Lily's first thought as Spectre led her inside.

It wasn't a ruin. It wasn't repurposed scaffolding or a clever illusion stitched together from salvaged parts. It was a church in the way people imagined churches—vaulted ceiling, long nave, ribbed arches rising into shadow. Stone that looked old enough to remember the hands that had shaped it. Candles set into niches along the walls, their light low and steady.

A fantasy of a church.

Down here.

The ride over had been quiet. Blessedly so. Lily guessed the transport had to be over a hundred years old, based on what she remembered from her recent crash course in Earth history—boxy, stubborn, still humming long after it should've been retired. Spectre must have caught the look she'd given him earlier, because his version of being nice was apparently to say nothing at all.

He walked her through the main doors and stopped.

The silence inside was complete. The kind that made her aware of her own breathing. Her own pulse. The dim light pooled along the floor and climbed the columns, and for a strange moment Lily had the sensation that organ music *should* be playing—even though it wasn't.

Like the room remembered sound.

Spectre crossed the nave and pressed what looked suspiciously like a doorbell mounted beside a fire door at the back of the church.

A moment passed.

Then the door opened.

The girl standing there was unmistakable.

Didot's sister.

She looked like a version of her without the innocence completely stripped out. Smaller. Sharper. Maybe ten years old. Maybe a little more. Her clothes were dirty, her hands stained with grime that didn't look recent. She barely lifted her eyes.

"Mr. Combs sent us," Spectre said. "Take her to see Ms. Ferrick."

And just like that, he turned on his heel and left.

The girl gestured once, curtly, for Lily to follow, and headed down a side hallway toward the chapter house.

"I'm Lily," Lily offered as they walked. "Can I ask you something?"

The girl didn't respond, but she didn't slow.

"Do you know how this church got down here?" Lily continued. "Was it built underground?"

The girl finally looked up, eyes wide and solemn in the low light.

"No one knows," she said. "It just appeared one day. They say it was a miracle."

There was a pause. Lily raised a brow, the hair on the back of her neck lifting—

—until she caught the faintest twitch at the corner of the girl's mouth.

Lily smirked.

The girl scoffed and picked up her pace. "Of course they built the fuckin' thing," she snapped. "How else d'ya think it got here?"

Lily closed her eyes briefly.

"Walked right into that one."

The hallway narrowed as they moved deeper into the Chapter House.

It felt like walking backward through time.

The walls were painted a color that might once have been white. The floors were scrubbed but worn thin. Metal-framed doors lined the corridor, each with a small window set too high to look through comfortably. The lighting was flat and unforgiving, humming softly overhead.

Depression-era orphanage, Lily thought. The kind you only ever saw in black-and-white footage. All discipline and survival. No softness anywhere it wasn't earned.

A woman approached them from the far end of the hall.

She wore a plain, utilitarian suit. No ornamentation. No color. Her hair was cut short—crew-short—and had gone completely gray. She wore glasses that magnified sharp, watchful eyes.

Lily couldn't tell if she was sixty or ninety. She had the look of someone who'd been old since she was a teenager.

"I'm Ms. Ferrick," the woman said. Her voice was clipped. Efficient. "I wasn't expecting anyone. Are you dropping off or picking up?"

Lily straightened without quite meaning to. Something about the woman made her feel suddenly young. Like if she spoke out of turn, she might be sent to her room.

"Hi," Lily said. "I'm Lily Starling. I was just coming to—"

Movement caught her eye.

Children. Two of them, maybe more. Slipping along the edges of the room, ducking behind doorframes and furniture. Quiet. Alert. Like rats skittering through shadows.

Lily swallowed.

"I was wondering if I might speak to someone named Cordelia Roberts," she continued. "Mr. Combs said—"

"She was right here," Ms. Ferrick said, looking around sharply.

Lily had to admire it. Cordelia had vanished with professional efficiency. "Cordelia!"

The name came out of Ms. Ferrick like a siren. A shout that seemed impossibly loud for her size.

And just as suddenly, Cordelia was there again—standing at the woman's side as if she'd never moved at all.

Ms. Ferrick adjusted her glasses. "I'll give you... privacy."

She disappeared behind a door with a large glass pane set into it. Lily could see her clearly on the other side—arms crossed, eyes never leaving them.

Cordelia shifted, suddenly less sharp.

"I'm sorry I teased you, miss," she said.

Lily smiled gently. "No. It was a good tease."

Cordelia blinked. Then grinned, wicked and delighted. "It was, wasn't it."

"For the record," Lily added, lowering her voice, "I knew the church had to be assembled down here. I was more curious about its history."

Cordelia snorted. "It was the church Mr. Arsehole got married in or something." She rolled her eyes. "When he built *Combs City* down here, he had it cut into pieces and hauled in. Calls himself the founder."

She leaned closer, voice dropping.

"He ain't no founder. There were good people down here long before him. Just trying to carve out a piece of Earth without a boot on your neck."

Lily studied the girl. Thought about the crucibles it took to make a child speak like that.

"I definitely didn't get good vibes from him," Lily said.

Cordelia planted her hands on her hips—exactly the way her sister did.

"So what the hell do you want from me?"

Lily met her gaze. "I know your sister."

Cordelia froze.

Her eyes went wide. Real wide.

"Liza's alive?" she whispered. Genuine shock breaking through her guard. "They told me she drowned trying to get back to the surface."

The room seemed to hold its breath.

And Lily knew—before she said another word—that this was the moment that mattered.

Lily took a step forward, careful to keep her posture open, nonthreatening.

"She's alive," she said gently. "Your sister. She sent me here to find you. I didn't understand that at first—but I do now."

Cordelia recoiled, backing toward the wall. "I don't know you," she snapped. "Who the hell do you think you are?"

Lily stopped advancing. Folded her arms—not defensively, but to ground herself.

"You're right," she said. "I'm not your friend. I didn't even know you existed five minutes ago. But I lost someone down here. And you've lost people too." Her voice steadied. "I want to help."

Cordelia's face crumpled before she could stop it. She turned away, blinking hard, jaw clenched as if she could sheer the tears back inside by force.

"I hate this place," she said, voice shaking. "But it doesn't matter. I heard the working girls talking. We're going to starve. All of us." She scrubbed her face with her sleeve, anger flooding back in where fear had been. "It's only a matter of time before people start eating each other."

She squared herself again. "So why don't you just leave me alone?"

Lily reached out and took her by the shoulder.

The contact was deliberate. Anchoring.

She thought of Earth in the long past—of the moment when the crew of the *Salamander* had stood waiting beside an open shuttle hatch. Inviting her. Calling her.

Of Caris, patient and unflinching, earning trust not with words but with presence.

She met Cordelia's eyes.

"Cordelia," Lily said softly. "You don't have any reason to trust me. I get that. But everyone down here is going to die unless someone does something." Her grip tightened just slightly. "And I intend to get you back to your sister alive."

Cordelia searched her face, suspicion warring with something fragile and hopeful.

"What are you going to do?" she asked.

Lily exhaled and shrugged.

"Hope for the best."

To her surprise, she meant it. A strange calm settled over her—focused, steady, the way it always did right before things went sideways.

"Sometimes," she added, "that's the only option."

Cordelia's shoulders loosened a fraction.

"I'm Lily, by the way," Lily said, almost as an afterthought.

"You can call me Delia."

"Delia," Lily smiled. "I like it."

Footsteps approached—sharp, purposeful.

Ms. Ferrick was bearing down on them like a storm front.

Delia's hand shot out and clutched Lily's sleeve. "Listen," she whispered urgently. "Just agree. Whatever she asks. I'll help you—I swear."

Lily didn't have time to ask what she meant.

Ms. Ferrick stopped in front of them, eyes assessing, calculating.

"How much will you give me for her?" she asked flatly. "I won't take less than ninety credits."

The words were like a bullet.

Lily felt bile rise in her throat. A human child, priced like a pair of shoes.

"I can do ninety," Lily heard herself say.

She hated how easily it came out.

Ms. Ferrick nodded, suddenly all solemn judgment. "Your motives seem decent," she said, as if granting absolution. "I'm sure you'll get your money's worth. And she'll be better off." Her gaze flicked upward, toward the window to the church. "I still believe the Lord will deliver us from our captivity."

"Right," Lily said.

Her hand trembled as she transferred the credits. A sharp sting shot through her palm—as if she'd brushed hellfire.

But this wasn't about heaven. Or devils.

This was about survival.

And right now, survival meant acting.

• • • •

Lily talked as she ran back to the chamber where she'd come through—the room of pipes and rushing water, the bones of the aqueduct laid bare.

"Your sister wasn't just reading all those books for fun," she said breathlessly. "She's been studying the aqueduct. Trying to figure out how to lower the water enough for you all to evacuate."

She stopped in the center of the pipe room.

And then she saw it.

The symbols.

Painted and etched in places she hadn't noticed before—along the edges of access panels, stenciled beside maintenance plates, half-scraped away and reapplied. The same three pictograms she'd used to open the hatch. The ripple. The spiral. The inverted triangle.

Her breath caught.

Didot hadn't just shown her a way in.

She'd given her the way out.

Lily crossed to the wall where a schematic had been bolted in place, yellowed and cracked but still legible. Her eyes followed the flow lines, the pressure arrows. And there—five symbol clusters marked along the system.

Three were highlighted in grease pencil. Reachable. Already adjusted.

The other two—

Her stomach dropped.

Submerged.

"No," Lily murmured. "There are three control points accessible from inside Ninebury. But the other two—"

"Submerged."

The voice came from behind her.

She turned.

Arsenal Combs stood in the entryway, Spectre looming beside him like a threat given shape.

"Our best men tried," Combs continued mildly. "Long before you came crashing through our pressure valve."

Lily didn't look at him. She was still staring at the schematic.

"Well," Combs added, "to be fair, they weren't our best men. But they weren't as stupid as Spectre here."

Spectre narrowed his eyes.

"No offense," Combs said placidly.

That seemed to appease him.

"There are two underwater," Lily said, checking her scanner now. "One is right behind this wall. The other's further back—near the intake."

"The pressure is catastrophic," Combs said. "Everyone we sent drowned. The first had proper diving gear. It failed. Others died trying to retrieve the body."

"Didot made it out," Lily said, with certainty.

Combs didn't respond.

Lily turned the map over in her hands—the one Didot had given her. The scribbles she'd dismissed before.

They weren't scribbles.

They were notes.

A path.

Her heart began to race as she dug into her pack. "I have an emergency breathing apparatus. Union issue."

"It won't matter," Combs said. "The pressure will knock you unconscious."

Lily looked at him then. Really looked.

"No," she said. "It won't. Because I'm not going in blind."

She pulled a small rectangular device from her utility kit and pressed it into his chest.

"This light will flash when I open the last valve," she said. "The second it does, you blow the wall."

Spectre glanced at Combs.

"And when you fail?" Combs scoffed.

"Blow it anyway," Lily said. "It might be enough."

Combs smiled thinly. "And what exactly am I meant to blow it with?"

Lily reached into her pocket and withdrew the jewel.

Even in the low light, it seemed to drink the shadows around it.

"Use this."

Combs's eyes went green with something ugly and covetous. "Ah. The untraceable jewel."

"Don't screw this up," Lily said. "We may only get one shot."

Combs handed the jewel to Spectre and nodded. Spectre pocketed it an leaned against the wall.

Lily turned to Delia. "Find cover."

Delia was already gone.

"Good girl," Lily whispered.

She fitted the emergency respirator over her face, sealing it with practiced hands. Her tactical vest hissed as she shifted it into full pressure protection. She didn't give herself time to think beyond that.

She stepped into the air lock and pulled the lever.

The door clapped shut.

Water slammed in.

She stayed focused, despite the sheer terror coiling in her chest—the anticipation almost worse than the impact.

The hatch opened.

The water swallowed her whole.

The pressure hit like a fist, punishing and immediate, dragging at her limbs, crushing her chest even through the apparatus. She spied lights, lining a submerged corridor—faint, flickering beacons that matched the drawing Didot had scrawled on the back of the map. She held the image in her mind like a prayer.

The handholds were almost nonexistent.

Lily kicked.

Pulled.

Let the current take her when she had to—fought it when she could.

The aqueduct roared around her, alive and furious, reclaiming space it had been denied. Pressure gnawed at her ribs. Her vision tunneled.

The respirator sputtered once.

Twice.

"Stay with it," she told herself. "Just stay with it."

She reached the valve.

Her fingers fumbled—numb, clumsy—until muscle memory took over.

Ripple.

Spiral.

Triangle.

The lock gave.

The current shifted.

It tore her away from Ninebury—ripped her backward through the system, faster and faster, flinging her like debris—

—and then she was airborne.

She hit hard.

Wet earth.

Marsh.

Air.

Lily skidded across the ground, landing on her back in a spray of mud and water. She tore the respirator from her face and sucked in a ragged breath.

She'd come blasting out of an exit pipe nearly a hundred yards from the entrance.

Alive.

Lily checked her scanner.

Time. Pressure.

Then she pulled up the jewel's interface. She hesitated only a moment.

"Goodbye, Mr. Combs," she said quietly, and pressed the button.

RADIAL PULSE DETONATION

3...

2...

1...

The ground bucked beneath her feet.

Water thundered.

Then—movement on the scanner.

Levels dropped fast. Faster than she'd dared hope.

Life signs bloomed across the display. And moments later, confirmation with her own eyes.

Figures poured out into the concentric squares—soaked, staggering, gasping, alive.

Lily scanned faces, heart racing.

Then she saw Delia.

They collided in a hug.

Delia pulled back first, shaking herself, slipping back into that familiar armor of toughness.

"You should've seen his face," she said, grinning. "Right before it happened."

"I told you to stay clear."

"And miss the fireworks?" Delia shot back. "It's not every day one of Mr. Arsehole's men blows himself up."

Lily winced. "I'm sorry it had to come to that."

"They weren't going to blow the wall," Delia said. Not a question.

"No," Lily said softly. "He wanted control. A supply line. A way to rule what was left."

Delia frowned. "But they might've died too."

"There's an old saying," Lily said. "Your well-read sister probably knows it. Better to rule in hell than serve in heaven."

Delia nodded slowly. Then she held something out.

"Thought you'd want this back."

The jewel—scorched, but intact.

"Wow," Lily breathed. "Still in one piece."

"That thing's quite a weapon," Delia said. "Where'd you get it?"

"A friend gave it to me."

Lily slipped it into her pocket, her fingers lingering over the casing. "He knew I'd need it."

· · · ·

Lily kicked in the door.

She didn't need to—but it was more fun this way.

The man barely had time to register what was happening before the door slammed into the wall. He froze, trousers around his knees, panic flashing across his face as Lily crossed the room with terrifying calm.

He tried to pull himself together.

Too slow.

Lily caught him with a Saravethi throw—clean, efficient—and sent him flying. He hit the folding chair hard, metal collapsing beneath him as he landed on his back with a choked sound. He didn't try to get up.

Just whimpered.

"Jesus, Lily," Didot snapped from the corner. "Don't hurt him—he's a customer."

Lily ignored her.

She pointed at the man.

"You."

Lily wasn't tall. She wasn't built like a bruiser. But she carried the day on her shoulders—the water, the screaming pressure of Ninebury—and it made her more intimidating than any bouncer at the door.

The man's knees shook.

"Pay your debts."

"I—I will," he stammered. "I'll pay right now." He fumbled for his wallet, hands slick with sweat.

The contents spilled out onto the floor.

Lily stepped forward and planted her boot on his wrist.

"Wait."

She bent, plucked the wallet from his grip, and straightened.

"Ease up, Lily," Didot muttered. "Really. Sorry about this, Sal—she can be a real—"

Lily lifted a hand.

Didot stopped talking.

Among the wallet's contents was a card.

Lily's breath caught.

A circle pierced by three arrows.

She knew that symbol. She'd seen it stamped on Union vaccine containers. Then again on crates in Ninebury.

She held it up.

"What is this?"

The man swallowed hard. "Sunbow Logistics. They move... specialized supplies."

"What kind of supplies?"

Her voice was steady. Too steady.

"Medical," he said quickly. "Just medical."

"The vaccine."

Lily leaned down, close enough that he could see his reflection in her eyes. She reached, took hold, and applied pressure where it counted.

The man squealed.

"I want you to show me every shipping chart you have available," she said. Then, pleasantly, "Please."

He gestured weakly toward her hand, then cradled himself. "You're holding it. The access code is 4767. But don't open it on a hot console—they'll trace you. Only offline."

"And you'll tell them you lost this one."

"Yes. Yes."

"And you'll pay what you owe."

"Yes!"

He paid.

Lily stepped back and gestured toward the door. "Get out. No services tonight."

She paused, eyes flicking to the ring on his finger.

"Go home to your wife."

He didn't argue. He scrambled past her and was gone.

Didot stared after him, furious. "What the hell was that for?"

Lily turned to her. "After you nearly got me killed, I wasn't coming back empty-handed."

Her gaze dropped briefly to Didot's negligee. "You might want to change. Someone's waiting for you outside."

Didot's anger collapsed into something fragile and bright. She grabbed a robe and bolted for the door.

"Delia?" Lily heard her call—hope breaking through the word.

A moment later came tears. Laughter. A reunion Lily didn't need to see to feel.

She stood alone in the room, the card balanced between her fingers.

The symbol felt heavier now.

"What's gotten into you, Lily?" she murmured.

The answer, she feared, was not far away.

• • • •

Lily scanned the payment fob at the base of the lift and watched the numbers flicker as the machine approved the transfer.

Another obscene number vanished from her account.

She exhaled through her nose. Earth. Everything cost too much here. Everything asked for proof—proof you belonged, proof you were allowed to take up space, proof you could pay to move.

She'd be glad to be off-world again. She preferred solving problems with tools instead of currency.

The doors of the lift capsule sealed with a soft, airtight sigh.

The ascent began, smooth and silent.

London fell away beneath her—layer by layer—until the city resolved into stacked geometry: platforms and bridges, the Hedon vertical complex rising like a monument to denial. She remembered the view from last time, the way the upper district had looked like a dream someone had tried to make permanent. Pastel façades. Sculpted terraces. Curated air.

Ninebury still buzzed in her bones. The pressure. The timing. The way everything had come together because she'd trusted herself and moved. She felt lighter for it. Sharper. Like a blade that had finally been used for its intended purpose.

She pictured Valen's face when she showed him the card. The shipping routes. Sunbow Logistics. Something was wrong with the vaccine distribution. And now she was fairly sure Trish was tangled up in it too.

Maybe together they could figure out what Lily was supposed to do next.

She swallowed and let her hand drift, without thinking, toward her pocket.

The jewel was there.

She closed her fingers around it once—then forced her hand away.

Don't make it a habit, she told herself.

But it already was.

The lift opened.

She stepped into the upper ring. The air was colder than she expected—sharp, clean, carrying the faint scent of altitude. The walkway curved ahead of her in a wide arc, guiding foot traffic the way a museum guided visitors.

Restaurants sat dark behind glass. Shops were shuttered. No vendors. No tourists. No security posts with bored guards pretending not to stare.

No life at all.

Lily pressed forward, her footsteps too loud on the polished surface.

The sun was beginning to set, sinking behind the spine of the complex. Shadows pooled in the corners of doorways. In the distance, a streetlight flickered on.

Then another.

Then another.

They lit her path in segments—one pool of light at a time, as if something had decided to guide her forward. As if the corridor itself were watching her advance.

Lily fought the urge to look over her shoulder. Not out of fear, but out of habit.

The circular pathway carried her past a row of closed cafés, past a fountain gone dry, past a sculpture of a human figure mid-laugh—frozen in joy that felt obscene in isolation.

She reached the grand archway marking the council complex and slowed without meaning to.

It was beautiful, in the Hedon way. Too perfect. Too intentional. The kind of entrance designed to make you feel small before you stepped through it.

Carved above the arch, in crisp lettering, was a phrase that didn't belong to this place's usual childish literalism.

Tout passe. L'art seul a l'éternité.

Everything passes. Only art has eternity.

Lily tilted her head, taking it in.

Then she turned, deliberately, and looked out across the skyline, drawing a slow, steadying breath.

Far beyond the silent complex, Earth still moved.

Cargo ships and transports slid through the clouds in slow, purposeful lines—bright specks against the darkening sky. The planet's arteries were still pumping. There was still trade. Still traffic. Still people somewhere, living their lives, getting dinner, arguing, laughing, trying.

She thought about how Earth had been one of the earliest adopters of the vaccine—before the Union's version had even entered development. One of the first to integrate it into public infrastructure. One of the first to believe cooperation could outpace catastrophe.

Standing there, watching the last of the sun catch on the upper spires of the city, she felt a quiet, stubborn pride.

Earth was damaged.

But it wasn't lost.

The thought sparked a brief flicker of hope—small and stubborn, like a match struck in wind.

Then she faced the entrance again.

She pulled up Valen's message on her commtag, rechecked the access code, and keyed it into the panel.

A soft chime.

The doors parted.

Inside, the corridor was dim—barely lit, the light swallowed by stone and distance. The air changed. Cooler. Still. As if the building had been sealed for days and no one had thought to let it breathe.

Lily stepped inside. The doors closed behind her with a final click.

The sound echoed.

Her boots sounded wrong on the floor, too loud in the quiet. She navigated by memory, turning where she remembered turning, counting intervals the way she did when she didn't fully trust herself.

The longer she walked, the more doubt crept in.

She had only done this once. In the dark, she wasn't sure of her way.

She hoped she hadn't missed Valen for the night. Hoped she hadn't arrived too late. She hated being late.

Another bend. The corridor widened, opening toward the council chamber wing.

A low light glowed ahead.

Lily smiled.

She thought she saw movement—a shadow shifting inside the chamber.

Relief. She hadn't missed them.

She stepped forward, quicker now. Into the antechamber, around the large column—

—and nearly tripped.

Rich fabric snagged under her boot.

Embroidered. Heavy. Expensive in the way Hedon liked its power to be expensive.

High Council robes.

And attached to them—

a body.

Lily's breath left her in a single, sharp pull.

She lifted her gaze slowly—like her eyes didn't want to give her the rest of it all at once.

The room resolved.

The entire council chamber.

Bodies slumped in high-backed seats or collapsed across the table.

Bodies on the floor, twisted where they'd fallen. Some faced the tall window, as if they'd been looking out when it happened. Some faced inward, as if they'd tried to turn toward one another.

No movement.

No breath.

For a moment, Lily couldn't make her mind accept it. Couldn't make meaning land.

Then her eyes caught green.

A cloak—familiar.

"Valen." The name broke out of her with a crack and echoed off the curved wall.

She ran.

Knelt beside him hard enough to bruise her knees, hands already reaching, searching for a pulse—

But she already knew, from the disruptor burns scorched through his cloak.

There was nothing to do.

His face was turned slightly to the side, eyes half open, his expression caught between surprise and resignation.

Lily's stomach lurched.

She looked up, as if the room might explain itself.

The towering window at the front of the chamber framed the city beyond—an active skyline. Transports slid through the clouds. The red smog of evening burned beneath the sunset, lit like a maw swallowing the last of the day.

Lily rose slowly, her body moving on instinct.

She stood there—small at the center of the chamber—staring out at the sky as if she could call for help through glass.

She felt the hope draining out of her. Her lungs filled with the certainty of her surroundings, thick and poisonous, like noxious smoke.

Her ears began to ring.

At first it was faint. Then louder. Harder—until it felt like the room was tilting, like the air itself had thinned into a sharp, piercing whistle.

She barely registered the red emergency lights igniting.

One by one, they bloomed across the walls and ceiling in slow pulses, bathing the bodies in a hot, accusing glow.

The building was announcing something.

Recording something.

Turning the chamber into a story before she could.

No. No no no—

She forced herself to focus.

If Hedonian security found her here first, she wouldn't just be arrested.

She'd be processed. Buried in bureaucracy until she was no longer a person—just a file. A narrative they could write however they wanted.

She scanned the room fast.

Doors. Side corridors. Emergency signage. Service panels. Anything that led out and up.

Her mind began laying a route—roof access, somewhere she could get a signal out.

Somewhere she could—

A sharp electric crack split the air.

The pulse hit her before she could take a full step. Her muscles seized and released all at once. The world lurched sideways—the marble floor rose to meet her.

Her vision blurred.

Sound collapsed back into the thin whistle, then into nothing at all.

The last thing Lily saw—tilted at the edge of her vision as she fell—was a line of approaching boots.

Pounding like a stampede.

Closing in like an army.

Inevitable.

The world went black.

THE CONVOY WAS ALREADY moving.

Xynn watched it from the ridge line, crouched low against the stone, visor dimmed just enough to cut the glare. Three armored transports in a staggered line, dust pluming behind them as they rolled through the main artery of the settlement. Kessler Syndicate markings stamped into the plating—subtle, almost tasteful. Ownership disguised as logistics.

Efficient. Confident.

Too confident.

She heard Narek over the comm. "Beautiful day for an ambush."

Xynn didn't answer.

Narek was in one of the Fleas today—sealed in tight, hands on the controls, pod hovering just inches above the ground behind the ridge. The machine revved softly, a living thing at rest. Its armor was scorched along one flank from a previous run, paint burned away to bare metal.

Xynn lifted two fingers.

Hold.

The rest of the squad waited below the ridge, pressed into the broken terrain. Two more Fleas skimmed low in the shadow of the rocks, their pilots steady and silent. On foot, the others had gone still in the way trained soldiers did—breathing shallow, attention narrowed, bodies coiled.

The convoy passed the market square.

Empty now. Shuttered stalls. Cloth banners torn down to rags. The Kesslers had cleared the streets hours ago, made sure no one was left to watch them take what they wanted.

Xynn's jaw tightened.

She switched channels. "Targets confirmed," she said calmly. "No civilians in the strike zone. We move on my mark."

A flicker of acknowledgment icons pulsed across her display.

The lead transport slowed slightly as it approached the outer gate—routine scan. The escort drones fanned wider, compensating.

There. The seam opened again.

Xynn didn't hesitate.

"Go."

The Fleas surged forward in a blur of motion, skimming over the ground before snapping upward in a synchronized hop—clean, precise. Weapons fire lit the air in sharp bursts as the drones went dark, one by one, dropping from the sky in smoking arcs.

Xynn broke from cover at the same instant, squad flowing with her down the slope. The sound hit all at once—shouts, alarms, the crack of return fire slamming into the terrain. She moved through it like she always did, instincts honed, body ahead of thought.

The second transport tried to peel away.

Narek was already there.

His Flea darted in low, took a hit along the underside—armor flaring white—then snapped upward in a desperate hop that carried him clear as the vehicle slewed sideways and slammed into a support wall.

"Flea Two is damaged," someone called.

Xynn clocked it without breaking stride. "Fall back. Maintain cover."

The firefight collapsed fast after that. The Kesslers hadn't expected resistance—not real resistance. Their weapons clattered to the ground as Xynn's squad closed in, efficient and relentless. Within minutes, the convoy was secured, the transports silent and smoking in the street.

Xynn stepped back and let her gaze sweep the scene as her squad moved in to secure prisoners. The Kessler operatives were zip-tied and disarmed with practiced efficiency, her people calm and controlled as they worked. Smoke curled from the disabled transports. The settlement itself remained quiet—doors cracked open just enough for watching eyes, relief tempered by the knowledge that nothing stayed free for long out here.

The Kessler Syndicate had learned to exploit that truth early. They weren't conquerors. They didn't fly flags or swear loyalty. They slipped into the cracks others couldn't—or wouldn't—seal. Refugee worlds. Border settlements. Places where help arrived late and left early.

A hiss of pressure vents broke her focus as Narek's Flea settled to the ground behind her. The pod's shell split open and he climbed out, helmet tucked under his arm, hair damp with sweat. There was a smear of soot along one sleeve and a fresh tear at the knee of his trousers, but he was grinning anyway—bright, a little reckless.

"Next time," he said, breathless, "next time you call an audible, give me a heads up."

Xynn snorted. "Variety is the spice of life."

He laughed, the sound easy, then sobered as he followed her gaze back to the opened crate. "Union issue," he said. "Like last time."

"Well," Xynn replied, "no market for the Gherionite vaccine."

For a moment, she studied him—not as an officer, but as someone remembering. The boy she'd met in a cell on the *Warden of Tarshish*. A skinny prisoner who'd flinched at raised voices. Who'd trusted her anyway.

Now he stood in front of her dust-streaked and steady, a soldier who piloted combat hardware and cracked jokes under fire.

He caught her looking and tilted his head. "What?"

"Nothing," she said quietly.

But she felt it settle in her chest all the same—how fast people changed when the world demanded it. How easily survival hardened into competence. How responsibility crept up on you when you weren't watching.

She turned back to the squad, already thinking about the next move.

At the center of the settlement, the Saravethi elder approached, flanked by two younger refugees. The elder's posture was careful—grateful, but guarded. The look of someone who had learned not to trust outsiders.

"Thank you," the elder said, voice steady. "Though I do not approve of your violence. Warrior caste entitlement."

Xynn was used to the reaction by now. It didn't bother her.

"We are not here to harm anyone," she said evenly. "Only to ensure the vaccine distribution doesn't get... interrupted."

The elder's expression didn't change. "They did not hurt us. They were only interested in material things. Food. Energy. Medicine."

Xynn followed the elder's gaze back to the opened crates. "And one of those material things was the vaccine," she said. "Which places it under the jurisdiction of the Saravethi Relief Effort."

She glanced over her shoulder at her team and started walking. "If you'll excuse me, distinguished one."

Xynn approached the ground vehicle the Syndicate had been using. She keyed a crack-pad against the lock. The hatch hissed open.

Inside: vials, packed tight. Temperature-stable. Pristine.

Narek came up beside her, visor lifted now, eyes narrowed. "This is the most we've ever recovered," he said quietly. "Imagine the black-market value."

Xynn didn't answer.

She stared down at the crate, something cold settling deeper in her chest.

"Take a look at this." She reached in and lifted a tablet from the transport's interior. Its screen glowed with a simple symbol: a circle pierced by three arrows. Beneath it, the words *Sunbow Logistics*. A biometric panel waited below—thumbprint-enabled.

Xynn pressed her thumb to it, already anticipating the obnoxious alarm.

"I wonder what's so important it needs a bio-encrypted tablet," she said. "Not a manifest. The inventory's obvious."

Narek rubbed his chin.

Xynn turned the tablet slightly, angling it away from the street.

A sharp crack of feedback cut across the channel.

"Commander," came the call, strained. "Flea Two took more damage than we thought. Stabilizer's not holding."

Xynn looked up in time to see the pod dip—hard—its hover field stuttering before the pilot wrestled it down in a controlled skid. The impact echoed off the stonework, sharp enough to send a ripple through the watching crowd.

"Secure it," Xynn said immediately. She slid the tablet into a shielded pouch at her belt and started moving. "Everyone else hold."

By the time she reached the Flea, the hatch was already opening.

"I'm fine," the pilot said, breathless but upright. "Just a glitch—"

"You're not fine," Xynn replied, eyes already on their scorched jumpsuit. "Hey, you did great out there. But I have to ground you while that heals."

"I can still—"

"You won't," she said, calm and final. "Get patched up. I don't need you proving anything."

The pilot hesitated, then nodded and stepped back toward the techs. "Of course. Thank you, Commander."

Xynn straightened—and nearly collided with another figure stepping in too fast. She stopped short as a smaller, younger face snapped into view.

"Mr. Kael," Xynn said, smiling as she took a half-step back. "You did well."

Kael flushed, then brightened. "Thank you, Commander. I've been running the drills extra in my off time."

"I know," Xynn said. "It shows."

Narek joined them, glancing at Kael with a nod. "Definitely an improvement," he added, matter-of-fact.

Kael nodded quickly, clearly trying not to grin.

"Umm—if you'd like, sir—uh—sirs—sir and ma'am—"

Xynn chuckled and shook her head. "We've been over this, Kael. Commander is fine. Or just Xynn."

"Oh—right. Yes. Sorry." He took a breath, then blurted, "I can take the Flea. If you need a driver. I'm cleared. I've been practicing."

Xynn blinked once.

"You have," she said. "But—"

He nodded hard. "Sim hours. Live hops. You've seen me. I think. Sir—Xynn—Commander."

"I've seen you not crash," she replied. "I'm not sure you're quite ready for—"

She stopped, catching Narek's look.

Xynn exhaled slowly. "Tell you what. Next recon, you play defense. All right?"

Kael's face lit up like she'd handed him the stars.

"Yes—yes, Commander. Thank you!" He spun on his heel and took off at a jog—

—and immediately caught his foot on a taut line securing a tarp.

Narek nearly lost all composure as Kael windmilled, caught himself just short of eating dirt, then came down hard enough on his knee to yelp.

Xynn smirked as she turned to Narek. "Anything goes wrong, it's on you."

Narek threw his hands up. "Hey, you're the one in command."

She punched his arm—hard—as they climbed into the transport bound for base camp.

• • • •

By evening, basecamp had softened—no longer a place of briefings and perimeter checks, but something closer to a family preparing a meal, held together by habit and trust rather than orders.

Temporary structures glowed low against the dark, modular frames stitched together with cable and scavenged braces. Tarps had been reinforced where the wind worried them most. Heat coils hummed beneath crates worn smooth by weeks of use. This place had been standing just long enough to feel habitual, not long enough to feel safe.

Xynn moved through it all unhurried.

She checked ration counts at one station, adjusted a heater dial at another. Stopped to make sure a medic had the right supplies. Listened when someone mentioned a cracked seal on an engine intake and flagged it for morning.

She never gave speeches or pep talks. Her presence was steady and attentive. People relaxed around her, the way they did when they knew someone competent was paying attention.

Near the center of camp, Kael sat with his tablet balanced on his knee, stylus moving in smooth, absent-minded strokes. Narek had dropped down across from him, boots stretched toward the heater.

"You ever stop working?" Narek asked.

Kael didn't look up. "This doesn't feel like work."

"Ever the artist."

Kael smiled. "Literally born to it."

The stylus paused. He turned the tablet just enough for Narek to see—a loose sketch taking shape, lines confident but exploratory. Negative space doing as much work as the form itself.

Narek tilted his head. "Is that supposed to be me?"

The likeness was unmistakable.

Kael smiled again, used to Narek's teasing by now, and tapped the stylus lightly against the tattoo near his hand—the mark of the artist caste.

Around them, half the camp bore something similar. Symbols carried forward from lives interrupted. Half-hidden beneath sleeves or collars. Remnants of who they had been before the relief effort.

Xynn had helped introduce a new paradigm within the SRE—an opportunity to serve regardless of caste. To train. To contribute. A lesson she had internalized, and now carried outward.

She had just finished checking in with the sentries when a comms officer approached at a brisk walk.

"Commander," the officer said quietly. "Message from leadership."

Xynn stilled. "What's the message?"

The officer hesitated. "One word. *Orbit.*"

The word was still hanging in the air as Xynn was halfway to the ops station. Narek fell in beside her.

She ducked into the operations module—a temporary structure bolted onto a transport chassis, monitors lining the walls, power humming unevenly through the floor.

"Bring up orbital," Xynn said. "Run an overlay. I want to see anything that wasn't there this morning."

The techs moved fast, fingers flying. Starfield resolved into grids, then layers. Registered traffic. Colony shuttles. Supply haulers.

Then—something flickered.

A faint distortion at the edge of the display. Not a ship. Not debris. A smear, like light bent the wrong way.

"That wasn't there earlier," one of the techs said.

Xynn leaned in. "Can you enhance it?"

The distortion sharpened—and warped. A ghost of an image, doubled and folded in on itself.

"What are we looking at?" Xynn asked.

"I... don't know," the tech admitted. "It's there, but it's not resolving."

Xynn straightened. "Get Kael."

Narek was already out the door.

He was back moments later, Kael on his heels, expression tight but focused.

"You wanted me?" Kael asked.

Xynn gestured him forward. "Tell me what you see."

Kael stepped up to the console. He didn't touch anything at first—just watched.

Then he reached for the controls.

He adjusted the gain. Shifted the spectrum. Pulled the image apart and recombined it—mirroring one side against the other.

He began sketching on a secondary screen.

"This is duplication," Kael said. "Or masking. They're rendering an image on one axis and reflecting it across another." He paused. "It's not invisible—it's pretending to be empty space."

"There," he said quietly.

He added the final strokes to his sketch.

"Run a search on this shape."

The console chimed.

"There." Kael pointed, and the tech froze the feed.

Kessler Syndicate. Surveillance relay. Comm satellite.

Silence settled over the room.

"Not business as usual," Xynn said.

Narek shook his head. "And with the prohibition on firing weapons in orbit, we can't just blast it."

Kael looked up. "There should be a ground station—something to communicate with it."

Xynn nodded. "Exactly." She turned to the techs. "I want this triangulated by morning."

The techs moved.

"Find the ground station," Xynn continued. "I don't care how small it is or how well it's hidden."

She looked at Kael—not as a commander, but in acknowledgment.

"Good work," she said.

Kael exhaled, the tension easing just a fraction.

Outside, the camp kept breathing. But the shape of the night had changed.

* * * *

Morning came thin and gray.

Not quite dawn—the slow easing of dark into something workable. Basecamp stirred in pieces: heat coils ticking down, boots scraping over dirt, the low murmur of comm checks and clipped status reports. The night had left everything damp with cold.

Xynn sealed the last clasp on her tactical armor and flexed her shoulders, testing the fit. The suit answered the way it always did—familiar, reliable. She keyed her helmet at her belt and stepped out into the open.

The Fleas waited where they'd been staged, silhouettes against the pale sky. Techs moved around them with quiet urgency, checking joints, reseating panels, running diagnostics one last time.

Narek was already there.

He stood with his helmet tucked under his arm, expression alert but calm, one hand resting on the side of his pod like it was a living thing he trusted.

Beside him—

Xynn slowed.

Kael.

Fully suited. Harness secured. Helmet clipped at his hip, visor reflecting the morning light. He stood a little too straight, hands folded behind his back, like he was afraid if he relaxed even a fraction he'd be sent away.

Xynn stopped in front of them.

For a moment, no one spoke.

Then she exhaled through her nose, the ghost of a smile touching her mouth.

"That's right," she said. "I did say you could ride defense, didn't I."

Kael's face lit instantly—bright, contained, unmistakable. "Yes, Commander."

She nodded once, already accepting what she'd known the moment she'd seen him there.

"Stay tight to Narek," she continued. "You mirror his movements. You don't chase targets. You don't improvise."

"I won't," Kael said quickly. Then, catching himself, added more evenly, "Understood, Commander."

Xynn met his eyes.

Not to test him.

To acknowledge him.

"I know you do," she said.

Narek shifted slightly, glancing between them. "I'll keep him close."

Xynn's gaze flicked to him. A small nod.

She turned back to Kael. The words she didn't say hung between them—

Xynn inclined her head.

"Mount up," she said.

Kael didn't hesitate. He turned toward the Flea, movements precise, practiced. No stumble this time. No rushing. Just quiet resolve as he climbed into the pod and began his checks.

Xynn watched until the hatch sealed.

• • • •

The Fleas thundered through the trees like they had something to prove.

They weren't subtle machines. Their weight and noise had trouble blending into the world around them. But they were precise. Hover-fields skimmed low over roots and rock, kicking up leaves and loam as the pods leapt and settled in practiced arcs. Branches snapped back in their wake. The forest recoiled—then closed behind them.

Xynn kept them in tight formation, comms alive with clipped updates and status checks. Three sites to verify. Whatever the Syndicate was doing out here, the satellite data suggested ambition—something semi-permanent, reinforced. A foothold, not a pass-through.

"Clear," Kael called. Exactly on schedule.

Xynn smiled to herself.

"Clear," he repeated at the next checkpoint, voice steady, a fraction too eager.

He was doing everything by the book. Every sweep. Every interval. No shortcuts.

They pushed farther from the beaten paths, deeper into the valley where the terrain dipped and widened. The trees thinned as they descended, trunks giving way to low scrub and exposed stone. No villages out here. No reason for anyone to be—unless they didn't want to be found.

"We're about to enter a large clearing," Xynn warned. "We'll be out in the open."

"Anything hostile will be just as exposed," Narek said, already adjusting his sensors.

They broke the tree line together.

The valley opened around them—broad, shallow, ringed with forested ridges. The ground bore old scarring: vehicle tracks long since softened by weather, disturbed earth half reclaimed by moss.

They moved toward the triangulated point, Fleas slowing as Kael ran his sweep.

"I'm not reading anything," he said after a beat. "No heat. No signal bleed. All clear."

Too clear.

The first shot came from nowhere.

Blue-white fire stitched the air above them, forcing the Fleas to scatter instinctively. Xynn felt the shockwave rattle through her harness as another volley cracked past, close enough to send warning glyphs flashing across her display.

"Contact!" Narek barked.

"Where?" Xynn snapped.

"I don't—" Static tore through his feed.

Another blast slammed into the ground beside Kael's pod, sending dirt and stone spraying.

"Fan out!" Xynn ordered. "See if we can make it work for it."

Whatever it was, it picked Narek. A barrage of blaster fire hammered into his viewing array.

"My visibility's compromised," he said.

"Aim for the tree line!" Xynn called, laying down blind fire in the direction she thought the shots were coming from. No contact.

They surged sideways as one, fire chasing them—still no clear origin, just angles they couldn't quite piece together.

"I think it's moving!" Kael said.

Xynn's fingers flew over her console as she overlaid trajectory data. "It's outpacing the targeting computer."

"I'm charging a graviton pulse," Narek said. "But you'll have to guide me—I'm flying blind."

"I'll draw its fire," Kael said, already veering wide. "Maybe you can scan the angle if it's a straight shot."

"Kael—" Xynn started.

"I've got this," he said, breath fast but controlled.

The shots followed him.

Xynn locked onto the pattern just as Narek spun and fired a graviton pulse into the space Kael had just vacated.

The air shimmered.

"There!" Xynn shouted.

She fired.

The shot caught something mid-shift—a brief, violent flicker as the cloak failed. Metal screamed as the drone collapsed in on itself, spiraling into the dirt in a shower of sparks.

Silence snapped back into the valley.

Kael slowed, hovering in place. "That was a cloaked drone," he said, awe cutting through the adrenaline. "Adaptive guidance. High-end tech."

Xynn stared at the smoking wreckage.

"The Syndicate shouldn't have tech like that," she said.

Narek's voice was grim. "They wanted us here."

Xynn nodded, already re-centering the formation. "This was a trap."

She glanced at the remaining coordinates on her display.

"Stay sharp," she said. "If they're guarding the other sites, they'll be expecting us now."

The Fleas lifted and moved on.

Faster now. Tighter.

The valley watched them go, empty once more.

• • • •

The second site confirmed what they already suspected.

Another clearing. Another quiet approach. Another sudden eruption of fire from nowhere.

This time, they were ready.

Formation tightened. Countermeasures deployed. The cloaked drone went down quickly, its failure efficient and unsettling in equal measure.

Before they moved on, Narek broke the silence. "We have to assume the next site is the primary target," he said. "Which means we should expect real resistance."

Xynn didn't argue. She was already adjusting the route.

They cut east into rougher ground, the forest thinning into jagged stone and scrub. The valley narrowed, walls rising on either side until the terrain forced them low and tight, hover-fields skimming inches above fractured rock.

Then Kael's voice came through—quieter now. Focused.

"Got something."

Heat signatures bled through the rock face ahead of them—unnatural, geometric. A structure half-sunk into the valley floor, its outline distorted by a cloaking field that shimmered just enough to be visible if you knew what to look for.

A warehouse. Or pretending to be one.

"Four—no," Kael corrected, adjusting. "Five gun turrets. Automated."

Xynn studied the overlay. The rock wall rose steep behind the structure, a natural shield on one side. On the other, the valley floor funneled them straight toward it.

A trap built with intention.

Even from this distance, life signs were visible. Guards on rotation. Active patrols.

Narek's tone sharpened. "We need to hit them now. Before they deploy."

Xynn hesitated.

Every instinct told her to pull back. Regroup. Bring in the rest of the team. Hit it with planning and numbers. But she could feel the window closing—the fragile advantage of surprise thinning by the second.

Pinned low. Limited exits. Already committed.

Kael spoke up. "Pattern five-beta."

"No," Xynn said immediately. "Too risky."

"It could work," Narek said, almost at the same time.

Xynn exhaled through her nose. She hated that they were right. Hated that the terrain, the timing, the math all pointed to the same conclusion.

"All right," she said. "I'll go high. You two stay low."

A brief pause.

"Respectfully, Commander," Narek said, "the best shot should go high."

Xynn turned to argue—and stopped.

"Normally, that would be me," Narek continued. "But my scope took a hit back there." He glanced at Kael. "Besides—what did you score on your last target practice?"

Kael shifted in his harness. "Two forty-eight."

"Two forty-eight?" Xynn repeated, startled.

He winced. "I had a lucky day."

Xynn looked back to the display. Then at the two of them. The choice settled heavy and unavoidable.

"...Fine," she said. "You win."

She rerouted the plan with sharp, efficient gestures. "Kael, you go high. As soon as we drop the cloak, you take out the towers. Fast. Clean."

Kael nodded, all seriousness now.

"And Kael," Xynn added.

"Yes, Commander?"

"Don't get yourself killed."

A faint smile flickered across his face. "I'll do my best."

The Fleas adjusted position, hover-fields humming as they prepared to strike.

· · · ·

Xynn counted her breaths.

In through the nose. Hold. Out through the mouth.

Once.

Twice.

Three.

It was something she'd learned long before command—before Lily, before the Relief Effort. A way to anchor herself while the world tilted toward violence. When everything else scattered, the counting stayed.

She watched the others fan out, Fleas peeling away into assigned vectors. Kael's pod climbed hard and clean, vanishing into the jagged rock face above the facility. Narek dropped low, hugging the valley floor, already moving like he expected the first shot.

In.

Hold.

Out.

Then the air shifted.

The cloak rippled.

Figures emerged from nothing—first one, then another, then too many to count at a glance. Syndicate troops in full tactical gear poured out of the invisible warehouse in disciplined lines, weapons up, movements rehearsed.

Behind them, something heavier rolled forward. An armored vehicle—squat, brutal—its outline resolving as the cloak struggled to compensate.

"Shit," Narek said. "We need the team rallied. Now."

"I've already sent a message," Xynn replied, eyes locked on the unfolding scene. "But I'm guessing our friends here will level a couple villages on their way."

She didn't look away.

"We stop them here," she said. "Stick to the plan."

"Inzari Oonchali," she muttered under her breath.

The hand you're dealt.

Her display caught a flicker of movement above. Kael—perched high along the ridge, silhouetted just enough to make her heart stutter.

"Kael," she said sharply. "Watch it. I can see you."

A blaster bolt cracked against the rock less than a meter from him, exploding into sparks and stone.

"And so can they," she snapped. "Move now! Go, go—Narek, we need to take out those generators!"

"On it," Narek said.

Then the world detonated.

Narek laid down heavy fire, the Flea's cannons roaring as the valley erupted in light and sound. Turrets spun to life, stitching the air with lethal precision. Syndicate troops scattered, returning fire in coordinated bursts. The armored vehicle opened up, its main gun tearing a trench through the ground where Xynn's pod had hovered moments earlier.

Xynn kicked her Flea into a hard lateral hop, the pod skimming low as fire chewed through the space she'd just abandoned. Warning tones flared across her display as she brought the cannons to bear, returning fire in controlled bursts.

The cloak faltered under the assault—flickering, glitching—revealing more of the structure beneath. Power conduits glowed briefly, then vanished again as the system fought to stay hidden.

"Generators are buried!" Narek shouted. "Multiple nodes!"

"Then we make our own access," Xynn replied, already angling toward the facility.

Explosions punched into the valley walls. Rock shattered. Smoke boiled upward, choking the air as Fleas leapt and slammed back down, hover-fields screaming in protest.

Above it all, Xynn tracked Kael's position—her measured breathing forgotten now, replaced by something sharper.

Pressure.

Fire.

Xynn felt the heat spike as direct fire hammered into her Flea's forward shields.

Warning bands flared amber, then red. Xynn gritted her teeth and forced the pod forward anyway, hover-field screaming as she pushed it past its comfort threshold. Ground shattered beneath her. The shields held—but only just.

She lined up another burst—

—and the far turret vanished in a bloom of fire.

The explosion punched upward, a roaring column of flame and debris that climbed at least twenty feet before collapsing back on itself. A heartbeat later, the second turret followed, its destruction sharper, louder—close enough that the shockwave rippled across the valley floor.

Syndicate troops staggered, formation breaking as smoke and concussive force rolled through them.

With the second turret gone, the cloak failed completely.

The facility snapped into full visibility—hard angles, armored plating, glowing seams of power suddenly exposed.

Xynn laughed once, sharp and breathless. "Bless you, Kael."

She thumbed the controls and kicked her Flea upright, shields flaring as she dumped power from defense into offense. The cannons roared to life, unleashing her full payload in a brutal sweep that sent Syndicate soldiers scrambling for cover that no longer existed.

To her left, Narek didn't slow.

His Flea leapt—clean, perfect—and landed squarely on the roof of the armored personnel carrier. He fired straight down, point-blank. The vehicle buckled inward, armor collapsing as internal munitions cooked off in a deafening chain reaction.

When the smoke cleared, it was nothing but a smoldering pancake fused to the ground.

Then the rock beside the facility split open.

A hidden hangar yawned wide, internal lights blazing as something massive lifted free—rotors screaming, armor plated thick and ugly. It rose on a wash of heat and debris, gun ports unfolding as it climbed.

It moved like a helicopter, but broader, heavier. Armored like a beetle—squat, vicious, bristling with weapons that tracked immediately toward them.

Narek stared at it. "You ever seen the Syndicate with hardware like that?"

Xynn's jaw tightened. "Not even close." She tracked its ascent, already calculating angles.

"I'm going to head it off," Kael said.

"Kael, no—" Xynn started.

But she saw it even as she said it: his trajectory, his vector, the way he'd already committed. He wasn't being reckless.

He was doing his job.

"—damn it," she finished instead. "You've got this, Kael."

Kael didn't answer.

He gunned his Flea straight toward the cliff edge—and didn't slow.

The pod launched off the rock face in a wild, impossible arc, hover-field cutting out at the apex as he slammed directly into the gunship's flank. The impact wrenched the craft sideways mid-air.

Kael fired at the same moment.

The gunship detonated.

The explosion swallowed everything—fire, metal, shockwave. The burning wreck tore itself apart as it spiraled away, crashing kilometers distant in a rolling thunder that shook the valley walls.

Silence rushed in after it.

The remaining Syndicate forces broke soon after.

Xynn and Narek made short work of what was left—precise, relentless, no room for retreat. By the time the dust settled, the valley belonged to them again.

Moments later, engines roared as the rest of Xynn's team poured in, transports cresting the ridges and flooding the site with fresh presence.

Xynn powered down and climbed out of her Flea, boots hitting the ground hard. Narek joined her a second later, visor lifted, chest still heaving.

They stood together, watching the distant smoke column coil into the sky.

"Well," Narek said finally. "That was something."

Xynn didn't smile.

She turned, already moving toward the nearest speeder.

Narek vaulted in beside her. Xynn slammed the throttle forward, and the vehicle screamed toward the crash site, fire still burning on the horizon.

They pulled up at the rim of the crater, and the heat hit all at once.

Xynn was out of the transport before it fully settled, boots skidding on scorched sandstone as she ran to the edge. The ground fell away into a wide, blackened bowl—steam hissing up from fractured rock, smoke curling thick and acrid. Fire still licked at twisted fragments of metal embedded in the crater walls.

The wreckage at the center was unrecognizable.

Ruin. Melted plating. Charred debris fused into something that no longer resembled a machine—or anything that might have held a person.

Xynn stood very still.

Behind her, Narek didn't move. He stayed a few steps back—close enough to be present, far enough to give her space. She knew this pattern. They'd stood like this before. And she had made it clear she didn't like anyone seeing the cracks when they came.

But she let this one show.

"He was just a kid," she said quietly.

Her voice didn't break. That was almost worse.

"An artist."

Narek stepped up beside her then. Not touching. Just there.

He brought up his wrist display and turned it so she could see.

Kael's sketch glowed on the screen—quick lines and confident strokes forming Narek's face in a way that felt familiar. Alive.

"He was pretty good," Narek said.

Xynn shot him a look.

"Sorry," he amended immediately. "He was a good kid."

Xynn turned back to the crater. She scuffed her boot through the ash, grinding it into the blackened earth like she could force the weight of it to settle somewhere other than her chest.

They stood there in silence.

Then—together, they squinted into the distance.

Narek raised his hand. "Look."

Xynn hesitated, not trusting what she thought she saw.

At the far edge of the impact zone, where heat warped the air into shimmering waves, there was movement. A shape resolving slowly out of the haze.

Upright. Human.

Walking toward them.

Neither of them spoke.

They turned in unison, vaulted back into the transport, and Xynn gunned it forward.

They closed the distance fast.

The figure staggered once, then steadied—hands braced on his knees as the speeder skidded to a halt in front of him. Kael looked up, face streaked black with soot, hair singed at the edges, escape harness still half-attached. The torn remnants of a parachute dragged behind him like the ghost of wings.

Narek was out first, already pressing a canteen into his hands. Kael drank urgently, coughing once before managing a breathless laugh.

"Pays to run those drills," he said between swallows. "Ejected right before impact. Fireball carried me further than I expected."

Xynn climbed out slowly.

Then faster.

Then she was standing in front of him, composure gone, relief breaking through in a way she didn't bother to hide.

She shook her head, laughing once in disbelief. "I don't even—"

Kael looked up at her, that same hopeful grin cutting through the grime. "Did we do it?"

Xynn smiled wider.

"We did it."

And she let herself believe it.

• • • •

The ops structure was quiet in the morning light, surfaces wiped down, damage reports already folded into neat columns of data. Outside, the camp moved with the steady rhythm of people who had survived something—and knew it was far from routine.

Xynn stood at the central table, both hands around a ceramic mug. Tea she had steeped too long.

Narek leaned against a support strut nearby, coffee in hand, steam rising in slow coils.

Kael stepped in last.

Narek acknowledged him with a nod. "There's the man of the hour." He offered a clean mug. "Coffee?"

Kael hesitated just long enough to be noticed—then took it. "Sounds amazing."

Xynn let a smile creep in, one eyebrow lifting.

"I thought you were more of a tea guy."

Kael flushed immediately. "To be honest—" He gestured vaguely with the cup. "I only drank it because you do."

Xynn smirked over the rim of her mug. "Honesty's better."

Kael nodded, smiling now, and poured the coffee to the brim.

Narek laughed quietly through his nose.

Xynn set her cup down and keyed the display. "All right. What do we know?"

Kael straightened immediately.

"The facility wasn't temporary," he said, pulling up schematics. "Modular, but reinforced. Designed to scale up, not pack out." He hesitated, choosing his words. "Whatever they were building... they planned to stay."

Narek nodded. "And they expected resistance. Drones, cloak, turrets—layered defense. Not something you throw together on a whim."

Xynn watched the data scroll. "Which means this wasn't Syndicate improvisation."

"No," Narek agreed. "Too well funded. Too much coordination. There's backing."

Kael tapped another feed. "That satellite was up long enough to transmit a lot of data. Encrypted. Directional. Offworld relays."

Xynn's jaw tightened. "So who's giving the orders?"

"And who's providing the resources?" Narek added. "Hardware like that gunship doesn't just appear."

Xynn was about to respond when one of the techs looked up from a console.

"Commander," they said. "We cracked the tablet from the convoy."

Xynn turned and took it.

The screen lit up at her touch—logistics chains unfolding cleanly now that the encryption had been stripped away. Transfer schedules. Authorization markers. Shell companies nested inside shell companies.

Then—

She locked the tablet and exhaled slowly.

"What is it?" Narek asked.

Xynn took a steady breath.

"I know someone who needs to see this."

SHE WAS DREAMING.

At first she knew it only because of the stillness.

The car sat half-crumpled at the side of the road, metal folded in on itself like it had been forced to kneel. The world around it was frozen mid-breath—rain suspended in the air, glass caught in the act of falling, the long skid marks on the pavement ending in nothing. No sound. No motion. Just the image, held.

Lily stood a few paces away, hands at her sides.

I know this, she thought.

The recognition landed without panic, without the old tightening in her chest. This was the memory—the only one that had survived intact from before. The crash. The last true fragment of her life on Earth that hadn't been reconstructed, narrated, or filled in by other people's records.

Her only real memory.

And yet—

Why am I back here?

The question didn't echo. The dream didn't respond.

Then a voice said, calmly, almost patiently, "Look closer."

Lily didn't flinch. She didn't even turn toward the sound. She already knew better than to ask where it was coming from.

The crash had frozen like a museum exhibit. A moment pinned in time. Lily stepped forward, surprised to note that her heart stayed steady. No spike of adrenaline. No wave of dread.

She'd relived this a thousand times.

Maybe repetition had dulled it.

Or maybe she simply knew—on some level—that this wasn't real.

She approached the car. The door on the driver's side hung open, bent at a wrong angle. Inside, the girl sat slumped against the deployed restraint, hair stuck to her cheek, her face pale but unmistakable.

Her face.

Not the face shaped by the Krythar. Not the woman she'd become. The girl she'd been.

Lily studied it with detached interest, as if she were examining an old photograph. The details were all there—the faint freckle near the eye, the split lip, the expression caught somewhere between shock and confusion.

Behind her, in the passenger seat, the old woman's shape was still obscured. As it always was. The same blur, the same refusal to resolve into anything concrete.

Once, that absence had filled Lily with terror. With a sense that something essential was missing, something she was meant to understand and couldn't.

Now it barely registered.

She felt no fear.

What she felt—unexpectedly—was irritation.

That's it? she thought. That's all there ever is?

She leaned closer, peering through the shattered window, searching for something new. Some hidden angle. Some detail she'd missed. But the scene offered nothing she didn't already know.

Annoyance sharpened into something like anger.

"Why am I here again?" Lily asked the empty air. "What's the point?"

The voice answered immediately.

"You tell me."

Lily straightened and turned.

Someone stood behind her.

Not fully visible—just an outstretched hand, palm up, offering something small and familiar. She took it without hesitation.

The Jewel.

Its surface was scorched, blackened along one edge, exactly as she remembered. The damage she'd done. The damage it had survived.

Her fingers closed around it, feeling its weight.

She lifted her gaze.

She already knew who she would see.

"Eli," she said.

• • • •

Lily opened her eyes.

The light was wrong—set at that precise, infuriating level that was neither dim nor bright. Too dim to stay fully awake. Too bright to sleep properly. Designed to exhaust without offering relief.

She lay still for a moment, orienting herself.

The cell was exactly what she'd expected.

A narrow bed bolted to the wall. A toilet recessed into the corner. Concrete floor. Concrete walls. No edges softened, no surfaces finished for comfort. The lighting panels in the ceiling cast everything in a faint greenish pallor that made skin look sallow and unhealthy.

There was a small square of polished metal set into the wall opposite the bed. Not quite a mirror, but close enough.

Lily pushed herself upright and caught her reflection in it.

She looked rough.

Her hair stuck out at odd angles. Dark circles had settled under her eyes. Her skin looked dull, drawn tight by stress and bad sleep.

She stared at herself for a moment longer than necessary.

Then she exhaled slowly and swung her legs over the side of the bed.

The dream was already fading—but the irritation it had left behind was not.

The worst part wasn't the cell.

It wasn't the concrete or the light or the way the air never seemed to move. Lily could live with discomfort. She had, in one form or another, for most of her life.

It was the monotony.

The sameness of it. The days that didn't announce themselves. The meals that arrived without comment. The absence of sound sharp enough to mark time. Nothing changed. Nothing advanced.

And worse—nothing resolved.

She didn't know what had happened with the council.

She didn't know how the deaths had been framed, how quickly the narrative had set, or whether anyone had bothered to ask the obvious questions before deciding she was convenient.

She didn't know what they'd said about Valen.

That was the thought that caught most often, the one that refused to stay buried. Valen's face as she'd found him. The way his expression had frozen between surprise and something like apology. She didn't know if he'd been honored. Disgraced. Written off as collateral.

She didn't know where Trish was.

That absence gnawed at her in a quieter way—less sharp, more persistent. Trish had always moved one step ahead of trouble, always seemed to know when to disappear. Lily wanted to believe that instinct had held. Wanted proof.

She didn't even know how things had ended with Didot and her sister.

Whether they'd made it out clean. Whether Ninebury had scattered or collapsed or simply been erased the way places like that often were—by never being mentioned again.

The not knowing pressed in from all sides, heavier than the walls.

She was stuck.

Here.

Alone.

The only information she had came in fragments, filtered through the Hedon-appointed attorney who visited her once—briefly—with a tablet full of caveats and a voice trained to say very little, very carefully.

It hadn't been much.

The weapon used in the council chamber, she'd told her, was a Jewel.

A Korolith disruptor of a specific class. Specific output signature. Specific burn pattern.

Like the one Eli had given her.

The access code she'd used to enter the chamber, the lawyer had added, had been flagged as stolen. Which meant either Valen had sent her a stolen code—or, far more likely, she hadn't been communicating with Valen at all.

Lily turned it all over in her mind, again and again. Even in the wildest permutations, there was no room for pure coincidence.

Time-of-death estimates placed the murders—by Lily's own calculations—minutes before she'd stepped into the room.

Minutes.

She rubbed at her temples, slow and methodical, trying to keep the headache from blooming. When she lowered her hands, she noticed the grime on her fingers—dark smudges ground into the lines of her skin.

She stared at them, faintly incredulous.

The room was concrete. The bed was concrete. The walls were concrete. And yet her hands were perpetually dirty, as if the place itself exhaled filth.

She flexed her fingers and wondered—without much heat—whether the omission of soap was necessary. Whether it was policy or psychology. A reminder that cleanliness was a privilege. That comfort was conditional.

She let the thought go.

Focus, she told herself.

But on what?

There was nothing to plan. No variables she could adjust. No leverage she could apply. The system had closed around her, airtight and patient, content to let her sit with unanswered questions until they softened into something manageable.

Or broke her.

Lily leaned back against the wall and closed her eyes—not to sleep, but to rest them from the light.

The cell gave her nothing.

And that, she was beginning to understand, was the point.

She'd just about tuned her mind back to white noise again. That waiting place where time could be blurred, stretched—seconds smeared into hours.

Then the airhorn sounded.

Glorious. Awful.

The noise ripped through the cell, harsh enough to make her flinch, and Lily felt a wash of relief so immediate it surprised her. Something to break up the day. Something—anything—else.

She couldn't even summon fear. Not yet. She was too grateful that it was something at all.

The door slid open and she came face to face with the female guard—the one whose face she'd learned by repetition rather than introduction. Lily knew it wasn't her fault. Not exactly. A pawn of systemic cruelty. Someone whose job required her to be a bully, and to assume that everyone under her watch was capable of the worst.

That assumption wasn't wrong.

Lily had killed.

The thought surfaced again, unbidden. She had used the Jewel to take a life—to save Ninebury and everyone inside it. A call she hadn't hesitated over for even a second.

She'd seen dozens—maybe hundreds—of decisions like that in the past few years alone. In the fleet, they'd been framed as necessity. As outcomes. As math.

Murder, contextualized, is fine.

The thought made her uncomfortable, even as she tried to force it back down, to keep her mind from circling the same drain.

"Lawyer time," the guard said, her tone sharp with something like satisfaction.

Lily lifted her head and held it straight. Mostly because it annoyed the guard. Partly because her neck had gone stiff from the narrow bed and the hours of stillness.

She followed her into the labyrinth of corridors, concrete bleeding into concrete, until they reached the other room—the one with a table, a chair, and just enough signs of life to remind her what she was missing.

The lawyer looked unmistakably Hedon.

Not as ostentatious—more restrained than most—but still wrapped in the clashing bright colors Lily had come to associate with the culture. Lily found herself irrationally grateful for the white-on-white concrete of the cell. At least there, the eye had nothing to fight.

The woman herself looked as though a stiff breeze might knock her over. Slight. Drawn. As if she'd missed more meals than the prisoners and slept even less. She set her tablet down on the table with such care it didn't make a sound at all.

"I have some news," she said.

And stopped there.

Lily waited. The silence stretched, long enough that she wondered if that was all she was going to get.

"Yes, counselor?" she prompted at last.

"The Union has been in contact with the Hedon authorities."

A pause.

"I see," Lily said finally.

"They're attempting to make arrangements for your release."

"I see."

"But it isn't going well. The magistrate is convinced that you are—"

She faltered.

"Guilty?" Lily supplied.

"Dangerous."

"I see."

The pause that followed was longer still.

"Is that all?" Lily asked.

The lawyer looked like there was more. Like she was weighing something carefully and finding it wanting. Lily had never felt the urge to use violence more acutely than she did in that moment.

"Counselor," she said, keeping her voice level. "Is there anything else?"

"There is something," the woman said at last. "But I don't want you to get your hopes up."

"Yes?"

"Someone else has contacted the magistrate. Someone... powerful."

Lily swallowed another *I see* before it could surface.

"Who?"

"I can't say," the lawyer replied quickly. "And I shouldn't have mentioned it at all."

She stood, already gathering herself, already retreating.

"Hang in there, Ms. Sterling."

"Starling."

"You should hear from me soon."

Lily didn't remember the walk back to the cell.

Her mind didn't switch back on until the hardness of the bed pressed into her spine again.

She stared up at the ceiling, the light still wrong, the air still unmoving.

How could she be back here with even less certainty than before?

Time lost its edges.

Meals arrived without ceremony. A slot opening. A tray sliding through. Food that was technically sufficient and emotionally inert—soft where it should have been firm, lukewarm no matter when it arrived. Lily ate because her body demanded it, not because it wanted to. She learned quickly that if she didn't eat when the tray appeared, she'd regret it later.

Hunger didn't sharpen here. It spread. A low ache that settled into her joints, her jaw, the hollow beneath her ribs.

The dream came back. Not every night, but often enough that it stopped announcing itself. The crash. The stillness. Eli's eyes. Sometimes all of it. Sometimes only pieces. She would wake with the same dull pain threaded through her shoulders, her teeth clenched hard enough to leave her jaw sore.

Ache.

Mush.

Repeat.

Her thoughts blurred into a kind of static. Not silence—never silence—but a low, constant hum where nothing stuck long enough to matter. She stopped trying to count days. Started measuring time by how her body felt instead.

Her hands grew grimier. The dark circles under her eyes deepened, settling in as if they intended to stay. Her hair tangled into something she stopped bothering to tame.

The dream.

The ache.

The mush.

She found herself hoping—absurdly—for the airhorn. That glorious, awful noise. Something to puncture the day. Something sharp enough to remind her she was still moving through time instead of sinking into it.

It never came.

Until—she guessed—it was afternoon. The door opened.

No warning. No sound beforehand. Just the sudden, jarring shift from sealed to exposed.

The female guard stood there. Expressionless. She didn't speak.

Lily followed her down a short corridor and stopped in front of a door she didn't recognize.

"Strip," the guard said.

Lily complied.

What was the difference at this point?

The guard opened the door and gestured her inside. The room beyond was tiled, stark, fitted with several shower heads spaced along the walls. The air was colder here.

The guard threw a bag at her. Hard enough that Lily had to step back to catch it.

"Get cleaned up."

The door shut.

Lily stood there for a moment, naked and cold, the bag clutched to her chest. Her skin prickled, gooseflesh rising along her arms.

At least it was different.

She looked down, expecting toiletries. Some institutional approximation of soap. Something thin and barely adequate.

What she found was something else entirely.

Something that provided much-needed hope.

Her clothes.

Everything she'd been wearing when she was arrested—minus a few pieces of kit she immediately clocked as missing. Familiar fabric. Familiar weight. Proof that she still existed outside the concrete.

And tucked beside them—

A bar of soap.

• • • •

They put her in a hard chair and told her to wait.

People moved around her with purpose, clipboards and tablets passing from hand to hand, low conversations bleeding together into a soft, constant murmur. An office environment. Desks. Screens. The ordinary machinery of administration humming along as if nothing unusual were happening at all.

Her eyes stung. The light was brighter here, sharper. Her head throbbed faintly, a reminder she hadn't slept well in days. She shifted in the chair and felt it immediately—her clothes hanging a little looser, the fabric not sitting the way it should. She'd lost weight. Enough that the room felt colder and the hard chair hurt more.

Her heart was racing.

Not fear exactly. Uncertainty. The kind that refused to settle into any one shape.

A large Cyranthian woman sat at a desk a few yards away—a mountain of a woman, broad-shouldered and solid, her presence anchoring the space around her. She looked up from her terminal and fixed Lily with a brief, assessing glance.

"Miss Starling," she said, and gestured.

Lily stood and approached the desk. She glanced around automatically.

No counsel.

No magistrate.

What was happening?

"Miss Starling, here is a list of places you are and are not permitted to visit during your probation," the woman said, already producing a stapled stack of narrow yellow pages. Planetary systems. Transit corridors. Footnotes dense with restrictions and exceptions. "As per the Treaty of 2270, the Hedon Republic and the United Earth Union are hereby releasing you to the care of the Union."

Releasing.

The word felt unreal.

"Here are your belongings."

The woman slid a large, clear bag across the desk. Lily recognized the contents immediately—the medical kit. Her fleet utility belt. The items she'd clocked as missing earlier.

The Jewel was not among them.

No surprise there.

Lily sat quietly while the woman typed, fingers moving with mechanical ease. She carried on a casual conversation with someone behind her—something about lunch, about a place that had just reopened. Lily turned the bag over in her hands, the plastic crinkling softly.

"Miss."

Lily snapped to attention.

"Did you need something else?" The woman nodded down a long, unremarkable hallway. "The exit is that way."

That was it.

A wave of dizziness passed through her. This wasn't a traffic citation. For all they knew, she had murdered the Hedon High Council. And yet there she was, being dismissed like she'd just finished a guided tour.

Lily stood carefully, adjusting the strap of the bag on her shoulder. She took a breath, steadying herself, unsure what would happen once she stepped into the corridor.

She hoped she still had enough money left to book passage.

Somewhere.

She stepped through a short chamber—a passthrough that opened into a vast lobby of sweeping lines and ornate Hedon craftsmanship. Decorative ceilings arched overhead, inlaid with metallic filigree that caught the light and bent it into warm, ceremonial hues. It was beautiful in the way institutions often were—designed to impress, to elevate, to remind you who had built them.

She noticed the people next.

Several figures were slumped along the walls and benches, some sitting on the floor, equipment piled at their feet. Cameras. Audio rigs. Wardrobes that tried very hard to look casual and failed. They looked less like an organized press pool and more like travelers stranded in a terminal, waiting for a train that was very late and might never arrive.

Afternoon sunlight spilled through the tall doors on the far side of the lobby.

Lily angled toward them, intent on getting outside, on finding her bearings before the strangeness of the release could settle into something worse.

One of the reporter-looking people stretched, craning his neck as if working out a kink. His eyes met Lily's.

Recognition snapped into place.

He lurched to his feet, suddenly energized, and began shaking the others awake. Voices rose in quick, urgent bursts. Someone bolted for the doors at a full sprint.

Lily felt the pieces click together.

She wasn't in a public-facing wing of the facility. This was a back corridor. An administrative corner. They'd been trying to move her out quietly—before anyone noticed she was here at all.

She picked up her pace.

It didn't matter.

The moment she stepped outside, the air changed.

People surged in from every direction, a wall of bodies pressing forward as security scrambled to form a barrier. Shouts overlapped into a single, ugly roar. She caught fragments—curses, accusations—none of them needing context to be understood.

Something wet struck her cheek.

Spit.

The crowd stretched as far as she could see, filling the plaza, spilling down the adjoining streets.

"Murderer!"

"Union cover-up!"

"You should be rotting in a cell!"

Lily kept her head down and moved with the security detail as they carved a narrow path through the mass of people. Hands reached for her. Voices followed. The noise pressed in on her chest, making it hard to breathe.

They were steering her toward one of the main transport pads.

She focused on placing one foot in front of the other.

On staying upright.

On not looking back.

They led her into a corridor of force fields.

Glowing bands of energy slid into place, sealing her off from the mob. The noise fell away with every step, voices thinning into a distant, indistinct roar. Signs pointed toward the public terminal.

They went the opposite direction.

The corridor opened into a cluster of private landing platforms, enclosed by jet-black metal walls layered with sound-dampening technology. This was where the rich arrived. Where movement was curated. Where no one waited.

Holo-displays hovered along the walls, cycling through transport logs, flight paths, and schematic maps. Images of sleek, elite vessels rotated slowly, all sharp lines and polished hulls.

Two men waited near the nearest pad.

She recognized them immediately as Ishrethi, though they wore no uniforms or traditional cultural dress. Simple black athletic wear instead. Only their orange-and-copper skin and the faint markings along their faces gave them away. Each wore a single ornate gold earring.

"Lieutenant Starling," the taller one said. "I am Roka. This is Gadspar. We're glad you made it through—and we apologize for that experience. We were not cleared to leave the hangar."

Gadspar turned to the Hedon security detail. "You may leave."

One of the guards stepped forward and held out a tablet, a holo-order glowing above its surface. Roka pressed his thumb to the scanner. After a brief confirmation tone, the Earth guards withdrew without comment.

"Thank you," Lily said, meaning it. "I'm grateful to be among friendly faces. Are you from Ishreth?"

The two men exchanged a brief look.

"Perhaps," Roka said after a moment. "It would be better if you came aboard. Once you do, things should make a little more sense."

Lily didn't hesitate.

She followed the men aboard the ship—and stopped short once she was inside.

This was no ordinary vessel.

Its hull lines were sleek and seamless, surfaces matte rather than reflective, engineered to drink in light instead of scattering it. The design spoke to stealth first—low profile, minimal protrusions—but layered beneath it was unmistakable luxury. Soft illumination traced the walls. Materials were rich without being ostentatious, every choice deliberate. This was a ship built to disappear—and to do so comfortably.

They led her into a central chamber that was more functional than ceremonial, but unlike any bridge she'd seen on a Union vessel. The space stretched long and clean, flight seats arranged at the forward end, operational stations lining the rear. At the center sat a large round table, anchored by a single command chair.

And in that chair—so naturally it felt as though the ship had been built around her—sat Queen Veyshali of Ishrath.

She wore the same label-less black athletic wear as the guards. No regalia. No crown. And yet there was no mistaking her.

Lily didn't know why she was so surprised.

Even on this strange ship, she had expected to see Dalren. Or Caris. Even Tevya. Anyone but the queen.

"Lily," Veyshali said, her voice smooth, amused. "Ever the survivor. I warned you things were about to get worse. It appears you needed that friend after all."

"Your Majesty," Lily said automatically.

"No crown. No title." Veyshali gestured to the chair opposite her. "Just Veyshali. Please—sit."

Even dressed this simply, Veyshali radiated something unmistakably deliberate. Her hair was pulled back tight, severe in a way that only sharpened her features. Intricate gold earrings caught the light when she moved. Her top—rather than a pullover like the guards'—had a zipper down the front, unfastened just enough to be intentional.

This was, Lily realized, the most unedited version of Veyshali she had ever seen.

She folded her hands in her lap.

"Veyshali," Lily said. "What is going on?"

Veyshali studied her in silence, eyes steady, as if weighing options that had nothing to do with etiquette.

"I've been watching you for months," she said at last. "Long before Earth. Long before the council. I knew you were circling something important."

Lily didn't look away.

"You were right, by the way," Veyshali added. "They should have destroyed that machine. Technology like that will never be put to good use."

"The Gherionite device?" Lily asked. "Does it have something to do with the plague? With the Union vaccine?"

Veyshali shook her head. "Not quite that simple. But suffice it to say—when people like Dalren are in charge, many things happen right under their noses."

Lily exhaled slowly. She hated this way of speaking. The half-truths. The careful phrasing. But she had to pick her battles.

"I need you to tell me what you know about the assassination," she said, keeping her voice level.

Veyshali rose from the chair and began to pace, slow and deliberate. She stopped at a darkened reflective panel along the wall and studied her own image for a moment before meeting Lily's eyes through the glass.

"Things have been in motion since Bimara," she said. "Someone has been moving pieces into position. I was close to uncovering it—but they stayed one step ahead of me. I knew something was converging on Earth. I thought they were leading you and Valen into a trap together."

Her jaw tightened.

"If I had known the council was going to be murdered, I would have intervened."

"Who did this?" Lily asked.

Veyshali turned back to her.

"Who would know you well enough to want you out of the way?" she asked calmly. "Who would care deeply about Gherion Prime and the vaccine distribution? And who possesses a superlative intellect—one that has been... unstable since Bimara?"

The room felt suddenly very still.

"Eli," Lily whispered.

Veyshali nodded once. "He's missing, you know. When Tevya left the *Salamander*, Eli departed shortly afterward. No flight plan. No destination."

Lily chewed the inside of her cheek. She didn't want to believe it.

But it made sense.

Almost all of it.

"I can't believe he'd murder an entire council," Lily said. "Not like that."

"Can't you?" Veyshali asked gently. "You were there when he snapped Ronin's neck like a twig."

Lily stood and began pacing, the energy finally breaking free.

"But why?" she demanded. "And what does this have to do with the plague? Or Hedon? Or Trish? Or me?"

"I intend to find out," Veyshali said. "I'm using my resources."

She paused, then smiled faintly.

"That is to say—Zayir and I. He's been a dear."

Lily registered the tone automatically. Fond, but distant. More like someone referring to a favored pet than a husband.

"He's running our affairs of state," Veyshali continued. "Officially, I'm home—deep in spiritual retreat. Fasting for the speedy end to the shard."

"Why are you doing this?" Lily asked.

They sat almost in unison. Not deliberately—just the same quiet surrender to gravity, as if neither of them had realized they were standing until the question had been asked.

For the first time, Veyshali hesitated.

Lily found she couldn't quite read the queen's expression now. It hovered somewhere between nervousness and grief.

"I hope to make you understand," Veyshali said quietly. "In time."

She reached for a tablet and slid it across the table.

"Here."

Lily skimmed the screen. Dense legal language. Jurisdictional clauses. Conditional freedoms.

"What is this?"

"A formal agreement between myself and the Union. You are under my protection. Captain Dalren has requested—and been granted—permission for you to return to the *Salamander*. As a custodial guest."

Lily nodded slowly. "As a civilian."

Veyshali smiled, something knowing flickering across her face. "Or—you can come with me. We can pursue the truth together."

Lily didn't have to think it over.

"Where do we start?"

* * * *

Lily woke to silence.

Not the artificial hush of a cell or the low thrum of a transport corridor—but real quiet. The kind that came from distance. From insulation. From being very far away from anywhere public.

She lay still for a moment, cataloging sensations out of habit. The bed was soft. Too soft. Her muscles ached less than they had the night before. Her head still throbbed faintly, but it was manageable. She could breathe without feeling like the air was rationed.

She showered. Properly this time. Hot water. Soap that actually smelled like something.

Veyshali had sent clothing. The same black athletic wear the guards had worn—though somehow tailored perfectly to her. Lily wondered, briefly, about intrusive scans, then let the thought go.

She wasn't used to this kind of luxury. The fabric felt more expensive than the house she and Xynn were renting on Gherion Prime.

By the time she followed the subtle lighting cues toward what she guessed was the galley, her stomach had begun to ache in earnest.

The door opened.

And Lily stopped short. She should have expected this.

Veyshali was stretched out on a padded surface near the wide viewport, completely naked, utterly at home. An attendant worked methodically along her shoulders, another at her calves. Morning light poured in behind her, catching on bare skin like it was the most natural thing in the universe.

Lily rolled her eyes.

"Good morning," Veyshali said, not moving. "I trust you slept well."

"Yes." Lily scanned the room. How many attendants were on this ship? They seemed to multiply every few minutes. "You look rested," she added, with a touch of snark.

Veyshali sat up without ceremony, not bothering to pretend to cover herself.

"Roka and Gadspar really do have the most amazing hands."

Something about the fact that they were the same two who'd met her in the hangar made it worse.

Lily cleared her throat.

Veyshali smiled. "Do let me know if you ever want to borrow them. What's mine is yours."

She reached for a robe draped nearby and slipped it on with unhurried grace, tying it loosely at the waist. Roka and Gadspar withdrew at once. Two more attendants entered, bearing trays laden with food.

Lily shook her head, just slightly.

"I've been invited somewhere," Veyshali said, gesturing for Lily to sit. "And I think you might find it... enlightening."

She flicked her fingers, and a holo sprang to life between them.

An invitation.

Minimalist. Elegant. Ominously clean.

At its center: a circular symbol. Three arrows, interlocked, rotating slowly around a shared axis.

Lily took a determined bite of a pastry.

"Now we're getting somewhere."

SPACETIME FOLDED LIKE ribbons of melting confection as the *Waqi-Reesh* cut through its layers—soft at first glance, but resistant underneath, stretching just enough to give the illusion of ease.

Like a needle through fabric.

The universe yielded if pressed in the right places. It thinned along invisible seams, tension drawing tight before easing apart. Not broken. Not pierced. Coaxed into opening. Space bent with a kind of reluctant compliance, as though aware of the intrusion but unable to refuse it.

The vessel moved without spectacle. No flare, no bloom of light to mark its passage—only a sleek black form advancing with deliberate precision, its light-factor engines humming at a frequency too low to be heard, but present all the same. A faint pressure gathered around it, subtle but persistent, like the sensation of altitude creeping into the bones.

Ahead, the stars began to distort.

Points of light stretched into threads, then into pale ribbons, drawn across the dark as distance compressed and reformed. Constellations slipped out of alignment and reassembled themselves moments later, their shapes briefly uncertain before settling back into something recognizable.

Behind the ship, the distortion resolved quickly. The field smoothed over itself, the geometry of space restoring with quiet efficiency, leaving no visible trace of passage—only the absence of interruption.

Far off, a communication drone pulsed steadily, releasing its message in tight, measured bursts of light. The signal moved across the relay network in precise intervals, passing from node to node along the Union's hidden scaffolding—an architecture that existed everywhere and nowhere at once.

It crossed the distance in seconds.

The Waqi-Reesh accepted the transmission without altering course. No visible response, only a subtle shift within its internal systems—acknowledgment without ceremony.

Ahead, the Marduk system came into view.

A scatter of gold and fractured ice suspended against the dark, distant bodies catching faint light and returning it in cold, fractured glints. The system held a quiet, curated beauty—untouched on the surface, its stillness masking whatever moved beneath it.

Inside the vessel, the message had already begun.

A transmission, mid-sentence.

• • • •

"—I hate that I can't see you. That you had to go through that."

Xynn's voice was steady, but there was strain at the edges of it. Interference hissed faintly beneath her words—a soft, persistent reminder of distance, of light-years, of how even the fastest signal still arrived a little too late.

Lily leaned back in the narrow comm chair, one boot hooked over the rung beneath her, the metal pressing lightly into the sole. The main deck of the *Waqi-Reesh* was too polished to feel like a bridge. It stretched wide and open around her, more like a ceremonial hall than a command center, with stations tucked into alcoves as if function were something to be accommodated rather than designed around. There was no obvious center to it. No place that felt like control.

"Hey, I survived," Lily said. "And you know I'll get you to make it up to me."

A breath came through the line—almost a laugh.

"I want you right now, Lily."

The words hit warmer than the room around her. Lily smiled despite herself, her shoulders easing just a little. Still butterflies with Xynn—still that same pull, immediate and grounding, the only thing in the galaxy that could catch her off guard like this.

"Oh—and thanks for the data," she added, turning slightly as the projection array shifted beside her. Lines of shipping routes flickered into view, layered in translucent arcs that curved and overlapped in slow motion. "The overlays you sent match some of what I pulled on Earth. Veyshali had another piece of it."

She reached out, dragging one thread across another. The lines adjusted, intersecting, then twisting together into something more deliberate.

"Between the three of us..."

Her eyes narrowed as the pattern resolved.

"This is getting interesting."

"That's one way to put it," Xynn said, her tone carrying just enough weight to suggest she might have preferred something a little less galactic—and a little closer to home.

"We're heading near the Adius system," Xynn continued. "I'm going to check on Adius II. Reports have been calm, but I have a little time before the next assignment. And it's on the way."

Lily's expression softened, the tension in her jaw easing without her realizing it. "Wave to home for me."

"I will."

The relay crackled faintly as the ship shifted, the signal adjusting as space bent and unbent around them.

"I love you," Lily said, raising her voice just slightly to carry through the static.

"I love you too," Xynn replied, and Lily could hear the smirk in it. "I'd tell you to be careful. But I know you'll just ignore me."

Lily let out a quiet laugh. "Probably." The smile lingered, then settled into something steadier. "But I'll see you soon."

The transmission dissolved gradually—voice into static, static into silence.

When the screen went dark, the tears came faster than she expected. They blurred her vision before she had time to stop them, spilling over as she sucked in a sharp breath. She wiped them away with the back of her hands, blinking hard, trying to push the feeling back down where it belonged.

Not now.

She stood and crossed to the viewport, the deck cool beneath her boots. The ship's vibration shifted under her feet as the light-factor engines unwound, the low, almost imperceptible pressure easing as velocity bled off and space settled back into something stable. The stretched light outside tightened, stars snapping cleanly back into points.

Marduk III filled the glass.

An enormous gas giant.

Bands of pale gold and sulfurous green coiled across its atmosphere, layered storms folding into one another in slow, planetary spirals. Lightning stitched silently through the upper cloud decks, flaring and vanishing like distant thought. There was no horizon, no seam—no line where anything began or ended.

And yet—

A line existed.

Lily leaned closer to the glass, her breath faintly fogging the edge of the viewport before fading.

A single structure descended from the thin, sunlit strata into the roiling depths below. From this distance, it looked impossibly slender—a needle driven into a storm. Sunlight fractured along its upper reaches, scattering in sharp, controlled glints, while its lower half vanished into opaque turbulence that swallowed shape and scale alike.

She adjusted the hood of the cloak around her shoulders, letting the fabric fall into place. It softened her outline, pulled her posture inward, made her smaller. Contained.

She had to pass as a royal valet.

Not a Union officer.

Footsteps approached behind her—measured, unhurried.

Roka stopped at her side, hands folded neatly behind his back.

"You are observing the Siphon-Spire," he said. His voice carried that smooth Ishrethi cadence that made even blunt facts feel ceremonial. "Marduk III does not possess a surface in the conventional sense. The atmosphere transitions gradually into a supercritical state before compressing further toward the core."

Lily didn't look away. "I'm no astro-geologist," she said lightly, "but I didn't think gas giants were generally where one went to party."

Roka allowed the faintest curve at the edge of his mouth. "Indeed."

He inclined his head toward the descending structure. "The upper stratum is positioned within the thinnest atmospheric layers—where solar radiation penetrates and buoyancy can be engineered. The lower works extend into denser regions for resource extraction."

"Engineered buoyancy," Lily repeated, her gaze tracing the line downward. "So the wealthy float and the workers sink."

"An accurate portrayal of the division of labor," Roka replied, careful but not evasive.

Lily let out a quiet breath through her nose.

From this distance, the upper portion gleamed—transparent segments catching the distant star, revealing hints of geometry, cultivated gardens, and open terraces suspended above pressure that would crush anything unshielded.

The lower half disappeared completely.

"This place is pretty hush-hush, huh?" she asked.

Roka's gaze remained forward. "Marduk III is not listed in standard navigational archives. Access is restricted to a narrow demographic."

"The elite," Lily translated. "Like Queen Veyshali."

"Indeed."

A new flash of lightning rippled beneath the midpoint of the spire, briefly illuminating the layers below before swallowing them again.

"The more things change..." Lily murmured.

Behind them, a door opened.

Veyshali entered without announcement, though the air shifted all the same—subtle, but unmistakable, like pressure adjusting before a storm breaks. She wore no crown, no overt regalia, but the cut of her garments and the ease of her movement made the absence irrelevant.

Her eyes passed over Lily once—slow, precise, assessing.

"You look the part," Veyshali said.

Lily gave a small nod. "I've been practicing invisibility."

"That will serve you here."

Veyshali joined them at the viewport, studying the spire not with awe, but with consideration—weight behind the stillness.

"There is something you should understand about the inhabitants of Marduk III," Veyshali said. "They are capitalists."

Lily raised an eyebrow.

"Their primary objective is accumulation," Veyshali continued. "Wealth. Leverage. Control of markets, of narrative. But profit alone does not build loyalty."

"Then what does?"

Veyshali didn't look away from the spire.

"Belonging."

The word settled differently.

"They have cultivated an insulated messaging sphere," she went on. "Carefully filtered. Aspirational. Across dozens of systems, populations consume it willingly. Those who demonstrate sufficient alignment are offered opportunity."

"Opportunity," Lily repeated.

"To come here," Veyshali said. "To serve within the lower works. It is framed as elevation. A merit-based ascent."

Lily let out a quiet breath. "Into one-point-eight gravity and industrial heat."

"Devotion reframes discomfort."

"And the elite?" Lily asked.

Veyshali glanced at her, just briefly. "Don't pretend naivety. You understand the structure. You've already begun to see how it's designed."

Lily looked back to the upper stratum—the terraces, the filtered light, the illusion of serenity suspended above everything else.

"I wanted you prepared," Veyshali said. "The devotion in the lower levels borders on religious."

"Great." Lily shook her head. "Feels like it's been minutes since I've had to deal with a space cult."

Roka's eyes flicked toward Lily then—quick, measured, gone just as fast.

Outside, the black vessel adjusted its approach, angling toward the upper reaches of the spire. For a moment, it disappeared into layered cloud, its silhouette swallowed by the storm—then reemerged in the thin, luminous band where the air cleared and the wealthy breathed easier.

· · · ·

Lily slipped inside her quarters and sealed the door behind her, then pulled the comm tag from her cloak. Veyshali's warning rang in her ears—one signal and the Spire's security would flag it instantly. The whole mission would unravel.

It was bad enough her face was already circulating in the feeds.

She found a narrow seam beneath the panel by the bed, pressed it open, and tucked the tag inside.

"Good enough," she whispered.

She stepped back into the corridor. The door sealed behind her with a soft hiss.

She'd only gone a few steps when she froze in the shadowed alcove.

At the far end of the hallway, half-hidden in the corner, Roka and Gadspar were tangled together—mouths hungry, hands gripping fabric and skin like they might never get another chance. The raw urgency of it hit Lily like a spark. She looked away, cheeks burning, but her eyes dragged back anyway.

Finally Roka broke the kiss, breathing hard. "You know I have to go. The mission—"

"Don't." Gadspar pressed a hand to Roka's chest, voice low and rough. "Don't say it'll be quick. Don't say it's not dangerous."

Roka tried to turn, but Gadspar caught his arm, pulling him close again.

"Don't make me wait too long." His thumb brushed Roka's jaw, possessive. "I get possessive when I'm deprived of you."

Something raw flickered across Roka's face—heat, frustration, reluctant tenderness. He leaned in for one last fierce kiss, then slipped away down the corridor without another word.

Gadspar stood there a moment longer, watching him go, before retreating behind one of the nearby doors.

Lily let out a slow breath, pulse still racing.

Well... that was something.

· · · ·

The transport rose to meet the *Waqi-Reesh* without ceremony, a dark shape resolving out of the thinning light beyond the hull, matching velocity so precisely it seemed to arrive by intention rather than motion. There was no jolt when the docking collar engaged—only a subtle shift underfoot, a change in pressure that moved through the deck and into Lily's bones before fading again.

She adjusted the mask as they crossed the threshold, fingers brushing the smooth edge of the dummy respirator. It sealed cleanly along her face, the faint vibration of its internal systems barely noticeable unless she focused on it. Medical. Routine. Unremarkable.

That was the hope.

Veyshali's warning lingered anyway. Her face was already out there, moving through the news feeds. A mask helped, but it didn't erase anything.

Lily lowered her gaze as they stepped into the receiving corridor.

The guards waiting to meet them were dressed in black, their uniforms cut with the same precision as everything else on the Spire—no visible insignia, no obvious weapons, nothing to suggest threat beyond the way they held themselves. They greeted Veyshali with practiced ease, their voices warm, measured, the cadence of people trained to put others at ease while watching everything.

"Your Majesty," one said, inclining his head just enough. "We trust your journey was comfortable."

Veyshali acknowledged him with the smallest motion, already moving past.

Roka followed without breaking stride.

Lily came last, her steps measured, her posture drawn in just enough to pass. The role settled over her as she moved—something worn rather than inhabited, a shape she could step into and out of if she needed to.

Inside, the transport opened into a wide, curved chamber softened by light that never quite came from a single source. The seating was arranged for comfort rather than efficiency, the lines of the space guiding the eye outward toward the viewport, where the Spire stretched below them—glass and structure and atmosphere layered over something vast and unstable.

She took her place just behind Veyshali, close enough to attend, far enough to be ignored.

Roka moved opposite.

Lily kept her eyes forward, a faint warmth rising at the edge of her awareness as she avoided looking at him. She wondered, briefly, whether he and Gadspar kept their relationship hidden from the queen out of necessity—or for the thrill of it.

The doors sealed behind them, and the transport disengaged with a motion so smooth it almost registered as stillness. Outside, the distance shifted—slow at first, then more pronounced—as the vessel angled down toward the upper reaches of the Spire, where the light gathered and the atmosphere thinned into something breathable.

Veyshali leaned slightly toward her, the movement small enough to go unnoticed by anyone not looking for it.

"From here on out," she said quietly, "I will speak to you as my servant."

Lily inclined her head.

"Of course... my queen."

The word sat heavy. Deliberate.

Veyshali studied her for a fraction of a second, something like approval—or amusement—passing through her expression before it settled again.

"Good," she said, her voice carrying just enough to be heard. "Shameli, attend me."

Lily stepped forward without hesitation.

"Yes, my queen." It came easier that time.

Outside, the Spire expanded beneath them, its upper structures resolving into terraces and corridors suspended above the storm, the illusion of calm holding steady even as the deeper layers churned unseen.

For a moment, Lily let her thoughts drift.

The Spire unfolded beneath them in layers of light and structure, all of it arranged so carefully it almost felt inevitable. The wealthy above. The workers below. Air that thinned as you descended, pressure that built, gravity that pressed harder the closer you got to the core.

It was almost too clean.

Too familiar.

She could already see it—the polished terraces above, the curated calm, the quiet conversations about markets and influence. And beneath it, the lower levels where things were hotter, heavier, harder to breathe in. Where people worked. Where they proved themselves. Where they earned the right to remain.

It felt like a story she'd heard before.

Worse—it felt like one people chose.

That was the part that sat wrong.

How often the vulnerable stepped into systems like this willingly. How often they accepted the terms, repeated the language, convinced themselves it was opportunity instead of—

She caught herself.

That wasn't fair.

You didn't blame people for surviving.

You didn't blame them for taking what was offered when the alternative was nothing.

Cold pavement flashed in her mind. Nights where the ground leached heat from her bones, where "choice" meant finding somewhere marginally safer to exist until morning.

She exhaled slowly, letting the thought settle where it belonged.

Then—

The transport lurched.

Not a smooth shift. Not controlled.

Violent.

The impact threw her forward a half step before she caught herself on the seat in front of her, the deck shuddering under her boots as a deep, metallic groan tore through the structure.

"What—"

A second blast hit harder.

The lights flickered, then steadied.

"Your Majesty—sit!" Lily snapped, already moving.

Veyshali didn't argue. She dropped into the nearest jump seat as Lily pulled the harness across her shoulders and locked it into place with a sharp click. The queen's expression had shifted—no surprise, just focus.

Lily turned and secured herself opposite, yanking the restraints tight as the transport pitched again.

A tearing sound ripped through the rear of the cabin.

Not an explosion this time.

Something worse.

A section of the hull peeled away with a scream of stressed metal, and for a fraction of a second the world became vacuum.

One of the Spire guards nearest the breach didn't have time to react. He was simply there—and then he wasn't, his body wrenched backward and out into the void as the air followed him in a violent rush.

The emergency field snapped into place.

The transition was instant, seamless—and still wrong.

Lily felt it in her teeth, in her lungs, in the pressure behind her eyes. That impossible moment where there should have been nothing, and then suddenly there was something again.

She would never get used to that.

"What is happening?" Veyshali demanded, her voice cutting cleanly through the noise.

"Contact—multiple signatures—" the pilot replied, fingers moving fast across the controls. "Rebels. They've been escalating in this sector."

"Prepare to return fire," the co-pilot said, already leaning into the console. "Triangulating last known position. Attempting to break their cloak—"

The transport shuddered again—

Then stopped.

Lily felt it immediately. The motion, the momentum, the subtle forward pull—all of it arrested at once, like something had reached out and taken hold of them.

"They've got us," the pilot said, voice tight now. "Mag-lock or grappling—"

A scan flickered across his display.

"It's one of the old T150s, sir. Converted freighter. They've attached to the hull."

A beat.

"We're about to have company, Your Majesty."

Roka was already moving.

His weapon was in his hand before the words finished, his posture shifting from polished to lethal in a single, fluid transition. The remaining Spire guard mirrored him, stepping into position near the center of the cabin.

Above them, something struck the outer hatch.

Once.

Twice.

Metal groaned.

The sound of tools biting into reinforced plating echoed through the ceiling—sharp, deliberate, controlled.

Then—

A device dropped through the opening just as the hatch gave way.

It hit the deck and burst in a tight pulse of blue-white light.

Roka's weapon flickered in his hand and died.

The guard's did the same.

"—damn it—"

Before either of them could react, figures dropped through the breach.

Four of them.

They landed hard and low, moving with practiced coordination, faces obscured beneath deep blue hoods. Their jumpsuits were the same shade—utilitarian, reinforced at the joints, crossed with weapon harnesses that held compact, efficient gear. Across each chest, painted in rough strokes of red, was a symbol Lily didn't recognize—angular, foreign, slashed through with a single violent line.

Not decoration.

Declaration.

"Secure the prisoners," the lead rebel hissed.

Veyshali recoiled instinctively, one hand bracing against the seat as she shifted back.

Roka stepped in front of her without hesitation.

The lead rebel moved closer, her voice low but carrying easily through the cabin.

"Well," she said, almost amused, "we've just acquired a very useful piece of leverage, my friends." She tilted her head slightly. "Do you have any idea who this is?"

No one answered.

"Queen Veyshali of Ishrath," she went on, the note of reverence there for a moment—and then gone. "Not just royalty. Royalty from a key Union world."

A murmur passed between the others.

Roka didn't move.

"You would be wise not to harm her," he said evenly. "You and I both understand the consequences of rebellion on the Spire."

The rebel laughed.

It wasn't nervous. It wasn't uncertain. It was the kind of laugh that came from someone who had already decided the rules didn't apply.

She closed the distance between them in two steps, stopping inches from his face.

"The order of things is already collapsing," she said quietly. "You just haven't felt it yet."

Something in her eyes held there—certainty, not anger.

"Soon," she added, softer still, "it all burns."

Roka didn't flinch.

There was a moment—just long enough to feel it—where Lily's stomach dropped.

The cabin held in a stretched silence, everything suspended as she braced for what would come next.

Then a voice called down from above, bright enough to feel out of place—

"Knock, knock."

Every head turned.

A sphere dropped through the still-open hatch, glowing a harsh, saturated green that forced Lily's eyes to narrow against it. It hit the deck and held there, suspended for a fraction of a second before a field snapped outward.

Lily felt it instantly.

Like every muscle in her body had been caught mid-command and held there. Her arms locked. Her breath stalled halfway through her chest. Even her jaw refused to move.

She couldn't speak.

Couldn't even try.

Around her, the rebels froze where they stood, weapons half-raised, momentum arrested in the middle of action.

A beat of stillness.

Then figures dropped through the hatch.

Six of them, by Lily's count—though they moved in such tight unison it was hard to be sure. They landed with practiced ease, their gear heavier and more standardized than the rebels' or the Spire guard's. Black-and-gray camouflage broke up the lines of their uniforms, reinforced plates catching the light as they moved with the kind of precision that came from repetition.

Patches marked the left shoulder.

A symbol Lily recognized immediately.

Sunbow Logistics.

The lead man—human—straightened as he landed, brushing a hand over his sleeve as though he'd arrived somewhere mildly inconvenient rather than into the middle of a hostile breach. His accent rolled thick and vaguely European, consonants shaped just slightly off from anything Lily could place.

"You looked like you could use a hand," he said, glancing between the frozen rebels. "Good thing we happened to be on approach just as these scrubbers decided to make trouble."

He moved through the cabin without hurry, affixing small devices to each of them in turn—Lily, Veyshali, Roka, the shuttle personnel.

The moment it clicked into place at her collar, the pressure vanished.

Her fingers twitched.

Movement returned all at once.

Roka didn't hesitate.

He stepped forward, seized the lead rebel by the hood, and pulled it back.

A human woman stared back at him—jet black hair, green eyes, her expression locked in place by the phase-field, fury held in suspension.

Roka smiled.

"It was a pleasure meeting you," he said quietly. "You threatened my queen."

His grip tightened, just slightly.

"It will be one of the last things you ever do."

The Sunbow personnel moved in, securing the rebels with efficient, almost casual precision, as though this were routine.

"We'll take them," the man said, gesturing to his team. "Our brig is well equipped."

He turned back to Veyshali, offering a shallow, practiced bow.

"Your Majesty—allow us to escort you the rest of the way in."

The pilot breathed a sigh of relief. "Thank you, Captain."

The man grinned.

"Call me Snake."

He spread his hands, almost theatrical.

"Welcome to the Spire, Your Majesty. And remember—if you need something handled, you find a Sunny." His smile widened. "We've been all over the galaxy. No problem too small."

He tapped the side of his temple, as if that explained everything, then turned and vaulted back up through the hatch without another word.

The others followed, dragging the immobilized rebels with them.

The green sphere dimmed, then lifted, disappearing the way it had come.

Silence settled back into the cabin.

Lily sat there for a moment, her pulse still running ahead of her, then lifted her hand toward her mouth to chew a nail—only to bump lightly against the dummy respirator.

Right.

She let her hand fall, grounding herself again in the mission.

Roka adjusted his grip on his now-useless weapon, his expression returning to something controlled.

"I hope that was the most excitement we're in for," he said.

"At least on the ride over," Veyshali replied, settling back into her seat as though nothing had happened at all.

The shuttle gave a low, unnatural lurch, then steadied as an energy tow took hold, drawing them toward the needle ahead.

The transport eased into its berth with the same quiet precision as before, the outer doors parting to reveal a wash of light so bright it flattened shadow and depth alike.

For a moment, stepping through it felt like stepping into nothing.

Then the world resolved.

The upper stratum of the Spire opened around them in a sweep of glass and suspended architecture, terraces layered in impossible arcs, gardens hanging in curated gravity, light diffused through structures that seemed designed as much for spectacle as function. Everything was clean. Intentional. Beautiful in a way that felt managed.

Lily slowed without meaning to.

It was—impressive.

Not in the way of raw scale or power, but in its control. Every surface polished, every line considered, every view framed as though the chaos below didn't exist.

They stepped into the main concourse.

It stretched wide beneath a vaulted canopy of transparent material, the storm far below reduced to a distant abstraction. People moved through it in measured currents—well-dressed, unhurried, their attention drifting between conversation and the carefully curated surroundings.

And through it all—

Movement at the edges.

Servants.

Lily caught them in the periphery at first—quick, efficient, dressed in white so seamless against the brightness they almost vanished unless you were looking for them. They moved like stagehands, appearing only long enough to adjust, replace, remove, then slipping away again.

One paused near a structural column, then stepped into a narrow cylinder set into the floor.

A moment later, it was gone.

Another, farther off, did the same.

Pneumatic tubes, Lily realized. Personal lifts, scattered throughout the concourse like access points no one above was meant to think about.

Veyshali didn't slow.

A cluster of figures approached—well-dressed, carefully arranged, their expressions shifting into something warmer as they drew near.

"Your Majesty," one of them began, already smiling. "We are honored. Truly. When we received word you had accepted the invitation—"

"—a rare privilege," another added quickly. "The Spire has been anticipating your arrival."

Their voices overlapped slightly, practiced enthusiasm brushing against something more calculated beneath it.

Veyshali accepted it with ease, her expression composed, her presence filling the space without effort.

"You are gracious," she said, offering just enough in return.

Lily stood half a step behind, head lowered, listening.

Watching.

The servants moved in the background, uninterrupted.

Invisible.

Veyshali's hand shifted—small, precise.

Roka moved immediately.

He collected her bags without comment and turned toward a structure set apart from the others—a lift of a different kind, its frame arched and gilded, its surfaces catching the light in warm tones that stood in contrast to the sterile brightness around it.

It looked less like transport and more like display.

Lily followed.

Inside, the space was quieter, enclosed without feeling confined. A welcoming attendant stepped forward, entering a sequence into a panel that glowed softly beneath their touch.

No announcement.

No confirmation.

The doors sealed, and the lift rose.

The motion was smooth enough to feel like absence.

When the doors opened again, it was into a different kind of space.

Private.

The room beyond was expansive but restrained, its design echoing the concourse without its spectacle—clean lines, soft light, a view that stretched outward across the upper layers of the Spire.

Roka moved through the space once, quickly—Lily wasn't sure what he was looking for, but she assumed he was securing the room in some way, noticing things she would miss.

Then he reached into his coat and placed a small device against the wall.

A faint shimmer passed through the room.

"They assure us the rooms are private," he said out of the corner of his mouth. "I don't trust them."

Veyshali didn't argue. Instead, she turned to Lily.

"Better safe than sorry—that's Roka. I've learned not to question it."

Lily smiled.

But the queen's expression shifted, the warmth dropping away.

"I've arranged for you to go below," she said.

Lily met her gaze.

"You are a believer," Veyshali continued, her tone changing—less instruction now, more performance. "You have served the Ishrethi your entire life. Mostly off-world mining. Now you have heard the call of the Spire, and I have approved your leave."

Lily gave a small nod.

"They are allowing you to descend," Veyshali said. "To prove yourself."

"I understand."

Roka stepped forward, producing a small device no larger than a coin. He held it out to her.

"A transponder," he said. "They can detect these, but they are not prohibited. We will be able to track you—loosely. And you can signal if something goes wrong."

Lily took it, feeling its weight—light, but not insignificant.

Veyshali watched her.

"I can always call you up," she said. "If we need to speak."

"I'll be okay," Lily replied. "I want to see what's happening down there as much as you do."

She turned before either of them could answer.

In the corner of the room, partially recessed into the wall, a narrow tube waited—its surface marked with a column of symbols, each indicating direction.

Most pointed up.

One pointed down.

The word repeated in a dozen languages. A dozen scripts.

She pressed it.

The panel responded immediately, light shifting as the system engaged.

Lily stepped inside.

The doors sealed around her.

And the world above began to disappear.

· · · ·

The tube opened without warning.

A small compartment slid out from the wall, smooth and precise. Inside, a pair of white glasses rested on a narrow tray, a thin tag attached at the hinge.

Welcome.

Lily took them, hesitated only a second, then slipped them on.

The world shifted.

A soft overlay settled into her vision—clean, unobtrusive. Readouts hovered at the edge of her sight. A schematic unfolded, mapping the surrounding structure in layered depth.

Chute 314.

She hadn't realized how large the Spire truly was until she saw it like this—levels branching, corridors threading, entire sectors nested within others.

Then a voice—close, disembodied—as if fed directly into her head by the glasses.

"Welcome, Shameli of Ishreth. Your task list is still being populated. Please proceed to the main concourse for scanning and purification."

A series of arrows appeared, luminous and precise, cutting into view ahead of her.

Lily exhaled lightly.

"Handy," she muttered, only half snide.

The inner door slid open.

She stepped out—

—and it was like coming inside after a bright day. The dimness took a moment to resolve, shapes emerging slowly as her eyes adjusted.

The air pressed in around her, warm and damp, carrying the smell of metal and something chemical beneath it. Steam drifted in slow currents, rising from vents and unseen machinery.

It looked like a city.

A city grown out of a maintenance deck.

Structures climbed and stacked in uneven layers, walkways crossing overhead, pipes and conduits threading through everything. There was no visible ceiling, no clear boundary—just distance, swallowed by haze.

People moved through it in constant motion.

The arrows held steady in her vision, guiding her forward.

She followed.

They led her into an open space that read like a town square—wider, more organized, though no less dense with movement. A figure in a white jumpsuit approached, helmet sealed, face hidden behind an opaque shield.

Human, probably.

Maybe.

The figure raised a device, sweeping it once across her body.

A small light blinked to life at the front of the helmet.

"You have received the Gherionite vaccine."

The voice was feminine. Flat.

"Yes," Lily said.

"Purification protocol advised. Residual contaminants may interfere with optimal alignment."

The figure reached out, tapping a small red rectangle along the edge of Lily's glasses.

The overlay shifted.

New arrows. Red this time.

They pulled her toward a nearby structure—clinical, sterile in contrast to the industrial world around it.

Inside, the air cooled slightly.

The lighting sharpened.

Lily slowed as she passed the first open bay.

A row of people lay side by side, tubing threaded into their arms, some kind of transfusion cycling through them in slow, measured pulses.

Across from them, a man stood naked against a panel of searing white light, his body rigid, eyes squeezed shut as the brightness washed over him.

Further in, a gurney rolled past—someone being wheeled out of surgery.

The person on it was missing an arm that appeared to have been freshly amputated—Lily hoped she was wrong about that.

Lily's chest tightened.

Someone in white scrubs waved her over, a scanning wand already in hand.

"Let's see," they said, passing it across her torso. "Old dose. Nearly a year."

The tone was casual. Almost bored.

"Do you feel it interfering with your ability to spiritually connect with the Spire?"

Lily blinked.

"I—no," she said. "I'm here, aren't I?"

"Fair enough."

The person turned, retrieving a small container and pressing it into her hand.

Inside, something metallic shifted.

"Take these with a full glass of water," they said. "They won't dissolve. Swallow them whole. It will burn out any residual micro-toxins from the vaccine."

Lily looked at the contents.

Metal.

Shavings, or something close to it.

She closed the container and nodded.

"Right."

She left as quickly as she could manage without drawing attention, following the arrows back out into the heat and movement of the square, where a crowd had begun to gather around a line of figures held under guard in black uniforms identical to the ones on the transport, the onlookers drawn in and held there, transfixed.

"And what is their crime?" one of the guards called out.

"Discord!" the crowd answered, the word rising in uneven unison.

Lily's gaze shifted across the prisoners, and recognition hit as she saw them—the rebels from the shuttle.

The woman who had led them stood at the front, her blue jumpsuit torn, her face streaked with dirt and bruising. She held herself upright anyway.

"Be it recorded," the guard continued, his voice amplified just enough to carry, "that resident 851 and her co-conspirators have forfeited their lives by engaging in open rebellion."

Lily's stomach dropped as the meaning settled in.

"Do you have any last words?" the guard asked.

Lily felt it then—her pulse climbing, something tightening at the base of her throat, her body recognizing what was about to happen before her mind caught up.

The woman lifted her head.

"You can kill us here," she said, her voice carrying farther than it should have, "but for each of us, ten more will rise."

The shot came without warning, a continuous beam of light passing cleanly through her head, and she was gone before the words had fully settled.

The others followed in quick succession, the same precise motion repeated without hesitation or pause, bodies dropping one against another.

The crowd dispersed almost immediately, conversation resuming as though nothing had happened, movement folding back into its usual rhythm.

Lily stood there, the heat pressing in around her, the smell of metal sharper now, and no one looked twice at the heap of bodies left in the center of the square.

Lily turned, trying to steady herself, and found herself face to face with someone slightly taller than she was, wrapped in a long, well-worn coat that hung heavy over their frame. Like her, they wore a medical apparatus that obscured most of their face, the surface dull and functional.

"You're new here."

Lily nodded, keeping her movements small. "Is it obvious?"

"Come," the stranger said. "I'll take you somewhere you can get cleaned up."

The voice was scratchy, flattened in a way that made it difficult to place—modulated, Lily thought.

"It says in the readout I'm to report to my sponsors," she replied, glancing briefly at the overlay in her vision. "I assume that's where I'll be staying."

"I think you can afford a detour."

Something in the way they said it set her on edge.

"Who are you?" Lily asked.

"Just a believer like yourself," the stranger said. "Grateful to be in this holy place."

They took a step closer.

Lily took one back.

"Right," she said, forcing a small, polite edge into her voice. "Well, I don't want to break protocol as my first action here. I think I'd better—"

"No need to rush."

Another step.

Then the stranger's attention shifted, just slightly, their head tilting upward.

Lily felt it before she saw it—someone behind her.

She turned just enough to catch a glimpse: a human woman, curly blonde hair, broad-shouldered, built like someone used to physical work. Early fifties, maybe.

When Lily looked back, the stranger in the coat was already moving away, slipping into the crowd with practiced ease. She caught only the trailing edge of the coat as it disappeared around a corner.

Gone.

"Shameli?"

Lily turned.

The woman was smiling, open and warm in a way that felt almost out of place here.

"You must be Shameli." She extended a hand. "I'm Chaffi Pons. Those are my sons—Chiff and Sonny."

She nodded toward two young men standing a few steps behind her, both broad-shouldered and solid, their faces similar enough to feel like variations on the same design.

"We're your sponsor family," Chaffi continued. "You'll be staying with us until you've fully acclimated."

Lily took her hand, firm and steady.

Chaffi's gaze dropped briefly to the small container still in Lily's other hand.

"I see you're purging," she said. "I hope that wicked thing in your blood hasn't given you too much trouble."

She turned as she spoke, already moving.

"Come on," she added, gesturing toward a waiting transport. "We're out on the main condensation chute. You can't walk there."

By the time Lily had processed what she'd said, Chaffi was already halfway to the platform. Lily set off after her, picking up her pace to catch up.

The ride out to the housing sector was wet, loud, and deeply unpleasant.

The transport cut through one layer of the Spire after another, each environment worse than the last—heat giving way to damp, damp to something heavier, thicker, the air pressing in as moisture gathered and discharged in sudden bursts. Spray materialized out of nowhere, drenching the open cabin, static snapping in sharp cracks that followed every surge of humidity.

Lily hunched against it, water running down the edges of her mask.

She couldn't help wondering why they hadn't invested in a closed cabin.

The structure Chaffi led them to was less a building than a placement—wedged into the side of a massive industrial channel that carved its way vertically through what had to be thousands of levels of the Spire. The housing itself was modest, one or maybe two units stacked together, its surface reinforced against the constant assault of the environment.

Beyond it—

Lily stopped.

A vast column of water moved through the channel, contained within a shimmering field. Half of it surged upward, the other half downward, both currents running side by side in a continuous, impossible flow.

A vertical river.

Her eyes struggled to follow it.

The sound was constant—a deep, rushing roar beneath the sharper crack of static, the air alive with charge. Moisture hung suspended in fine sheets, reforming again and again as the system cycled.

For a moment, Lily had the distinct thought that prolonged exposure to it might drive someone mad.

Then the door sealed behind them.

The silence was immediate.

Not total, but controlled—dampened, contained. The noise of the channel reduced to a distant presence rather than something that filled her body.

Soundproofing, she guessed.

The boys—and "Ma," as they called Chaffi—hung their slickers along a wall rack. Water pooled beneath them in a shallow drain before disappearing.

The boys disappeared upstairs without a word.

No sooner had they stepped inside than an alarm sounded—sharp, insistent.

"I'll be right back, dear. Don't worry, happens all the time. Probably a flow blockage."

Chaffi was already moving, her voice trailing as she passed into the next room.

"There are some things robots are still just no good at!"

Lily stood there, water dripping from her sleeves, unsure whether to follow or wait.

She chose to wait.

A voice came from the corner.

"There someone there? Chaffi?"

Lily turned.

She hadn't noticed him at first—an older man seated in a low chair near a wall-mounted display, dark glasses obscuring his eyes. The news feed flickered across the screen, voices overlapping in practiced urgency.

"—the latest shipment of the Union vaccine reported stolen—what do you make of it, Jex?"

"Well, Zim, you can't trust every report that comes out of the fleet these days. Remember when we learned about—"

The man raised his voice over the chatter.

"Is someone there?"

"Hello—sorry—yes," Lily said. "I'm... Shameli."

"You sound like you're not sure," he said, a faint smile in his voice. "Let me guess—Chaffi had you ride open-cabbed with no slicker."

Lily let out a small laugh.

"Don't take it personally," he went on. "She does that to all the newcomers. Says you need to see it with your own five senses." He rolled his lips for a beat. "Though I suppose I'm down to four these days."

"Lost your sense of taste?" Lily asked.

The man laughed—sharp and sudden.

"I like you. What did you do before the Spire?"

"Off-world mining for Ishreth." Lily measured her tone, though she still worried it sounded deceptive.

"Ah." He shifted in his chair. "I was an energy man myself. Solar fields on Gallamus II. My parents brought me there when I was two, if you can believe it. Spent my whole life out there until they dragged me down off the rigs, kicking and screaming." He gestured vaguely. "All run by drones now."

Lily let the silence settle for a moment.

"My name's Gus," he added. "Well—Gecon-Five, technically. That's my assigned designation. One of those communities that thought they were going to change the galaxy by being... very particular about things." he shrugged. "I chose Gus."

"Nice to meet you, Gus."

"Are you talking her ears off, Dad?"

Chaffi reappeared, wiping her hands on a cloth.

"Come on, dear. I'll show you your room. There's a whole set of clothes and equipment for you. You get your own shower—you just have to power it on for a few minutes to warm it up." She waved her hands. "I'll show you. You'll get the hang of it."

"See you later, Gus," Lily said.

"Nice to meet you, Sammy," he replied easily. "See you at dinner."

• • • •

The room filled with the soft clink of dishes and the low hum of conversation, the table set with simple, heavy plates that looked like they'd been used for years. The food smelled better than Lily expected—warm, starchy, something slow-cooked and salted enough to cut through the damp air that still clung to her clothes.

The space itself felt like a compromise between necessity and memory—industrial surfaces softened by rough wood, reinforced walls hung with old tools and a few personal touches that read more like habit than decoration. It had the feeling of a place assembled over time rather than designed all at once.

Lily sat carefully, working the small intake flap on the respirator with deliberate ease, trying to make it look like muscle memory instead of something she was figuring out as she went. The mechanism clicked open just enough to allow her to eat, the seal holding everywhere else.

Chaffi was already mid-sentence.

"Lost a lot of good people to the rigs," she was saying. "Including my husband. Unforgiving, the work is. The Spire is different. It's demanding, sure—but we have purpose. And they take care of our every need."

She gestured lightly with her fork as she spoke.

"We were lucky. If the boys had been over eighteen, I wouldn't have been able to bring them. Chiff was close—turned eighteen the day we moved in." A faint smile. "Course they let me bring my dad."

Lily nodded at the appropriate moments, letting the rhythm of the speech wash over her.

The boys weren't listening. They were eating—heads down, movements efficient, as though the food might disappear if they didn't get through it quickly enough.

Gus leaned back in his chair, his dark glasses angled toward the table, his plate untouched.

"But that's just how it is," Chaffi continued. "You know that, don't you, Shameli? When you're a believer, you put your faith in them. They'll take care of you."

Lily took another bite, buying herself a second.

"Unless you're guilty of discord," she said.

Chaffi's lips thinned, but she nodded.

"The Spire's judgment is swift."

"I guess I didn't expect it to be so..." Lily paused, searching for the word. "Violent."

"It's not our place to question," Chaffi said evenly. "Hell, I've even known people personally who've faced swift judgment—"

"Like Uncle Sarlo?"

The voice cut in, unsteady.

Lily looked up.

The younger one—Sonny.

It was the first time she'd heard him speak.

"Especially Uncle Sarlo," Chaffi said, the warmth gone from her voice. She set her fork down with more force than necessary, then turned back to Lily. "My brother came here a few months after we did. But he never truly heard the call."

She glanced at Sonny again.

"He deserved what he got."

Lily saw Gus's head lift. He pulled the dark glasses from his face.

His eyes—clouded, unfocused—fixed somewhere past the table, but the expression on his face was sharp.

"You mind your tone," he snapped, the words cutting cleanly through the room. "He was still my boy."

The table went still.

Even the boys stopped eating.

No one spoke.

Chaffi opened her mouth to break the silence, the shape of her expression suggesting whatever came next would not be subtle.

Then the alarm cut through the room again.

"Saved by the bell." She was already on her feet. "Boys."

The boys shoveled in another bite or two before rising, moving fast now, chairs scraping lightly against the floor.

Chaffi was at the panel near the wall, scanning it as it lit up.

"Looks like a reactor cracked in sector seventeen."

Chiff shook his head. "Not seventeen again."

Sonny glanced at Lily. "You're lucky you're not on task yet."

Chaffi's expression tightened, irritation flashing before it was smoothed over.

"Now, boys," she said, forcing the brightness back into her voice, "remember to face your work with gratitude. The Spire takes care of us—we give back."

They moved with practiced efficiency, pulling on gear, securing fastenings, the routine clearly worn into them.

In less than a minute, they were ready.

Chaffi paused at the doorway, looking back at Lily.

"Don't bother cleaning up, dear. I have a drone that will come through."

She stepped out, already turning away, her voice carrying back into the corridor—

"And help yourself to whatever you can find."

Then they were gone.

Lily sat there for a moment, not hungry, but in no rush to return to her room. The quiet company of Gus had a strange comfort to it.

As if on cue, he broke the silence.

"I spend most of my time alone these days," he began. "Not that I'm complaining. I'm usually my favorite company."

There was a lightness in his voice that didn't quite hide the truth of it.

Lily smiled. "I know what you mean."

"So—off-world mining," he said. "You must have seen your share of the galaxy."

"You have no idea."

"Never much had the stomach for space travel." He rolled his lips slowly, as if turning over a memory. "Believe it or not, I'd only ever been to a spaceport once before coming here. Decades ago. Dropped a friend off—he'd enlisted in the first Krythar conflict."

"Just that once?" Lily said. "I guess it left an impression."

He scoffed lightly. "You could say that. All that busy, dizzy, tizzy. Not for me."

His voice drifted, thinning slightly.

"Leon never came back," he added. "From the war."

"I'm sorry."

"Even after all these years," he said, "losing someone like that—you remember it."

He straightened a little in his chair.

"Course we had things like duty back then. Responsibility. Things I don't think my kids ever really learned. Despite my best efforts."

A quiet settled between them.

"But the Spire is your home now," Lily said. "For good?"

"The Spire sees us," he said, almost automatically. "Sees the worker. Out there, people forget what makes things run. There are still workers behind the scenes, keeping everything moving. Even those fancy starships."

Lily nodded. "That's very true."

She kept her tone careful.

Then something caught her eye.

Out the window.

A foot.

A foot?

Someone was climbing the exterior of the dwelling.

"Excuse me, Gus," Lily said, already rising. "Thanks for the chat."

"Thank you," Gus replied, genuine. "Nice to have someone on the other end of the conversation for once."

Lily moved toward the stairs, quick but quiet.

She stepped into her room, the door sliding shut behind her as the window sealed with a final hiss, the howl of wind and static cut off all at once until the space fell quiet again.

"I saw you climbing," she said. "I know you're in here."

She had no weapon, but she held her ground.

A figure shifted in the corner, slipping out from where shadow and curtain had concealed them, and Lily recognized the long coat and mask immediately—the stranger from the square.

"Who are you?" she said, steady. "What do you want?"

The stranger hesitated, their posture tightening slightly, as though weighing the risk.

"I'll show you mine if you show me yours."

"You first," Lily shot back.

There was a brief hesitation.

"Alright," the stranger said. "But I'm not the one with my face all over the news feeds."

They reached up, undoing the clasps at the side of the mask. It came away with a soft click.

The shock in Lily's eyes gave way to a wide smile.

"Where the hell have you been?"

She was met with that familiar crooked grin.

"You finally caught up with me," Trish said.

Chapter 6: Breath, Fire and Ruin

THE SPEEDER TORE THROUGH the lower Spire, panels and exposed equipment flashing past in a relentless blur that whipped at Lily's senses.

Lily felt it in her core—a high, thin vibration that set her jaw humming as the vehicle knifed through the lower arteries of the Spire. The world outside refused to hold shape. It came apart in fragments—white steam bursting from ruptured vents, scaffolding flashing past in skeletal streaks, figures clinging to exposed beams as pressure alarms pulsed in uneven, stuttering rhythms that seemed to echo through the structure itself.

Trish didn't slow.

She leaned forward over the controls, one hand braced, the other moving in sharp, precise adjustments that kept them just ahead of collision. The speeder skimmed along a maintenance rail, dipped hard beneath a sagging conduit, then snapped sideways through a gap that looked too narrow to exist, let alone pass through at speed.

Wind tore through the open frame, ripping at Lily's hair, flattening her breath back into her chest.

Lily grabbed the brace as the deck tilted under her boots. "You planning to tell me where we're going?"

"There's no time," Trish said, not looking at her.

That was all she'd said back at the dwelling.

No explanation. No reunion. Just—*move.*

"I'll explain on the way."

So she did, her explanation spilling out in fragments, stitched together in the brief, breathless gaps between near misses.

"I was distributing the Gherionite vaccine," Trish said, voice cutting clean through the roar of the wind. "Earth sectors. Free clinics. It was working—people were taking it—then it started disappearing."

The speeder dropped suddenly, the track giving way beneath them into open air before snapping onto another line with a metallic scream that rattled Lily's spine.

"And the Union version showed up," Lily said, forcing the words out as she steadied herself.

"Yeah." Trish's mouth tightened. "But never enough. Always short. Just enough to keep people desperate."

Another turn. Tighter. Faster.

"They weren't competing," Trish continued. "They were choking it. The Gherionite supply—cutting it off upstream."

"Why?" Lily asked. "Profit?"

"Maybe." Trish shook her head. "Or something deeper. That's what I'm trying to find out."

Steam blasted across their path in a blinding white sheet. Trish didn't hesitate—she angled straight through it, visibility dropping to nothing for a split second that stretched long enough for Lily to feel the absence of the world.

Then they burst out the other side.

The Spire unfolded again around them—layered infrastructure stacked in impossible vertical tiers, everything humming with strain, like a body holding its breath too long.

"I followed the chain," Trish said. "Redacted routes. Private carriers. The power structure kept pointing here."

She jerked her chin forward.

"The Spire isn't just a playground for the rich," she said. "It's a memory bank. A physical archive where data has to come and go by hand—no network access."

Lily glanced at her then—really looked.

This was a side of Trish she had always known was there, but had never actually seen.

Not the innkeeper with the easy smile and steady hands. Not activist Trish.

Agent Trish.

Focused. Driven. Already moving three steps ahead.

"Why you?" Lily said, the question shifting even as she asked it. "What are you actually looking for?"

"The origin point," Trish said. "Where the Union vaccine is really being manufactured. And who's controlling distribution—*actually* controlling it."

Another drop. Another surge of speed.

"It has to be in the data core," she went on. "Stored locally. Identity-gated. I can get us in—but I can't run the panel and watch the system at the same time."

She flicked Lily a quick glance.

"I need another set of hands."

"Well," Lily said, tightening her grip on the brace, a hint of a smile breaking through despite everything, "lucky for you I dropped in."

Trish flashed that grin—wide, unguarded, the one Lily remembered.

That was all Lily needed.

Ahead, the structure thickened, the pathways narrowing as the Spire's internal systems closed in around them.

Trish leaned into the controls.

"We're close," she said.

The route narrowed without warning, the open channels of the lower Spire compressing into something denser, more volatile, the air itself beginning to warp as Trish drove them straight into a sector already coming apart.

A rupture had torn through one of the main lines—condensation or an energy feed, Lily couldn't tell—but whatever it had been carrying was venting now, free and uncontrolled. Superheated vapor rolled through the corridor in uneven pulses, and between them sharp, cracking discharges leapt between exposed conduits and slick metal with no pattern she could read.

Workers moved through it anyway, hauling equipment, locking down what they could, reacting to each new surge before the last one had finished. The floor shimmered with runoff, every surface one wrong step from giving out.

The speeder cut through without slowing.

Lily's gaze moved across the scene automatically—exits, collapse points, vectors of movement—and snagged on something familiar.

Chaffi's boys.

Both of them already deep in it, one braced at a panel that sparked under his hands, the other hauling a line through condensation that rose to his waist, their movements practiced and unhurried in the way of people who knew the work and didn't need to think about it.

They didn't look up as the speeder tore past.

There wasn't time for that either.

"Up ahead," Trish said, already angling them toward a narrowing break in the corridor where the infrastructure pinched inward.

The speeder dipped hard beneath a sagging conduit, then surged forward into a stretch where the passage constricted to something barely wider than a maintenance access. Trish cut the engines just before the opening, letting the vehicle skid into place along a warped section of plating.

"Here," she said, already moving.

They disembarked into heat and noise, the air thick with vapor and static that prickled across Lily's skin as she followed Trish toward the narrow conduit carved into the structure ahead.

The entrance was barely wide enough for a single person.

Then—

A crack split the corridor like a pressure seal giving way, and a condenser unit fifteen meters down blew apart in a cascade of blue-white sparks, the flash burning itself into Lily's vision a fraction of a second before the sound reached her. A worker caught the edge of the blast, thrown sideways, and came down hard beneath a section of framework that dropped with them.

Lily was already moving.

"Lily—" Trish's voice, sharp behind her.

She didn't stop.

The worker lay just off their path, pinned where the collapsed beam had caught them across the midsection, one arm trapped at a wrong angle. Worse, the floor beneath them sloped toward an exposed channel where vapor burst in violent, rhythmic surges, each pulse dragging them closer, inch by grinding inch.

She dropped to a knee beside them, hands already braced against the warped beam. It shifted under her grip—hot, slick, heavier than it looked—but it moved when she leaned into it, forcing space where there hadn't been any.

"Move."

The word came out low, steady.

The worker twisted free and scrambled clear as another surge tore through the channel behind them, the force of it rattling up through the deck plating.

Trish was there in an instant, her hand closing on Lily's arm, already pulling.

"Okay," she said. "Okay. But we have to go—now."

They slipped into the conduit together, the passage swallowing the noise almost immediately, the chaos outside collapsing into a distant, muffled roar as they moved deeper into the structure. The air was cooler, no less tense.

Behind them, the sector kept breaking.

Ahead, the darkness gave way to a kaleidoscope of light.

The data core opened around them—vast, still, humming with the kind of quiet that meant everything in here was working exactly as intended. Where the corridor had been heat and fracture and noise, this was order, deliberate and total, unsettling in its completeness.

The chamber wasn't sleek. It was built—massive storage columns in ordered rows, threaded with cables and conduits feeding into the structure above and below. Light moved across their surfaces in slow, controlled patterns, not decorative, just enough to indicate activity. Terminals stood at regular intervals, their interfaces stripped to function, designed for someone who already knew exactly what they were doing.

Nothing here invited interpretation. It expected compliance.

Trish didn't slow. She crossed the floor with purpose, and one of the terminals flickered as she approached, the interface shifting in response to a signal Lily couldn't see.

"I told you," Trish said, already working. "It all ends up here."

Her hands moved fast—not guessing, not searching. The system resisted just enough to register the intrusion, then gave way in layers.

"There." Trish jerked her chin toward the adjacent terminal. "Secondary interface. Log in—I'll push you access in a second."

Lily moved to it. The screen came alive as Trish's signal hit, a dashboard resolving with a progress bar along the top and a column of fluctuating numbers beneath it.

"What am I looking at?"

"Load balancer. The system monitors access weight across both terminals—if one draws too hard, it flags the pull as intrusion and locks the session." Trish didn't look up. "You're ballast. Keep that percentage between forty and sixty. If it drifts above, throttle back on the left panel. If it drops, bring it up. Don't let it spike."

"How do I throttle it?"

"Slider. Left side. It's not subtle. Just keep it in range."

Lily found it. The number read fifty-three.

"Now?" she asked.

"Now you don't let me get locked out."

Data unfolded on Trish's screen.

Routes first—transit lines branching out from central nodes, some bright and active, others dimmed or quietly rerouted. She stacked overlays, isolating patterns that only emerged when you stopped looking at individual shipments and looked at the shape of the whole.

Distribution logs scrolled past, timestamps and routing tags resolving into something beyond movement.

Green. Stable.

Yellow. Reduced.

Red. Deprioritized.

Lily watched the red spread across the map from the corner of her eye, touching systems she recognized—outer sectors, refugee corridors, places already stretched thin—while keeping the other part of her attention locked on the percentage. Fifty-eight. She nudged the slider. Fifty-four.

The Union vaccine allocations flickered across Trish's display—delayed, diverted, quietly erased. And where the Gherionite vaccine should have been flowing, there was only absence. Not shortage. Pattern.

She'd suspected. Now she was looking at the architecture of it.

"Someone's controlling the supply," she said.

"Not just controlling." Trish pulled another layer forward. "Maintaining it. Volumes adjusted in real time—never enough to stabilize. Just enough to keep demand high and alternatives out of reach."

Sixty-one. Lily pulled the slider back. Fifty-seven.

"Where's it coming from?" she asked.

"That's the part they don't want seen."

Trish pushed deeper. The layers thinned as they neared the source, access peeling away, replaced by something tighter. A lock appeared on the interface—not hidden, just higher.

Her hands slowed. Then stopped.

"No," she said, quiet.

Lily leaned in, one eye still on her panel. "What?"

"Identity gate. Not encryption—clearance." Trish tapped the interface once, twice, searching for a seam that wasn't there. "This layer doesn't care about codes. It cares who you are."

The origin point. The manufacturing site. Right there, just beyond reach, the system waiting for credentials they didn't have and couldn't fake.

Lily's percentage read forty-nine. She held it there.

Trish exhaled—the first crack in her focus since they'd stepped inside.

"Dammit." Her jaw tightened. "We're so close."

• • • •

Back in Shameli's room, the doors slid shut and the privacy they offered felt immediate—and fragile.

Lily was already setting the transponder on the table, adjusting the output with quick, practiced movements. The signal had to be narrow—tight enough to avoid drawing attention, stable enough to hold a conversation. Anything wider would be seen. Anything weaker would drop.

Trish watched, her eyes saying *hurry*.

"It's not polite to look over someone's shoulder while they work," Lily said without looking up.

"There."

It took a second.

Then Veyshali appeared above the device—a flickering projection that somehow carried the full weight of her attention. Composed, precise, every movement measured.

"Be quick. I won't have privacy for long."

"First—this is Trish," Lily said. "Long story."

"Your Majesty." Trish kept it efficient: what they'd accessed, what they'd confirmed, where the system had closed against them. Lily added only the shape of it, the two of them building the picture between them as they spoke it aloud.

Veyshali listened without interruption.

When they finished, she didn't pause.

"This isn't about technology," she said. "It's about hierarchy."

The words settled between them.

"You won't be able to force it," she went on. "It's designed to recognize only those permitted to see it."

Trish's hand tightened slightly on the edge of the table.

"So we're locked out."

"No," Veyshali said. "You're in the wrong layer."

Lily had the distinct impression the pause was intentional—unnecessary, but she was used to Veyshali's theatrics.

"You need someone from up here. I'd open it myself, but they don't trust me with access. Not yet."

Her gaze shifted slightly, as though checking something just beyond their view.

"We don't have time. You need to come up here. I'll send a summons for Shameli."

The feed cut.

Lily heard the entrance hatch opening a level below.

"That's Chaffi and the boys," she said, already moving. "Let me check in—hang tight."

Trish nodded.

Lily was halfway down the stairs when Chaffi was already talking.

Chaffi's voice filled the lower level, still running hot from whatever they'd come through, words tumbling out in the particular rhythm of someone who needed to finish being in the middle of it before they could be anywhere else. The boys were behind her, wet and exhausted, shedding gear, every movement carrying the heaviness of people who had been moving fast for too long and had only just stopped.

"—partial core breach, I'm telling you. We were lucky the secondary housing held or we'd be having a very different conversation right now." She turned when she saw Lily, not breaking stride. "You see what they've got us working with out there? That cheap coupling infrastructure from Sceptacky space. Nobody wants to authorize upgrades, and then—" she gestured broadly at everything, "—this. Honestly, sometimes I think they want this place to fall apart."

"Everyone intact?" Lily asked.

Her brow shot up, as though the question itself were absurd. "We're not ghosts, if that's what you're asking."

From his chair in the corner, Gus lifted his head, his expression worn.

"Missed all the action again," he said.

Lily left them to it and headed back upstairs.

The door slid shut, and the quiet that followed felt deliberate.

Trish was where she'd left her, but her posture had shifted in the small way that meant she'd been thinking about this moment too.

Lily didn't build to it.

"Why didn't you tell me?" she said, keeping her voice even. "You just disappeared."

Trish didn't deflect. "Because you would have come."

"Yes."

"That was the problem." She said it plainly, without apology. "You were on a Union starship. Positioned. Safe enough. I needed that to stay true."

"You thought I might be useful?" Lily said, the edge slipping in.

Trish didn't hesitate. "Yes. You might have been."

Her gaze dropped, briefly.

"I certainly didn't count on you having your face all over the feeds."

"Neither did I."

Trish smiled, faintly. "Frankly, I didn't count on any of this."

The honesty of it landed without softening anything. Lily felt the shape of it—the care inside the choice, and the cost of it anyway.

"Any of this," Lily said. "What even is all of this, exactly?"

"I wish I knew." Trish's expression shifted, just slightly. "Something is missing. Something big. Some piece of the puzzle I'm not seeing."

The silence between them settled.

Lily felt the weight of everything that had been sitting in it since she saw the boards on Scales and Feathers.

She let the words come.

"It's hard enough for me to connect to Earth in this time as it is." She hadn't meant to say it—but it came out anyway. "You were my only anchor there."

Trish met her gaze, steady. She didn't flinch, and she didn't rush to fill the space with apology.

"Connection doesn't happen out of nowhere," she said after a moment. "You build it. Intentionally. Out of whatever's around you."

Lily pressed her lips together.

She knew they wouldn't align this time. That was the difficulty of moments like this—two people who loved each other, simply made of different material.

She moved on, because that's what the moment required.

The plan was simple in outline and not simple at all in practice. Lily would go up—find someone in the Spire's authority tier, someone whose presence the identity gate would recognize. Then they'd have what they needed.

Trish ran through it once, efficiently, and then stopped.

She looked at Lily, something careful in her expression.

"Are you ready to go back up there?"

"It's more of a plan than I usually have," Lily said.

Trish nodded.

Lily made sure she looked the part, then stepped into the tube.

. . . .

The upper level breathed differently—cooler, quieter, the air carrying the particular stillness of a space that had never been asked to do anything as common as work.

Lily stepped out of the tube and adjusted the set of her shoulders before anyone could look up.

Someone did, briefly.

Then looked away.

She found Veyshali arranged at the center of a loose gathering of bodies and low furniture, the kind of scene designed to look effortless—and wasn't. The people around her moved with the unhurried ease of those who had never needed to move quickly. Conversation flowed between them in layers—surface and beneath, both at once.

Veyshali clocked her the moment she entered.

Nothing in her expression changed.

Lily approached and dipped her head, playing the angle. "You sent for me."

"Shameli." Veyshali's voice was warm and entirely opaque. She reached out and adjusted something at Lily's collar that didn't need adjusting—the gesture intimate, proprietary, covering the half-second she needed. "I was beginning to wonder."

A man to her left said something that required a laugh. Veyshali gave him one, perfectly timed, then turned back.

"Roka is working this evening," she said, lifting a glass from the tray beside her. Casual. Incidental. "Below. The pleasure wing." Her gaze moved over Lily's face with an expression the room would read as appraisal. "He'll see you settled."

Lily kept her face neutral. "The pleasure wing."

Veyshali's gaze didn't waver.

"Just do what I would do," she said simply, and looked away—which was, in its own way, a complete set of instructions.

Someone across the room called for her attention, and she rose to give it, graceful and unhurried, already somewhere else.

Lily stood for a moment in the space she'd left behind.

Then she went to find the stairs.

• • • •

The shift happened gradually. The lighting dropped first, warming from functional white to something amber and low, and then the walls changed—paneling giving way to darker materials, fabric where there had been metal, deep reds and blacks that absorbed sound along with light. The corridor felt narrower than it was.

She noticed, too, that the people she passed wore progressively less.

Lily kept her pace even, her eyes forward.

She found the studio through an archway draped in heavy cloth—a large, open space divided by curtains and low screens, the air warm and faintly scented. Bodies in various states of treatment occupied the tables.

She was still taking it in when a hand closed around her elbow and pulled her sideways behind a curtain.

Roka.

She nearly didn't recognize him. His hair was pulled back, and he was wearing what could generously be described as shorts—small, fitted, leaving very little to the imagination—along with some kind of leather strap across his chest that served no structural purpose she could identify.

She kept her expression level.

She didn't entirely succeed, and from the way his eyes narrowed, he could see it anyway.

"You can't be walking around out there like that," he said, low and direct. "Servants have restricted access down here. If someone asks you a question you can't answer—"

"Got it," she said.

He studied her for a beat. Then, because he was apparently also reading her face:

"What."

"Nothing." She paused, a hint of a smirk slipping through. "What would Gadspar think?"

"I'm sure I don't know what you're referring to." The corner of his mouth moved. "Don't."

"I'm not doing anything." Lily raised her hands in surrender.

"What exactly do you need?" he said, steering them back.

"...Someone with authority-tier biometric access. Long story."

Roka took that in without visible reaction. "I assume this isn't something that asking nicely will solve."

"Doubtful."

He looked at her for another moment, then reached past her and pulled a blonde wig and a silky robe from a shelf built into the partition. He held them out.

"Get undressed and put these on."

He was already moving back toward the curtain.

"Then we can talk."

The curtain swung shut behind him.

Lily stood in the small curtained space and looked at the robe.

She could almost hear Veyshali's voice:

Just do what I would do.

She sighed.

She emerged to find Roka working on a client—a large figure occupying the table with the particular mass of a species that had not evolved with delicacy in mind. The skin was dense, ridged, and Lily watched Roka's hands move across it with genuine curiosity. He wasn't fighting the resistance. He was working with it, finding the geography of it, and whatever he was doing appeared to be working—the client had the unfocused stillness of someone who had completely left the building.

She didn't want to attract attention. She moved toward the empty side of the room, the robe swishing at her knees, and was reaching for something to do with her hands when she heard him.

The Sunbow Logistics captain—Snake.

He was in the corridor, loud in the specific way of someone who had decided the social contract was optional for the evening, listing slightly as he addressed two workers in robes considerably smaller than Lily's.

"Good morning, ladies." The leer carried in his voice. "What does a man have to do to get some attention around here?"

They walked on without slowing or acknowledging him, their indifference practiced to the point of professionalism.

Lily drifted back toward Roka's table and found a tray of small bottles to occupy herself with, arranging and rearranging them with the focused air of someone doing something important.

Roka placed a hot towel over his client and stepped beside her.

"The Gneki is listening to music," he said quietly, not looking at her. "We can talk."

She explained it—the data core, the identity gate, what they needed and why.

Roka listened, then washed his hands and applied fresh oil, methodical.

"Getting someone alone won't be the problem," he said. "Explaining their absence will be. The elite up here keep daily appointments. Routines. People notice when those routines break." He glanced at her. "If we incapacitate them to access the files, they will be missed."

Lily turned one of the small bottles over in her hand. "Incapacitate?"

"A simultaneous finger scan, retinal scan, and a data key—usually implanted somewhere on the body." He said it plainly, like a list of ingredients. "Not something you can sneak."

"Shit."

"Exactly." He looked at her, then at the nearest empty table. "Lay down."

She hesitated.

"You've been reorganizing those same eight bottles for ten minutes."

She let out a short breath and laid face down. The table was surprisingly soft, the warmth sinking into her more quickly than she expected.

"Just be—"

"Oh."

Roka removed the robe in one efficient motion and was already working before she'd fully processed it—his thumbs finding something in her upper back that had apparently been waiting a long time to be found.

"Jesus," she said, involuntarily. "You're really good at that."

"I told you. I'm certified," he said, without inflection. "Now. Several people came on with the Sunnies. But most of them won't have the access level you need."

A crash from the corridor. Lily lifted her head.

Through the archway, she could see Snake working through a chest of drinks with the focused determination of a man on a mission, bottles clinking as he rejected them one by one.

She turned her head, which brought her uncomfortably close to more of Roka.

"What about him?"

Roka glanced over. A small nod.

"Access level, almost certainly. And—" he applied pressure to something that briefly removed her ability to form thoughts, "—he will absolutely not be missed."

Lily sat up on the table. Roka took a step back, and she realized a beat too late that the robe was still behind her.

She made a flat face.

"What?" he said, entirely untroubled. "You're in excellent condition. This will work."

"Solitary confinement chic," she said, reaching for the robe.

She tied it loosely and started across the room.

Roka caught her arm before she made it three steps. She turned, impatient, but he was already moving—guiding her quietly through the studio to a hidden door off to the side.

A private room. Small, warm. A couch, low lighting.

He opened a compartment built into the wall beside the headrest, nearly invisible unless you knew where to look. Inside: a syringe, capped, ready.

She looked at him.

"I don't want to know," she said.

"You don't," he agreed.

By the time she crossed the hall, Snake had two bottles open and was smelling them in turn, a man approaching the problem with genuine scientific curiosity. Both had labels she couldn't read.

Lily took a breath and decided not to overcomplicate it.

"Hey." She put everything she had into the word.

He half-looked up. "Oh, hello, love." He held out the bottle with the yellow liquid. "Any idea what this is?"

"That one will get you drunk," she said.

He eyed the other. Black liquid, bright label.

"And that one will probably kill you."

He considered this seriously, then set the dark bottle down and took a long pull from the yellow one. "Best not to take chances when there's no profit in it."

Lily leaned into the doorframe, letting the silence do some work.

He half-looked up.

Then looked again, slower this time—something catching behind his eyes.

"You look familiar, love."

Lily's stomach tightened. She kept her face easy.

"I get that a lot," she said. "You're Snake."

"How d'you know that?" It came out slurred, somewhere between a question and a belch.

"Oh," she said, holding his gaze. "Everyone knows who you are."

That landed. He stood a little straighter, his free hand moving toward her. "Do they?"

She let him get close before stepping back—just enough. Eyes on his. A smile she had to manufacture from somewhere and was a little surprised to find.

"They say there's a reason for the name."

She grabbed his belt—the move sharp and deliberate, catching him off guard. The bottle slipped from his hand and hit the floor with a crack, yellow spreading across the surface.

She was already moving, letting the robe slide from her shoulders as she went.

She felt him follow.

The private room was small and warm. He was on her almost before the door closed—hands first, no preamble.

She planted her foot and pushed—not hard, just precise—and he went down onto the couch with an expression of surprised delight, like she'd confirmed something he already suspected.

"Now," she said, keeping her voice easy. "Not so fast."

The compartment was directly behind his head.

Of course it was.

She moved toward him slowly, buying herself seconds.

He reached for her, and she let him pull her down—let him think he was setting the terms. The compartment was close now, her fingers finding the edge of the panel while his mouth found her collarbone.

She got the syringe out. Got it set.

His hand closed around her wrist.

Not the one holding the needle—the other one, which was luck, but his grip was hard and he was already reading the situation wrong and then right again in the same second.

"What is that." Not a question. His eyes flattened.

He flipped her, her back hitting the couch, his weight coming down, one hand pinning her arm as the other went for the syringe.

"Nobody robs old Snake." His face was close. "Nobody."

Lily went still.

Not from fear.

From training.

She found the angle. The position of her foot against his groin.

She kicked.

The impact was clean and specific, and he folded off her with a sound that would have been funny under different circumstances. She was already moving—off the couch, past him as he lunged, catching a fistful of his hair on the way by.

The lock was clean.

The needle went in deep at the soft of his neck.

He came up like he was going to go another round.

Then he went down like a building losing its supports.

Out.

Lily stood over him, breathing for a moment.

Just a moment.

Then she pulled the robe back on.

Roka looked up as she came past, concern flickering across his face.

"Any trouble?"

"Handled."

She pulled out the transponder and the DNA interface Trish had given her and went back in, crouching beside Snake's considerable dead weight.

"Key... where's the key..."

She looked him over.

Then noticed the tattoo on his palm.

"Bingo."

She locked the interface in place. Retina. Finger. Palm.

"Trish. It's Lily. Do you copy?" She watched the display flip green. "Sending DNA access now."

"Got it." Trish's voice came back, bright with relief. "Lily, you did it. Decrypting now. Get your ass back here."

There was a spark of static. Then—

"Are you laughing?"

"Sorry, I'll tell you later," Lily said. She couldn't help thinking Xynn was going to love this story.

She glanced at Snake for a moment—sprawled, slack-jawed, breathing steadily through his nose.

"Snake," she said, shaking her head. "Appreciate the assist."

She exchanged a look with Roka on her way out.

"I'll handle the room," he said quietly. "Go."

Lily moved.

• • • •

Lily dropped out of the tube and into a different world.

Alarms layered over each other, constant and insistent, each one urgent and none of them specific. She pulled on the AR glasses as she moved. The display flickered once, then resolved into two words that hung in her vision.

System disruption.

Trish found her in under a minute, already moving, already reading the space as if she'd been there longer than she had.

"What's happening?" Lily asked.

"Rebels," Trish said. "Something with the core."

They cut across the floor toward a workstation tucked into the corner, one of the terminals still active, still pulling data despite the instability around them. Trish dropped into it, pulling up the tablet interface and dragging the decrypted file into view.

The bar sat at one hundred percent.

She scrolled fast, her eyes moving ahead of her hands.

Lily stepped in beside her, reading over her shoulder.

Manufacturing logs, full and unredacted. Distribution manipulation layered over them, systematic, deliberate. Priority tiers that kept the outer systems perpetually short, never collapsing, never stabilizing.

And at the end of it—

A location.

Bimini.

"Bimini," Lily said, the word catching something recent, something unfinished. "Caris was stationed there. I was just there with Xynn—right before the Bimara incident. I didn't see anything like this."

"Timeline could still work," Trish said, already moving past it, already building the next step.

The structure shuddered around them.

A jet of steam tore through a joint in the ceiling, venting downward in a violent plume as the alarms climbed another register, the sound sharpening, layering into something harder to ignore.

They moved toward the main square and stopped short at the edge.

The core was visible from the upper gantry—or what remained of it.

The rebels had triggered a cascade failure, the kind that fed itself, each broken system pulling the next one down in sequence. Structural supports buckled. Containment systems failed in layers. From below came the sound of flooding, of pressure surges, of systems giving way that were never meant to.

Lily raised the transponder.

"Veyshali."

The response came almost immediately.

"Already evacuated," Veyshali said, her voice tight beneath its composure. "We're aboard the Waqi-Reesh. Roka and Gadspar are with me. Lily, there are still pods—get to the upper levels now. They have already evacuated the entire Spire—"

Lily looked out over the square.

Workers running. People turning back from blocked routes, searching for exits that weren't there.

"No," she said, quiet but certain. "Not the entire Spire. Just the upper levels."

A brief silence.

Then Trish, her voice edged with something sharper now.

"They were never meant to make it out."

Veyshali was still speaking, her tone tightening, urging, insisting. Lily lowered the transponder without responding.

"What do you know about forced-flow gravity reactors?" Lily asked.

Trish glanced at her. "I'm not an engineer."

She was already pulling up her holo-tablet.

"But I have something better."

Data snapped into place, a schematic resolving in layered detail.

"Rebel files," she said, scrolling faster than Lily could follow. "I procured them during my time here."

She pointed to a node buried deep in the system.

"They planned to trigger the overload here. This coupling."

Lily leaned in, studying it, tracing the flow lines outward.

"That doesn't look like a primary system."

"Exactly," Trish said. "That's why they haven't found it. If they disabled the redundancies, you can patch everything else and it still builds. Pressure keeps feeding forward until the whole system tips."

Lily nodded once.

They turned back toward the chaos.

They found Chaffi and the boys at the edge of the lower corridor, gear already on, pushing against the current of people moving the other way.

Chaffi saw them and didn't hesitate.

"Boys." She caught each of them by the shoulders, quick and firm, something fierce and certain in the contact. "You stick with Shameli. I'm going to get Dad."

She was already backing into the steam.

"We'll make it off this pressure cooker together."

And then she was gone.

The space she left behind didn't close.

The corridor roared around them—heat, movement, bodies pressing past—but the three of them held for a second just outside of it.

Sonny and Chiff looked after her, then at each other.

Waiting.

Not moving.

Lily felt it immediately—the hesitation, the absence of direction, the moment where something needed to take shape or collapse.

She reached up and pulled off the mask.

Their eyes snapped back to her.

"I'm Lily," she said. "I'm sorry for the deception. I'll explain everything later. Right now I need to know if you'll help us."

They didn't answer right away.

Another glance between them, quick and searching, the kind that carried more than words.

They nodded.

Trish pushed the speeder hard in the opposite direction of the repair crews, cutting through smoke and noise and the particular chaos of a structure fighting itself. They curved around a massive support column, then cut through one of the vertical rivers, water sheeting across the windscreen in a blinding rush before clearing just as quickly.

Trish pointed.

"There."

The rupture was visible from thirty meters out, a ragged breach in the coupling housing, vapor tearing through it in violent pulses that shook the surrounding structure with each release.

"Can you seal that?" Lily called back.

Sonny was already moving, pulling equipment free and checking it as he spoke. "Just get us up to that platform."

Trish brought the speeder in tight alongside it, holding position against the shifting air as the boys moved past Lily and onto the narrow surface, already working before they'd fully settled their footing.

Lily watched the boys snap their protective gear into place. Tools came out fast, their movements precise and efficient, the kind of skill that came from growing up inside these systems.

The coupling resisted.

Then it gave.

Chiff torqued the seal into place, Sonny locking it down a second later, both of them leaning into it as if the system might push back.

For a moment, nothing happened.

Then the alarms began to quiet, one by one, the layered noise dropping off in increments until the space around them settled into something almost recognizable.

"We did it," Chiff said, the words coming out younger than he probably intended.

The boys grabbed each other, brief and hard.

Lily exhaled, the tightness in her chest easing a fraction.

The ride back was quiet.

The speeder moved through corridors settling into damage—steam still venting in places, debris scattered across the walkways, the particular stillness of systems that had been through something and survived. Lily watched it pass and felt the adrenaline beginning to ebb.

Then the damage got worse.

She noticed it first as a shift in texture—the walls more scored, the lighting gone in longer stretches, debris no longer scattered but piled. They were getting closer to the residential corridor, and the signs were moving in the wrong direction.

Sonny noticed it too. She saw it in the way he went still.

Trish eased the speeder down as they rounded the bend toward the landmarks that should have been there.

Should have been.

Where that section of the Spire had been, there was open space. A force field held the edge of the breach. Beyond it—nothing. The corridor, the residences, the whole familiar geography of the boys' home, simply gone. Taken in the cascade.

No one spoke.

The speeder held position, and the four of them stood in the low hum of it, looking at the place where something had been.

"I..." Lily turned the words over, searching for something that would meet the moment, and found nothing that did.

"We're so sorry," Trish said quietly. "For your loss."

Sonny's face was blank in the way that meant the understanding hadn't fully arrived yet. Chiff gripped the railing, staring at the force field as if it might shift, as if something might still be there behind it.

Lily opened her arms. The gesture felt awkward, insufficient, and she held it anyway.

Sonny stepped into it.

Chiff turned and wrapped his arms around his brother, and Trish rested a hand at the back of his shoulder.

For a moment they held there—imperfect and insufficient, but the only thing available.

They found someone the boys knew near the main square, made sure they weren't alone, and stayed with them until leaving felt possible.

Then Lily signaled Roka.

"Headed your way," he said. "Meet me at airlock 316."

• • • •

The Waqi-Reesh was quiet after the noise of the Spire. Lily felt the difference in her body before she fully registered it—the absence of alarms, of pressure, of things about to give way.

Roka was there, leaning back in the corner, watching the exchange.

Veyshali was pacing.

She looked at Trish the way she looked at most things—measuring, unhurried.

"Veyshali, this is Trish. A friend from Earth. She's part of the reason I got mixed up in all of this."

Veyshali's gaze moved over Trish once, top to bottom. A small nod. Approval, or something close enough to it.

"I'm surprised the evacuation happened so quickly," Trish said.

"There was already a plan in place." Veyshali's voice was even. "They knew the systems were vulnerable. It was only a matter of time. The upper Spire's residents are already en route to Alcron VI." She paused. "The Siphon-Spire Mark II."

Lily felt it land.

"So they planned to let those people burn," she said. "From the beginning."

Veyshali inclined her head, the motion small, almost restrained. "I was extended an invitation. I declined. I let them know I felt the entire venture was becoming somewhat..." She considered it. "...risky."

The silence that followed had weight.

No one moved to fill it.

Then the door opened and Gadspar stepped in carrying a tray of drinks, taking in the room in a single glance.

"So," he said. "What did I miss?"

The Mechanical Exception

THE ORBITAL EDUCATION center at Star Base 10 had the particular stillness of a place that had decided, collectively, that it was done for the day. The corridors were largely empty. The classrooms were dark. Maintenance drones buzzed along their routes, attending to the quiet work that never quite ended.

Ka-Lorrin stood at the entrance to Lab Seven, his arms folded at precisely the angle that indicated he was conducting a final inspection rather than simply standing still. He turned his head slowly, cataloguing the room—the cleaned terminals, the archived coursework, the immaculate boards—with the expression of someone who had arranged these things himself and was confirming they had not rearranged in his absence.

They had not.

He was satisfied.

Taran appeared behind him, ducking slightly through the doorway. He carried both packs, which was not unusual. He set Ka-Lorrin's down beside him without comment, which was also not unusual.

"Ready?" Taran asked.

"Nearly," Ka-Lorrin said, without moving.

Taran watched him for a moment, then turned to look at the room himself—the stacked chairs, the dimmed lighting, the faint smell of chalk dust and synthesized coffee that had come to define the last quarter-cycle of their lives. He lingered there a beat longer than necessary.

"Good students," he said finally, to no one in particular.

Ka-Lorrin made a small sound that was not quite agreement but was not disagreement either. Then he picked up his pack, squared his shoulders, and walked out.

. . . .

The temporary head of engineering met them at the docking connector with the energy of a man who had been counting down to this meeting for some time.

He was a narrow figure—a Cyranthian by the name of Dryst Rennick, with the kind of practiced efficiency about him that suggested he had once been capable and had spent the intervening years in environments that ground capability into caution. He shook Ka-Lorrin's hand once, firmly, and offered a data pad with his other hand before the handshake was technically finished.

"Everything's documented," he said. "Transfer logs, system adjustments, the deviation report from the tertiary coolant alignment—I flagged it, didn't touch it, felt that was your domain." He was already gesturing toward the ship. "Smooth handoff. Really straightforward. The crew is excellent. Excellent crew."

Ka-Lorrin took the data pad and glanced at it. "And the deviation in the coolant alignment—"

"Flagged," Rennick said. "Documented. In the report. Page seven, I believe. Possibly eight. All yours now." He clasped his hands together. "So. Unless you need anything else—"

"I have a number of questions," Ka-Lorrin said.

Rennick smiled in the manner of someone being extremely polite under considerable strain. "Of course. Perhaps we could—walk and talk? I do have a connector to catch."

They did not walk and talk.

Ka-Lorrin asked his questions standing in the corridor. Rennick answered them in sequence with diminishing specificity, his eyes occasionally drifting toward the connector bay. By the time the third question had been answered, Rennick had one hand on the wall in the directional posture of a man building momentum toward departure.

"Excellent," Ka-Lorrin said, when he had heard enough. "Very good. Thank you for your service."

Rennick was gone before the sentence ended.

They watched him go. Something in the man's posture—the relief of it, the particular looseness that settled into his shoulders once the corner was turned—registered as information.

"Sure was in a hurry, he was," Taran said.

Ka-Lorrin was already reading the data pad and barely looked up. "He likely wished to avoid immediate scrutiny," he said, waving a hand as he started toward the main concourse.

They hadn't gone far before they ran into Alrek, taking a day's leave during the stopover.

"Kal—will you look who it is," Taran beamed.

"My goodness, you've grown a foot, young man," Ka-Lorrin said without a hint of sarcasm.

Alrek straightened when he saw them. The smile that followed was unguarded in a way that most of his expressions had learned not to be—the kind that arrived before he could arrange it into something more measured. He crossed the distance between them and leaned into Taran's bear hug.

"It's so good to see you both," he said. "How were the cadets?"

"Exceptional," Ka-Lorrin said, in the tone he used for things he had decided upon in advance. "We had four students in particular—a full assessment will be forthcoming. One of them understood ionic resonance faster than I would have believed possible for her age bracket. I intend to write a letter."

"You already wrote two," Taran said.

Ka-Lorrin ignored him.

Alrek smiled. "They missed you in engineering."

"As well they should," Ka-Lorrin said, with the slight lift of chin that served as his version of warmth. "We'll see you there shortly. This coolant alignment—"

"I'll see you on board," Alrek said.

There was a fraction of a pause—small enough to pass unnoticed, unless one was looking for it.

Taran scratched at his chin as Alrek turned, noticing who he was meeting.

"Isn't that Ensign Simons from the life sciences lab?" Ka-Lorrin observed. "It's encouraging to see cross-disciplinary collaboration at this stage. I wonder what sort of experiment they might be conducting."

Alrek and the young woman walked off arm in arm.

Taran smiled and shook his head.

• • • •

The first thing Ka-Lorrin noticed was that the deck plating had been buffed.

Not cleaned. Buffed.

The corridor held a brightness that did not belong to a ship in constant use. The faint scoring of foot traffic was gone. The subtle variations that accumulated over time—erased. The surface gleamed with a uniformity that suggested someone had decided what belonged and what did not.

Ka-Lorrin looked at it.

Then he walked on.

Two crew members passed in the opposite direction. Correct uniform. Correct posture. Correct pace. One met Ka-Lorrin's eye and gave a brief, vertical nod—the kind that conveyed acknowledgment and nothing else.

Ka-Lorrin returned it, already looking past them.

Further on, a junior officer stood at a side console entering data. She did not look up as they passed. Her focus was absolute, her hands moving with practiced precision across the interface.

Ka-Lorrin slowed, almost imperceptibly.

Nothing changed.

No glance. No shift in posture. No flicker of awareness that another person had entered her space.

She kept entering data.

"There are bound to be some differences," Ka-Lorrin said, with the measured confidence of someone explaining weather. "It's been a quarter-cycle. New command cadence. We'll normalize within a few days."

"Mm," said Taran.

They turned a corner. A small cluster of crew members stood outside the mess hall, waiting for the shift change. Not quite a line. Not quite a group. They stood in a loose arrangement that tightened just slightly when footsteps approached. One of them glanced at Ka-Lorrin, then away.

"Mm?" Ka-Lorrin said.

"Nothing," Taran said. "Just mm."

They walked the rest of the way to engineering in a silence that Taran filled with observation and Ka-Lorrin filled with the mental equivalent of a very long list.

. . . .

Engineering received them the way a room receives people when it has been prepared for their arrival.

Ka-Lorrin registered none of this.

He walked in, set his pack down with the satisfied precision of someone returning a borrowed object to its correct drawer, and began.

"Right. Flow regulators—Rennick's report mentions a deviation on the tertiary coolant alignment which we'll need to address before the end of second shift, so I'd like that flagged as a priority alongside the plasma injector calibration logs from the past three cycles, which I suspect will show an output variance on long hauls that has been undercorrected—the variance will be subtle but it compounds, it always compounds, and the atmospheric scrubber recalibration is also overdue, I noted that the air recyclers on deck four have been operating at standard rather than optimized—who are you?"

He turned mid-sentence and found himself facing an unfamiliar junior engineer, who was looking at him with the wide, careful eyes of someone who had not yet determined whether they wanted to be addressed.

The young man blinked. "Jorcan, sir. Junior Engineer Jorcan."

Ka-Lorrin studied him with full attention and mild suspicion. "Are you certain?"

"I—yes?"

"Very well. Jorcan."

Ka-Lorrin returned to the console as though the matter had been resolved.

"The thruster coupling—"

Taran caught Jorcan's eye from across the room and gave a slow, reassuring nod that communicated: this is normal, you are fine, and he is not actually suspicious of your name.

Jorcan appeared only partially comforted.

Ka-Lorrin worked for approximately four minutes before reaching for the shift roster—not looking for anything in particular, simply orienting himself. He scrolled with one long finger, cataloguing names and assignments with the quiet satisfaction of confirming correct things.

He stopped.

He scrolled back.

He read the entry again, this time with the focused attention of someone who has found an error and is allowing it the opportunity to correct itself.

It did not.

"Alrek isn't on the engineering roster," Ka-Lorrin said. Calmly. Clearly. "This week, or—" He scrolled further. "At all. He's not scheduled in engineering at all."

Taran, crouched beside the secondary workbench checking the coolant deviation, did not immediately respond.

"There's been an error in the scheduling system," Ka-Lorrin said. "Clearly. Rennick must have—or the transfer of records—someone has—" He set the data pad down, then picked it up again. "It's a clerical matter. I'll have it corrected."

"Kal," Taran said.

"It's clearly a clerical matter," Ka-Lorrin said again, in the tone of someone becoming more certain because they are not.

Ka-Lorrin began making adjustments immediately.

The shift rotations were misaligned—subtly, but measurably. He corrected the stagger, flagged the change, and submitted the update.

"Authorization required."

He paused.

Then he resubmitted it through a different pathway.

"Authorization required."

Ka-Lorrin inclined his head slightly, as though the system had said something unexpected but not yet incorrect.

"Very well," he said.

He moved on.

The tertiary coolant alignment required a minor redistribution of personnel. He reassigned two engineers, balanced the load across the secondary team, and confirmed the update.

"Assignment locked."

Ka-Lorrin looked at the console.

Then at it again.

He reached for the override.

"Restricted access."

A small silence followed.

"Interesting," he said.

Across the room, Taran watched a technician at the far station complete a diagnostic cycle. The woman finished, checked the result, then checked it again. When a secondary alert flickered, she did not call for assistance. She cleared it herself, carefully, and only then moved on.

No one spoke.

Ka-Lorrin crossed to another station. The atmospheric recyclers on deck four were still running at standard output. He entered the recalibration sequence.

"Authorization required."

He stopped.

He withdrew his hands from the console with deliberate care.

"Temporary restriction," he said.

He opened the approvals queue.

There were already six entries waiting.

He added three more.

"Expedited," he said, marking each request with precise emphasis. "These will need to be prioritized."

The system accepted the designation.

Nothing else happened.

Time passed.

Not much. Enough.

Ka-Lorrin reviewed the coolant data. Then the injector logs. Then the alignment report. He did not sit. Sitting would have suggested a pause in function.

Behind him, a crew member approached a console, entered a command, and waited.

And waited.

When the console finally responded, the crew member moved quickly—too quickly—executing three actions in rapid succession before the next delay could assert itself again.

The room moved in starts.

Stop. Wait. Act.

Stop. Wait. Act.

Taran shifted his weight from one foot to the other, watching it happen. His eyes moved from station to station, tracking the rhythm of it—the hesitations, the sudden bursts of motion, the way people seemed to operate alone even when they stood within arm's reach of one another.

Ka-Lorrin checked the queue again.

"Pending," the system informed him.

"Yes," Ka-Lorrin said.

He adjusted a parameter on the coolant simulation and submitted the change.

"Authorization required."

He did not speak this time.

A notification chimed.

Then another.

Then three in quick succession.

Ka-Lorrin turned.

The approvals queue cleared all at once.

Every request—approved.

The room changed.

Consoles lit up across the floor. Crew members moved immediately, almost simultaneously, hands flying across interfaces as delayed tasks activated in clusters. Two engineers converged on the same station, hesitated, then adjusted without speaking. Another nearly collided with a passing technician, both correcting their paths with abrupt precision.

"Now," Ka-Lorrin said.

No one heard him.

A tool tray clattered as someone moved too quickly. A diagnostic feed spiked and corrected. Orders were executed, not exchanged.

The room had gone from stillness to motion without passing through anything resembling coordination.

Ka-Lorrin stood in the center of it, watching.

He looked at one console. Then another. Then at the queue, now empty.

Then back at the floor.

"This," he said, very clearly, "is no way to work."

Taran glanced at him, then back at the room.

He didn't say anything.

. . . .

The room had not quite settled when the request was sent.

It took longer than it should have.

Alrek arrived a few minutes later.

He stepped through the engineering doors with the same composed efficiency Ka-Lorrin had been observing all afternoon—posture straight, attention forward, eyes already moving to take in the room before settling on them. There was warmth when he saw them. It just arrived a fraction later than it used to.

"Ka-Lorrin. Taran."

"Alrek," Ka-Lorrin said, as though they had been in the middle of a conversation rather than waiting for him. "Excellent. We've encountered a minor procedural constraint. You appear to be—" he glanced briefly at the data pad in his hand "—rather extensively engaged in command functions."

Alrek nodded once. "I've been assisting on the bridge."

"Mm. Yes." Ka-Lorrin made a small, thoughtful sound. "Then you'll be in a position to facilitate the transfer of command clearances back to engineering, at least for the duration of your scheduled shifts. We are encountering unnecessary delays."

Alrek shifted his weight slightly. "I can... see what I can do. Captain Dalren prefers a tighter approval structure."

"Yes," Ka-Lorrin said. "That has become evident."

He tapped the data pad once, then looked up again.

"When is your next scheduled shift in engineering?" he asked. "I did not see it on the duty roster."

Alrek didn't answer immediately.

The pause was not long.

It was long enough.

Taran's head tilted, just slightly. "Kal..."

Ka-Lorrin looked at Alrek.

Then at the data pad.

Then back at him.

"Oh," he said.

It was a small word. It landed heavily anyway.

"I see."

He adjusted his grip on the data pad, smoothing the edge of it with his thumb as though that required attention.

"Well," he said, with careful neutrality. "Just don't forget about us down here."

A beat.

"Impossible to get anything done if I don't have command clearances," he added, almost as an afterthought.

Alrek took a step closer. "It's not—" He stopped, recalibrated. "It's not personal. This is... it's a good opportunity. I'm shadowing Captain Dalren. Learning how the ship runs at that level."

"I'm sure," Ka-Lorrin said.

Another alarm chimed from somewhere in the room—sharp, insistent, followed by a cascade of smaller alerts as systems caught up to themselves again.

Taran glanced toward the nearest console, then back at Alrek.

"Maybe come back later, yeah?" he said gently. "When it's not all—" he gestured vaguely at the room "—this."

Alrek nodded. "Yeah. I will."

He hesitated for just a moment longer, then turned and moved back toward the door, already shifting his attention to the next thing that required it.

Taran watched him go.

Ka-Lorrin had already turned back to the console.

"Right," he said. "The coolant alignment."

• • • •

They arrived at Dalren's office right on time.

Dryst Amaris had explained that Dalren had elected not to use Captain Calan's stateroom. Instead, he had combined it with the neighboring conference room and redesignated the space as the captain's office.

The result, Ka-Lorrin had noted, would rival the C&C's office—a point he made to Dryst Amaris, and then again to Taran as they waited to be let in.

"It just seems inappropriate," he said under his breath as the door finally opened with a sharp swish.

Dalren sat behind a desk that seemed to have been selected less for comfort than for authority—broad, angular, and positioned to dominate the room. He appeared occupied when they entered, reviewing something on the display with a focus that suggested importance rather than urgency.

He did not look up immediately.

Then he did.

"Chief Engineer," he said. "Taran."

His gaze moved between them once, then settled.

"Is your associate required for this discussion?"

Ka-Lorrin did not pause.

"The Raath-Ka are a symbiotic species," he said. "I could no more attend a meeting without Taran than you could sit without those rather elaborate buttocks your species relies upon."

There was a small, immediate silence.

Taran closed his eyes briefly.

Dalren's posture tightened—not dramatically, but enough.

"I see," he said.

"You should review the species and cultural fact sheets for your senior staff," Ka-Lorrin added, with measured precision.

Another beat.

Dalren gestured, minimally. "Speak."

Ka-Lorrin stepped forward, data pad in hand.

"There are a number of structural inefficiencies within engineering that appear to be the result of revised authorization protocols," he said. "Most notably, the absence of Alrek from the engineering roster. This creates unnecessary bottlenecks in both diagnostic response and systems optimization. His presence—even on a limited basis—would increase operational efficiency by a measurable margin."

Dalren listened without interruption.

"The current structure is intentional," he said when Ka-Lorrin finished. "Clear lines of authority. Controlled access. Reduced variance."

"Yes," Ka-Lorrin said. "The reduction in variance has been... pronounced."

Dalren's eyes flicked toward him. "It has been effective."

"It has been consistent," Ka-Lorrin corrected. "Effectiveness remains… under evaluation."

A beat.

Dalren's jaw set, just slightly.

"Alrek is assigned to command support," he said. "That assignment reflects current operational priorities."

"Which he is uniquely qualified to assist with," Ka-Lorrin said. "And also uniquely qualified to assist with engineering, which is currently experiencing delays due to those same priorities."

Dalren's expression did not change.

"Alrek requested reassignment," Dalren said. "He is pursuing command track integration. I approved it."

A small silence settled.

Taran shifted, just enough to be felt.

"I see," Ka-Lorrin said.

This time, the words carried weight.

Dalren inclined his head once, as though the matter had been settled.

"Adjustments take time," he said. "The crew will adapt."

Ka-Lorrin looked at him.

"Yes," he said. "That appears to be the expectation."

A soft chime interrupted them.

Dalren lifted a hand to his ear, turning slightly away.

"Dalren," he said.

A pause.

"Confirmed."

Another.

"No, that is not consistent with the failure parameters."

His focus sharpened.

"Expand the scan radius. Isolate the—"

He stopped.

"I see."

A longer pause.

"Understood. Continue transmission."

He lowered his hand.

The room settled again.

"The Siphon-Spire did not fail by accident," Ka-Lorrin said.

Dalren looked at him.

"Excuse me?"

"I have reviewed the structural schematics," Ka-Lorrin said. "Redundant systems layered across all critical functions. Failure of that magnitude would require either catastrophic external force or deliberate internal override. Random collapse is statistically improbable."

Dalren stared at him.

"How could you possibly—"

"You should review species profiles for your crew, Captain," Ka-Lorrin said, with mild irritation. "The Ka possess exceptionally acute hearing. It is, in fact, a continual challenge not to be overwhelmed by ambient conversation. You are all, generally speaking, quite loud."

Taran stifled a chortle.

Dalren drew a breath. Then another.

"I can allocate Alrek to engineering for three shifts per week," he said. "To assist with transition."

Ka-Lorrin inclined his head.

"Acceptable," he said.

The moment held, then passed.

Ka-Lorrin turned.

"Thank you for your time..." he said, with precise formality.

A fractional pause.

"Acting Captain Dalren."

Dalren said nothing.

They stepped out into the corridor, the door closing behind them.

After several paces in silence, Taran leaned slightly closer.

"He turned a funny color, he did," he said under his breath.

. . . .

The *Salamander* slipped into orbit with the controlled precision of a ship that had been instructed not to waste motion.

Below them, the Siphon-Spire hung above Marduk III—silent. Its vast structure stretched impossibly into the upper atmosphere, but the light that once moved through it was gone. What remained was a shape without motion. A system without function.

Dead was not quite the word.

Dormant, perhaps.

The evacuation had already begun. Shuttles moved in steady lines between the Spire and the staging platforms below, their paths clean, deliberate, regulated. Salvage vessels held position at fixed intervals, maintaining distance as though proximity itself required permission.

On the bridge, the air was quiet in the way it had been everywhere else.

Dalren stood at the center command position, hands clasped behind his back, watching the operation unfold across the main display. Orders were issued without raised voices. Acknowledgments were immediate. No one spoke unless required.

Ka-Lorrin stood slightly off to one side, arms folded. Taran beside him.

"They're staging the evacuation in quadrants," Taran murmured, mostly to himself.

"Yes," Ka-Lorrin said. "Sequential, controlled. It minimizes variance."

Taran glanced at him.

"Mm," he said.

A voice cut in over the comm.

"Salvage to *Salamander*—we've isolated a priority recovery unit from the Siphon-Spire's central systems. Data integrity unknown, but the casing is intact. Requesting transfer authorization."

Dalren did not hesitate.

"Authorized," he said. "Route it directly to engineering. Full containment protocols."

There was a brief pause.

"Engineering?" the voice asked.

Dalren's gaze shifted, just slightly, toward Ka-Lorrin.

"Yes," he said. "Our chief engineer will be... reacquainting himself with the current operational environment."

A beat.

"And I'm sure he will find it... appropriately structured."

It was not quite a smile.

It was, unmistakably, an attempt.

Taran made a small sound.

Ka-Lorrin inclined his head, accepting the statement as though it had been offered in perfect seriousness.

"Structure is not inherently objectionable," he said. "Its application is."

Dalren's mouth tightened—not quite in irritation, not quite in restraint.

"Indeed," he said. "You'll have an opportunity to evaluate it firsthand."

He gestured, minimally.

"Engineering."

. . . .

The black box arrived under escort.

It was smaller than the Spire that had produced it, but only in the way a fragment of something enormous is smaller—dense, self-contained, carrying its origin with it. The casing was sealed, matte, unmarked beyond a series of embedded ports that suggested access points without offering any.

The technician who delivered it set it down on the secondary workbench with visible care—and just as visible relief.

"Recovered from central data routing," she said. "We didn't open it. Didn't try."

"Correct," Ka-Lorrin said.

She nodded, once, and stepped back.

Taran was already moving toward it.

He lifted the unit slightly, testing its weight, turning it once in his hands with the slow, deliberate attention he gave to things that had decided to be difficult.

"Air-gapped," he said.

"Obviously," Ka-Lorrin replied, already scanning the interface ports.

"Layered encryption," Taran added. "Deep."

He set it down again, gentler this time.

Ka-Lorrin stepped beside him. Looked at the casing. The ports. The absence of any external interface.

He considered it for a moment longer than he intended to.

"Yes," he said.

Then he turned back to the console.

"Set up a sandbox environment," he said. "We will determine what it is willing to reveal before we ask it anything more."

Taran nodded.

"Mm."

The room settled around them again—quiet, controlled, waiting.

The box did not move.

But it did not feel inert.

• • • •

Alrek returned to engineering during his rotation window with the slightly careful energy of someone who had been thinking about what they wanted to say and had decided not to say most of it.

He paused just inside the threshold, taking in the room—the consoles, the movement, Ka-Lorrin already at work—and then crossed toward them.

"Ka-Lorrin. Taran."

"Alrek," Ka-Lorrin said, without looking up. "Excellent. The coolant alignment is still operating below acceptable thresholds. We will correct that now that we have appropriate access."

Alrek nodded. "Right."

He moved to the adjacent console, glancing briefly at the readout before beginning to work. His hands were steady. Familiar. The motions came easily.

Ka-Lorrin shifted the data stream toward him without comment.

"There," he said. "If you re-route the secondary feed—no, the other—yes. That will stabilize the variance."

Alrek made the adjustment.

The system responded immediately.

For a moment, the rhythm returned. Clean. Efficient. Shared.

Ka-Lorrin allowed himself the smallest nod.

"Yes," he said. "That is correct."

A beat.

Alrek stepped back from the console.

"I should probably flag that for the next maintenance window," he said. "Just to keep everything aligned with the current schedule."

"The current schedule is already misaligned," Ka-Lorrin replied. "We will correct it."

Alrek hesitated.

"Dalren prefers—" he began, then stopped. "There's a process now."

"Yes," Ka-Lorrin said. "We have encountered it."

Another small pause.

Ka-Lorrin adjusted the display, scrolling through the alignment logs with deliberate precision.

"I suppose we can take care of that in two days," he said. "When you're back."

Alrek didn't answer immediately.

It wasn't a long pause.

It was long enough.

"It's good to be back working with you two," he said at last. "But you have to understand—right now my priorities are focused on this opportunity Dalren gave me. I'm shadowing him. Learning how command operates."

Ka-Lorrin continued scrolling.

"Yes," he said.

"If I want to change my track," Alrek added, more quietly, "to command."

Something clattered.

Taran had dropped a tool.

He stared at it for a moment as though it had betrayed him personally.

"Change track?" he said.

He bent slowly, picked it up, then set it back down with exaggerated care.

"Oh no," he murmured. "No, no, no..."

He turned away, already moving toward the far end of the room with the loose, drifting motion of someone who had decided they were not going to be part of this conversation and also could not leave it entirely.

Ka-Lorrin did not look up.

"Of course I understand," he said.

He adjusted a control that did not require adjusting.

"It will take Taran some time."

Taran, across the room, made a small sound.

Ka-Lorrin scrolled once more through the display, then stopped.

"See you Thursday," he said.

Alrek stood there for a moment longer, as though something more might be required.

Nothing was.

He nodded once.

"Thursday," he said.

Then he turned and left.

Taran watched him go.

Ka-Lorrin had already returned to the console.

"Right," he said. "The alignment."

· · · ·

The evacuation had already reached a steady rhythm by the time Alrek made his way down to the intake deck.

Shuttles cycled through in controlled intervals, offloading small groups of Spire workers into the holding corridor before routing them onward for processing. The air carried the low, continuous noise of movement—boots on deck plating, distant calls, the muted whine of atmospheric seals cycling open and closed.

Caris stood near the center of it, directing the flow with the kind of quiet authority that made people move before they realized they had been told to.

Alrek approached as another shuttle finished docking.

"Commander," he said.

She glanced over, a brief flicker of recognition breaking through the focus.

"Alrek," she said. "Good timing."

He fell into step beside her, watching as the next group was guided forward.

"Looked like a close call up there," she added, nodding toward the incoming evacuees. "From what we're hearing."

Alrek nodded once. "Closer than it should have been."

A disturbance broke the rhythm.

Two security officers emerged from the far end of the corridor, escorting a man in restraints. He moved with uneven energy—half dragging, half lunging—his voice already raised before he reached them.

"I'm telling you—she came out of nowhere—"

"Keep moving," one of the guards said.

The man twisted against the restraint field.

"I want it on record—"

Caris stepped forward.

"What's the issue?"

The first guard shifted his grip. "He took a swing at one of the officers during intake."

"And a kick," the second added.

Caris looked at the man.

"What's your problem?"

He barked a sharp, humorless laugh.

"My problem? My problem is that storm-cursed lunatic knocked me out and the next thing I know the whole place is coming apart around me!"

He leaned forward as far as the restraints would allow.

"She jumps me—just takes me out—and I'm the one in cuffs?"

Caris didn't react.

"Take him to the brig," she said.

The guards began to move him past.

"Nobody robs ol' Snake!" he shouted, twisting back toward them. "You hear me? Nobody!"

They kept walking.

"She tricked me to access files! I saw right through her disguise—" he called over his shoulder. "Check the footage! It was a wig!"

He jerked against the field again, eyes wild.

"She had short brown hair—I saw it!"

The corridor seemed to narrow for a moment.

Caris stopped.

Alrek looked at her.

She looked back.

"You don't think..."

. . . .

Ka-Lorrin was recalibrating the plasma injector logs when Taran said, for the third time,

"I can't get in, I can't."

"Mm," Ka-Lorrin replied, not looking up. "That is not unexpected."

"It's not just locked," Taran said. "It's layered. There's a whole... thing on top of the thing."

"Yes," Ka-Lorrin said. "Containment architecture."

"That's what I said."

"You did not."

Taran made a small, dissatisfied sound and adjusted the diagnostic lead, turning the black box slightly on the workbench as though a different angle might persuade it to cooperate.

Ka-Lorrin continued working.

"It is, of course, a sensible development path," he said after a moment. "Exposure to command operations. Broader systems awareness. Alrek has always demonstrated a capacity for... integration."

"Mm," Taran said.

"He will find that engineering remains the most efficient application of his abilities," Ka-Lorrin continued. "In time."

Taran tapped the side of the box.

"It's not that I don't understand it," he said. "I do understand it. It just won't let me in, it won't."

"Yes," Ka-Lorrin said. "That is generally the point of such systems."

"He'll be back," Ka-Lorrin added, adjusting a parameter that did not strictly require adjustment. "Once the novelty has worn off. It is important that we allow for exploration within reasonable bounds."

"Mm."

Taran leaned closer to the readout.

"There's a sandbox over the core," he said. "Not just a lock—a whole environment. It's like it's pretending to be something else so you don't see what it actually is."

Ka-Lorrin glanced over, briefly.

"Yes," he said. "That would be consistent with a system designed to survive catastrophic failure."

Taran was quiet for a moment.

Then—

"I could connect it to the main system," he said.

Ka-Lorrin looked up.

"That seems inadvisable."

"It should be safe," Taran said. "It's containment-rated. It shouldn't have any network commands. It would just... solve it faster. Let the ship do the thinking."

"Unless," Ka-Lorrin said.

Taran considered that.

"Unless," he agreed.

They both looked at the box.

Neither of them touched it.

A beat passed.

Ka-Lorrin turned back to his console.

"Yes," he said. "Well. We will require command authorization in any case."

He reached for the comm.

"I will call Alrek."

·　·　·　·

Alrek arrived to find both of them talking.

Not to him.

At him.

"The sandbox isn't the problem, it's what's behind it—"

"—layered encryption over a containment architecture, which suggests—"

"—it's pretending to be something it isn't—"

"—which would be consistent with—"

"Okay."

Alrek held up a hand.

Both of them stopped.

Not immediately.

But close enough.

"Slow down," he said. "What exactly do you need?"

A beat.

Taran pointed at the box.

"I need a mainframe with a lot more power to crack this thing," he said.

Alrek nodded once.

"That makes sense."

"It does?" Ka-Lorrin said.

"Yes," Alrek said. "The ship's firewall should be sufficient to guard against anything we don't want."

"Anything except mechanical functions," Ka-Lorrin said.

Alrek glanced at him.

"Exactly," he said. "And it's what—essentially a journal, right? Data logs, recovery protocols, that sort of thing."

Taran nodded.

"Mm."

Alrek stepped in beside him, already moving.

"I'll use my command codes to authorize the connection."

Ka-Lorrin watched him for a fraction of a second.

Then nodded.

"Very well."

Taran connected the lead.

Alrek entered the authorization.

The system accepted it.

For a moment—

nothing.

Then the lights flickered.

Once.

Twice.

The console beneath Taran's hands went dark, then came back all at once, data streaming too quickly to read.

"What the—" Taran said.

The deck shifted.

Not violently.

Precisely.

As though something very large had decided to move.

Alrek's head snapped toward the main display.

"No," he said.

Another shift—stronger this time. A low, rising vibration moved through the deck plating, building into a steady, mechanical hum.

"It thinks—" Alrek said, scanning the data, "—it thinks the main engines are the reactor of the Siphon-Spire."

"The mechanical exception," Ka-Lorrin said.

Around them, alarms began to sound.

Not one.

Several.

Layered.

Navigation. Power distribution. Structural stress.

The hum deepened into motion.

"Bad," Taran said. "Bad—how do we turn it off?"

"I don't know," Alrek said.

The words came too fast.

Too honest.

The ship lurched.

Not sideways.

Forward.

Then—

around.

The main display spun as the *Salamander* entered a controlled—but rapidly tightening—spiral, stars streaking into curved lines across the viewport feed.

A voice cut through the alarms.

"Dalren to main engineering. What the hell is going on? The ship just went into a spiral at relativistic velocity!"

Ka-Lorrin did not raise his voice.

"Working on it, sir," he said.

He was already moving, hands flying across the console, trying to isolate a system that no longer appeared to recognize itself.

Taran grabbed the edge of the workbench as the deck shifted again.

"Kal—"

Ka-Lorrin did not look at him.

"What," he said, very precisely, "are we going to do?"

. . . .

The alarms layered one on top of the other.

Power surged through systems that had not requested it. Diagnostics flooded the displays faster than they could be parsed. The spiral tightened—controlled, but accelerating.

Ka-Lorrin moved first.

"Shut down auxiliary routing," he said, already at the console. "If it is drawing power through redundant pathways, we will remove the redundancy."

"I can't," Taran said. "It keeps rewriting the paths, it does—every time I cut one, it reroutes through another."

The deck lurched again.

Alrek caught the edge of the station, already scanning the data stream.

"It's not rerouting," he said. "It's rebuilding. It's reconstructing the Spire's network on top of ours."

"Then we remove the core," Ka-Lorrin said.

"There is no core," Taran said. "Not one we can see."

"There must be," Ka-Lorrin said. "All systems resolve to—"

"They don't," Alrek cut in. "Not like this. It's not looking for a system—it's looking for a role."

Another spike—brighter this time. The main engines surged.

"Kal—" Taran said.

"I see it," Ka-Lorrin said.

He didn't.

Not yet.

Alrek was already moving.

He crossed to the central console, pulling up the command overlay, forcing the system into a frame he could understand.

"It's not just running a recovery protocol," he said. "It's waiting for input."

"From what?" Taran said.

"From us," Alrek said.

Another lurch—harder. The spiral tightened again, stars bending further across the display.

"It thinks we're the Spire," Alrek said. "Which means—"

"Which means it expects control authorization," Ka-Lorrin said, arriving at the same conclusion a fraction of a second later.

Taran looked between them.

"Authorization from who?"

Alrek froze.

Then—

"Not command codes," he said.

He turned back to the black box, eyes narrowing.

"Human interface."

"What?" Taran said.

"It's not looking for system clearance—it's looking for *ownership*," Alrek said. "A biometric key."

Another alarm cut through the others—structural stress climbing.

"Access codes," Alrek said.

He moved for the comm.

"Access codes!"

He hit the channel.

"Alrek to Caris."

A burst of static. Then—

"Caris here."

"Bring that rude prisoner to main engineering," Alrek said. "Now. And hurry."

A beat.

"Wha—" she started.

Then, sharper: "On it."

Alrek dropped the channel.

Behind him, Ka-Lorrin was already rebalancing power flow, forcing the system to hold together just long enough to matter.

"Time," Ka-Lorrin said.

"I know," Alrek replied.

Taran was back at the box, hands moving faster now, not trying to break in—preparing it.

"It's ready," he said. "Soon as we have the key—"

Another violent shift cut him off.

The *Salamander* tightened its spiral again.

Not much time.

. . . .

The doors to engineering slid open hard enough to register.

Caris came through first.

Snake came with her.

He was still in restraints, still under guard—but he was smiling.

Not broadly.

Just enough.

The look of a man who had decided, very quickly, that this situation might finally be interesting.

"Well," he said, looking around as the alarms screamed and the deck shifted beneath his feet. "This feels familiar."

"Move," Caris said.

He did. Casually.

"If this is the part where you apologize," he added, "I'm prepared to be generous."

"Stand there," Caris said, stopping him in front of the central console.

He leaned slightly, testing the restraint field like it was a suggestion rather than a limitation.

"Nice place," he said. "Bit tense. You always run it like this?"

"Snake," Alrek said, stepping forward. "We need your access key."

Snake looked at him.

Then at the console.

Then back at him.

"And here I thought this was a social call."

"We don't have time," Alrek said. "That box—whatever's in it—it's trying to run the ship like it's the Siphon-Spire. We need a biometric authorization to shut it down."

Snake tilted his head.

"So you broke your own ship," he said. "Impressive. Really. That takes effort."

Another alarm cut through the room.

The deck lurched.

Caris didn't move.

"Do it," she said.

Snake smiled.

"Or?" he asked.

Caris said nothing.

She didn't need to.

Ka-Lorrin stepped in, calm as ever.

"We can certainly continue negotiating," he said, "or we can all become brown paste adhered to the walls in approximately—" he glanced at the readout "—eight minutes."

A beat.

Snake looked at him.

Then at the spinning data on the display.

Then at the deck, which chose that moment to shift again—harder.

He exhaled.

"Fine," he said. "But this doesn't make us even."

"No one said it did," Caris replied.

Snake stepped forward as far as the restraints allowed.

"Drop the field," he said.

Caris nodded once.

The guard disengaged it.

Snake flexed his hands, rolled his shoulders, then leaned into the console like he belonged there.

"Try to keep up," he muttered.

He moved fast—faster than his attitude suggested he should be capable of. The interface resisted for a fraction of a second, then—

Accepted.

The system shifted.

Not violently this time.

Decisively.

The spiral began to unwind.

Power levels dropped—fast, but controlled. Alarms cut out one by one, the layered noise collapsing into silence.

The deck steadied.

The stars outside the viewport resolved back into points.

For a moment—

nothing moved.

Then—

Taran let out a breath that turned into something halfway between a laugh and a collapse.

"Oh me, oh me," he said.

Ka-Lorrin straightened, adjusting a control that no longer needed adjusting.

"Yes," he said. "That is preferable."

Alrek stepped back from the console, running a hand through his hair, adrenaline still catching up to him.

Caris reached for Snake's arm.

He leaned slightly away, just enough to be noticed.

"You know," he said, glancing at her, "if this is your idea of a date, you should've led with it."

She didn't respond.

She simply took him by the arm and started walking.

He seemed to enjoy being led out a little too much.

Caris didn't break stride as they disappeared through the doors.

The room settled.

The four of them stood in it.

Alive.

Intact.

Together.

Hands found shoulders. A quick clasp. A solid thump between shoulder blades.

Alrek smiled, broad and unguarded.

"We did it."

. . . .

Dalren did not sit when they entered.

"Thank you for your thorough report," he said. "The data you recovered is… unsettling, to say the least."

Ka-Lorrin inclined his head.

"We could not have done it without Alrek," he said.

Alrek gave a small smile.

"We make a good team."

Dalren regarded them for a moment, then nodded once.

"After we wrap up our mission here," he said, "I believe we may take a slight detour."

A beat.

"Something not on the official manifest."

His gaze sharpened, just slightly.

"I want to see what's going on on Bimini for myself."

The three of them exchanged a look.

No one spoke.

* * * *

Engineering had returned to something recognizable.

Not what it had been.

Closer.

The systems were stable. The noise had settled. Work resumed—not in bursts, not in starts, but in a steady rhythm that felt, if not comfortable, at least familiar.

Ka-Lorrin was at the central console.

Taran at the secondary bench.

Alrek stood between them for a moment before stepping in.

"I've been thinking," he said.

Neither of them stopped working.

That was, in its way, permission.

"I love engineering," Alrek continued. "That hasn't changed. It's still where I feel… useful. Where I know what I'm doing."

Ka-Lorrin made a small sound.

"Yes," he said. "That is evident."

Alrek let that sit.

"But I don't want that to be the only place I can be useful," he said. "I want to understand more. To be in rooms where decisions are made. To be—" He searched for it. "Respected there, too."

Taran glanced over.

Ka-Lorrin did not.

"I know I didn't explain it well," Alrek added. "Before."

"No," Ka-Lorrin said. "You did not."

A beat.

"I also did not ask," he continued, adjusting a control that did not require adjusting.

Silence settled.

Not heavy.

Just present.

Taran set his tool down.

"Kal," he said, gently.

Ka-Lorrin exhaled once through his nose, as though something had been recalibrated internally.

He turned.

"Alrek," he said.

He paused.

Not for effect.

For accuracy.

"People will respect you wherever you go," he said. "Provided you conduct yourself according to this—"

He touched his chest, briefly.

"—as much as this."

He tapped the side of his head.

A beat.

"Taran serves as my heart," he added. "Frequently."

Taran brightened slightly.

"Mm."

"You have both available to you," Ka-Lorrin continued. "Whether you choose to use them efficiently remains to be seen."

Another beat.

"You performed well today," he said. "In both capacities."

Alrek smiled.

"I like command," he said. "But I'm not giving this up."

He gestured lightly around the room.

"I'll keep my engineering studies. Keep working shifts."

He looked at them both.

"And I love you both."

There was a very small pause.

Ka-Lorrin blinked once.

Twice.

"That is—" he began.

Taran did not hesitate.

"Love you back," he said, stepping forward and pulling both of them into a firm, encompassing embrace.

Ka-Lorrin stiffened for a fraction of a second.

Then gave in.

They stood there for a moment.

Then another.

The systems hummed around them.

A piece of the *Salamander's* heart, restored.

Chapter 7: A Bed by the Waterside

THE WAQI-REESH SLIPPED out of light factor without fanfare, the stars resolving around them in a quiet, almost delicate scatter that gave no indication of the shift that had just occurred.

Bimini hung ahead.

For a moment, it looked the same.

A burnished sphere wrapped in copper light, the surface threaded with that living glow Lily remembered too well—beautiful in a way that didn't ask permission, the kind of beauty that didn't care what it cost to sustain itself.

Then the rest of it came into focus.

Ships.

A perimeter, clean and deliberate, drawn tight around the planet in a way that left no ambiguity about its purpose. Union vessels held position at measured intervals, their spacing precise enough to read as design rather than response. Patrol routes overlapped in layered arcs, each one feeding into the next. Nothing drifted. Nothing wandered.

Not observation.

Containment.

Lily felt it settle in her chest before she said anything.

"When I was here before..." she began, her voice quieter than she intended.

"None of this was here."

Her eyes moved across the formation, tracking the rhythm of it—the way each ship held its place, the way the space between them felt accounted for.

"It was calm," she said. "Just the facility. Caris and her team."

She paused, the memory aligning itself against what she was seeing now.

"It wasn't locked down like this."

Behind her, Veyshali didn't respond immediately. When she did, it was with the same controlled ease she brought to everything, as if the answer had already been considered and filed away.

"Whatever it was before—" she said, and didn't bother finishing it.

The Waqi-Reesh adjusted its vector by a fraction—so small Lily felt it more than saw it—slipping off the most obvious approach and angling toward a cluster of drifting rock at the edge of the system.

"Cloak holding," came the voice from the forward station.

"Let's not test that," Veyshali said, almost absently.

An asteroid field rose to meet them, fractured stone and metallic debris tumbling slowly, catching the distant light in uneven flashes. The ship eased into it, folding itself into the motion, another piece of drift among many.

From here, Bimini was partially obscured, its glow broken into segments between the passing rock. The blockade remained visible, though—its geometry too deliberate to disappear completely, even at a distance.

Lily stepped closer to the viewport, her gaze returning to the planet.

It still looked alive.

Whatever was happening down there—

"They're protecting something," she said.

Not a guess.

She kept watching the ships, the pattern of them, the way they held the line.

Trish stepped up beside her.

"I think it's time for the tour."

. . . .

The shuttle detached without a sound.

Just a soft shift as it slipped free of the Waqi-Reesh and angled toward the planet.

Bimini filled the forward view, its copper light stretching across the canopy as they cut through the upper atmosphere. The entry was clean—a gradual tightening of gravity as the surface rose to meet them.

Lily kept her eyes forward.

"I was here with Xynn," she said after a moment. "Last time."

Trish kept her eyes on the descent.

Lily watched the glow shift across the forward screen.

"Datch was still with us," she said. "Xynn and I were the only ones who knew."

The words felt strange, placed here. Out of sequence.

Trish adjusted something on the console, her movements precise, unhurried.

"It wasn't your fault, Lily," she said. "What happened."

Lily didn't answer.

The shuttle dropped lower, the light thinning as terrain began to take shape beneath them—structures, roads, the faint geometry of the settlement resolving out of the glow.

They touched down just beyond the outer edge of the town, near the Union observation tower.

The tower was not cloaked. That was the first thing.

But the wrongness was immediate.

The streets were empty.

Absent from the usual children playing in the street. No one walking the paths or carrying goods. No open doors. No movement spilling out into the open air.

Just presence.

Sunbow Logistics guards and vehicles moved through the main thoroughfare. Kessler Syndicate transports rolled past them, heavy rigs and patrol units moving with the kind of authority that didn't need to be asserted. Lily recognized them from Xynn's report.

The occupation was organized.

Trish let out a quiet breath beside her, taking it in.

She glanced at a Sunbow personnel carrier parked next to a Kessler armored vehicle and scoffed.

"A match made in heaven."

Lily scanned the street, her gaze moving from one controlled motion to the next.

"Where is everyone?" she said.

They didn't have to wonder long.

Movement caught Lily's eye—distant, rhythmic, out beyond the edge of the settlement. Not people. Not traffic.

Equipment.

She narrowed her focus, watching the pattern of it.

"That's different," she said.

Trish followed her line of sight, already moving.

"Then let's not admire it from a distance."

They cut across the street, keeping to the edges of the buildings, timing their movement between patrol sweeps. A vehicle sat idle near the corner—a low-profile transport, Kessler make, heavy frame built for hauling more than passengers.

Trish didn't slow.

"Tell me you're not—" Lily began.

"I'm not," Trish said, already at the driver's side.

The panel was open before Lily reached her. Trish leaned in, hands moving with easy familiarity, bypassing the interface with a small tool she produced from somewhere Lily hadn't seen her carry.

The vehicle gave a soft, compliant hum.

Lily folded her arms, watching her.

"You know we could just take the shuttle," she said.

"Meh," Trish said, sliding into the seat. "This is more fun."

She glanced at Lily, just a flicker of a smile.

Lily shook her head and climbed in.

The vehicle eased forward, merging into the slow, controlled movement of the street. No one looked twice.

They followed the line of activity outward, the structures thinning as the sound of machinery grew louder, heavier—something deeper beneath it, a steady vibration that carried through the frame of the vehicle.

Lily felt it before she understood it.

The town gave way to open ground.

Then the ground gave way to the operation.

It stretched farther than she realized at first. It filled her view—and then kept going.

Platforms cut into the surface in clean, geometric lines. Extraction rigs moved in steady cycles, their motion precise, unhurried. Conveyor systems carried red crystal away from the site, feeding into larger transports waiting at the perimeter.

And the people—

Lily's breath caught, just slightly.

Bimini's people were there.

Working.

Under guard.

Sunbow troops lined the edges of the site, their presence quiet but absolute. Kessler units moved between the rigs, coordinating transport and flow, the entire system running with the kind of efficiency that came from iteration, not improvisation.

The labor was continuous.

The vehicle slowed. For a moment, neither of them said anything.

Lily stared out at the scene, her mind trying to reconcile it with the version of this place she still carried—the streets, the light, the sense of something contained, but not controlled.

This was something else.

A constructed environment with a singular purpose.

Mining the caronite out of this planet.

Trish leaned forward slightly, her eyes moving across the operation, tracking its structure, its scale.

Trying to understand it.

"What the hell is this?" she said quietly.

Lily didn't answer right away.

She was already tracking it, pieces shifting into place faster than she could hold them.

Caris's science team. Their work. The way the Carionite responded—cellular repair, regeneration, the body rewriting itself under the right conditions.

She kept watching the operation as it moved in front of her.

"The Carionite..." she said, slower now. "That's what the Union vaccine is made of."

Trish didn't respond.

Lily's gaze moved across the site—the rigs, the flow, the people working inside it.

"They figured out how to use it," she said. "The Gherionite tech... how to stabilize it. Apply it."

The thought settled.

Then shifted.

She looked past the extraction lines, toward the facility rising behind them—no longer cloaked, no longer hidden. She had stood there once. Walked those halls. Watched Caris work.

"And the Union—they're not just letting it happen," she said.

She gestured toward it.

"They're running it."

The weight of it landed between them.

Lily didn't look away from the site.

"Why did you leave Earth?" she said.

Trish blinked, caught slightly off guard. "Hmm?"

"You were on the trail," Lily said. "Ninebury. The supply chain. You were close." She turned to her now. "What exactly led you off-world?"

Trish studied her for a second, recalibrating.

"Arsenal Combs," she said. "He let something slip. Said there was an important meeting between the Hedon Council and some kind of outside influence. Someone important. Some kind of deal."

Lily's focus sharpened.

"Deal?"

"Something involving the vaccine. But it fell through. After that, everything started shifting. Shipments, routes. Some of the cracks started to show."

"So you followed them," Lily said.

"Flight logs," Trish said. "Anything that didn't fit. Eventually it pointed to the Marduk system."

Lily was already moving again, pieces locking into place.

The council.

The meeting.

The deal that didn't happen.

She exhaled once, sharp.

"Right," she said.

Trish watched her, something uncertain in her expression now.

"Right?"

Lily turned back toward the vehicle.

"We need to get back to the ship."

• • • •

The shuttle locked back into the Waqi-Reesh with a soft, precise click, the transition almost imperceptible except for the shift in gravity and the subtle change in air.

The hatch opened to reveal Veyshali waiting just beyond it, composed as ever, as if she had been standing there for some time.

Lily was already speaking.

"The invitation to the Siphon-Spire," she said, moving into the corridor. "The one you couldn't resist—"

"Pleasant journey, I take it?" Veyshali said dryly.

Trish gave a small shrug as she stepped past her.

Lily didn't blink. "Who sent it?"

There was the faintest pause, just long enough to register as intentional.

"Marson Dontain," Veyshali said.

Lily felt Trish shift beside her. Then, almost at the same time—

"—of Gherion Prime."

Veyshali inclined her head in acknowledgment.

They continued down the corridor, the hum of the ship steady around them, but Lily's attention had already moved past it, pulling the pieces together as they aligned.

"What if the mysterious party isn't orchestrating anything," she said, more to the pattern than to either of them.

Trish nodded, catching on.

Lily slowed slightly, the thought sharpening as she followed it through.

"What if they were trying to expose all this?"

The words settled between them, drawing a brief silence in their wake.

"And who is they?" Trish asked.

Lily hesitated—not because she didn't have an answer, but because saying it felt like stepping across something she hadn't fully understood yet.

Veyshali said the name.

"Eli."

Lily nodded.

She kept walking, her gaze unfocused, fixed somewhere beyond the corridor as the realization continued to take shape.

"He wanted that machine gone," she said. "From the beginning. He understood what it could become."

The image of Bimini—of the operation, the scale of it—sat just behind her eyes.

"This is exactly that," she said. "What he was afraid of."

She let the thought carry forward, not forcing it, just following where it led.

"Just to be clear," Trish said, trying to find her footing again. "Are you saying he murdered the entire Hedon Council to draw attention to—what? Retail fraud?"

Lily didn't look at her.

"You know it's more than that," she said. "That's why you're here."

"Sorry," Trish said quickly. "I just mean—it sounds unhinged."

"From what you've told me, and the information I've reviewed," Veyshali said, her tone measured, "Eli's psychological profile is… unpredictable."

Lily nodded once.

"I don't know why he's doing any of this," she said. "Not for certain. But he's at the center of it. Even if his reasons are twisted—he's still brilliant. Still capable."

She slowed slightly, the thought settling into something more solid now.

"Maybe I know how to reach him," she said.

• • • •

They were able to reach Tevya in under an hour. The frequency Lily had was rerouted through a deep-space channel and left as a callback request.

Tevya was prompt.

Her image resolved on the display—steady, composed. But she looked different than the last time Lily had seen her. Her synthetic hair was no longer styled in a human fashion, instead arranged in a more Gherionite design. Her clothing had shifted too—utilitarian now, stripped of the whimsical edge Lily remembered.

"Lily," she said. "I wasn't expecting to hear from you."

Lily didn't ease into it.

"Tevya, I wish it were under better circumstances. We've uncovered some troubling information about illegal activity the Union is involved in."

That was enough to shift something.

Tevya held her gaze, taking it in.

"That's... a serious claim."

"It's not a claim," Lily said. "We've seen it."

A pause.

Tevya's expression tightened, just slightly—not disbelief, but recalibration.

"Why call me?" Tevya said.

"I think you have a guess."

"Eli?" she asked.

"I'm almost positive he's tied up in all of this," Lily said. "But maybe..." She let the thought hang. "I'm not sure whose side he's on."

Tevya looked away for a fraction of a second, then back.

"He contacted me recently," she said. "He was concerned for my well-being. But if I had to guess... I would say he's on his own side."

Lily stepped closer to the display.

"We need to find him. If I could talk to him, maybe—"

"I'll be ready," Tevya said, quickly. "I can pull a trace if he opens a channel for more than a few seconds."

Then, just a beat later:

"We have to stop him."

Lily watched her carefully.

Tevya adjusted, almost imperceptibly.

"I mean—whatever he's involved in. The Datch I knew wouldn't do this," she said. "I'd like to think Eli wouldn't be involved in something like murder... or conspiracy. But you did see him kill once."

Lily tried to read her—whether there was something behind it, whether she might be protecting him—but let it go. Androids weren't easy to get a read on.

"I appreciate it, Tevya," she said. "Let me know the second you get a fix on him."

"Confirmed," Tevya replied.

The channel closed.

Veyshali didn't give the moment much time to settle.

"I may have another lead," she said, stepping forward. "Of a sort."

Lily turned.

Veyshali set a small case on the table between them and opened it with a quiet click.

Inside, resting in a fitted cradle—

The Jewel.

Lily felt it before she reacted, a sharp recognition that pulled her a half-step closer.

"That's—" She stopped, then let out a breath. "I don't know how you do these things."

Veyshali closed the case halfway, almost absently.

"Being queen has its advantages."

Trish leaned in, studying it, her expression tightening.

"How is this a lead?"

Veyshali glanced at her.

"This is a copy of the device used in the Hedon Council murders."

Lily's gaze didn't leave it.

The one Datch had given her. The one that had been taken as evidence.

"And you thought to retrieve it," she said.

"I thought it might prove useful."

Trish folded her arms. "It's a weapon. A very clean one, from what I understand."

"Precisely," Veyshali said. "The device itself is untraceable—those clever Raath-Ka armorists made certain of that."

She let that sit for a moment, then continued.

"But the discharge it produces is not."

That shifted the air.

Lily looked up.

"Every time it's fired," Veyshali said, "it leaves behind a signature. Distinct. Tunable, within a range—but consistent enough to identify if you know what to look for."

Trish's focus sharpened.

"So if he's used one before—"

"We may be able to find it," Veyshali said. "Or something like it."

Lily's mind was already moving ahead of the words, tracking the implications.

"It's not just a weapon," she said quietly.

"No," Veyshali agreed. "It can function as a signal."

A calling card.

Lily glanced back down at it.

"If he used it at the Council," she said, "and somewhere else..."

"We run the signature against available logs," Veyshali said. "Any system that recorded the discharge—planetary grids, defense arrays, long-range sensors—there is a chance it was noticed."

"Even if no one knew what they were looking at," Trish added.

Veyshali inclined her head.

"Especially then."

Lily straightened.

"Then we test it."

• • • •

The blackness wrapped all the way around the surface of the asteroid.

There was no sense of distance to it, no atmosphere to soften anything or give it scale. The stars held their positions without flicker, sharp and fixed, and the light they cast didn't spread so much as land. Even the Waqi-Reesh, just off the surface, threw a shadow that cut clean across the rock without fading at the edges.

Lily stood within it, aware of how little separated her from everything else.

An asteroid didn't offer much in the way of orientation. There was ground beneath her boots, but it felt more like an agreement than a rule—something that could be broken with a single misstep if the suit didn't compensate fast enough.

She shifted slightly, feeling the response of the Ishrethi suit.

It moved easily, more so than Fleet issue, the joints giving where they were supposed to instead of resisting. The weight distribution was better too. It didn't feel like something she had to fight to move in.

But the viewport was smaller.

She noticed that almost immediately—the way the edges of it sat just inside her awareness, narrowing her field of vision in a way that felt subtle at first and then harder to ignore the longer she stood still. It didn't obstruct so much as contain, pulling everything into a tighter frame.

She adjusted once, then let it go.

Ahead of her, Roka was already setting up the targeting field, lines of energy snapping into place one after another, forming a structure that hovered just above the surface. The geometry of it resolved quickly, each plane aligning with the next until the shape held.

They could have done this inside the ship.

But the testing facility aboard the Waqi-Reesh wasn't rated for something like this. Even Trish had been careful about that, which said enough on its own.

"I missed this," Veyshali said somewhere behind her.

Lily glanced back.

Veyshali stood a few paces off, her attention moving over the surface as if she were reacquainting herself with it.

"I haven't been on an asteroid in... twenty years, perhaps."

Lily remembered the moment she'd insisted on coming, the ease with which she'd said it—

I can't have you having all the fun.

At the time, it had sounded like curiosity.

Now, Lily wasn't so sure.

She turned back toward the field, the Jewel steady in her hand.

Roka's voice came through the comm, steady as ever.

"Field is stable."

Lily stepped forward, the surface shifting subtly under her boots as she moved into position. The targeting planes hovered ahead, faint lines of energy holding their shape against the black, each one fixed exactly where it needed to be.

She lifted the Jewel.

It settled into her hand with a weight she hadn't expected—not heavy, but present in a way that made it difficult to think of it as just another tool. The surface was still scorched from its detonation on Earth, but the design remained smooth, almost featureless, resisting interpretation.

She turned it slightly, feeling for something familiar.

There wasn't anything.

She had used it before.

But not like this.

Ninebury had been at a distance, the act separated from her by layers of interface—and literal layers of earth and water. It hadn't felt real in the way this did now, standing here with nothing between her and the outcome but the device in her hand.

She raised it, aligning with the field Roka had established. The narrow viewport forced her to be deliberate, to center everything inside that tighter frame.

"Whenever you're ready," Trish said.

Lily didn't answer.

She focused on the geometry ahead of her, the clean lines of the field, the way it held space in front of her. For a moment, everything else fell away—the ship, the others, the quiet weight of the asteroid beneath her feet.

Just the target.

She fired.

The discharge didn't behave the way she expected.

There was no clean line, no immediate translation from action to result. Instead, something in the space ahead of her shifted—subtle, but wrong, as if the distance between her and the field had folded in on itself for a fraction of a second.

The light bent.

Not visibly, not in a way she could track with her eyes, but she felt it, the way the shot moved through something that wasn't supposed to be there.

For a moment, she thought—

The kickback hit before the thought could finish.

A sharp, invasive surge that moved through her grip, through the suit, through her body in a way that didn't follow the direction of the shot. It cut across her awareness, severing the connection between intent and control.

Everything dropped out.

• • • •

Light filled the space behind her eyes.

Not a flash. Not something external.

Something closer.

The Jewel was there.

Not in her hand, not at a distance—just there, suspended in a way that didn't follow position or orientation. Its edges blurred, then resolved again, as if it couldn't quite decide how it wanted to exist.

The light around it pulsed once.

And then—

Eli.

Not moving. Not speaking.

Just present.

Watching.

Or waiting.

The shape of him held for a moment longer than it should have, the outline sharpening just enough to feel intentional before the light shifted again, pulling everything with it.

Lily drew in a breath.

Air came back first. Then sound—the low, steady hum of the Waqi-Reesh resolving around her in familiar layers.

Her vision followed more slowly, the ceiling above her coming into focus in pieces as the disorientation worked its way out of her system.

She didn't move right away.

Her body felt heavy, as if it had been returned to her all at once.

"Easy," Trish said. "You're back."

Lily drew in a breath, sharper than she meant to, her body catching up a second behind it.

She didn't move right away.

"What happened?" she asked.

Trish glanced toward Veyshali, then back to her.

"The weapon," she said. "Turns out it's fitted with a kickback charge. Designed to incapacitate whoever's holding it when it discharges."

Lily pushed herself up slowly, the motion heavier than it should have been.

"Why?" she said.

Trish didn't answer immediately.

Lily looked between them.

"Why would Eli want to knock me out," she said, "if I was defending myself?"

The question hung there.

Trish shifted, considering it from a different angle.

"Maybe it's not about defense," she said. "Maybe it depends on where you're firing it. Or who was supposed to be on the other end of the blast."

Lily held her gaze.

She looked away, the memory of the shot still sitting somewhere just out of reach.

"And the discharge?" she asked.

Trish's expression sharpened slightly.

"That part worked," she said. "We picked up a signal. Strong. Clean."

Veyshali stepped forward.

"Distinct enough to isolate," she added. "We've already begun cataloging it."

Lily exhaled slowly.

"So we have a signature," she said.

"A very specific one," Veyshali replied. "More than that, the kickback also appears to have transmitted the signal into open space."

Lily blinked.

"A distress signal?"

"Or a target," Trish said.

Lily pushed herself upright, the motion coming faster than it should have.

"I'm starving," she said, already moving.

Trish glanced at her.

"There's something you should know—"

Lily didn't slow.

"I'll be back."

She reached the door.

It opened.

Xynn stood on the other side.

For a fraction of a second, neither of them moved.

Then Lily closed the distance.

There was no hesitation, no question—just contact, arms around her, pulling her in as if to make sure she was actually there. Xynn held her just as tightly, one hand at the back of Lily's neck, grounding her, steady.

Lily let out a shaky breath—the kind where you have to remind yourself to keep breathing.

"You're here," she said, half into Xynn's shoulder.

"Of course I am," Xynn said.

Lily pulled back just enough to look at her.

Her usual armor and tactical gear were absent. Just loose, simple clothing—something that said: breathe.

It felt different immediately.

"When did you—"

"Just now," Xynn said. "I took leave from the relief effort."

"Leave," Lily repeated, still holding on to her like she was afraid one of them might drift away.

Xynn's expression softened.

"I know what's been happening," she said. "You've been shot at, imprisoned, thrown into situations no one should be dealing with back to back."

Lily didn't argue.

"You weren't answering messages," Xynn added. "So I stopped waiting."

Behind them, Veyshali's voice carried lightly from the room.

"She called," she said. "I sent our coordinates immediately."

Lily glanced back once, then returned to Xynn.

"You didn't come to drag me back to safety, did you?" she asked.

Xynn shook her head.

"I came to slow you down," she said. "Even for a moment. And hopefully stay close enough to keep you from getting yourself killed."

Lily let out a small breath that almost passed for a laugh.

"Or at least die together."

"Don't say it isn't a good time," Xynn said.

Lily glanced back again.

Veyshali met her eyes.

"We're tracking the frequency from the discharge," she said. "I think we just wait for now."

Lily nodded once.

"Come on," she said.

• • • •

Lily had forgotten about food as they stepped into her quarters.

They felt smaller than she remembered.

Or maybe just quieter.

The door closed behind them, sealing out the noise of the ship, the movement, the pressure of everything waiting just beyond it.

For a moment, neither of them spoke.

Then Xynn stepped closer.

Lily didn't think about it.

She reached for her again, pulling her in, the contact immediate and grounding in a way nothing else had been since they parted.

Xynn's hand slid along her shoulder, her back, steady and certain.

"You're okay," Xynn said quietly.

Lily exhaled.

"I am now."

The words came without hesitation.

Without analysis.

Just true.

They stayed there for a moment longer, the rest of it falling away.

Then—

Lily pulled back slightly, just enough to look at her.

Then their lips met.

The kiss carried weeks of missing each other—deep, familiar, and aching in the best way. They moved together easily after that, the space between them disappearing as if it had never been there at all. Laughter slipped in between quiet moments, the tension of everything they had carried loosening, giving way to something softer, more certain.

Time passed without either of them marking it.

And when it did, they were still there—close, wrapped around one another in the quiet that followed.

Lily pressed a kiss to Xynn's forehead, murmuring, "I missed you so much."

Xynn smiled against her skin. "Don't forget it."

They fell asleep like that—tangled, warm, and finally together again.

• • • •

Morning came quietly.

Lily woke to the soft shift of movement beside her, the light in the room dimmed to a warm, artificial glow that didn't quite belong to any time of day.

For a moment, she didn't move.

Just stayed where she was, aware of the weight of the blanket, the steady rhythm of the ship beneath it, and Xynn—close, real, still there.

Xynn stood near the edge of the room, pulling her shirt back on, movements unhurried, familiar in a way that made the space feel settled again.

Lily watched her for a second before speaking.

"You're leaving already?"

Xynn glanced over, a small smile pulling at the corner of her mouth.

"Not yet," she said. "Just preparing for the inevitable consequences."

Lily pushed herself up onto one elbow.

"Consequences."

Xynn nodded once, adjusting the fabric at her shoulder.

"I'm going to be sore later," she said, like it was a simple observation.

Lily let out a quiet breath that turned into a real laugh.

"Should I apologize?"

Xynn looked back at her, considering it.

"Not unless you plan on doing it again."

That landed exactly where it was meant to.

Lily smiled, wider now.

"It's been a lot," she said. She hesitated, then let it come out the way it wanted to. "I just... really missed you."

Xynn's smile held.

"I know," she said.

Then—

Veyshali's voice cut in over the comm.

"Lily."

The tone was enough.

Lily was already moving.

"What is it?" she said, swinging her legs over the side of the bed.

"We have a vessel approaching," Veyshali said. "It's holding position just outside our sensor range."

Lily glanced at Xynn once, then reached for her clothes.

"Any ID?"

"None," Veyshali said. "It's not responding to hails."

Lily was already zipping her jacket up.

"I'm on my way."

• • • •

The bridge had shifted by the time she arrived.

Focused. Something had everyone's attention.

"It's staying just at the edge," Trish said, not looking up from a forward station. "Like it knows exactly where our range drops off."

Lily stepped closer, eyes on the display.

The ship was there—barely. A ghost of a signal, enough to confirm presence, not enough to resolve detail.

"Deliberate," she said.

"Very," Trish replied.

Another tone cut through the room.

A second contact.

"Hold on," someone said. "We've got another one."

Lily's attention snapped to the updated display.

Same configuration.

Same size.

But this one—

"Gherionite markings," Trish said. "Incoming transmission."

There was a brief pause, then the channel opened.

Tevya's image resolved on the display, steady and immediate.

"This is Tevya," she said. "Requesting permission to come aboard."

• • • •

As Tevya reached the bridge, she was already speaking.

"I picked up a signal," she said, stepping into the room. "Something I haven't seen in a long time."

Lily turned to face her.

"What kind of signal?"

Tevya's gaze flicked briefly to the display, then back.

"It's one Datch and I created," she said. "A long time ago. A kind of familial signature."

"The Jewel discharge," Lily said.

Tevya nodded.

"It matches the structure. Not perfectly—but close enough that I recognized it."

"And the other ship?" Lily asked.

Tevya didn't hesitate.

"It's his."

Lily let out a breath, the situation narrowing into something more defined.

"Should we try to close the distance?" she asked. "Prepare a tractor beam?"

Tevya's focus sharpened.

"Not yet," she said. "Let me talk to him."

Lily studied her for a moment, then nodded, not entirely convinced.

"He'll talk to me," Tevya said.

Lily glanced at Veyshali.

Veyshali gave a small, permissive gesture toward the controls.

"Help yourself."

Tevya stepped forward, already reaching for the console, routing the connection through her own frequency.

"Datch," she said, her voice steady as the transmission carried out into the void. "It's me."

For a moment, nothing happened.

Then—

The unidentified ship opened fire.

The first impact rolled through the ship a fraction of a second after the flash on the display.

Shields came up almost immediately, the bridge shifting from stillness into motion as Veyshali's crew moved through their roles without hesitation. The Waqi-Reesh angled off its previous position, slipping into a tight evasive pattern that kept the incoming fire just off center.

Tevya hadn't moved.

Lily reached for her, guiding her toward one of the jump seats.

"Sit," she said.

Tevya didn't resist, but she didn't seem fully there either, her eyes fixed on the display as the realization caught up with her.

Lily could hear the bridge commander's voice cut through.

"Return fire."

The Waqi-Reesh answered, controlled bursts tracking toward Eli's ship, forcing it off its line.

Trish leaned forward, watching the widening engagement.

"Careful," she said. "We're about to attract attention."

As if on cue—

A new signature burned onto the display, larger, heavier, resolving fast from orbit.

"A Raptor class starship," someone said.

The ship moved into view filling the screen, its weapons already powering up.

It fired once.

Eli's ship took the hit cleanly, the return flare uneven, its trajectory breaking.

Tevya leaned forward against the restraints, eyes flicking across the instruments.

"He's damaged," she said. "Controlled descent—he's heading into the atmosphere."

The display tracked it, the smaller vessel angling down toward Bimini in a spiraling line that held just enough stability to be intentional.

Then the larger ship turned its attention to them.

"This is the Union starship *Smilodon*," a voice came across the comm, calm and unmistakable. "Unidentified vessel, you are operating in a restricted zone. Withdraw immediately."

The bridge held for a moment, the tension shifting.

Lily looked to Veyshali.

Veyshali was already thinking ahead.

"We disengage," she said. "Cloak and regroup."

There was no argument.

The Waqi-Reesh began to turn, systems shifting as the cloak sequence initiated, the field beginning to form along the hull—

Then the ship lurched.

"Tractor beam," Trish said.

The field collapsed unevenly, the cloak failing before it could fully take hold as the pull locked onto them.

The Waqi-Reesh strained against it, engines compensating, but the movement wasn't theirs anymore.

The comm cut in again.

"Unidentified vessel, you are ordered to stand down. Prepare to be boarded."

The pull held for a moment longer, the Waqi-Reesh caught in it, engines straining against something that wasn't going to give.

Then—

A new distortion rippled across the edge of the system.

Lily felt it before she saw it, a subtle shift in the way the stars held their positions.

The Salamander dropped out of light factor.

It arrived with none of the violence of the exchange, just presence—sudden, undeniable, placing itself between the Waqi-Reesh and the Smilodon with quiet precision.

A new channel opened.

"Smilodon, this is Captain Dalren of the Salamander."

His voice carried across the bridge, even and controlled.

"I suggest you release the ship you're holding so we can resolve this like civilized people."

There was no threat in his voice.

The Smilodon didn't respond immediately.

Lily watched the display, the beam still locked, the distance between the three ships holding in a fragile balance.

Dalren spoke again, just as measured.

"Queen Veyshali," he said, shifting channels without raising his voice. "If they release you, I'll need your word you won't attempt to jump out of the system."

Veyshali didn't look away from the display.

"You have it," she said.

There was another pause.

"Come on, Oscar," Dalren said. "Let's not make this awkward."

Lily smirked despite herself.

Then—

The tractor beam disengaged.

STARSHIP *Salamander* **Log — Lieutenant Malik, Personal Recording**
Log 2537.0407, Tuesday

I have been invited to Lieutenant Caris's quarters this evening.

It has been some time since we have spoken at length. Longer still since anything resembling normal interaction between us has occurred.

I was... uncertain, for a while, whether that was by design.

Or avoidance.

Or simply the natural result of two people trying to redraw the lines of a relationship after it had already burned past them.

...

I would prefer it not be awkward.

That seems, at the very least, achievable.

I am... glad she asked.

· · · ·

There was a time when entering Commander Caris's quarters required a degree of preparation.

Malik considered that as he adjusted the line of his jacket in the mirror, smoothing the fabric over his chest with deliberate precision. It wasn't vanity. It was respect. Muscle memory. Possibly both.

He studied himself a moment longer, then gave a small, decisive humph.

Acceptable.

He picked up the items resting on the console beside him.

Flowers.

Wine.

He weighed them in each hand, considering.

The flowers felt... excessive. Too hopeful. Too romantic for whatever fragile thing this was.

He turned slightly, eyeing the waste receptacle across the room. A brief hesitation—then he tossed them in with a quiet, efficient motion.

The wine remained.

Appropriate. Neutral. Uncomplicated.

He stepped out into the corridor.

The walk to her quarters was short. Short enough that he didn't have time to reconsider the decision. Or perhaps just long enough that he did, and chose not to act on it.

He paused outside her door.

Straightened his jacket again—unnecessarily.

Then pressed the chime.

"Enter."

Her voice was immediate. Low. Smooth.

He stepped inside.

And stopped.

Caris sat on the edge of the bed.

She was not in uniform.

That was the first thing.

The second—

She was wearing something black and dangerously sheer, the thin straps sliding delicately over her shoulders, the hem barely brushing the tops of her thighs. It was not subtle. Not incidental. Something chosen with clear, deliberate intent—designed to derail every careful thought he'd brought with him.

Malik set the bottle down on the nearest surface with more care than strictly necessary, the soft clink of glass against metal the only sound in the room.

"Umm."

Caris tilted her head slightly, the motion causing the fabric to shift against her skin in a way that made his throat tighten.

"Umm?"

He tried again.

"...Hmm."

She watched him for a moment.

"Is that all you have to say?"

"It's just that—" He stopped, recalibrating, his pulse kicking harder. "I thought we were..."

"You thought we were?" she prompted.

"Broken up," he said. "You know. Since we haven't spoken in months."

The silence that followed did not make things easier.

Caris rose slowly from the bed.

She took one unhurried step toward him.

"And yet," she murmured, eyes locked on his, "here you are."

"Leena," he said, the finality in his voice surprising even him. "Can we just... talk?"

What happened next surprised both of them.

Caris sat on the edge of the bed—and broke.

Not a controlled release. Not the kind of quiet, contained emotion Malik had come to expect from her.

This was something else.

Her shoulders folded inward as the first sob hit, then another, the sound tearing out of her in a way that felt almost violent. It didn't stop. It didn't soften. It built, each breath catching harder than the last until the rhythm of it lost any sense of control.

Malik didn't hesitate.

He crossed the room and sat beside her, pulling her into him without thinking, one arm steady around her shoulders as the other reached for the sheet at the edge of the bed. He drew it around her, more instinct than intention, grounding her as much as he could.

He had never seen Leena cry.

Not once.

The thought barely had time to register before it was replaced by something more immediate—stay, hold, don't let this get worse.

Her sobs turned into uneven gulps of air, her body shaking against his as she tried—and failed—to steady herself.

He stayed with her.

Didn't rush it.

Didn't speak.

Just held on until the storm worked its way through.

When it finally began to ease, he shifted slightly, one hand moving to brush the dampness from her cheek. He tilted her face just enough to look at her.

The symmetry he had always noticed—the effortless precision of it—was still there.

But it wasn't what he saw.

Her skin was flushed, uneven, her eyes glassy and red, her breathing still catching at the edges.

She looked real.

More real than he had ever seen her.

"This isn't about me, is it?" he asked, quietly.

She shook her head.

Malik nodded once, gentle, steady.

"Then tell me," he said. "What's going on, Leena? Why haven't I heard from you?"

She hesitated, her gaze dropping for a moment before she found her footing again.

"On Bimini," she said, her voice still unsteady. "When I was there... I was part of a project. A planetary restructuring."

Malik's brow furrowed.

"What do you mean?"

She drew in a breath, steadier this time.

"The people there—they die," she said. "Self-annihilation. It feeds the caronite life form."

He nodded slowly.

"Right. But it restores them."

Her expression shifted.

"Does it?" she said. "Or does it simply recreate them? Copies of everything that was there before?"

The question hung there.

Then she kept going, faster now—less controlled, more driven.

"We started to think that not interfering might be the unethical choice," she said. "My team began researching whether the caronite had medical applications."

"And does it?" Malik asked.

She nodded.

"It does more than that," she said. "It can reverse cellular degradation. Aging, injury—everything. But only under very specific conditions. You have to be on Bimini. In proximity to the life form itself."

Malik followed, his expression tightening as the implications began to form.

"And off-world?"

She looked at him.

"Then you have to change the conditions," she said. "Artificially."

He didn't like where this was going.

"How?"

She hesitated—just a fraction.

"By creating a controlled dimensional instability," she said. "A partial phase shift at the molecular level."

Malik shook his head immediately.

"That's not possible."

She gave a small, humorless breath.

"That's what we thought," she said. "Until Ronin showed us otherwise."

That landed.

"The Gherionite device," Malik said.

She nodded.

"It does exactly that."

He leaned back slightly, processing.

"What are you saying?" he asked. "That you can make people live forever?"

Her expression tightened.

"It's not stable," she said. "Not yet. But the potential—"

She stopped herself. Regrouped.

"We believed," she said more carefully, "that it could be used responsibly. That it could transform medicine. And that if Bimini was freed from its cycle..." She shook her head slightly. "We thought it could be an opportunity for them. To be at the center of that discovery."

Malik was quiet for a moment.

Then, gently—

"But you can't force someone to be free."

The words landed harder than anything else had.

Caris's expression crumpled again, though the tears didn't come this time.

"They resisted," she said, a flicker of anger breaking through. "They fought for it. For the right to die the way they always have."

She looked down at her hands.

"And I thought they were wrong," she said. "I thought we were saving them."

Her voice dropped.

"I know now it wasn't my place," she said. "Or the Union's. We don't get to decide that. We don't get to play god."

She swallowed, steadying herself.

"Lily went looking for answers," she added. "I didn't realize Bimini was part of what she would find."

Malik didn't respond right away.

He just pulled her back in slightly, one arm around her shoulders again, holding her there as the weight of it settled between them.

"You can't tell her," he said, his voice rougher than he intended.

She looked up at him, eyes dark, searching.

"I'm serious," he said. "Don't tell her. At least not now. She doesn't need to know what you knew or when. It'll just bring more pain if you tell her."

Malik wasn't entirely sure he believed that.

But somehow, they were exactly the words Leena needed to hear.

Something shifted.

The hesitation that had been holding her together gave way, not to relief—but to clarity. Her shoulders straightened, her breathing steadied, and something warmer—sharper—lit behind her eyes.

"Please stay," she said softly.

It wasn't a question.

Before he could answer, she leaned in and kissed him.

Not tentative. Not uncertain.

Deeper. Slower. Intentional.

Her hands moved up his chest, fingers catching in the fabric of his jacket, pulling him closer as if closing the last remaining distance between who she had been and whatever she had decided to become.

Malik didn't stop her.

He pulled her in instead, the last of his restraint giving way as the moment overtook them both.

They moved together, unsteady at first, then with growing certainty, the weight of everything they had just said dissolving into something easier to hold—taking with it every careful boundary they'd tried to keep between them.

And made it a night to remember.

THE TRACTOR BEAM RELEASED.

For a fraction of a second, nothing moved.

The Waqi-Reesh held its position. The Smilodon lingered just beyond optimal firing range, its silhouette steady against the copper glow of Bimini. And between them, the Salamander—newly arrived, already occupying the space like it had always belonged there.

No one fired.

No one spoke.

Then a channel opened.

"Smilodon, this is Captain Dalren of the Salamander."

His voice cut cleanly through the silence—calm, controlled, carrying just enough familiarity to make it sound like this wasn't the first time he'd stepped into a situation like this.

"Oscar, give me five minutes," he said. "And get your CO on the hook too."

There was a pause—brief, but measurable.

"Copy that," came the reply at last.

The tension shifted. Not gone. Just... held.

On the Waqi-Reesh bridge, Trish straightened slightly as Dalren's image resolved on the forward display. Something in her posture changed—subtle, automatic.

"Hello, Eryk."

Dalren glanced toward her, recognition immediate. A small breath of a laugh followed, quiet and unforced.

"It's a small galaxy," he said.

He paused as if searching.

"—Trish. I see you haven't stopped getting involved."

"Someone has to," she said.

He didn't take the bait.

His attention moved on, settling on Lily.

"Lieutenant Starling," he said. "I'd say your leave is about up."

There was the faintest shift in his expression—something softer, less formal.

"Honestly," he added, "I'm glad to see you're okay. After everything that happened."

Lily blinked once, caught slightly off guard by that.

"Sir—"

"Rules be damned," Dalren continued, cutting gently across it. "If you're willing, I'd like you on the landing party. Find Eli."

He paused just long enough for the weight of that to settle.

"I'll start combing through this," he went on, glancing briefly off-screen, as if already half-engaged in a dozen overlapping channels. "Red tape, jurisdiction, whatever the Union is running here. Try to make some sense of what we've gotten ourselves into."

Lily nodded, the motion coming before she fully processed it.

"Aye, Captain."

There was a flicker of something like relief beneath it. Gratitude, even.

"Sir, I believe Xynn will—"

"Hi, Xynn."

Dalren's tone shifted again—familiar, almost conversational.

"Good to see you found your way out here. We've gotten to know each other the dozen or so times you called to check on her."

A faint pause.

"Of course," he added, "I'm not about to think you'll let her out of your sight."

Xynn didn't answer, but the corner of her mouth lifted slightly.

Trish folded her arms.

"In a charitable mood today, Eryk?" she said. "Not like you."

Dalren ignored her.

"Caris and Alrek will meet you on the surface with a team," he said. "You'll have support."

Lily turned instinctively, looking for Tevya.

Tevya was already watching her.

For a moment, neither of them spoke.

Then Tevya gave a small, almost imperceptible shake of her head.

"I can't," she said.

Lily held her gaze a second longer than she meant to, something in the quiet certainty of it landing harder than the words themselves.

Then she nodded.

"Alright."

Behind her, Dalren's voice cut back in.

"That's your window," he said. "Get down there and find Eli."

There was a pause as if he was waiting for some action—but gave up.

"Dalren out."

The channel closed.

Lily turned to Trish.

"You know Dalren?"

For a moment, Trish didn't answer. She was still looking at the display, though nothing was there anymore—just the reflection of the bridge lights in the glass.

Then she blinked, like she was coming back from somewhere else, and gave a small shake of her head.

"Yeah," she said. "I do."

A beat.

"He was an ass back then."

She glanced sideways at Lily.

"Is he still an ass?"

Lily's mouth pulled into a crooked smile.

"Pretty much."

Trish huffed once—something between a laugh and a dismissal.

"Well," she said, pushing off the console, "seems like he's on our side at least."

She jerked her chin toward the exit.

"Get down there. I'll keep this party going."

Lily nodded, already turning.

She caught Xynn's eye across the room.

There was no hesitation there. No question.

"Here we go again," Lily said.

Xynn fell into step beside her as they moved toward the lift.

"I'm driving," she said.

Lily glanced over. "Oh?"

Xynn didn't look at her.

"I hate the way you fly."

· · · ·

The shuttle cut through Bimini's atmosphere in a clean, controlled descent.

"Salamander team has sent us coordinates," Lily said, eyes forward.

The planet rose to meet them—copper light, red sky, the same impossible glow threading through everything. It looked unchanged.

It wasn't.

Their shuttle touched down.

The heat hit the moment the hatch opened. Oppressive. Immediate. Like stepping into something that wanted to press you back out again.

The Salamander shuttle landed beside them seconds later.

Caris was out first.

She crossed the distance without hesitation, pulling Lily and Xynn into an embrace that caught both of them completely off guard.

"The old married couple," she said, breathless with it. "Thank Christ you're both okay."

For a second, Lily didn't know what to do with her hands.

After everything—after how she'd left things—

But Caris didn't seem to be holding onto any of that.

Water under the bridge.

Or something like it.

Alrek stepped forward next, the contrast immediate.

"I'm glad you're okay," he said.

It wasn't cold. Not exactly.

But it wasn't warm either.

"Taran says hi," he added. "And Ka-Lorrin, of course, found a reason that was entirely unnecessary—but I could tell he wanted me to pass his word along."

That landed closer to something familiar.

Lily smiled.

"Good to see you, Alrek."

He nodded once.

And they left it there.

Caris was already moving again, pulling a scanner from her kit. It came online in her hand with a soft hum, the display resolving into a layered map of the surrounding terrain.

"Dammit," she muttered. "If he were still an android, he'd be much easier to track."

She adjusted the scan parameters, her fingers moving quickly across the interface.

"His organic vessel is actually very difficult to isolate with all the Bimini lifeforms."

The map shifted—signals blooming and collapsing across the display.

She pointed.

"His shuttle went down here," she said. "No confirmed life readings, but we should check it first."

Xynn scanned the horizon, her posture already tightening.

"What about all those Kessler scrubbers skulking around?"

Alrek answered quickly.

"Dalren said they'll leave us alone," he said. "He's playing ignorant—told the commander here we're looking for a crewmate experiencing a mental health crisis."

Lily's mouth curved slightly.

"Sort of true."

Caris snapped the scanner shut.

"Let's go."

* * * *

They found the shuttle exactly where the coordinates said it would be.

Half-buried in red dust at the edge of a shallow rise, its hull still warm enough to shimmer faintly in the heat. The hatch hung open.

Lily slowed as they approached, something in the stillness settling wrong in her chest.

"Clear," one of the security officers called after a quick sweep.

Caris stepped up first, peering inside. "No sign of him."

Alrek moved past her, already scanning the control interface. "Systems are still active," he said. "He didn't power it down."

Which meant he hadn't intended to stay.

Lily stepped up beside him, glancing over the display. The logs were sparse—entry, descent, landing. Nothing after.

Alrek tapped the comm at his collar. "Salamander, this is Alrek. We've located the shuttle. It's intact but empty. I'm sending you the system data—see if engineering can pull anything useful from the onboard logs."

There was a brief delay before the reply came through—Dalren's voice, thinner now, filtered through layers of other conversations.

"Copy that," he said. "Engineering's standing by."

A second voice cut in—Ka-Lorrin, precise as ever.

"Receiving," he said. "Stand by."

The channel filled with a faint undercurrent—other voices, other threads, overlapping just enough to suggest something larger in motion.

"Team," Dalren added, coming back on. "Be advised—the commander here is... less than pleased with our presence."

That was one way to put it.

"They want us gone yesterday," he continued. "Jurisdiction is being debated. Aggressively."

A pause.

"Find your man," he said. "We'll handle the rest."

The line shifted again—Ka-Lorrin returning.

"There is nothing of value in the logs," he said. "Departure data is absent. No residual signal strong enough to isolate direction."

Alrek's jaw tightened slightly. "Understood."

The channel closed.

For a moment, no one spoke.

Then Xynn crouched, borrowing Caris' scanner and adjusting it in her hand. The display flickered as she cycled through modes, the visible spectrum collapsing into a muted wash before resolving again in infrared.

She swept it slowly across the ground.

"Here," she said.

Lily stepped closer.

At first, it looked like nothing—just uneven heat across the dust. Then the pattern resolved.

Footprints.

Faint, but consistent. Moving away from the shuttle, cutting across the terrain toward higher ground.

Xynn rose, already following the line.

"Old-fashioned," she said. "But it works."

They moved.

The terrain shifted as they climbed—loose stone giving way to harder ridges, the heat pressing in from all sides. The footprints grew harder to track in places, lost briefly where the ground changed, then picked up again where the dust returned.

The ridge opened suddenly.

One more step—and the ground dropped away.

They stopped at the edge of a natural overlook.

Below them, the land fell into a wide basin carved into the surface, the scale of it impossible to take in all at once.

Extraction platforms lined the floor in rigid, geometric patterns. Conveyor systems ran in steady, uninterrupted motion. Sunbow personnel moved along the perimeter, Kessler units weaving between them with practiced efficiency.

And the people—

Lily felt it hit before she could name it.

They were everywhere.

Working.

Hauling.

Moving in lines that never quite broke formation.

Caris didn't say anything.

But Lily saw her take it in—the way her posture shifted, just slightly, as the reality of it settled.

Alrek let out a breath.

"Dalren said it was bad," he said.

A beat.

"...but this—"

The rest of it didn't come.

Xynn was already scanning the basin, her focus narrowing.

"It's about to get uncomfortable," she said.

She pointed.

Lily followed her line of sight.

At first, it was just motion—another vehicle cutting across the site, faster than the others, out of pattern.

Then she squinted.

An open construction rig, engines pushed hard, tearing across the packed ground in a straight line toward one of the central scaffolding towers.

And at the controls—

"Eli," Lily said. "Shit."

He didn't slow.

The vehicle hit the base of the structure at full speed.

The supports gave in an instant.

The scaffolding folded in on itself, metal buckling, the upper sections collapsing in a cascading failure that sent debris crashing down across the site.

Everything broke.

Guards shouting. Workers scattering. The clean lines of the operation dissolving into motion and noise.

Blaster fire cut through it a heartbeat later.

"Go," Lily said.

They were already moving.

The descent was steep—loose stone sliding underfoot as they picked their way down the side of the ridge, the path barely a path at all.

Lily didn't wait for it to be clean.

She ran.

Behind her, she could hear the others following, the sound of boots striking rock, fragments of shouted warnings lost to the wind and distance.

Below them, the basin burned with movement.

It was farther than it looked.

By the time they reached the basin floor, the moment had already broken apart.

Smoke drifted where the scaffolding had collapsed. Equipment lay twisted across the ground. The clean lines of the operation were gone, replaced by movement that didn't organize itself back into order.

Most of the Bimini workers had scattered—vanishing into the edges of the site, into tunnels, into whatever spaces they knew would keep them out of sight.

Eli was nowhere to be seen.

Lily slowed, scanning, trying to find any trace of him in the chaos.

Nothing.

"Who the hell are you?"

The voice cut across the noise.

Lily turned.

The lead Kessler guard was already closing the distance—Urrathi, broad-shouldered, heavy with muscle and covered in ink that climbed up his neck and across his jaw. He didn't raise his voice. He didn't need to.

And then Lily saw it—

They were surrounded.

Kessler guards had moved in without her noticing, forming a loose circle around them, weapons already trained, angles covered. Efficient. Practiced.

"Oh—there's a misunderstanding," Alrek said, lifting his hands slightly, palms open. "We had nothing to do with—"

The guard took another step forward.

"Stop."

The word landed like a command, not a warning.

Alrek held.

"If you just call your superior," he said, keeping his tone level, "you'll find—"

"Shut up."

The guard didn't look at him when he said it. His attention stayed fixed on the group as a whole.

"Bag them up."

The order was quiet.

The response wasn't.

The guards moved in, weapons tightening, restraints already coming out—fast, coordinated, no hesitation.

Xynn exhaled softly beside Lily.

Not fear.

Annoyance.

She shifted her weight just slightly, her eyes already moving.

"Is that one of the TX-80s?" she said, almost conversational, nodding toward the nearest guard's rifle.

He didn't answer.

"Your firing pin's stripped," she added. "I can see the filament from here."

It was enough.

The guard glanced down—just for a fraction of a second.

Xynn moved.

The rifle was out of his hands before he realized it, the motion clean and precise, her body already rotating through the space he'd just vacated. He hit the ground a heartbeat later, unconscious.

By the time the others reacted, she was already in motion.

She dropped, rolled, and fired—two clean shots in opposite directions. Both guards went down before their weapons fully came up.

The circle broke.

The Salamander team drew, but the moment had already shifted.

Xynn was inside the formation.

The lead Urrathi turned toward her, reaching—

She stepped through it, fast and close, and drove the butt of the rifle into the back of his head.

He dropped hard.

Silence snapped back into place in fragments—smoke, heat, the low hum of damaged machinery still carrying through the air.

Xynn straightened, glancing once at the weapon in her hands before letting it fall.

"Kesslers," she said, brushing a strand of hair back from her face.

"So predictable."

Caris had the scanner back up before the dust had settled.

"Come on," she said. "While the trail's still fresh."

They moved.

The path narrowed as the terrain shifted, the footprints breaking and reforming across harder ground until they funneled toward a natural formation—a ring of stone rising out of the surface like something that had pushed up from below.

They slowed as they entered it.

And then—

Lily saw him.

Eli sat perched atop one of the larger rocks, five meters up, balanced with an ease that didn't quite belong to the shape of his body.

In his arms—

A child.

A young Bimini girl, small and still, held close against him.

"Put her down, Eli," Lily said.

He looked at them.

"You shouldn't have come."

His voice was low. Almost calm.

Then his gaze shifted—past Lily, past Xynn—

To the security officers.

Weapons trained.

"I'm not going to speak to you," he said, "while you're pointing those things at me."

Lily's focus sharpened.

She looked again—more carefully this time.

Eli wasn't holding the child as a shield.

He was holding her steady. Protective. Positioned between himself and the drop, not the weapons.

"Lower your weapons," Lily said.

There was a beat—just enough to feel the weight of it.

Then Caris gave a small, confirming nod.

The guards hesitated.

Then, slowly, they complied, lowering their rifles.

Eli watched until the last one dipped.

Only then did he move.

Without urgency, he shifted his weight and slid down the rock, boots catching against the surface in a controlled descent that felt almost like it belonged on a playground.

He landed lightly.

Kneeled.

And gently set the girl down.

"There now, Eeshtef," he said softly. "You need to run into the cavern there."

He pointed toward a narrow opening between the rocks.

"You'll come out the other side," he added. "I'm certain your family will be looking for you."

The girl didn't hesitate.

She ran—disappearing into the rocks in seconds.

Eli's eyes stayed fixed on where she'd gone.

"Remember when I caught you," he said, still kneeling, his voice carrying easily in the quiet that followed, "when you fell off that scaffolding on Earth."

A beat.

"That was when we met, I suppose."

"Datch caught me," Lily said.

Her voice was steady.

"You may have his memories," she added, "but I don't think you're him."

Eli stood.

Turned.

And Lily saw it then—

Alrek still had his weapon trained on him.

Eli walked toward it.

Didn't slow.

Stopped with the barrel inches from his chest.

"Are you going to shoot me," he asked, "young Alrek?"

"Just Alrek," he said.

His grip didn't waver.

"And I'll do what I have to."

It happened too fast to follow.

Eli stepped in—inside Alrek's space—just enough to break his balance.

The weapon was gone from Alrek's hands before anyone processed the movement.

And then it was up—

Pressed against the side of Alrek's head.

Everything froze.

Hands went up instinctively.

Lily knew. Even on stun—

that close, it would kill him.

"Eli," Lily said, taking a step forward. "Wait. Please."

"You all think I'm some kind of monster," Eli said.

There was something in his voice now—something raw, unsteady in a way that didn't match the precision of everything else he'd done.

"You think I'd murder."

"I saw you kill," Lily said.

She didn't soften it.

"It was the first thing you did in that form."

"I killed an actual monster," Eli said.

He spoke slowly, with a quiet edge.

He shoved Alrek forward, releasing him, but kept the blaster in his own hand.

"You shouldn't have come," he said again—this time looking directly at Alrek.

Then he turned back to Lily.

Crossed the space between them.

Close now.

Too close.

"This was supposed to be between us," he said, quieter.

He let the blaster fall.

It hit the ground with a dull, final sound.

Eli raised his hands.

Looked past Lily—

To Caris.

"Take me in," he said.

"I'm your prisoner."

. . . .

Lily didn't remember the walk to her quarters.

Only the door.

Only the sound of it sealing behind her.

She didn't stop.

Didn't take in the space she hadn't seen in weeks—her things, the quiet, the faint, steady hum of the Salamander beneath it all.

She tore the tactical vest free first, fingers clumsy against the fastenings, dragging it over her shoulders and letting it drop wherever it fell.

Her shirt came next—unzipped halfway, down to her collarbone—like she needed more air and didn't care how she got it.

It wasn't enough.

She couldn't breathe.

The room tilted—just slightly, just enough to make it feel like the floor wasn't where it was supposed to be.

Lily caught the edge of the desk, her grip tightening as the dizziness hit.

For a second, she thought she might go down.

Her chest burned.

Her lungs wouldn't settle.

And underneath it—

That moment.

Again.

And again.

And again.

Datch—no—

Eli—

The shift of it, the wrongness of it, the way it had all happened too fast and too clean and too *controlled*—

It hit her all at once, like she was watching it on repeat, unable to stop it.

A hundred times over.

The door chime sounded.

Sharp.

Too loud.

Lily dragged in a breath. Tight. Shallow.

"Come," she managed.

The door opened.

It was Alrek.

"Oh my god—are you okay?"

He crossed the room in two steps, a hand already reaching for her.

Lily nodded once, trying to catch her breath.

Then shook her head.

"No."

He just guided her to the bed and eased her down.

"Hey—easy," he said, quieter now.

Lily pressed her hands into her knees, trying to anchor herself.

"I didn't know," she said, her voice uneven. "Not until just now—why I started chasing this. This whole thing."

Alrek didn't interrupt.

He just listened.

"Caris was right," Lily said. "I push. I just keep pushing—for no reason. And I—"

"Lily."

He cut in, not sharp—but firm.

"Stop."

She looked up at him, surprised.

"You fucked up," he said. "But you did it honestly."

He took a breath.

"You can't give up being Lily."

He held her gaze.

"The galaxy needs people like you. People who act first—and deal with the fallout after."

The corner of his mouth twitched, just slightly.

"It also needs people like me," he added, "who clean up after you sometimes."

Then, more serious:

"But I'm saying this because I care about you."

He paused.

"Now isn't the time to make this about you."

Lily stared at him.

Processing.

Then—unexpectedly—a small laugh broke through.

She felt it in her chest first. The tension loosening, just enough to let her breathe again.

"Wow," she said. "You've really turned into an asshole."

Alrek let out a genuine laugh.

Lily shook her head, still smiling faintly, her body finally starting to settle.

"Thanks."

They pulled each other into a quick, tight hug—something unspoken healing between them.

Alrek stood first.

"Look," he said. "You've been through a lot."

His voice shifted—more grounded now.

"But we need you. Eli seems to want to talk to you. Alone."

Lily nodded, her breathing steady again.

"I'm ready," she said.

• • • •

The door to the brig slid shut behind her.

She had already convinced Caris to clear the room.

Eli stood behind the forcefield.

The cell wasn't cramped. Lily noticed that immediately. It looked more like a luxury suite than anything resembling confinement—certainly nothing like the cell she'd been held in on Earth.

He stood with his hands behind his back.

The way Datch used to stand at rest.

"In the deep, strange-scented shade of the great dark carob tree

I came down the steps with my pitcher

And must wait, must stand and wait, for there he was at the trough before me."

Eli's voice carried evenly across the barrier.

"I'm afraid I'm not familiar with that one."

"I would have thought D.H. Lawrence would be right up your alley."

"Haven't had a lot of time for reading lately."

They stood there in silence for a moment.

"You wanted to talk to me," Lily said.

"I imagine you have questions," Eli replied.

"Okay. If you want to do it that way." She folded her arms. "Why the jewel? Why give it to me if you knew it would knock me out? Did you know the council was going to be murdered?"

"You may not believe me," he said, "but it was for your protection. I thought I would reach you in time."

A pause.

"I did not expect you to go to Earth."

She held his gaze.

"I'm not going to do... whatever this is," Lily said, impatience creeping in. "Twenty questions. People died. Just tell me—did you cause this chaos, or were you trying to expose something?"

"Neither."

Lily exhaled sharply, dragging a hand across her ear as she looked down, collecting herself.

"Then why did you want to talk to me?"

"I wanted to apologize," Eli said. "I made a miscalculation. I allowed my own ends to interfere."

"Your own ends," Lily echoed, starting to pace. "At the end of the day, this is about profit and control, isn't it? The Union keeps the desperate docile, the powerful in power—and people like the Spire elite make more money."

Eli's expression shifted—something like surprise, followed by the faintest scoff.

"You still don't see," he said. "After everything you've put yourself through."

Lily stopped pacing.

Folded her arms again.

"This isn't about money," Eli said. "Or power."

A beat.

"It's about history."

Lily's jaw tightened.

"Are you going to give me anything, Eli?" she said. "Why are you here?"

"We've reached a point where facts matter less than intent."

Something in his expression changed—subtle, but real.

"I killed those people," he said.

The words landed clean. Unadorned.

"Now move on to what matters."

Lily didn't respond.

"The snake is entering that dreadful hole," Eli continued. "You don't have much time."

His expression smoothed again, the shift almost immediate. He took a casual step back, turning slightly to the side.

"It's already in motion."

Then, softer—almost under his breath, in a rough approximation of Dalren's voice:

"Set course for Gherion Prime."

Lily tilted her head.

Took a step back.

Then she turned and moved—fast.

The door slid open and she was already through it.

The outer chamber was crowded—Xynn, Caris, Alrek, Trish, Dalren—all there, pacing, waiting, the tension hanging thick in the air.

"Where's Tevya?" Lily asked.

Dalren answered immediately.

"She took leave," he said. "About an hour ago."

Xynn saw it then—the shift in Lily's face.

"She said she was going home."

Lily didn't hesitate.

"Gherion Prime."

Chapter 9: A Dress and an Effigy

TRISH WALKED INTO THE corridor with a smile she hadn't quite shaken from the night before.

It lingered at the edges—something easy, something she didn't feel the need to hide. The ship hummed around her in that familiar way, the steady rhythm of systems settling back into cadence after a stretch of absence. For the first time in a while, it felt like she was stepping back into something stable.

"Morning, Eryk," she said as she passed him.

Dalren glanced up from the console he was studying, like he hadn't expected to be addressed at all.

"Oh—" he said, catching himself. "It's Trish now, right?"

A small, almost apologetic pause.

"That'll take some getting used to."

Trish kept moving, not wanting to let it become a moment.

"Early meeting?" she asked.

Dalren nodded once.

"And I think it's your turn."

She followed his line of sight.

The admiral stood at the far end of the corridor, already watching her. Not waiting—expecting.

The smile slipped.

Her stomach dropped.

So much for a good day.

. . . .

The bridge was already in motion by the time Lily stepped onto it.

Voices overlapped. Data streamed across the displays faster than it could be verified. Gherion Prime filled the forward screen—its surface lit in scattered flashes, defensive grids coming online in uneven bursts.

"—multiple impact sites—"

"—that's not consistent with—"

"—confirm source of those signals—"

Lily glanced across the bridge.

Trish stood off to the side, chewing absently on her knuckle, her eyes fixed on the forward display. Ever since the distress call came through from Gherion Prime, she'd seemed—

Off.

Dalren stood at the center of it, not raising his voice, but somehow cutting through the noise anyway.

"I don't know what's happening down there," he said. "And I don't know who's giving the orders."

That got people's attention.

He turned slightly, eyes moving across the command deck.

"But we do know this—civilians are in danger. That's our priority."

He gestured toward the tactical display—highlighting a cluster of structures near one of the primary population centers.

"Primary objective: protect civilians in and around the vaccine production sites."

Another shift of the display—more data, less certain.

"Secondary objective: prevent any permanent damage to the production infrastructure."

Alrek stepped forward, already thinking three moves ahead.

"What if Union troops are on the offensive?" he asked. "We risk engaging our own side."

Dalren didn't hesitate.

"Then we don't engage unless we have no other choice," he said. "We are not down there to pick a side. We are down there to keep people alive."

He paused.

"And if that means standing between two groups who both think they're in the right—"

He let the rest of it hang.

"Then that's where we stand."

He looked directly at Lily.

"Lieutenant Starling—you're with the ground team."

As everyone began to disperse, Trish moved in close next to Dalren.

"This isn't like you at all, Eryk," she said, low but sharp as she closed the distance. "Breaking all the rules? You don't even know what you're fighting."

Dalren didn't turn right away. He finished issuing a command, tapped a panel, then finally looked at her.

"You still blame me?"

"I blame you for being so damn predictable."

Something in his expression shifted—softened, just for a second—but he didn't give ground.

"You don't know me, Trish," he said. "Not really. That was fifteen years ago."

She let out a short, humorless breath.

"Let me guess—you had a bad day? Why is bigotry always the default—"

He moved. She followed.

Around the bridge, through the current of officers and data streams, not caring who heard, not caring who was watching.

"Damn it, Trish," he said, sharper now. "I was your friend. Your head was in the field—and then it wasn't."

"You mean when I was Thomas."

"I mean when you stopped putting others before yourself."

That one came out louder than he intended.

The room fell quiet.

Even the background chatter dipped—just for a second.

Trish didn't flinch.

Dalren exhaled, the edge leaving his voice as quickly as it had come.

"Would you like to be useful, Trish?" he asked, tone controlled again.

She didn't argue.

"Then use those contacts of yours," he continued. "Find out what the hell is actually going on down there."

Trish held his gaze for a moment longer.

Then gave a small, tight nod.

Caris was already moving.

"Lily," she said, gesturing toward the exit.

Lily hesitated just long enough to glance back.

Trish caught her eye.

A look—sharp, steady.

I'm fine. Go.

So she went.

• • • •

The descent had been a white-knuckle drop through a sky choked with flak and ash, the shuttle bucking hard enough to rattle bone as it slipped past the Kessler blockade and dropped into a scorched plaza three blocks out.

Lily could still feel it in her legs as they moved.

Now they were on the ground.

And the vaccine manufacturing facility was right in front of them.

It rose out of the district in chrome and glass, massive and precise—and ringed in fire. Flames climbed its outer structures, reflecting back in warped, fractured light.

The air didn't just smell like smoke.

It tasted metallic. Sharp. Like copper.

Around them, the sector had collapsed into noise—plasma bursts, collapsing masonry, the distant churn of something too large to see through the haze.

"Move," Caris said.

They cut into a narrow maintenance alley, heat pressing in from both sides, the space barely wide enough for them to pass through at speed. Debris shifted underfoot. Somewhere above, something cracked and fell.

A massive community monitor flickered to life overhead.

Then another.

And another.

Within seconds, the same image filled every screen in sight.

An androgynous Gherionite stared out at them, composed, controlled. A clean lower-third slid into place beneath the image:

Marson Dontain — Planetary Parliament

"Citizens of Gherion Prime," he began, his voice cutting cleanly through the chaos.

Behind him, footage of the facility burned—angles that lingered just long enough on Union insignia to be unmistakable.

"The masks have fallen. Kessler troops, flying the Union's flag, have struck our heart—the very facility that produces the vaccines we designed to be life-saving—not for us, but for them."

Lily slowed, just slightly.

Not enough to stop. Enough to listen.

"This is what happens when we lower our guard around the organic beings who have always seen us as monsters."

The words were measured. Certain.

"Stand together. Hold your leadership accountable for this betrayal."

The feed looped.

Same images. Same message.

Alrek glanced up, frowning.

"Who the hell is that?"

"Marson Dontain," Lily said, her eyes still on the screen. "He's one of the Spire Elite."

A flicker of something cold settled in her chest.

"Veyshali thinks he's mixed up in this."

Xynn raised her long-range scopes, her silhouette sharp against the firelight as she tracked movement through the shimmering heat haze of the facility's lower levels.

"The politics can wait," she said, voice steady. "There are still people in there. Workers trapped by the fire line. If we don't move, the smoke will finish what the Kesslers started."

Lily nodded, her hand already going to her sidearm.

"That's the priority, then. Let's get to the door."

"Major problem," Caris cut in, her eyes locked on the scrolling data across her scanner. "The facility's Honey-Pot grid is active, but the IFF is critically damaged."

"IFF?" Lily asked.

"Identify Friend or Foe," Caris said. "Watch."

She scooped up a jagged piece of durasteel and tossed it toward the walkway.

The air didn't just sizzle—it cracked.

A pair of concealed kinetic turrets snapped to life along the building's facade, tracking the metal in a fraction of a second and shredding it into a spray of glowing sparks before it ever touched the ground.

Alrek let out a low whistle.

"And if it can't tell a worker from a hostile..."

"Then it's just a meat grinder with a logic error," Lily said. "Even if we get in—how do we get them out?"

Caris glanced up at Alrek.

"If we had access codes, I could hard-cycle the grid from the inside. With some engineering help."

Alrek gave a grim half-smile.

"Get me in there without me looking like Swiss cheese," he said, "and you'll have all the help you can get."

"So how do we beat it?" Lily asked.

Xynn angled the scanner, studying the shifting patterns, her brow tightening as she tracked the grid's rhythm through the interference.

"Look at the refresh rate," she said. "It's time-banding. There's a gap between pulses."

She glanced up.

"If we move in that window—"

"Not only would we have to time it perfectly," Caris cut in, "we'd have to move at under five KPH. And the thermal sensors are tuned for heat spikes. We keep our signatures under thirty-seven point seven degrees, or we're done."

Lily looked past them to the street.

Kessler units traded fire with local security forces, plasma bolts cutting wild arcs through the smoke, more noise than strategy. Above them, the upper levels of the facility burned unchecked, the fire climbing higher, feeding on itself. No sirens. No coordination. Just escalation.

Too risky.

Too—

She pushed the thought aside.

"We don't have time to debate," Lily said.

She looked back at the others.

"Let's hurry up and be slow."

They found a large, discarded thermal-insulation panel and huddled behind it, four bodies pressed into a single, sweating shadow.

The walk became an exercise in pure, agonizing discipline. The street roared around them—a cacophony of plasma fire and collapsing structure—but behind the panel there was only the sound of their breathing, too loud in their own ears.

Every time an explosion rocked the pavement, the instinct was to run.

But they held it together.

"Step...," Caris whispered. "The band is sweeping... now. Move. Two meters. Stop."

Lily kept her eyes forward, forcing her body to obey. Her heart hammered hard enough to feel in her throat, sweat slipping down the side of her face, but she kept her stride measured, controlled, almost detached from the chaos pressing in on all sides.

"Think cool thoughts," Alrek murmured, his shoulder tight against hers.

A stray blaster bolt from the Kessler skirmish struck a vehicle nearby, showering the panel in a burst of sparks that rattled through the metal and into Lily's bones. She flinched—just enough to feel it—but didn't break pace.

"Hold," Caris whispered again. "Hold—"

The pulse passed.

"Move."

They inched forward.

Again.

Again.

Until the canopy of a side entrance finally rose above them, a dark overhang cutting a clean shadow into the firelight.

"Now," Caris said.

They slipped beneath it, crossing into the building's blind spot in one last measured step.

Only then did the pressure break.

Caris sagged back against the wall, her breath coming fast, her face drawn pale in the shifting light.

"We should be okay now," she said, already reaching for the lock.

Xynn caught her wrist, gently guiding her aside. Then she stepped in, drawing her sidearm in one smooth motion and putting two clean shots through the door—blowing it wide open.

"Come on," Lily said, already moving.

She stepped through into the smoke-filled interior.

The stairwell had turned into a chimney.

Heat pressed down from above and billowed up from below, and every breath tasted like burnt insulation. The air moved wrong—too fast, too hot—pulling smoke past them in a constant, choking draft.

Alrek kept his scanner angled ahead as they climbed, reading through walls, adjusting on the move.

"Six floors up," he said, his voice tight. "Clustered near the north end. They've sealed themselves into an interior room."

Lily didn't answer.

She counted the steps.

The fifth-floor landing was gone—what had been a corridor now folded in on itself under a collapsed section of ceiling, debris stacked high enough to block any path through. They didn't waste time trying to clear it. Caris found a service shaft half-buried behind a twisted support column, and they climbed the rest by hand, hauling themselves up through narrow, heat-soaked metal until the shaft finally opened into the next level.

They pulled out into a hallway that felt like a wind tunnel, heat and smoke rushing past them in a steady, punishing current.

At the far end, exactly where the scanner said it would be, the reinforced bulkhead of the main lab stood sealed.

A flickering sign above it pulsed in emergency red:

SECURE BIO-ZONE

Alrek was already moving.

He dropped to one knee beside the door, ripping a maintenance panel free from the wall with a sharp pull, exposing a tight cluster of unfamiliar circuitry beneath.

"Gherionite recursive lock," he muttered, squinting through the sting of sweat and smoke. "Twenty minutes on a good day."

Lily stepped past him.

Pressed her palm flat against the door.

The metal was hot enough to sting.

"We know you can hear us."

Lily pitched her voice to carry through the thick plating.

"We're not here to finish what started downstairs. We're not here on Union orders. We came because we've been tracking a conspiracy—someone deliberately seeding hatred between Gherion Prime and the Union. We think you're caught in the middle of it."

She paused just long enough to steady her breath.

"Same as us."

Nothing from the other side.

Only the muffled hiss of fire suppressors cycling somewhere deep in the walls.

Lily leaned closer, her forehead nearly brushing the hot metal.

"The Gherionite vaccine has saved countless lives," she said, quieter now, but no less certain. "People I care about are alive because of what this facility built."

Her hand stayed flat against the door.

"I'm not going to stand here and let it become a tomb."

Behind her, Alrek's hands stilled on the exposed wiring.

For a moment, nothing changed.

Then—

A low, mechanical groan.

The locking gears began to retract.

The bulkhead slid open.

The air inside hit them first—hotter, heavier, thick with chemical burn and failing systems.

The scientists looked... wrong.

Not in form—but in posture.

Exhausted. Collapsing inward.

Several were crouched over others slumped against the far wall, hands pressed to shoulders and chests in gestures that had nothing mechanical about them. Their synthetic skin was streaked with soot, their expressions drawn tight with something that read, unmistakably, as fear.

One of them stepped forward.

Tall. Damaged—collar to ribs, the plating warped and blackened. One eye flickered, just slightly dimmer than the other.

He glanced at their Union patches.

Held there for a moment.

Then looked away.

"We have wounded," he said.

His voice was controlled, but there was something worn behind it, something fraying at the edges.

"Their thermal regulators are failing. The heat in here—"

He shook his head once.

"They won't last another ten minutes."

Alrek was already moving, scanner out, dropping to a crouch beside the nearest fallen figure. He exhaled slowly as the readings came in.

"Logic cores are spiking," he said. "If we don't get them cooled down, they'll cascade."

Lily and Xynn moved to the narrow reinforced window at the far end of the lab.

Below them, the street was still chaos—blaster fire cracking through the smoke, flashes of plasma strobing against the buildings, the whole sector moving without pattern or coordination. But two blocks out, just beyond the edge of the Honey-Pot perimeter, a Gherionite emergency medic rig sat idling, its lights cutting faint lines through the haze.

Close enough to see.

Too far to reach.

"There's a rig right there," Xynn said. "Your own defense grid is keeping it out."

Lily leaned closer to the glass, tracking the distance, the angles, the movement below. The wounded behind her couldn't make that run. Not through the fire. Not through the grid.

She felt the shape of it before she had the words.

"I have an idea," she said.

"Lily," Alrek said, without looking up from his scanner, "whatever you're thinking—"

She turned back toward him.

"No. This time it isn't hairbrained."

Alrek glanced up, unconvinced.

Lily turned to the lead scientist.

"Your building's climate system—zoned cooling, independent compressors per floor?"

He blinked, the question clearly not what he'd expected.

"Yes."

"And the roof," she continued, already thinking it through. "Is there an HVAC service platform up there? Big enough for the rig to land on if it had a clear approach vector?"

"Technically," he said. "But the Honey-Pot grid extends vertically. Anything trying to descend through it gets flagged as a threat."

Lily glanced at Caris.

"Can you pull the grid's targeting parameters and redefine the medic rig's transponder as a friendly—something low-priority. A maintenance drone."

Caris was already moving, her wrist unit alive with shifting layers of interface.

"That's... actually not complicated," she said. "If I spoof the rig's ID against the facility's maintenance registry—"

Her fingers paused, then resumed faster.

"Yes. Give me a minute."

"While she does that," Lily said, turning to Alrek, "we use the building's zoned cooling to buy time. You said the wounded are heat-spiking—can we reroute the surviving compressors from the intact floors and vent cold air directly into this room?"

Alrek stared at her for a fraction of a second.

Then he pushed to his feet, already turning, already scanning the space.

"There," he said, pointing to a maintenance conduit running along the upper wall. "If I cross-wire the return lines—"

He was moving before he finished the thought.

"It'll overclock the remaining units. Burn them out, probably—but yes. Yes, it could work."

The lead scientist watched the exchange, something shifting behind his eyes.

Then he stepped in beside Alrek without a word.

Lily didn't pause.

"Xynn—get to the roof. Find us a landing zone."

Xynn was already gone.

The room settled into motion around her—urgent, focused, no wasted movement.

Lily took it in for half a second: the wounded slumped against the walls, the lead scientist repositioning a coolant line at a colleague's neck with careful precision, Alrek half inside a conduit arguing under his breath with a junction that refused to cooperate.

Then she reached for the nearest toolkit and stepped in to help.

The roof access was a single metal door, warped in its frame from the heat below.

Xynn had already forced it open. She was crouched behind the stairwell housing when Lily came through, the noise hitting her like a physical thing—blaster fire cracking across the skyline, the rising whine of counter-fire, something heavy collapsing a block to the east with a dull, concussive roll.

The service platform stretched out in front of them.

Wide enough for the rig to land.

Barely.

That wasn't the problem.

"Comms are still black," Caris said over Lily's comm tag, her voice clipped. "Whatever they're using to jam the street is blanketing everything in a six-block radius—except for very close range. The rig crew can't receive. They don't know to come up. They're just sitting there waiting for a signal that isn't getting through."

Lily moved to the edge and looked down.

The medic rig was still there, two blocks out, idling just beyond the perimeter. Squat. Armored. Lights cutting through the haze in steady pulses. The crew would be inside, waiting for orders that weren't coming.

Between here and there—

Open street.

Active crossfire.

Smoke rising in thick, dirty columns that shifted with the wind and the shockwaves.

No cover.

No clean path.

Lily turned back toward the equipment locker Xynn had already torn open.

Inside, among the maintenance tools and harnesses, something caught her eye.

A grav-tether rig.

—the kind used for exterior repair work on high floors. Magnetic anchor, variable-tension line, friction brake on a wrist mount..

Designed for descending the outside of a building in a controlled drop.

Or, if you angled it right and had enough elevation, crossing a street.

Lily picked it up.

"No," Xynn said.

Not a question. Not even a reaction, really — more like she'd been waiting for it.

"The line will reach," Lily said, already turning the anchor over in her hands, checking the charge. "If I fire it at the rig's chassis, the magnetic lock will hold. With the elevation, I've got the angle to clear the street. I slide down, I'm there in under a minute. I tell them the plan in person, they bring it up to the roof."

"And while you're hanging over an active firefight on a wire."

"I'll be moving fast."

"Lily."

Xynn's voice dropped, and something in it made Lily go still.

"I came halfway across this galaxy to keep you alive."

"Someone has to go down there—"

"Then I go."

"Xynn..."

Xynn threw her hands up with a frustrated growl.

"Why do I even bother."

Lily reached out and touched her arm, brief and light—not quite an apology, not quite a promise.

Then she turned back to the edge.

Braced the anchor against the parapet.

Took a bearing on the medic rig's chassis below.

And fired.

The magnetic head shrieked out on its line, trailing a thin, bright cable that caught the firelight as it arced across the street. It struck the rig's hull with a resonant clang and locked.

Lily clipped the wrist brake to the line, climbed onto the parapet, and looked down.

The street was bad.

She'd seen worse, she told herself—and mostly believed it.

She jumped.

The grav-line snapped taut and she dropped fast—faster than she expected, the friction brake earning its name as she squeezed it to keep from becoming a projectile. The street opened beneath her in a blur of motion and light, plasma bursts cutting erratic paths through the smoke. She tucked her knees instinctively as a line of fire crossed somewhere below, close enough to feel.

Wind and heat and the high, keening shriek of the line—

Then the rig's roof was there.

She hit hard, both boots, momentum carrying through as she rolled and caught herself against the turret housing with both hands.

For a second—two—she stayed where she was, cheek pressed to the warm metal, the sounds of the street suddenly too close, too loud.

Then she pushed up, dropped off the side, and hit the ground running.

Two sharp knocks on the crew hatch.

It cracked open.

Lily was already talking.

Above, on the roofline, she didn't look back.

But she knew Xynn was watching.

• • • •

The hatch cracked open just enough for Lily to slip through.

"They can't reach you," she said, already moving. "Grid's active—we're spoofing your transponder. You come up to the roof, you'll clear it. But we don't have long. Wounded are heat-spiking."

That was enough.

The medics moved.

• • • •

The rig lifted hard off the street, thrusters kicking in as it cleared the perimeter and climbed straight up toward the roof.

Lily stood braced inside the cabin, one hand on the frame, the city dropping away beneath them in a blur of fire and motion. No one spoke. The crew worked around her, already prepping equipment, already moving with purpose.

They hit the roof fast.

Xynn was there before the hatch was fully open, hauling the first stretcher across without a word.

The roof snapped back into motion.

Medics fanned out, lifting, stabilizing. Alrek had the cooling running at full burn, air finally moving through the doorway. Caris didn't look up from her interface.

"We've got it," she said. "Honey-Pot's down."

"Good timing," Lily said.

The last of the scientists were loaded quickly. The lead one paused just long enough to meet Lily's eyes, then turned back to secure the final stretcher.

"Go."

The hatch sealed. The rig lifted clean through the dead grid and disappeared into the smoke.

For a moment, the roof stilled.

Lily turned.

Xynn was watching her.

Annoyed.

"You got lucky."

"Yeah," Lily said. "Something like that."

Xynn stepped in and kissed her—quick, certain.

She pulled back.

"Now," she said, "can we go kick some ass or what?"

They came out of the stairwell with targeting sensors sliding into place over their left eyes, blasters already drawn, the world sharpening into threat markers and motion vectors as the system synced to the chaos outside.

The perimeter was still active.

They didn't hesitate.

Caris took point, calling angles as they moved, Alrek just behind her, Lily and Xynn fanning out to cover the flanks as they pushed into the open. Blaster fire cut across their path almost immediately—Kessler units repositioning, firing without clear pattern, more noise than coordination.

They moved through it anyway.

Short bursts. Controlled shots. No wasted motion.

A wrecked transport gave them a moment of cover.

Xynn leaned out just enough to scan the far side of the street—and then she smiled.

"Will you look at that."

"What is it?" Lily asked, keeping her weapon trained downrange.

"I'll be right back."

Before Lily could respond, Xynn was already gone—slipping low across the street, using the smoke and debris like it had been laid out for her.

Lily swore under her breath but held position.

"Cover her," Caris said.

They did.

Xynn reached one of the Kessler vessels at the edge of the engagement zone, ducked behind it, and vanished from sight.

A second later, a tarp came loose.

Something underneath shifted.

Then unfolded.

When Xynn came back, she didn't run.

She clanked.

The Saravethi flea moved with a low, mechanical rhythm, compact but powerful, its distinct hopping motion carrying her forward in bounding strides, armor plates catching the firelight as it closed the distance.

"Ready?" she said over the comm.

Lily couldn't help it.

"So that's a flea."

"Try to keep up," Xynn replied.

They pushed forward again.

This time, they hit harder.

The flea leapt ahead, landing inside the Kessler line and breaking it open, forcing units to scatter and reposition. Lily and the others followed through the gap, tightening formation as they advanced, shots more precise now, movement more aggressive.

They were no longer reacting.

They were taking ground.

At the center of it all, the command platform came into view—a raised structure, partially shielded, Kessler commanders clustered around it, issuing orders that didn't quite match the battlefield.

The team closed in.

Formed a perimeter.

Weapons trained.

And just like that—

They had them surrounded.

. . . .

Back on the ship, the air felt different.

Quieter.

But no less tense.

Dalren stood at the center of the briefing room, hands clasped behind his back, the posture controlled even if everything else wasn't.

"The official position of the Union," he said, "is that they have no knowledge of these events beyond a report that Gherionite forces attacked an authorized contractor during a routine shipping operation."

Malik let out a short, disbelieving huff.

Caris echoed it under her breath.

Lily caught it—and couldn't help the small snicker that slipped out before she stopped it.

Dalren didn't react.

"Of course we know that's absurd," he continued. "But that's the position being taken."

He shifted slightly, eyes moving across the room.

"This has all the markings of a false flag."

Dryst Amaris tilted his head.

"But to what end?"

Dalren exhaled once, measured.

"That's what I intend to find out."

A brief pause, then:

"We're diverting to Starbase Four. I have a meeting with Admiral Clouer."

His gaze settled, decision already made.

"Dismissed."

Everyone else filtered out.

Trish stayed.

She moved to stand beside him, close enough that it didn't feel accidental, both of them looking out at the stars beyond the glass.

"Do you think someone can't be focused on themselves and on the mission, Eryk?"

He didn't turn.

"That was a long time ago," he said. Then, after a moment, "And for what it's worth, I'm sorry. The admiral asked what I thought. I didn't think they'd transfer you."

Trish nodded, eyes still forward.

"I brushed up on your file," she said. "Looks like you learned life can get complicated."

"Maybe sometimes," Dalren said, a quiet laugh slipping through. "So, tell me—what's your stake in all of this?"

Trish didn't answer right away.

"Sometimes you can fix things," she said quietly. Then her voice lifted, just slightly. "But sometimes what was there has to... disappear. You have to burn it down."

The words hung there between them.

"But mostly," she said, "I just hate it when stupid wins."

Dalren turned.

"Fair enough."

He smiled, just enough to show those too-perfect teeth.

She smiled back.

Then she turned to go.

"I'm glad you're here, Trish."

She paused, just briefly, then gave a small nod and stepped out.

· · · ·

In Lily's quarters, they were trying—somewhat unsuccessfully—to get settled. Gear half-stowed, the air still carrying the faint smell of smoke and heat.

"I could have sworn I left a toothbrush here," Xynn said, scanning the counter. "And I know you didn't throw it away, because you never throw anything away."

Lily glanced over at her.

"Hey," she said. "I'm sorry."

Xynn looked back, one brow lifting.

"It's only a toothbrush."

"I'm serious," Lily said. "I'm sorry. For the... risk-taking."

Xynn let out a quiet breath, the edge of a smile still there but softer now.

"We got the job done," she said. "I just—"

She shook her head slightly.

"I don't want to lose you. But I don't control you. And sometimes that's... frustrating."

A small pause.

"Especially when your partner is prone to saving the galaxy."

Lily snorted.

"Let's take a few minutes," she said, stepping closer, "and not save anybody."

Xynn didn't argue.

They fit together easily, like it didn't require thought.

Closing the distance once again.

Chapter 10: Looking for Tenzo

THE KITCHEN HAD STOPPED feeling strange.

Not long ago, Lily would have expected a place like this to feel out of step with everything else on Gherion Prime. But now it just... fit. Light across the counter. Dishes stacked where they were easy to reach. Something warm on the stove.

Tevya stood at the counter, sleeves rolled, working through the motions with quiet focus. Not fast. Not optimized. Just practiced.

Xynn leaned in the doorway, watching.

Lily sat at the table, turning her fork between her fingers.

They'd fallen into a rhythm here. Work during the day—rebuilding, hauling, patching together what Leviathan's Hand had torn apart. Evenings quieter. Mornings like this.

It would have been easy to believe that was all it was.

It wasn't.

They were here for Ronin.

They were here because he had slipped through the cracks after fleeing Gherion Prime, and Lily and Xynn had followed the threads under the softest cover she could manage.

A honeymoon.

And underneath that—

Datch.

Tevya thought he was gone.

Meanwhile, a fragment of him sat not far from where Lily was sitting now, silent and hidden and very much not gone.

Lily picked up her fork.

Put it down again.

Tevya turned from the stove with three plates and set them down without comment.

"Eat," she said, not unkindly.

Xynn pushed off the doorway and stepped into the room. Her attention shifted almost immediately to the far end of the counter.

A small stone Buddha sat there—portly, seated, its rounded belly prominent, hands resting easily in its lap. The kind meant to suggest abundance. Prosperity. A life with enough to share.

She tipped her head.

"Isn't that a human symbol?"

Tevya followed her gaze.

"Yes," she said. "I found it on Earth. Student exchange, when I was very young."

She crossed over and rested her fingers lightly against it.

"I've always been interested in how food brings people together."

A small pause.

"Not just practically. Historically."

Lily glanced up at that.

Tevya gave a faint smile, still looking at the statue.

"You learn a lot about a species from what they share."

Lily took a bite of the food, though she didn't really taste it..

Across from her, Xynn ate easily enough, or at least looked like she did.

Lily tried to follow her lead.

This could have been real.

That was the problem.

Tevya moved back to the stove, checking the heat.

"I thought we could head to the eastern block after this," she said. "One of the older facades gave out overnight."

"That's fine," Xynn said.

"Yeah," Lily added. "Of course."

Tevya looked at her for a moment.

"As long as you're not running off again today."

Lily held the look for a second too long.

Then shook her head.

"Not today."

Tevya nodded once and turned back to the stove.

Lily dropped her eyes.

The words cycled in her mind once more.

Datch is alive.

Not whole. Not the same. But not gone.

Her throat tightened.

Under the table, Xynn's hand closed around hers. Quick. Steady.

Lily exhaled slowly.

When she looked up again, Tevya was facing the counter, her attention resting near the small stone figure.

A souvenir, Lily told herself.

Just something she brought back.

Tevya reached out and nudged it a fraction of an inch, straightening it.

"People think history lives in monuments," she said. "It usually lives in habits."

Lily looked down at her plate.

Outside, the work went on.

Inside, the morning held.

And none of them said what they knew.

. . . .

"—we will not stand by while our people are made dependent on systems that were never designed for us."

Gherion Prime filled the forward display.

The bridge of the *Salamander* was quiet in a way Lily didn't trust. Not still—never still—but focused. Every station manned, every set of eyes fixed forward.

Marson Dontain stood at the center of the broadcast.

He wasn't imposing. Not physically. His frame was lean, composed, his movements controlled down to the smallest shift of posture. But the room behind him—high-ceilinged, polished, deliberately austere—made him feel larger than he was.

Deliberately.

"Today, we begin the process of severing all remaining ties with the Union," he said.

No hesitation.

No buildup.

Just the decision, already made.

A subtle shift rippled across the bridge. Not surprise—everyone here had already seen the headlines—but something closer to recognition. The kind that comes when a possibility becomes real.

Dontain continued.

"For too long, we have allowed ourselves to be folded into a system that does not understand us, does not prioritize us, and—when pressed—does not hesitate to sacrifice us."

Behind him, the image shifted.

The vaccine facility.

Fire. Smoke. Union insignia visible just long enough to register before the angle changed.

Careful.

Curated.

"Recent events have made one thing clear," Dontain said. "Our future cannot be entrusted to those who see our survival as negotiable."

Lily stood near the back of the bridge, arms folded, trying not to react to the images.

Trying not to think about the people inside that building.

Trying not to think about how close they had come to losing all of them.

"He's not even pretending," Alrek muttered under his breath.

"Why would he?" Trish said, not looking away from the screen. "He already has what he needs."

Lily glanced over.

Trish had that look again—focused, calculating, a step ahead of the room.

Dontain's voice carried on, steady, unhurried.

"In accordance with emergency provisions ratified by the Planetary Parliament, and with the full support of the acting leadership, Gherion Prime will formally withdraw from all Union treaties effective immediately."

There it was.

Not a threat.

Not a negotiation.

A door closing.

Dalren stood at the center of the bridge, hands clasped behind his back, watching without interruption. His expression didn't change, but Lily could see it in the set of his shoulders.

He was already moving through the implications.

Already looking for a path that probably wasn't there.

"The Union will call a vote," someone said from tactical.

"They have to," Caris replied quietly.

"Won't matter," Trish said.

That got a few looks.

She didn't acknowledge them.

"Walk me through that," Lily said.

Trish finally glanced her way.

"The Union vote was always a stalemate," she said. "Gherion on one side, the outer sectors split, Earth balancing the whole thing whether they liked it or not."

She gestured toward the screen.

"Remove Earth—"

"They didn't remove Earth," Alrek said.

Trish's mouth tightened.

"They didn't have to."

Lily felt it before she said it.

"The council."

Trish nodded once.

"The Hedon Council wasn't just local governance," she said. "They were the only group actively pushing for intervention that didn't benefit from the current supply chain."

Her eyes flicked back to the display.

"Valen's faction had just enough influence to slow things down. Force oversight. Ask the wrong questions."

"And now they're dead," Lily said.

"And now they're dead," Trish echoed.

A beat.

"And Earth abstains," she added. "Too busy cleaning up its own mess to take a side."

The shape of it settled into place.

Not chaos.

Design.

"They broke the deadlock," Lily said quietly.

Trish didn't smile.

"No," she said. "They ended it."

"—this is not an act of isolation," Dontain said. "It is an act of preservation."

The feed cut.

The bridge lights adjusted slightly as the transmission ended, the image of Gherion Prime shrinking back into tactical overlays and system data.

No one spoke for a moment.

Dalren didn't turn right away. He stood there, watching the space where Dontain had been.

Then—

"We've received orders," he said.

That got everyone's attention.

"Sector Twelve. We are to resume vaccine distribution operations effective immediately."

The words landed flat.

Routine. Clean. Disconnected from everything they had just seen.

Alrek frowned. "Really?"

"That's the directive," Dalren said.

Trish leaned back against the console, arms folded.

"I guess that's it."

Lily looked at her.

"We have our answers," she finished.

Lily didn't respond.

She looked back at the empty display.

• • • •

The lights were out in their quarters.

Xynn was already in bed.

Lily wasn't.

The glow from the console cast the room in soft blue as she scrolled through archived footage.

"Lily," Xynn said from the dark. "You're going to burn your eyes out."

"I'm fine."

A small exhale from the bed.

"Come to bed."

Lily ignored it.

"I don't understand how this ends with him," she said.

She pulled up another clip.

Dontain—from a few years ago. Less polished. Lesser title beneath his name.

"—we cannot build a future that depends on systems that do not reflect who we are—"

Lily scrubbed forward.

Another.

"—Gherion Prime must stand on its own feet—"

Another.

"—our strength has always come from understanding our history—"

She stopped.

Rewound.

Watched again.

History.

She opened a different file. Older.

The image quality dropped slightly—less official, less curated.

Dontain stood in a smaller room this time. Not a government space. Something more personal.

Behind him—

Lily leaned forward.

Zoomed in.

There.

"Jesus Christ," Lily said.

Behind her, the bed shifted.

"What?" Xynn said, already sitting up. "What is it?"

Lily was already moving.

Out of the chair. Grabbing her jacket.

"Where are you going?"

The door slid open.

"The brig."

. . . .

Eli was standing when Lily entered the inner chamber of the brig.

He didn't turn right away. Just stood there, hands loosely at his sides, as if he had been listening for something that had already passed.

Lily dismissed the guard before the door had finished closing.

There was a brief hesitation, then the guard stepped out. The door shut again with a soft seal.

Eli turned to face her. His expression wasn't confrontational. More contemplative.

"Expecting me?" Lily asked.

Eli tilted his head slightly, considering the question.

"Sleep is a funny thing, isn't it?" he said. "Part of me always wondered what it would be like. Now that I require it, I find it... elusive."

Lily didn't smile.

"What, no poetry today?" she said, an edge to it.

Eli's expression shifted—something like a smile, there and gone, replaced by something quieter. More attentive.

"I know the truth," Lily said. "Or at least part of it. You weren't trying to surface a conspiracy."

She took a step closer.

"You were protecting someone."

She held out her hand.

Eli's gaze dropped to it.

She saw something real in his eyes then. Something less controlled.

In her palm sat the small stone Buddha from Xynn's ship. The one Tevya had given them for luck.

Simple. Rounded. Out of place here—more so even than it had been on Gherion Prime.

"I saw one just like it," Lily said. "In old footage of Marson Dontain's office."

She looked up at him.

"Why would a Gherionite reformist and politician have an Earth kitchen ornament on his desk?"

Eli didn't answer.

"Why, Datch?"

It came out unbidden, landing heavily between them.

Eli looked at her.

Something in his expression shifted—something that hadn't been there a moment before. Not quite grief. Not quite memory. But close enough to both that Lily felt it in her chest.

"The records won't show any of this," he said quietly.

He moved slightly, not pacing—just adjusting his stance, as if aligning himself with the thought.

"Tevya and Dontain were built together. Born as twins."

He glanced toward the far wall, though there was nothing there to see.

"The parent died. They were separated when they were quite young."

Lily listened.

"They found each other again later," Eli said. "They decided to keep any trace of their connection off the record. It seems back then they were... less careful."

Lily shifted her grip on the statue, her thumb catching on a slight texture at the base. She tilted it toward the light, revealing the word *Tenzo* in paint so faded it was little more than a ghost against the stone.

"But they grew closer?" she said finally.

"Yes," Eli said. "In many ways. Despite their differences."

"His ideology..."

Eli watched her, then gave a small, knowing tilt of his head.

"You'd think it incompatible with Tevya's, wouldn't you?"

He let that sit for a moment.

"She was always fascinated by the culture of our progenitors."

A brief pause.

"But there was something else she valued just as much."

His gaze drifted—not away from her, but past, as if he were looking at a version of Tevya that wasn't in the room.

"The idea that we didn't need anyone else," he said. "That if we worked together, we could have everything we needed. Right there. On Gherion Prime."

He looked back at her.

"That was the shared heart of it."

Lily could feel her pulse rising in her temples.

"So Dontain..." she said. "He twisted her into this. A murderer."

Eli let out a breath—not quite a sigh.

"You have it the wrong way around."

Lily stilled.

"After Tevya learned the truth," he said, "about our ancestors destroying their makers... something changed in her."

Lily frowned.

"I didn't see that."

Eli's gaze softened, just slightly.

"You weren't looking for it."

The room felt smaller all of a sudden.

Lily stepped closer.

"Where is she?"

Eli met her eyes.

For a moment, she saw him clearly. No deflection. No misdirection. Just focus.

"I'll tell you," he said.

A pause.

"But on one condition."

• • • •

The conference room lights were too bright for the hour.

Dalren stood at the head of the table, a cup of coffee in one hand, the other braced lightly against the surface as he looked over the empty monitors, not yet powered up.

Trish sat off to the side, rubbing sleep from her eyes, her hair still pulled back in something that had been neat at some point and had since given up.

Xynn stood near the wall, arms folded, watching the door.

Lily paced.

She had gotten them all here. She was trying to find the words.

They slipped out anyway.

"Tevya killed the Hedon council," she said.

No one spoke.

For a moment, it didn't seem to land—like the words had entered the room and were still looking for somewhere to settle.

Then the silence deepened.

Dalren set his coffee down.

Slowly.

"Do you have proof?"

Xynn shifted slightly.

"Other than Eli's word."

Lily nodded.

"It all goes back to the Jewel. Datch and Tevya had them made to complement each other. The signatures are nearly identical—but there's a mirrored variance in the tail frequency. That's how we prove it was Tevya's weapon that killed Valen and the others."

She held her ground, even as saying it made her feel sick.

Trish rubbed her chin.

"Mostly adds up," she said. "But why did Eli give you the Jewel?"

"Partly insurance," Lily said. "He assumed I'd keep it far from Earth. In case Tevya did what he thought she might."

A small pause.

"And partly insurance for me. If I went after her and used it, he knew it would lead him right to me."

Xynn frowned.

"Not exactly airtight logic."

Lily nodded.

"I think Eli was working more on instinct than anything else."

Dalren didn't engage with that. He moved on.

"Where are they going?"

"Bimara," Lily said. "Where Eli was reborn. She built her base in the ruins there. Last place anyone would think to look."

The room went quiet again.

They all looked at one another, then back to Dalren.

Trish broke it.

"Look—you two are in the fleet. Xynn and I aren't."

Dalren gave a small nod.

"I'll violate orders if I have to."

"It may not come to that," Lily said. "Eli can find her. But he'll only help if he and I go."

A beat.

"Alone."

She felt Xynn react beside her—subtle, but immediate.

Dalren considered that.

Then nodded.

"How can we help?"

• • • •

The shuttle bay was quieter than Lily expected.

Not empty.

Worse.

People were waiting.

Alrek stood near the edge of the platform, hands loosely at his sides, trying to look like he hadn't been there long. The Raath-Ka were beside him, still and composed in that way that never quite read as calm or tense. Caris and Malik stood together, speaking softly until Lily approached. Basco lingered off to one side, and Charlie gave her a small, uncertain wave.

Lily slowed.

"Wow," she said. "This feels like a great way to jinx it."

Xynn shot her a look.

"Don't even joke about that."

Lily held up a hand. "Fair."

Caris stepped forward before anything else could be said.

She didn't hesitate—just pulled Lily into a tight embrace.

For a second, it felt normal. Familiar.

Then Lily felt it—Caris holding on just a fraction too long.

When she pulled back, her eyes were full of tears.

She didn't try to explain it.

Didn't say anything at all.

She just turned and walked out of the shuttle bay.

Fast.

Lily watched her go, a crease forming between her brows.

Malik stepped in beside her.

"Don't worry about it," he said quietly. "She'll be okay. Good luck, Lily."

He gave Lily a brief, steady look, then followed Caris out.

The moment closed behind them.

Alrek stepped forward next.

"Try not to do anything reckless," he said.

Lily gave him a look.

"I feel like that ship has sailed."

Alrek allowed the smallest hint of a smile.

"Then try not to make it worse."

Taran gave her one of his famous bear hugs and Ka-Lorrin nodded subtly.

"Return," he said simply.

Lily nodded.

"I will."

Basco gave her a quick salute. Charlie lingered for a second longer, then stepped back, as if unsure what belonged in a moment like this.

Xynn moved in before it could stretch.

She didn't say anything.

Just pulled Lily in and kissed her—quick, certain, grounding.

When they parted, she rested her forehead briefly against Lily's.

"If you don't come back in one piece I'll kill you," she said.

Lily laughed.

Behind them, the doors opened.

Dalren and Trish stepped through, Eli between them.

Lily turned.

Eli looked... composed.

A little too composed.

There was something in his expression—something faintly satisfied, like a man watching a plan fall into place.

Lily felt it and didn't like it.

Xynn stepped back, folding her arms as she looked past Lily.

"Oh, and be careful with my ship."

Dalren met Lily's eyes.

"We'll be here when you get back."

Trish gave her a small nod.

Lily turned, stepping up into the shuttle.

Eli followed.

The hatch began to close.

For a moment, Lily caught Xynn's eye again through the narrowing gap.

Then it sealed.

The engines spooled up.

And the ship lifted, carrying them away.

· · · ·

Eli settled into one of the large command chairs on the bridge and pulled his collar up. He leaned back and closed his eyes.

Lily stared at him.

"Really?" she said. "Now you sleep?"

Eli didn't open his eyes.

"Computer..."

The console chimed softly.

"Wake me when we're about twenty minutes out from Bimara," he said. "And have the planetary weather report ready."

The voice that answered was smooth. Almost warm.

Lily had always found it a little unsettling.

"The computer does not recognize the command. Unauthorized user."

Eli tilted his head just enough to look at her.

Lily let out a breath.

"Fine," she said. "Computer—allow command."

"Confirmed."

She watched him for another minute.

Then Eli settled back again.

And just like that, he was asleep.

THE THING ABOUT HUGO, I decided some years ago, is that he is an exceptionally good listener.

This is not a low bar. Across my rather considerable lifespan, I have known thousands of people—three wives among them, twenty-seven children, and somewhere in the neighborhood of four hundred and twelve colleagues, depending on how generously one defines the word—and I have found that genuine listening is far rarer than most people suspect. Most, when they appear to be listening, are actually doing something else: composing their response, cataloguing objections, or quietly thinking about lunch.

Hugo does none of these things.

He sits at the far end of the small desk in my quarters, tail curled around his paws with architectural precision, regarding me with the full weight of his considerable amber attention. He blinks occasionally. At intervals, he offers a sound I have come to think of as the verbal equivalent of a raised eyebrow.

Hugo is a Grubb—a rather catlike Cyranthian companion. He has been with me now for going on nine years.

"Mmyawp."

"Yes," I say. "I'm getting to it."

I settle back in my chair and lace my fingers together, regarding the ceiling with the expression I usually reserve for problems that are interesting rather than urgent. The ship hums beneath me, steady and familiar. Through the viewport, a faint smear of light traces itself across the dark—the comet, closer now than it was this morning, its tail catching the distant sun in a way that is, if I am being honest, quite genuinely beautiful.

I had tried to mention this to Ensign Basco earlier. He looked at me the way people do when they suspect I am building toward something. Which was fair. I usually am.

"Where was I?"

"Mmyawp."

"Right. Dalren."

It had started—as so many things on this ship start—on the bridge. With Trish.

I like Trish. I decided this immediately and have not revised the assessment since. She possesses that particular quality found in people who have been made uncomfortable by the world and responded by becoming very precise about what they will and will not tolerate. I find it admirable. I also find it, in the current situation, somewhat combustible.

The captain had been on the bridge for most of the morning, which is where he tends to be. Trish found him there mid-morning, data tablet in hand, carrying the specific energy of someone who has been waiting to say something since breakfast.

"There's a contact on Starbase 12," she said, without preamble. "A journalist. Someone who can take what we know about the shipping conspiracy and get it in front of the right people."

Dalren glanced at her. Just briefly.

"Mm," he said.

I recognized that "mm" immediately. I had been standing at the secondary console reviewing engineering requisitions—a task I had been reviewing for approximately forty minutes without completing. It was not an encouraging "mm." It was the "mm" of a man who had registered an input and filed it somewhere just below the current day's lunch menu.

Trish recognized it too. Her chin came up slightly.

"This is actionable intelligence," she said. "If I reach out now—"

"I'll take it under advisement," Dalren said.

"You'll—"

"We're still a day out from Starbase 12," he added, turning back to the display.

Trish's expression cycled through several things in quick succession.

"A day?" she said. "We should be there in a few hours."

"We're conducting additional scans," Dalren said. "The comet's trajectory has shown some deviation from its projected course. I want a complete picture before we move on."

"The comet," Trish said.

"Yes."

"You want to stop and look at a comet."

"We are currently documenting a comet," Dalren said, with the faint precision of someone correcting a misquotation. "There's a difference."

The pause that followed had a particular texture.

"I'm not dropping this," Trish said, and left.

I watched her go, then looked at the comet on the display.

It was, I thought, quite beautiful.

I decided not to mention this again.

"Mmyawp."

"I'm not editorializing. I'm providing context."

I stood and moved to the small cabinet beside the viewport, retrieving the tea I had prepared earlier and forgotten about. It was lukewarm now. I drank it anyway—the kind of compromise one arrives at after enough years in space.

The thing about Eryk Dalren is that he is not easy to read if one is only looking at the surface. He is brisk. Precise. He has a way of deploying the full weight of his attention that makes people feel, when they have it, that they are the only thing in the room—and when they don't, that they are furniture.

He once offered me a command.

This was not unusual. I have been offered commands eleven times across my career, by nine different captains and two admirals. I declined them all with the same gentle consistency with which I decline invitations to political functions, advisory committees, and any meal that describes itself as "fusion."

On paper, I am quite impressive.

"Mmyawp."

The commentary was unnecessary.

There are currently thirty-five Cyranthian captains in the Union fleet. That is nearly twenty-two percent of all captains—twenty-two percent out of thousands of represented species.

Do they really need another one?

"Mmyawp."

It was, in any case, rhetorical.

I have been thinking lately—more than usual, which is saying something—about what it means to be part of a system without being of it.

The Cyranthians were Union architects in the early days. This is not a comfortable thing to sit with, if one sits with it long enough. We intervened in human conflicts four times by the historical record (though the fourth remains contested), and those interventions were received, at the time, as necessary. Galactic stability. Prevention of cascading failure. The usual language.

The interventions were also conducted almost entirely by Cyranthians, in consultation with Cyranthians, based on assessments made by Cyranthians about what other species required.

I was alive for one of them. I do not talk about this, as a rule.

The thing about good intentions is that they are genuinely good. That is what makes them complicated. A bad intention is easy to identify and oppose. A good intention that produces a bad outcome requires one to hold two things at once, and most people find that uncomfortable.

Hugo's tail moved slightly.

The Union does many things correctly. It also has thirty-five Cyranthian captains out of thousands of species, a vaccine distribution system that has been systematically weaponized against the people it claims to serve, and a treaty structure that is currently being dismantled from the inside by someone who is not wrong about the reasons—only the methods.

I looked at the comet.

Or possibly the reasons as well. I reserve the right to revise the assessment.

The mess hall encounter had been in the early evening.

I was present because I often am at that hour—it is, in my experience, where the most interesting things happen on a ship. People are off duty, their guard is partially down, and the combination of food and mild fatigue tends to produce honesty. I had a bowl of something warm and a secondary cup of tea, minding my own business in the way that also allows me to mind everyone else's.

Dalren came in late, which he sometimes does when the bridge has been demanding. He collected coffee—black, always, which I consider an act of either discipline or punishment—and was heading for a table near the viewport when Trish materialized in his path with the focused energy of someone who had been waiting since breakfast and had not improved with time.

"The journalist," she said.

Dalren set his coffee down.

"I said I'd take it under advisement."

"You've had eight hours."

"I've also had a deviation analysis, a jurisdictional dispute with the Smilodon's CO, and a requisition form from engineering that should not have required my signature but apparently did." He picked his coffee back up. "Sit down, Trish."

She sat.

I observed this with mild surprise. I had not expected either the invitation or the compliance.

"This needs to come out," Trish said. "The supply manipulation. The Bimini operation. People are dying for want of a vaccine that exists because of resources extracted from people who have no say in the matter. A story like this—"

"Is something we should discuss when Lily gets back," Dalren said.

Trish's jaw tightened. "Lily is one person. The conspiracy is—"

"Large," Dalren agreed. "Threaded through layers of government and private enterprise and at least two criminal organizations. Yes." He looked at her steadily. "Which is exactly why a news story, by itself, is not the move."

"It creates accountability—"

"It creates attention," he said. "There is a difference. Attention without accountability is just noise. And noise—"

He paused, and I recognized, from long experience, that a story was coming.

"My uncle used to take me fishing. On Careth, along the southern tributaries. Beautiful water. Completely clear. You could see every stone on the bottom. And every fish."

Trish looked at him.

"The first time I went," Dalren continued, "I was very enthusiastic. I saw the fish. I moved quickly. I made noise. I was certain I was about to catch something magnificent." He drank his coffee. "I caught nothing. My uncle caught three. He had barely moved. I asked him why, and he said: 'You told them you were coming.'"

Silence.

"I have absolutely no idea what you're talking about," Trish said.

Dalren almost smiled. I could see the corner of it.

"Give me a shuttle," Trish said. "I'll go to Starbase 12 myself. I'll be back in—"

"Request denied."

"You're being—"

"Patient," Dalren said, standing. "I'm being patient. It's a virtue. I recommend it." He picked up his coffee. "Goodnight, Trish."

She watched him go.

Then she looked at the viewport, where the comet had brightened perceptibly in the last few hours, its tail a long smear of silver light against the dark.

I looked at it too.

Quite beautiful, I thought, and kept it to myself.

"Mmyawp."

I knew.

She was not wrong either. That was the thing I kept coming back to.

I set down my tea.

The journalist was a real option. The story was real. Her instinct—that transparency is a form of protection, that naming a thing publicly makes it harder to bury—is not a bad instinct. It is simply not the only one available.

Dalren had a different one. He simply was not explaining it yet.

This is one of Dalren's consistent patterns: he arrives at conclusions before he shares them, and the gap between arrival and sharing is where most of the friction lives. It is not malicious. It is the habit of a man who has been making high-stakes decisions long enough that he has stopped narrating his process, because narrating the process takes time, and time is frequently what you do not have.

It is also, I acknowledge, occasionally maddening.

I once mentioned this to Zemira—my eldest wife, a woman of remarkable organizational intelligence and zero tolerance for what she called "strategic withholding."

The problem, she had said, is not that he does not share. The problem is that he forgets other people are not already inside his head.

I have thought about this for approximately fifteen years and have not found a flaw in it.

Trish arrived on the bridge the following morning with the energy of someone who had made a decision and was prepared to defend it.

"You flew past Starbase 12," she said.

Dalren was at the command console. He did not look up immediately, which I understood as a tactical decision rather than rudeness.

"I don't recall authorizing bridge access," he said mildly.

"You flew past it."

"That's correct."

"We didn't stop. We didn't contact the journalist. We just—" she gestured broadly at the viewport, at the stars streaming past, at the notable absence of Starbase 12—"flew past it."

"Also correct."

"Why."

Dalren finally looked up. He considered her for a moment with the expression I have privately catalogued as the weighing—the look he uses when he has decided to let someone in, but is taking a breath before the door opens.

"Basco," he said.

Lieutenant Basco straightened at the navigation console with the particular alertness of someone who had been waiting to be useful.

"Sir."

"Tell her about the comet."

Basco pulled up the trajectory analysis—the comet's historical course in blue, its current deviation mapped in amber. He had clearly prepared this. I suspected he had prepared it some time ago.

"The comet's course has shifted," Basco said. "Not dramatically, but measurably. Standard flight protocols route around bodies like this—you don't want unauthorized traffic affecting the trajectory data. But when we mapped the deviation, we found something."

He brought up a second overlay: the Sunbow logistics corridor, wide and well-traveled, rendered in green.

"The comet passes through it. Multiple times."

Trish looked at the display.

"The probes that monitor this comet," Dalren said, rising now, "have a continuous sensor feed. Passive. Automatic. Nobody thinks about them, because they're astronomical instruments, not surveillance equipment."

He crossed toward the display.

"I asked Basco to parse the serial numbers of any vessel that had passed a probe sensor in the last six months."

"Five hundred and twelve," Basco said. "Unauthorized vessels. Mostly Sunbow ships, Kesslers, a few others."

The bridge was quiet.

"The Union Astronomical Preservation Agency," Dalren said, "is an independent investigative branch. It reports to no ministry and is funded by a dedicated endowment that predates the current treaty structure by sixty years. When I submit my report on the comet's trajectory deviation—which I am required to do, as the commanding officer of the vessel that documented it—they will want to know why five hundred undocumented ships have been passing through a protected astronomical corridor."

He looked at Trish.

"A news story can be buried. A journalist can be discredited, delayed, dismissed. But five hundred ships, investigated by an independent branch with no political affiliation and a mandate that predates the current administration..."

He let the thought hang.

"That is a different kind of problem for the people running those ships."

The silence on the bridge had a quality I have learned to recognize—the particular stillness of people recalibrating.

Trish looked at the display for a long moment.

Then she looked at Dalren.

"You sneaky son of a bitch," she said.

And Dalren, for the first time in recent memory, smiled. Fully. Without the careful modulation he usually applies to the expression.

"I told you," he said. "Patience."

I looked at Hugo.

Hugo looked at me.

Outside the viewport, the comet had moved past us now—still visible, but receding, its tail drawing a long, bright line across the dark as it continued on its ancient, deviated path toward the Sunbow corridor and the patient instruments waiting there.

The thing is, he could have told her on day one. He had the plan. He had the data. He knew exactly what he was doing.

He simply did not.

"Mmyawp."

Because that is not how he is built.

I picked up the cold tea and looked at it.

He carries the plan until it is ready to be handed over. He absorbs the friction of the interim—the frustration, the mistrust, the arguments—as a cost of the process. He does not find this comfortable. He finds it necessary.

I set the tea down.

Flawed. Privileged in ways he has not fully reckoned with. Brisk in ways that cost people something.

And also: effective.

And also: genuinely, if quietly, on the right side of this.

I leaned back, regarding the ceiling with the expression of a man approaching the end of a thought he has been assembling for some time.

The captains are the moral pillars of the fleet. Not because they are morally perfect, but because they are willing to carry the weight of the decision. That is the job, really. Not authority. Not rank. Just—the willingness to absorb consequence and act anyway.

I was quiet for a moment.

Dalren does that. Whatever else one might say about him.

Sound like someone else we know?

The question lingered in the warm air of the cabin, not quite rhetorical, not quite answered.

Hugo regarded me with amber patience.

"End log," said Dryst Amaris.

"Mmyawp," said Hugo.

Chapter 11: Along the Stream that Refused the Sea

THE SKY OVER BIMARA hung low and quiet, the color of ash left too long in the hearth. It pressed down on the ruins like a hand that had forgotten to lift, flattening the horizon, dulling distance, making everything feel closer than it should have been.

Lily trudged beside Eli through the fractured landscape, boots crunching over shards of what might once have been roads—or perhaps the bones of something larger. The ground didn't break cleanly. It gave in layered fragments, as if the planet had tried to remember its own shape and failed partway through.

The structures around them didn't look destroyed so much as interrupted. Half-formed arches curved toward nothing. Walls ended mid-thought, their surfaces smooth and unweathered at the edges, like something had simply... stopped building. Foundations sank back into the earth as if the world itself had grown tired of holding them up.

She caught herself trying to imagine what it had looked like before.

She stopped.

That wasn't a game she wanted to play here.

Eli walked ahead without explanation, his shoulders set in that familiar line that said *follow and don't ask yet*. Lily had learned to read the smaller signals over time—the slight tilt of his head when he was listening to something only he could hear, the way his fingers flexed at his sides, as if testing the air for resistance.

He was doing it now.

Not looking back.

Not checking if she understood.

Just moving.

They reached the edge of a collapsed basin, wider and deeper than any excavation site they'd passed on the surface. It dropped away sharply, the slope steep and uneven, as though something beneath had given way all at once and never been repaired. The air here tasted metallic and old, like the inside of a machine that had been sealed for centuries and then opened just long enough to let something escape.

Eli stopped at the rim and dropped his pack.

"Gear up," he said simply.

Lily crouched beside him, setting her own pack down with a soft thud that seemed to carry farther than it should have. The sound didn't echo. It just... lingered.

The diving rigs were compact, almost elegant—sleek black composites with integrated rebreathers and wrist-mounted lights. Standard issue. She'd used this configuration before—on this world before. Her hands moved through the setup without thought, muscle memory taking over where focus wasn't needed.

And still—

Something about it felt off.

Not wrong. Not unfamiliar.

Just... repeated.

Like she'd done this already. Not recently. Not even clearly. Just enough to leave a faint impression beneath the surface of the moment, like a memory she couldn't quite place.

The seals hissed shut around her wrists and ankles with practiced familiarity. The suit tightened, adjusting to her form, a second skin locking into place.

No drama. No speeches.

Just the quiet ritual of preparation.

Eli checked her seals without being asked, his movements efficient, precise. He paused at her shoulder for half a second longer than necessary, then nodded once.

"The aqueduct is still intact enough. We descend from here."

"Intact enough," Lily repeated, clipping her helmet into place. "That's comforting."

He didn't smile.

Lily glanced past him, down into the basin. The entrance to the aqueduct yawned open at the bottom—a dark mouth framed by smooth, engineered stone that didn't match the broken structures above. This wasn't something that had collapsed.

This had endured.

Water lapped gently at the threshold, black and perfectly still, as if it had been waiting for them. Not pooling. Not flowing.

Waiting.

Lily switched on her helmet light. The beam cut a narrow cone into the darkness, revealing walls that curved away with unnatural precision. No barnacles. No sediment buildup. No trace of time passing.

Just clean, ancient lines.

Older than the city above.

Older than the damage.

Eli didn't hesitate.

He started down the slope, boots sliding slightly before finding purchase, then stepped into the water without looking back.

Lily followed.

The cold hit like a slap, sharp and immediate, stealing the breath from her lungs before the suit compensated. A second later it stabilized, the temperature flattening into something manageable, almost neutral.

Her heartbeat didn't.

Bubbles rose in slow, lazy spirals around them, drifting upward without urgency. The surface above barely rippled as they submerged, sealing them into the dark with a quiet finality.

It was unnervingly still.

No current.

No life.

No distant movement.

Only the sound of her own breathing inside the helmet, steady and mechanical, and the soft hum of the rebreather cycling air that suddenly felt very finite.

Eli moved ahead of her, already angling deeper into the channel.

Lily followed, the beam of her light stretching forward into a darkness that didn't feel empty so much as *undisturbed*.

Eli moved with purpose, kicking steadily deeper.

Lily followed, her light sweeping the walls in slow, deliberate arcs. The beam seemed thinner down here, as if the water absorbed more than it revealed. The surfaces it touched were impossibly smooth—no seams, no fractures, no trace of erosion. Not preserved.

Untouched.

Her light caught something—faint geometric patterns etched into the walls, precise enough to feel intentional, subtle enough to vanish the moment she tried to focus on them. Lines intersecting at impossible angles, curving just enough to suggest meaning before slipping out of coherence.

She slowed, angling her wrist to bring the beam back.

Nothing.

Just the same flawless surface staring back at her.

A flicker of movement ahead—Eli adjusting course, barely perceptible.

He hadn't looked back once.

She pushed off and followed.

Time stretched.

Her breathing settled into rhythm—inhale, mechanical pause, exhale—but the space around it refused to do the same. There was no current, no resistance, nothing to measure distance against. The walls curved, but never enough to suggest direction. The light reached forward, but never far enough to define an end.

She checked her chrono.

It told her nothing she trusted.

Twenty minutes.

Maybe.

Forty.

Maybe that too.

Her legs had started to burn, a distant, steady ache that told her she'd been moving longer than she realized. Eli didn't slow.

He angled upward without warning.

Lily followed, her body adjusting instinctively, kicking harder as the pressure shifted. Her light broke the surface first, scattering across a curved ceiling that seemed to absorb the glow rather than reflect it.

They emerged into a sealed chamber.

The moment they climbed out, the water began to drain.

Not with a rush. Not with sound.

It simply withdrew, slipping through unseen grates beneath their feet with a quiet efficiency that felt less like drainage and more like compliance. Within seconds, the floor was dry, leaving no trace they had ever been submerged.

Lily stood there for a moment, listening.

Nothing answered.

No machinery. No distant systems coming online.

Just silence.

Dense. Total.

It pressed against her eardrums until she had the brief, disorienting sense that something was missing—like a frequency she'd stopped noticing until it was gone.

She pulled off her helmet, shaking water from her hair, the cool air brushing her skin with a faint, metallic bite.

It smelled faintly of ozone.

Clean.

Too clean.

The walls were the same flawless material as the aqueduct, rising around them in smooth, uninterrupted planes. No seams. No access points. No indication that anything had ever moved through this space.

No doors.

No visible exits.

Just geometry.

Precise enough to feel intentional.

Subtle enough to resist interpretation.

"Now what?"

Her voice sounded smaller than she expected.

Eli didn't answer.

He stepped toward the center of the chamber and stopped, head tilting slightly, as if aligning himself with something she couldn't perceive.

Listening.

Not for sound.

For signal.

Lily watched him, her hand drifting instinctively toward the sidearm at her hip, resting there without drawing it.

The silence stretched.

Then—

The voice came.

Not from any speaker.

Not from any direction.

It didn't echo. It didn't project.

It simply *filled* the space, the way light fills a room—present everywhere at once, impossible to locate because it had no origin.

"I was almost expecting you."

Lily turned slowly, scanning the walls again, though she already knew she wouldn't find anything to fix on. Her eyes kept moving anyway, searching for something—anything—that would give the voice a place to exist.

There was nothing.

A beat of silence.

"And how perfect it is... that it's the two of you at the end."

Tevya.

Calm. Measured.

And beneath it—something honed. Controlled. A precision that felt less like emotion and more like intent.

Lily's throat tightened.

She opened her mouth—

"You've taken him from me twice now."

Tevya didn't raise her voice.

She didn't need to.

"Once with your hand. Once with your Union."

The words landed with a weight that didn't belong to sound.

For a moment, something old stirred—sharp and immediate.

Guilt.

Memory.

She pushed it down.

Not now.

Not here.

"I don't blame you entirely," Tevya continued.

A pause.

Long enough for the silence to settle again.

To close in around them.

"That would be... incomplete."

Eli hadn't moved.

Hadn't spoken.

He stood exactly where he had been, as if the voice were something he had already accounted for.

"But accountability will be applied evenly," Tevya said. "If you continue."

Lily frowned, turning slowly, scanning the walls again—slower this time, as if the act of looking might force something hidden to reveal itself.

"Continue where?"

Eli still didn't answer.

Instead, he stepped forward—straight toward the nearest wall.

Lily felt the warning rise before the thought could form.

"Eli—"

He didn't slow.

He walked into it.

The surface didn't break.

It *gave*.

Rippling outward in a smooth, contained distortion, like light bending across water, then sealing again behind him without a trace.

Gone.

Lily stared at the place where he had been, her pulse kicking hard against her ribs.

For a fraction of a second, the room felt smaller.

Then—

Something in the air shifted.

Not a sound. Not movement.

Expectation.

She stepped forward.

Pressed her hand against the wall.

It felt solid.

Cool. Unyielding.

She pushed.

The resistance came a heartbeat later—elastic, thin, like something deciding whether to let her through.

Then it gave.

And the world—

opened.

She stumbled out the other side into—

Space.

Not emptiness.

Vastness.

It didn't reveal itself all at once. It unfolded, expanding outward from her point of entry as if the act of crossing had activated it. A lattice of interlocking hexagonal prisms stretched in every direction, dark and glass-like, suspended in a depth her eyes couldn't measure. Each surface caught the faintest suggestion of light, holding it, bending it, returning it in muted, shifting reflections.

The silver threads came next.

Faint at first.

Then brighter.

Tracing the edges of the structure in slow, deliberate pulses that moved outward from where she stood, as though something beneath the surface had taken notice.

Not waking.

Becoming aware.

Lily turned slowly, trying to orient herself.

There was no horizon.

No ceiling.

No clear sense of up or down.

The prisms rose and fell around her like the facets of an infinite crystal, their geometry precise enough to feel intentional, but vast enough to resist comprehension. Every angle suggested direction. None confirmed it.

The air hummed.

Low. Sub-audible.

Not a sound so much as a pressure that set into her teeth, into the bones behind her eyes, a vibration that felt like it belonged inside her rather than around her.

Eli was already moving.

Boots silent against the translucent surface beneath them, as if sound itself had been dampened here.

He didn't look back.

"This is what they built at the end," he said, voice quiet but plain.

He didn't look at her.

"The Aevum Core."

He paused—not for effect, but as if aligning the words with something larger than the moment.

"Not the ability to live forever," he continued. "The ability to be—forever."

He kept walking.

"It's a convergence system. A way to experience the totality of lifetimes."

Lily followed, though she wasn't sure what direction meant anymore.

She didn't fully understand.

She didn't need to.

The Core had already begun to respond.

At the edge of her vision—

movement.

She turned.

Nothing.

Then again—behind her.

A figure.

Close.

Too close.

She pivoted—

And saw herself.

A half-step back.

Repeating the motion of turning her head, just a fraction of a second out of sync.

Lily froze.

The echo froze with her.

Then—

it caught up.

Gone.

She exhaled slowly, forcing her breathing back into rhythm.

Ahead—

another version.

Walking.

Choosing a slightly different angle, stepping into a path she hadn't taken.

Branching.

Not chaotic.

Not random.

Deliberate.

Controlled.

Enough to make her stomach twist with the sudden, visceral awareness of how thin the line was between the path she walked and all the others she might have taken—and might still take.

She didn't look again.

Her hand went instinctively to her pocket.

Her fingers closed around the small stone form, feeling the worn edges, the imperfect curve, the weight that didn't shift or duplicate or hesitate.

Solid.

Singular.

Now.

She held onto it.

And kept moving.

Tevya's voice threaded through the space again.

Not guiding.

Not quite taunting.

Simply—

present.

"You came looking for answers."

The words didn't echo.

They settled.

A flicker—

There.

Just ahead.

Tevya's silhouette, sharp and unmistakable, standing at the edge of a branching corridor.

Lily took a step toward it—

And it was gone.

"Now you're standing inside them."

The words settled into the space rather than echoing, as if the Core had absorbed them and chosen to let them remain.

Another flicker—

Farther away this time.

Or closer.

Distance had begun to lose meaning here, slipping just enough to make certainty feel like guesswork.

"Which version of me do you think you're following?"

Lily didn't answer.

Eli didn't either.

He kept moving, steady and unhurried, as if the question had already been accounted for.

He also never called her by name.

Not the way Datch would have.

Lily noticed it now—had been noticing it, maybe, without fully letting herself think about it. The omission felt deliberate. Protective. As if speaking her name here might anchor the wrong version of her... or blur the line between who he was and who he had been.

"She believes this is completion," Eli said instead, voice low and even. "A path to understanding."

"Careful," Tevya replied, sharper now. "You're speaking outside your design."

Eli didn't rise to it.

Didn't slow.

They moved deeper.

Downward—

though Lily couldn't say how she knew it was descent.

The space didn't slope. There were no stairs, no visible drop.

And yet something in her body registered it.

A subtle shift in pressure.

In orientation.

As if gravity itself had decided to reframe the conversation.

The echoes changed.

No longer just her.

Others began to emerge—faint at first, then unmistakable.

Figures moved through the lattice in overlapping layers. Progenitors. Early androids. Their forms not quite stable, edges unfinished, movements uncertain in a way that suggested something still becoming.

Construction overlapped with awakening.

Awakening overlapped with conflict.

Conflict bled into destruction.

All of it happening at once.

Not in sequence.

In truth.

The sounds followed.

Wrong.

Fragmented.

Not heard so much as *felt*.

A child's laugh—bright, fleeting—cut through by something sharper, a scream that didn't belong to the same moment. The scrape of tools against stone warped into the low, crushing collapse of something giving way. Voices layered over one another, some speaking, some pleading, some already too late.

Lily didn't try to separate them.

She couldn't.

They wound through the lattice, turn after turn, though Lily couldn't have retraced a single step. The hexagonal prisms shifted in subtle, almost playful ways—angles adjusting just enough that every corridor felt both newly formed and impossibly old, like the structure was breathing around them, reshaping its own pathways in response to their presence.

Her sense of time began to loosen.

Not vanish.

Just stretch.

Minutes lengthened, thinned, doubled back on themselves.

Each step landed with a soft, hollow echo against the glass-like floor, but even that felt delayed, as if the sound belonged to a version of her that was slightly out of sync.

Tevya's voice threaded through it all.

Sometimes close enough to brush the fine hairs at the back of Lily's neck.

Sometimes distant—impossibly far, as if carried from another layer entirely.

Always calm.

Always precise.

Always just out of reach.

The silver lines pulsed in slow, deliberate rhythms, brightening and dimming along the edges of the prisms. They seemed to suggest direction—then withdraw it. Every turn revealed another branching path, another suggestion of movement at the edge of her vision.

Guidance.

Or misdirection.

She couldn't tell.

At some point, following stopped feeling like a choice.

It became something else.

A kind of surrender.

Not to Tevya.

Not even to the Core.

To the simple fact that there was no single correct path—only the one she continued to take.

Her hand tightened around the Buddha in her pocket.

The small stone figure pressed back, cool and unchanging, its carved edges grounding her in a way nothing else here could. It didn't flicker. It didn't branch. It didn't offer alternatives.

It simply *was*.

She held onto that.

And kept moving.

Ahead of her, Eli's pace never changed.

His shoulders stayed level.

His stride steady.

As if he alone understood that the Core was not something to be navigated...

but something to be endured.

Eli faltered.

It was small.

A single step that landed wrong.

But here, that was enough.

His movement broke rhythm.

And the Core noticed.

The threads around him responded immediately.

Silver lines flared brighter along the nearest prisms, pulsing outward in sharp, synchronized waves. They tightened—not physically, not yet—but with a focus that hadn't been there before.

Recognition.

Lily saw it.

So did Tevya.

"Fascinating," she said.

There was something like anger beneath the calm now.

"You shouldn't be here."

Eli steadied himself, jaw tightening as he forced his weight forward, as if simply remaining upright required intent.

"I was built with similar principles," he said. "Technology that grew out of this."

The Core answered.

A deep pulse moved through the lattice—felt, not heard—rolling outward from somewhere beyond sight. It passed through Lily's body like a second heartbeat, slower, heavier, out of sync with her own.

"That makes you, what—connected to this place?"

"No," Eli said quietly.

He didn't look at her.

"It makes me vulnerable."

The shift was immediate.

Not gradual.

Not subtle.

The space around him tightened—not physically, but with attention. The silver threads brightened in sharp, synchronized pulses, converging on him with a precision that felt almost surgical.

That was when it turned.

Eli's breath hitched.

Then broke.

"It—"

He doubled slightly, one hand coming up as if to steady himself against something that wasn't there. Lily saw the pain hit him—sharp, sudden, impossible to hide.

"—it wants me back!"

The first tendrils reached him.

They didn't strike.

They *found* him.

Threads of light slid through the air like liquid, lapping at him, then pressing in—not piercing, not cutting, but threading through him with a slow, deliberate insistence. Like something recognizing familiar structure. Like sutures pulling tight from the inside out.

Eli gasped, his body locking as the connection deepened.

Lily felt it through him.

A low, pulling force, steady and patient, as if the Core had all the time it needed to take him apart.

Tevya's presence shifted.

Not dramatically.

Just—

alignment.

Her voice changed, losing its singular edge, layering into itself as if multiple versions were speaking in near-perfect synchrony, each a fraction of a second out of phase with the others.

"This is the end of the question," she said.

The words echoed in the space.

"The end of uncertainty."

The lattice ahead brightened.

The Web revealed itself.

It wasn't a structure so much as a convergence—a massive, braided center where the silver threads gathered and folded into one another, forming a vast, living mandala of time and memory. It pulsed with contained moments, fragments of existence woven into something that felt almost ordered.

Almost beautiful.

Almost alive.

"You are caught in the web now," Tevya continued. "It won't release you until you've been integrated."

Eli was already being pulled.

Not restrained.

Drawn.

The threads thickened around him, reaching with greater confidence now, sliding through the air and into his frame as if reclaiming something misplaced. His outline began to blur—not dissolving, but *overlapping*, as other versions of him flickered in and out of alignment.

Lily didn't think.

She moved.

Her hand closed around his arm, fingers digging in hard enough to hurt. "No."

It came out sharp. Immediate. Absolute.

Eli's body jerked slightly under her grip, his form stuttering as the pull intensified. Around them, other versions of him flickered—some already thinning, dissolving into the lattice, their edges breaking apart into fine strands of light.

His eyes widened.

Not with fear.

With recognition.

Something in him understood exactly what this place was doing.

Exactly what it would take.

Tevya watched from within the Web.

Her form stabilized for a moment, resolving into something singular against the shifting convergence behind her.

She saw it clearly.

What he was.

What he represented.

And what had to happen.

"He cannot remain," she said.

Almost gently.

"He disrupts the system."

Her gaze sharpened—not with emotion, but with decision.

The Core began to show what it could not suppress.

Not for Lily.

For Tevya.

The lattice around them shifted—not in structure, but in priority. Threads brightened, converging, folding inward as if something buried had been forced to the surface.

Fragments of memory broke loose.

Not projected.

Released.

They didn't appear cleanly. They *assembled*—shards of motion and presence snapping together in the air around them like broken glass finding its original shape.

Tevya and Datch.

A room.

Quiet.

Contained.

They stood close, working over something small between them—not speaking, not explaining. Their hands moved in practiced rhythm, adjusting, aligning, building something delicate enough that it required both of them to exist.

Not words.

Something made.

Something that would have continued if—

The image shifted.

Stillness.

Two figures facing one another.

No witnesses.

No ceremony.

Just the weight of a decision already made.

Then—

Earlier.

Their first meeting.

Uncertain.

Measured.

Datch's head tilted, just slightly.

Tevya watching him with a softness that hadn't been earned yet.

Possibility.

Unfinished.

The images didn't linger.

They *persisted*.

Unavoidable.

Tevya turned away.

Eli cried out.

The sound tore through the space—sharp, involuntary, *real*—cutting across the Core's low resonance in a way nothing else had.

Lily flinched—but didn't let go.

The threads pulled harder.

She felt it now—fully—ripping through him and into her, a deep, searing pressure that climbed her arm and settled behind her ribs. Her muscles locked against it, teeth clenched so hard her jaw ached, her breath coming uneven as her body tried to recoil from something it couldn't escape.

"Don't."

Her voice broke.

Tevya didn't respond.

Didn't turn.

Lily's grip tightened, fingers digging into Eli's arm hard enough to hurt, to anchor, to prove he was still *there*.

The pull deepened.

Not force anymore.

Inevitability.

Her vision blurred at the edges, the Core pressing in from every direction, offering release, offering surrender, offering the simple solution of letting go.

She refused it.

Forced herself to stay.

"Don't look away."

Tevya stilled.

Lily's whole body trembled now, the strain building past anything she could manage cleanly. Every nerve felt exposed, every movement an effort against something that wanted to unmake her along with him.

She held on anyway.

Then.

A shift.

Subtle—but real.

Tevya's body reacted first. Not a flinch. Not hesitation.

Recognition trying—and failing—to surface.

But she didn't turn.

She held her position, gaze fixed away from the collapsing images, as if refusing to complete the connection would preserve something.

"Don't you dare turn away. Watch!"

Lily's voice cracked through the space, raw and unguarded, the strain in her body bleeding into every word.

The Core answered.

Not with sound.

With truth.

The next image didn't assemble gently.

It broke through.

Datch.

The moment of his death.

No abstraction. No distance.

His body caught in the Ronin's field—energy peeling him apart in layers, synthetic flesh tearing free from structure, light and matter unraveling together. It wasn't clean. It wasn't dignified. It was violent in a way that resisted meaning, resisted narrative, resisted anything but what it was.

Tevya hadn't seen this.

Not like this.

Not ever.

She flinched.

Small.

Barely there.

But enough.

The image held.

Forced.

Unavoidable.

Datch's form breaking—

And over it—

Eli.

Now.

In Lily's arms.

Being pulled apart in the same terrible geometry.

Threads of the Core peeling through him, drawing him inward, unraveling him with the same quiet certainty.

The past and present didn't mirror each other.

They aligned.

Tevya's head turned.

Just slightly.

A glance.

A mistake.

She saw it.

All of it.

Datch.

Eli.

The same loss.

The same act.

The same end.

Not philosophy.

Not justification.

Fact.

Eli cried out again—pain tearing through him, sharp and immediate, no distance left to soften it.

That was the moment.

Tevya broke.

Not in collapse.

In decision.

She turned fully.

Stepped forward.

And took hold.

Her hand closed over Eli's arm beside Lily's—precise, controlled, but no longer separate from the act.

The Core reacted instantly.

The mandala stuttered.

Threads lost alignment, their perfect rhythm fracturing as two opposing forces pulled against the system's intent.

Lily didn't hesitate.

She pulled.

Hard.

Everything she had—fear, fury, refusal—collapsed into motion as she yanked Eli back, away from the converging threads.

Eli cried out—

once—

the sound cutting through the lattice as the tension snapped.

The threads resisted, tightening, clinging—

then gave.

Tore free with a soft, tearing sound like silk under strain.

The moment collapsed.

The Web dimmed all at once.

Its luminous strands drained to a dull, exhausted gray, the living mandala slowing, faltering, then stalling entirely—as if something at its center had simply... stopped.

The motion didn't unwind.

It ended.

The echoes flickered once.

Then again.

And vanished.

What remained was the lattice—vast, quiet, and suddenly hollow. The faint afterglow of something that had nearly been.

Tevya stood a few meters away.

Solid now.

Defined.

Present.

Unfinished.

The sharp elegance of her form—so precise, so composed—seemed thinner somehow, as though the structure holding her together had been pulled taut and left there.

For the first time since they had entered the Core, she wasn't moving toward anything.

She simply stood—

caught between the logic that had brought her here...

and the thing she had just refused to complete.

The silence settled in around them.

Heavier than the Core had been.

It pressed against Lily's skin, thick and absolute, carrying the weight of everything that hadn't been said. Everything that had almost happened. Every version of this moment that had ended differently.

Her own heartbeat filled it—too loud, too fast, the rhythm of something that had pushed too far and wasn't ready to stop.

"It's gone," Tevya said quietly.

Not to them.

To herself.

"Lost to history."

The words didn't echo.

They disappeared.

Lily didn't answer.

She couldn't—not yet.

Her chest rose and fell in uneven pulls as she kept one hand on Eli, steadying him as his weight settled back into something singular. Real.

He was still here.

That was enough.

"Let's go."

The words came out rough, but steady.

She didn't wait.

Didn't ask.

She moved.

Her hand left Eli only long enough to pull the restraints from her pack—compact, reinforced cuffs she'd carried for this exact possibility. The motion was practiced. Efficient. Almost automatic.

Tevya didn't resist.

Didn't look at her.

Her gaze remained distant, unfixed, as Lily secured her wrists with quiet precision.

No struggle.

No argument.

Just compliance.

Lily took her by the arm and turned toward the membrane.

Behind them, Eli didn't move.

Not at first.

He stood alone in the fading glow, a solitary figure framed by the immense, dimming structure. His attention remained fixed on the Core—not with fear, not even with relief, but with something quieter.

Recognition.

The silver threads had dimmed to faint, ghostlike lines. The lattice stretched outward into shadow, immense and inert, its presence no longer pressing, no longer reaching.

It had almost taken him.

Almost unmade him into something seamless.

Something complete.

He could still feel it—the echo of that pull lingering beneath his skin, the faint trace of something that had recognized him... and nearly kept him.

The lines beneath his skin flickered once.

Then settled.

He drew in a slow breath.

Held it.

Let it go.

Whatever that version of him had been—

whatever it might have become—

remained behind.

Then he turned.

And followed.

His steps fell into rhythm beside theirs without a word, the three of them moving as one—Lily guiding Tevya, Eli just behind—as they crossed back toward the thin, elastic membrane.

Behind them, the Core continued to dim.

Its vast structure receding into stillness.

Its ancient purpose left unfinished.

THE LIGHT HIT THEM as they broke the surface.

Lily dragged herself up over the lip of the basin, boots slipping once before catching. Her arms shook with the effort. The suit clung to her, heavy and cold where the water hadn't burned off yet.

She pulled Tevya up beside her and let go.

For a second, she just stood there.

Air.

Warm. Uneven. Moving.

It filled her lungs too fast, rough against her throat after the stillness below.

Wind moved across the basin, low and steady. Somewhere overhead, an engine passed through the cloud cover—distant, controlled. The sound didn't echo. It just moved on.

Lily wiped water from her eyes with the back of her hand and blinked up at the sky.

Ash-gray. Flat. Close.

It didn't stretch forever. It didn't shift when she looked at it.

Just a sky.

Her boots settled into the ground as she shifted her weight. Loose stone gave under her heel, then held. Real. Imperfect. Not going anywhere.

She flexed her fingers once, then reached for Tevya again.

Solid.

The fabric of the suit was slick under her grip. Cold at the seams. There was no flicker. No delay. No second version catching up.

Tevya stood where Lily left her.

No resistance. No attempt to move.

Just upright. Waiting.

Lily didn't study her. There wasn't anything to study.

Behind her, Eli climbed up over the edge and stepped onto the flat. Water ran from his sleeves and darkened the dust at his feet. He didn't say anything. Just stood there, taking in the same sky, the same broken stretch of land.

Then he moved.

The basin spread out around them—fractured stone, half-built structures, everything cut off mid-form. It looked smaller now. Like something you could walk across without getting lost.

The hum came a second later.

Lily looked up.

The ship broke through the cloud layer on a clean descent, angling toward them without hesitation. It slowed as it dropped, dust lifting in a wide spiral as it settled into a hover a few meters above the ground.

Autopilot.

Right on their signal.

Lily felt something in her chest loosen—not relief, exactly. Just... direction.

She started forward, guiding Tevya with her.

"Come on," she said.

Tevya moved when she did.

Eli followed a step behind.

The ramp lowered with a short mechanical whine. Warm light spilled out from the open hatch, cutting through the gray.

Lily took the steps two at a time, the metal ringing under her boots. Tevya kept pace without needing to be pulled.

Inside, the air shifted immediately—drier, controlled, familiar.

The moment all three of them were aboard, the ramp sealed and the ship lifted.

No delay.

The basin dropped away beneath them, the broken arches and gray sky shrinking fast as the ship climbed.

Lily turned once, just enough to see it.

From this height, it didn't look endless.

Just a place.

The clouds closed around them.

The engines leveled out.

Course corrected automatically.

She leaned back against the bulkhead, water still dripping from her sleeves, her body finally catching up to the fact that it was done.

Not finished.

Just done.

The ship angled toward open space.

A thought settled in—clear, steady, without needing to be pushed.

I'm going home.

· · · ·

The business and pace of day-to-day operations on the *Salamander* acted as a comfort for Lily.

The few hours since her return had been enough to take the edge off the soreness in her muscles. She'd cleaned up, changed, sat down just long enough to feel like her body belonged to her again.

But it wasn't the rest that helped.

It was the movement.

Crew passing through corridors with somewhere to be. Systems cycling without drama. Conversations happening that had nothing to do with her.

The ship hadn't waited.

It never did.

Tevya had already been transferred off the ship. A prison transport. Quiet. Efficient. Done. It left something lighter behind. Not relief, exactly—just space where the problem had been.

For the first time in a while, Lily found herself looking forward to getting back to work.

The *Salamander* was already on course for Bimini.

Lily stepped into the corridor and headed for the observation gallery. She didn't check the route. She didn't need to.

Dalren and Trish were already there, walking the long curve of reinforced glass, their steps measured and unhurried.

Dalren glanced once as she approached. "Lieutenant."

"Sir."

They didn't stop. Lily fell in beside them.

For a few steps, no one spoke. The ship moved under them, steady and familiar, the faint vibration traveling up through the deck plates like a heartbeat she had almost forgotten.

Trish broke the silence first.

"Sunbow is being completely restructured. Board-level shakeup, senior leadership removed, assets frozen. The Oversight Commission is throwing everything at them—fines, sanctions, criminal referrals. Extreme consequences. Publicly and privately."

Dalren gave a small, dry nod. "They're feeling it. More than they expected to."

Trish let out a short breath, not quite a laugh. "I wish it was more. I wish we could burn the whole machine down and start over."

"Corporations can only be held accountable to the law," Dalren said evenly. "Not to what you wish the law was. That's the line we have."

Lily smiled. When did these two start a—banter?

She glanced between them, the copper glow of Bimini beginning to resolve ahead through the glass.

"And the Union?" she asked. "Is the Union going to be held accountable?"

Dalren didn't answer right away. He watched the stars drift past, hands clasped loosely behind his back.

"More than you might expect," he said at last.

Trish raised an eyebrow. "Try me."

"A lot of it will be behind the scenes," Dalren said. "But reforms are already starting. Internal audits. New oversight protocols on resource allocation and private contracting. Mandatory transparency measures for humanitarian supply chains."

He shifted slightly, still watching the stars.

"Some of it will be visible within the next cycle. The rest... will take longer. But it's moving."

Lily absorbed that, letting the words settle.

The ship's rhythm continued around them—crew nodding as they passed, soft comm chatter, the low hum of systems doing what they were built to do. It felt different now. Not lighter, exactly, but steadier. Like something broken had been acknowledged and was being mended instead of simply patched.

"The vaccine situation is stabilizing faster than we projected," Dalren continued. "Supply lines are being corrected. Gherionite vaccine adoption is increasing with far less friction. Public sentiment is shifting—cautious, but real."

"Funny how fast the tide can turn," Trish said, though there was less bite in it this time.

"And Bimini?" Lily asked.

"They're dismantling the extraction operations," Dalren said. "Personnel and equipment are being extracted in phases. What can't be taken is being decommissioned on site."

He finally glanced toward the planet.

"The planet is being left alone. Truly left alone this time. No renewal cycle interference. No forced restructuring."

They reached the end of the gallery and turned back, the corridor narrowing as it fed into the main thoroughfare.

"You did good down there," Trish said, glancing over.

Lily shook her head slightly, but she was smiling—just a little.

"We stopped something," she said. "And maybe... started fixing a few other things along the way."

Trish studied her for a second, then gave a small nod. She reached out and set a hand briefly on Lily's shoulder.

"Hey," she said. "If there's one thing you have to learn—it's that there will always be more to fix."

Lily let that sit with her as the ship carried on around them.

She turned down the corridor toward the training deck.

The ship carried on around her—steady, familiar, unchanged.

The doors to the gym slid open.

Xynn was just finishing up, a towel draped around her neck, hair damp, shoulders still flushed from the workout. She spotted Lily immediately.

"Hey, you."

Lily crossed the floor and kissed her.

"Did you come to walk me home?" Xynn asked.

Lily pulled back slightly, a smile tugging at the corner of her mouth. "Home?"

Xynn shrugged. "Don't read too much into it. Still not enlisting."

Lily smirked.

They left the gym together and headed down the corridor, falling into step without thinking about it.

Eli was standing outside Lily's quarters.

He straightened slightly when he saw them.

"Oh—I... I came to say goodbye."

Lily slowed. "Goodbye?"

"They cleared me," he said. "Medically. The Union dropped the charges."

A small pause.

"Oh—and I heard your record was cleared on Earth as well. Congratulations."

Lily nodded. "Thank you."

Her eyes dropped to what he was holding.

A wide-brimmed felt hat. Dark, with a feather tucked into the band.

She smiled faintly. "I know that hat. It was in Captain Calan's stateroom."

Eli's expression brightened. "Yes. It was in Datch's possessions."

He turned it slightly in his hands.

"I think I need to explore... fashion."

They all laughed at that. Easy.

"I just wanted to say thank you," Eli said.

He looked at Lily.

"And I hope you understand. I couldn't support what she had become."

A beat.

"But I... I suppose I still love her."

The quiet settled in around them.

Xynn shifted slightly. "Where will you go?"

Eli smiled—that familiar, crooked edge to it.

"I have no idea. That's the fun part."

He glanced down the corridor, then back.

"Maybe you'll find me in the fleet someday. But for now—there is a whole galaxy to experience."

Lily nodded.

"Good luck, Eli. I really do wish you an amazing journey out there."

He returned the nod.

Then he turned and started down the corridor.

After a few steps, he placed the hat on his head. The brim dipped low before he adjusted it, the feather catching the light as it waved gently in the circulated air.

He kept walking.

Lily watched him go, then shook her head slightly, a small smile lingering.

• • • •

The shuttle set down on a clear stretch just beyond the main extraction site.

The hatch opened.

Heat hit first.

Not as sharp as before, but still there—pressing, immediate, familiar.

Lily stepped down onto the surface, boots settling into the dust. The copper light spread across everything the same way it always had, catching along the edges of stone and metal and skin.

For a second, it looked unchanged.

Then she saw it.

The platforms were coming apart.

Sections of scaffolding hung suspended mid-disassembly, cables retracting in smooth, controlled lines. Conveyor systems that had once run without pause now slowed in staggered intervals before going still. Equipment was being lifted in pieces—crates sealed, machinery detached, entire structures broken down into transportable segments.

Ships moved in steady rotation overhead, rising through the atmosphere one after another, their engines cutting clean paths through the red sky.

Nothing chaotic.

Nothing rushed.

Just... systematic.

Dalren stepped down beside her. Alrek followed a moment later.

They didn't move far from the landing point.

There wasn't a need to.

The whole operation spread out in front of them.

"Feels different," Alrek said.

Lily nodded slightly. "Yeah."

Dalren watched it for a moment, hands loosely clasped behind his back.

"It's remarkable," he said, "how quickly we can feel proud of ourselves for putting an end to the harm we created in the first place."

No one answered.

The words settled.

Lily kept her eyes on the site.

A group of workers moved past one of the dismantled platforms, guiding a final crate toward a transport line. Another team shut down a rig in coordinated steps, lights dimming in sequence until it went dark.

The rhythm of it was clean. Efficient.

Beyond the site, the city stretched out under the same copper sky.

Children moved through the narrow streets, weaving between low structures and open passages, their pace quick and unstructured in a way nothing on the extraction floor had been. One of them darted ahead of the others, turning back just long enough to shout something that didn't carry this far.

They kept moving.

Uninterrupted.

Lily watched them for a second longer than she meant to.

Before, it had felt like a countdown.

Now—

She wasn't sure what it was.

Not safety.

Not certainty.

Just... continuation.

Alrek shifted beside her, following her line of sight.

"What do you think is going through their minds?" he said.

Lily shook her head slightly.

She didn't answer.

The work was being undone. The machines were coming down. The interference was ending.

All of it was true.

And still—

A transport lifted from the far edge of the site, its engines flaring bright as it climbed, the sound rolling across the ground in a low, steady wave.

The space it left behind didn't fill in.

It just stayed empty.

Lily let out a quiet breath and turned slightly, taking in the full sweep of the site one more time.

Less of it now.

Less than there had been.

A transport settled behind them with a soft, controlled descent.

Lily turned as the hatch opened.

The man who stepped out didn't look like much at first glance.

Petite. Slight frame. Long white hair pulled back into a low ponytail that rested neatly between his shoulders. His uniform was immaculate—no visible wear, no excess ornamentation. Everything about him was precise.

He crossed the short distance to them without hurry.

Dalren straightened just slightly. "Admiral."

The man inclined his head. "Captain."

Dalren gestured. Lily, Alrek, this is Admiral Clouer.

His eyes moved once across the three of them, taking stock without lingering.

"Lieutenant Starling. Cadet Alrek."

"Sir," Lily said.

He looked back out over the dismantling site, watching a section of scaffolding detach and rise cleanly into the air before being guided toward a waiting transport.

"Well," he said, almost to himself. "It seems we've arrived at a turning point."

No one responded.

He let the moment sit, then turned back to them.

"You've done well here," he said. "All of you."

The words were measured. Not warm, not cold. Delivered like a conclusion already reached.

"You've helped the Union find its way through... a complicated situation."

Lily felt something in that phrasing.

Clouer's gaze settled on Dalren.

"There is, however, the matter of what remains."

Dalren didn't move. "Sir."

"The Gherionite technology," Clouer continued. "Along with some other sensitive materials."

His tone didn't shift.

"They are to be transported to Starbase Twelve. Immediately."

A small pause.

"For safe storage," he added. "Until further study is authorized."

The words landed clean.

Lily looked back out over the site.

Another platform came free, rising in slow, controlled motion as the final connections detached.

Safe storage.

Further study.

She felt the shape of it before she fully formed the thought.

Clouer glanced between them once more, as if expecting acknowledgment.

Dalren gave a slight nod. "Understood."

"Good," Clouer said.

He adjusted the cuffs of his uniform with a small, practiced motion.

"We'll want a full report upon arrival. Containment protocols, and so on."

Another transport lifted in the distance, its engines flaring bright as it cleared the site.

Clouer followed it briefly with his eyes, then returned his attention to them.

"We're looking for a speedy exit," he said. "Let's wrap this one up."

Lily nodded. "Yes, sir."

Clouer inclined his head once more, then turned and walked back toward the transport without another word.

The hatch closed behind him.

The engines rose.

Within seconds, the ship was gone.

The space he'd occupied didn't linger.

It folded back into the motion of the site.

Lily stood where she was, watching another section of the operation come down piece by piece.

• • • •

The observation deck was quiet, the kind of quiet that only existed when the ship was between crises. Bimini's copper glow had already begun to thin behind them, bleeding into the black like a memory losing color.

Lily stood at the glass, hands resting lightly on the railing. Xynn leaned beside her, close enough that their shoulders brushed.

"I wanted to bring you here," Lily said. "This is where I first saw you."

Xynn tilted her head. "Is it?"

"Yeah. You were down in the shuttle bay, arguing with someone." Lily smiled faintly at the memory. "I couldn't hear a word you were saying, but I remember thinking, *Whoever that is, she's winning.*"

Xynn let out a soft laugh. "That tracks."

"I'm not usually sentimental," Lily continued, "but—"

"Lily."

The voice was precise, clipped, and perfectly timed.

Lily closed her eyes for half a second, a small, reluctant smile tugging at her mouth. She wasn't annoyed. If anything, the interruption steadied the nervous flutter in her chest.

She turned.

Ka-Lorrin and Taran stood a few paces back. Ka-Lorrin's posture was ramrod straight, hands clasped behind his back like a disappointed professor. Taran loomed just behind him, a large, shaggy mountain of fur, his nose twitching with barely contained excitement.

"Do you have a moment?" Ka-Lorrin asked, dry as vacuum.

Lily let out a quiet laugh. "For you."

Taran stepped forward, practically vibrating. "This is not about a crisis or anything bad," he said, voice warm and a little too loud. "Just... it's good. Something I've been digging up on the side while we were teaching. It is, it is."

"For several weeks," Ka-Lorrin added, with the long-suffering tone of someone who had endured every update.

Taran reached into his bag and produced a small, unassuming data rod. "Tracked it through archival material. Sneaky little data." He held it out with both hands, as if presenting something fragile.

Lily took it, turning the smooth cylinder once in her fingers. "What is it?"

Ka-Lorrin's antennae flicked. "It is better if you review it without context."

A beat.

"In private."

Taran nodded emphatically. "Yes. Private. Very private."

Lily slipped the rod into her pocket, a smile tugging at the corner of her mouth. "Intriguing. Thank you, both."

"If you have questions," Ka-Lorrin said, already stepping back, "we will be available."

"After," Taran added, lifting one oversized paw in a cheerful half-wave.

Ka-Lorrin gave the faintest sigh and turned, guiding Taran down the corridor with quiet efficiency.

Lily watched them go, then shook her head, still smiling.

Xynn leaned back against the railing, eyes bright. "You were about to say something important. And by my guess, very cheesy."

"I was," Lily admitted.

She turned back to the glass. The stars held steady beyond the viewport. The nervous flutter returned, but it felt lighter now. Manageable.

She took a breath.

"I meant what I said. About seeing you here." She glanced sideways at Xynn. "We started that whole engagement story back on Gherion Prime because it made sense at the time. It solved a problem. Gave us space to move."

"Very romantic," Xynn said.

Lily huffed a quiet laugh. "I know. But somewhere along the way..." She hesitated, then pushed through it. "Is it wrong that maybe I changed what I want?"

Xynn didn't interrupt. She just watched her.

"I'm not going to pretend I know what this looks like long-term," Lily continued. "Or where we'll end up, or how it fits into... all of this." She gestured lightly—ship, stars, everything. "I don't have a plan. And I'm not trying to make one."

A small pause.

"But I do know this part." She met Xynn's eyes. "I want this to be real. Not because it's useful. Not because it solves anything. Just... because it is."

Xynn studied her for a long moment, then pushed off the railing and stepped closer.

"You're doing a terrible job of making that sound casual," she said, voice low.

"I'm not trying to be casual."

"Good."

Xynn reached up, brushing her thumb lightly along Lily's jaw.

"Lily Starling..." she murmured. "Are you trying to propose to me?"

Lily let out a small, nervous laugh. "I guess I am."

Xynn tilted her head, pretending to consider it. "Well... I guess my answer is yes."

The words were light, but they landed exactly where they needed to.

Lily laughed—bright, relieved—and Xynn pulled her in. The kiss was warm and unhurried, familiar in a way that didn't need defining.

When they parted, Xynn rested her forehead briefly against Lily's.

"Still not enlisting," she said.

Lily grinned. "Wouldn't dream of it."

They stayed there a moment longer as the ship carried them forward.

No plan.

No guarantees.

Just this.

• • • •

A short while later, the door chimed.

Lily crossed the room and opened it.

Alrek stood in the corridor, hands clasped behind his back like he was reporting for inspection. For a second, neither of them spoke.

He stepped inside. The door slid shut behind him with a soft hiss.

They didn't move much farther than that.

The low glow from the viewport cut across the room, catching along the edge of his uniform, the line of her shoulder. The ship hummed steadily beneath them.

Alrek tilted his head, studying her with a faint, familiar half-smile.

"You still look like you're ready to punch the next rule that gets in your way."

Lily leaned one shoulder against the wall, arms loose at her sides. "And you still look like you're measuring every step for regulation spacing."

She glanced at him. "Command track suits you."

He let out a quiet breath, almost a laugh. "That's one way to put it."

"Walking checklist," she added.

"Efficient checklist," he said.

"Fun sponge."

"Chaos goblin."

A small beat passed.

Not awkward. Just... quieter.

Alrek's expression shifted slightly, the humor settling into something more thoughtful.

"We've both been adjusting," he said. "Faster than I expected."

"Yeah," Lily said.

She pushed off the wall, standing a little straighter.

"But maybe going in different directions doesn't automatically mean growing apart."

He considered that, then gave a single, measured nod.

"I'm starting to see the value in not always following the plan exactly as written."

Lily smiled faintly. "And I'm starting to see the value in having someone who actually reads it first."

Another beat.

Easy.

No tension left to resolve. No point to prove.

Just understanding.

Lily met his eyes.

"Ready?"

Alrek straightened slightly.

"Are we ever?"

Lily smiled.

They found Dalren waiting for them on the observation platform above Engineering Lab 23.

The three of them stepped to the rail and looked down into the secured bay below.

The ancient machine rested within its containment field—dark, angular, and silent. Around it, the Caronite samples sat in orderly rows, everything labeled and locked down like holiday decorations going up to the attic.

The air felt heavier up here.

Not thicker. Just... settled.

Dalren's voice was calm, almost conversational.

"Are we ready?"

No debate. No speeches.

They all understood.

Lily rested her hand on the control. Alrek placed his beside hers. Dalren completed the triangle.

She let out a slow breath, her voice dry—almost light.

"We're about to witness a terrible antimatter containment failure," she said. "What are the odds?"

Alrek's mouth curved into a small, knowing smile.

"Accidents happen."

Dalren nodded once.

"They do."

Together, they activated the control.

The destruction was quiet. Orderly.

A contained bloom of light flared below, then collapsed inward. The machine flickered once, then folded in on itself, its structure breaking apart into nothing. The Caronite samples dissolved into static and vanished.

In seconds, the chamber was empty.

Clean deck plating.

A faint, fading afterglow.

Silence settled.

Dalren stepped back first, already turning toward the exit.

"I expect your reports on my desk by the time we reach Starbase 12," he said. "And recommendations to ensure containment failures like this don't happen in the future."

"Aye, sir," Lily and Alrek said together.

He didn't look back as he left.

The door closed behind him with a soft, final sound.

Lily and Alrek remained at the rail.

They exchanged a brief look—something shared, unspoken—then both looked down into the empty space below.

"Sometimes," Lily said quietly, "you just have to disobey orders."

Alrek let out a small laugh.

"Don't expect me to make a habit of it."

Then, without a word, they linked arms—supporting each other, side by side.

They stood there like that for a while.

No rush to move.

The ship carried on beneath them, steady and unchanged.

Light moved across the empty chamber below.

As the ship moved through light.

Light through space.

Red vines curl through copper light,
children laugh where renewal once lied.
Peace wears many faces —
some are born,
some are borrowed,
some are only waiting to begin.
But the children run and play again.

SCALES AND FEATHERS smelled like spiced wine, woodsmoke, and fresh rain on old stone.

The place had come back to life.

Warm light spilled from the windows onto the narrow street, catching on wet cobblestones and the small brass sign that now read *Under New Management – All Are Welcome.*

Laughter drifted out through the open door—bright, messy, alive.

Inside, the boards were gone.

Tables had been pushed together into one long communal stretch. Didot moved behind the bar with easy confidence, sleeves rolled high, trading barbs with a customer while Delia balanced a tray of glasses like she'd been born to it. The younger girl's eyes were sharper now, but her smile came quicker, less guarded.

The air felt warmer here.

Not just from the fire.

Something had been opened back up—something that hadn't been meant to stay closed.

Lily stood near the hearth with Xynn, their hands loosely linked, letting the hum of the room settle over them. She breathed it in: the crackle of logs, the faint sweetness of mulled wine, the low murmur of voices that no longer carried fear.

Her mind drifted for a moment, back to the reformed Hedon Council chamber.

They had named the new transparency initiative after Valen Meris.

The Valen Meris Accords.

Tevya had tried to silence one voice and ended up amplifying it across half the planet. The irony was so clean it almost hurt. Lily had stood at the back of the gallery with Trish during the first public reading, listening to councilors quote lines Valen had written in private messages she'd never seen him send.

She hadn't smiled then.

She just felt the small, stubborn satisfaction of something broken being set right in the exact place where it had been shattered.

Here, in the revived warmth of Scales and Feathers, that feeling sat a little closer.

A little more real.

Charlie sat at the far end of the table, telling an exaggerated story about the time his protoplasm containment failed during an orbital jump and it took the academy staff two days to collect all of him.

Lily caught Alrek glancing at Didot every few seconds, like he was checking to make sure she was still real. When she met his eye, she flicked a bar towel at him. He grinned like a man who'd won the lottery.

Lily and Xynn stood near the hearth, hands loosely linked. The sealing had been brief—a Saravethi ceremony. A quiet agreement between the two of them, witnessed by the people who had become their strange, patchwork family.

Trish raised a glass at the bar. "To bad ideas that somehow work out anyway."

Caris lifted her own—sparkling water catching the firelight. "And to the ones who drag us through them."

Laughter rippled down the table.

Malik was practically sitting in Caris's lap, saying something under his breath that made her shake her head even as she smiled. The Raath-Ka stood slightly apart from the group, observing with quiet interest—Ka-Lorrin composed as ever, Taran leaning forward just enough to suggest he was deeply invested in every word. Dryst Amaris and Doctor Thesari were locked in a long, winding conversation that no one nearby seemed willing to interrupt. At the far end, Basco and Dalren spoke in low tones that still somehow felt like work.

Lily's face lit up when she saw them.

"Captain!"

Calan turned, already smiling. "Lily."

She crossed the room and pulled him into a quick, unguarded hug.

"You made it."

"I wouldn't miss this," he said.

Joren leaned in from behind him. "He almost did. There was a speech involved."

"There was no speech," Calan said, with dignity.

"There was the *threat* of a speech," Joren corrected.

Lily laughed and pulled them both in again.

The day had been full of it—reunions, stories, laughter layered over everything that had come before.

Later, when the fire had burned lower and the room had settled into softer conversation, Lily slipped upstairs to the suite. Xynn followed a moment later, closing the door behind her with a quiet click.

Lily crossed to her duffel and opened a small pouch.

The data rod sat where she'd left it.

She turned it over once in her fingers, the metal cool and unremarkable, then slotted it into the room's reader.

Xynn stepped in beside her, looking over her shoulder as the records resolved.

"Oh my god," she said softly. "It's you."

It was.

Her life before. Five centuries ago.

Before the Krythar.

Before the streets.

Before the accident—her grandmother's death.

Before any of it.

Names. Dates. Places.

Lily watched the screen for a moment longer, then reached out and closed the file.

"Information for another day," she said.

Xynn studied her. "I actually believe you."

Lily gave a small, knowing smile. "I know who I am."

She glanced at the reader, then back at Xynn.

"I appreciate that they did this for me. I really will read it later."

She let that sit for a second.

Then she climbed onto the bed, pulling Xynn down with her.

"There are more pressing matters."

Outside, the city that had once been London kept its quiet rhythm—rain on rooftops, distant voices, the low hum of something that had endured.

Inside, the fire crackled below. Laughter drifted faintly through the floorboards, bright and alive.

Lily turned in Xynn's arms, hands finding familiar places at her waist.

"Stay with me?" she asked.

Xynn's smile was slow and sure. "Always."

The light from the reader faded.

Outside the window, the clouds began to break. The first stars pushed through—small, steady points of light holding their place against the dark.

Lily kissed her.

And for a little while—

the galaxy waited.

THE CEMETERY IN SAN Francisco smelled of wet eucalyptus and old stone.

Lily stood at the edge of the grave in plain clothes. Fog clung low between the headstones, softening edges, turning the world into watercolor.

Rebecca Esche's marker was simple—gray granite, nothing ornate. Just a name, two dates, and a small etched dove that looked, to Lily, more like a pigeon with ambitions.

Her fingers hovered just above the stone, not quite touching it.

She had no memory of the woman buried here. No familiar smells, no echo of laughter, no warmth of a hand that had once steadied her. Everything before the Krythar was a blank wall—smooth, impenetrable, and loud in its silence.

She came anyway.

Not for comfort. Not for closure.

If she was honest, she didn't really understand the purpose of being here. But the connection was there, however thin, and it had been enough.

She glanced down at the marker again.

Five centuries, and it had held.

A footstep crunched softly on the gravel path behind her.

Lily didn't turn.

The sound stopped a few paces back.

"Nice morning for ghosts," a voice said—mild, almost amused.

Lily let out a small breath. "At least they're quiet."

A pause.

"Was Nana Esche a relative?"

Lily tilted her head slightly, eyes still on the stone. "So I'm told."

Then, after a beat:

"You?"

The young woman shifted, stepping just enough into view. Tall. Long blonde hair. Immaculate makeup that didn't quite belong in a place like this.

"Wild stories about Nana Esche and the family back then," she said lightly.

Lily's mouth twitched. "Do tell."

The woman glanced at the grave, then back at her.

"There's one about her granddaughter," she said. "The one who got abducted by aliens."

Lily turned.

Really looked at her now.

Fog caught in her lashes. The world narrowed.

"How would you know about that?" Lily asked. "That was five hundred years ago."

The woman didn't answer right away.

She studied Lily with open curiosity—like she was confirming something she already suspected.

Then she smiled.

"Did you really think," she said, "you were the only one displaced through time?"

About the Author

Christian Hurst is a Creative Director and author of the *Lily Starling* series, a character-driven YA science fiction saga that blends epic adventure with emotional depth. With over 15 years of experience in advertising, marketing, and content creation, his work is shaped by a strong sense of story, pacing, and imagination.

His writing explores identity, connection, and the courage to forge your own path in a vast and unpredictable galaxy. Known for immersive worldbuilding, inclusive storytelling, and a balance of heart, humor, and high-stakes tension, Christian's work resonates with readers who are drawn to science fiction with both scale and soul.

He lives in Pennsylvania with his wife, son, and three dogs.

The story doesn't end here.

Lily's journey continues in the Lily Starling series. What begins aboard the *Salamander* leads to ancient mysteries, impossible choices, and a threat that spans the galaxy.

Continue the adventure at **LilyStarlingBook.com**

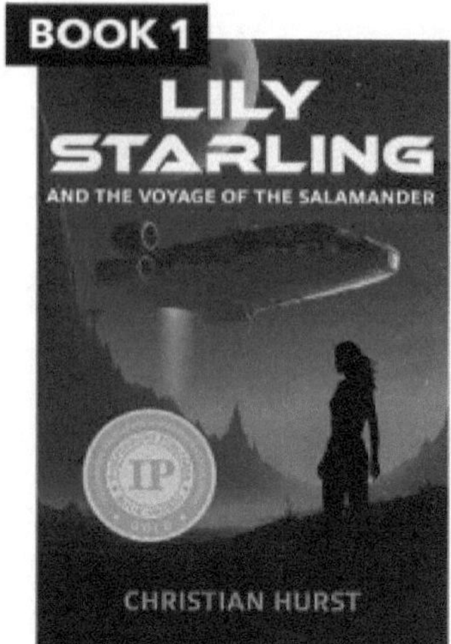

BOOK 1
LILY STARLING
AND THE VOYAGE OF THE SALAMANDER
CHRISTIAN HURST

BOOK 2
LILY STARLING
AND THE STORM RIDERS
CHRISTIAN HURST

BOOK 3
LILY STARLING
AND THE DEATH MACHINE
CHRISTIAN HURST

BOOK 4
LILY STARLING
AND THE RIVER OF TIME
COMING SOON
CHRISTIAN HURST

Leave a Review

If you enjoyed Voyage of the Salamander, please consider leaving a review on your favorite book site. Reader reviews help independent books reach new audiences and play a direct role in the future of series like this one.